PHOENIX RISING

By

Glenda C. Finkelstein

Final Destiny Press
Plant City FL.

Final Destiny Press
Plant City Florida 33565

Edited by Dr. Tammy L Ferrante

Cover Art by Dreamstime.com, © Philcold

Used under Free Royalty License

Cover Design by Tony E. Finkelstein

ISBN-13: 978-0-99140-900-6

Library of Congress Control Number: 2014930358

PHOENIX RISING

Prolog

Captain Conrad Banes is sitting in the brig staring at the floor contemplating his pending execution when a visitor comes to call. He lifts his brown eyes to see who it is. It's his old instructor and surrogate father from his Academy days, Admiral Griffin. Against advice from his lawyer, Conrad agrees to speak with the Admiral alone. His lawyer leaves along with the guard after the Admiral assumed responsibility for the prisoner.

"Thank you for coming," Conrad opens the conversation straightening his brown hair to present himself neat and tidy before his old mentor.

"Don't thank me. I just wanted you to know before you're brought out for all to see and displayed like a traitor that I'll be presiding over the proceedings. I can't say what's on my heart and for what it's worth, I believe your story."

"That means a lot."

"It means nothing, but I wanted you to know that your sacrifice is for the greater good of all mankind…I wish there was…" Griffin stopped talking. He's unable to share his heart knowing in just a few moments he will preside over this man's death. The Admiral signals for the guard to come and open the cell so he can take a few moments to compose himself before reporting to his post.

In the Great Hall located on the Epsilon 6 Command Station, the condemned prisoner was to stand before the Tribunal, various dignitaries, and the Rundi representative to face judgment. Six drummers tapped out a rigid cadence as the prisoner was escorted into the arena below with President Patton looking on from above. The chains connecting Conrad's shackled ankles kept an eerie rhythm with the tempo of the drums. The most decorated officer in the Rundi War was standing with hands and feet bound in shame and his uniform replaced by an orange jumpsuit.

Captain Banes gazed up into the crowd. He saw the familiar faces of his crew watching with confused expressions from the stands. Just a few short days ago he and his unit were being cheered by the people, now those same people cried out for the blood of their Captain while they were left alive to bear the shame of it all. None of the Phoenix crew had been re-assigned, and most were still being debriefed. What was worse was the way people stared at them as if they, too, were conspirators in what they considered trumped up charges.

The drums ceased and the room fell silent. A trumpet announced the entry of Admiral Griffin. The people stood to their feet when he entered. Admiral Griffin approached the podium and motioned with his hands for them to sit down. The Admiral was an imposing man. His face was etched with the lines of time and the weight of his responsibility. His silver streaked short black hair was combed neatly back, and his crystal blue eyes gazed into Conrad's face with both pain and duty.

Captain Banes stood there with his eyes facing down and feeling like a broken man, but before engaging the Admiral's stare straightened himself with shoulders back. Even in this moment Conrad wanted Admiral Griffin to be proud of him. He then locked his brown eyes with the Admiral as his former mentor pronounced his sentence.

"Today we are here to pronounce sentencing over Captain Conrad Banes who has been charged and convicted of High Treason. In addition to the former charges brought against him, he has been found responsible for drawing first blood in our war with the Rundi who were only defending themselves from our aggression."

The crowd gasped in shock and began to murmur amongst themselves growing louder with each passing second. This information was new to the people and only added to the outlandish rumors of collaboration with the enemy at the Battle of the Breach that had been circulating.

"Silence!" the Admiral yelled, calling the room back to order. After they quieted, he continued addressing the prisoner. "Do you wish to make a last testament before sentencing is pronounced?"

Conrad shook his head no, his eyes never leaving that of Admiral Griffin's.

"Very well, the Tribunal condemns you to death by immediate execution and any honors previously received are revoked."

His former crew interspersed among the crowd responded with shouts of anger protesting the sentence pronounced over their beloved captain. The trumpets blared out to regain control of the crowd again. The guard standing next to Conrad offered him a blindfold. He shook his head no. Breaking protocol, the guard saluted the prisoner with a tear in his eye. Conrad nodded his appreciation then returned his gaze to that of Admiral Griffin. The executioners, reminiscent of a firing squad of old, but using lethal lasers instead of projectile weapons took their position. The Master at Arms started to call out each command slowly and deliberately.

"Attention! Make ready! Aim! Fire!"

There was little sound emitted from the weapons, but very quickly Captain Banes was lying on the floor. There wasn't much blood either as the lasers quickly cauterized any wound created. A coroner dressed in white came out, knelt down, and checked his vital signs. He nodded at Admiral Griffin.

"Let it be recorded that on the seventy-ninth day in the cosmological year of 2991, former Captain Conrad Banes of the Phoenix was executed for High Treason against the human race and aggression against the Rundi people. Let it be known to all, that his execution lays the foundation of the long awaited peace with the Rundi," Admiral Griffin announced as protocol dictated with the last word sticking in his throat. The assembly applauded, but none of them realized the true cost of this peace, nor its tenuous longevity.

Chapter 1

Conrad's best friend since Academy days, Captain Rico Sanchez, the second most decorated captain of the Rundi war, wasn't aware of Conrad's situation until it was too late. When he heard about his friend's execution and the charges brought against him, he made a vow to confront Admiral Griffin on Epsilon 6 Command Station to find out what actually happened so he could clear his friend's name. Rico's ship, the Falcon, and his crew was considered the best and the bravest in the fleet second only to the Phoenix, whose reputation now lays in shambles.

Captain Sanchez has been sitting in his dimly lit office for the past three days mourning the death of his friend staring at a photo of him and Conrad the day they got their commissions. He wouldn't even leave to eat taking all his meals inside his office. The doorbell rang several times before he unlocked the door to allow entry. Rico was not at all surprised when his first officer, Lt. Commander Lindsay Macalister, walked in. Her expression of concern gave away her pretense of a simple duty call. Her response to his person caused him to take a quick glance at himself in a nearby decorative mirror. He was not reflecting his usual spit and polish image. His uniform was wrinkled and his shirt untucked. He was sporting the beginnings of a full beard. His deep brown eyes were dull and reflected none of their usual mischievous delight. They peered out from behind dangling locks of wavy black hair that had long since lost its styling crème. Before returning his attention to her Rico noticed the stack of uncollected food trays in the corner. He had lost track of time.

Rico noticed that she was waiting patiently for him to speak, but he refused to ask why she came to his office forcing her to begin the dialog. She took a deep breath, and then stated her purpose.

"I've come to report that the major repairs have been completed, and we are back underway to Epsilon 6 with estimated time of arrival at 14 hours and 15 minutes."

"You could've informed me of that via intercom," he commented, knowing full well the real reason she was there.

"Yes, but I thought…"

"You'd check up on me," Captain Sanchez said, completing her sentence.

"I can't get anything passed you. Can I sir?"

"If you could, I wouldn't be the captain. Is the coffee machine in the mess hall working yet?"

"No, Sir. The entire unit needs replacing, and what supply you had on hand in your quarters leaked out inside the wall. At least that's what Zeveney told me."

His disappointment was evident. The captain loved his coffee, but realized that he would survive. He started to look down at his desk and return to what he was doing when he noticed that she hadn't left. He looked back up at her and saw that insatiable need to communicate.

"Speak your mind," he instructed, capitulating to her unwavering stare.

"I'm concerned about you."

"What's there to be concerned about? The war is over, and when we arrive at Epsilon 6, everyone gets two weeks furlough."

His tone didn't agree with his words, and he knew that Lindsay knew, that he was blowing smoke. Although some first officers would allow their Captain that luxury, he knew she wasn't about to.

"That's the problem, Sir. Everyone is ecstatic, except you. Correction, you were happy until the news of Captain Banes' execution came down. I know how close you two were by all the stories you've told me about your antics at the Academy. His execution took us all by surprise."

"I assure you that my issues are unrelated," Rico quickly defended, knowing that his swift response gave himself away. Trying to recover his controlled visage, he continued, "and nothing that a couple of weeks of furlough on the beach can't cure."

"Why don't I believe you sir?" she asked with that coy, '*you really don't expect me to believe that do you?*' look upon her face. It's a look that he had received many times during the past several years.

"Because you've got good captain instincts," Rico acknowledged. "But since I still out rank you, you'll have to accept my word that I'm fine."

"I'll accept it under one condition."

Rico lifted his eyebrow, his patience beginning to wane slightly. He could see the battle raging in her mind behind those bright green eyes wondering if she had become too bold. He didn't let her struggle too long before giving her a wink indicating that he was more intrigued than he was offended. It was her boldness that he liked so much, and her willingness to pursue when others would drop it that caught his eye when she was a lowly ensign nine years ago. This was just one more confirmation that she was ready for a command of her own and made a mental note to write a recommendation for her when he returned from furlough.

4

"What's the condition?" He asked, wanting her to get on with it.

"That you take a bath, sir." Her request caught him slightly off guard, but then realized she had a point.

"I can do that."

"Thank you, sir."

"Dismissed."

She saluted, turned in proficient military manner, and began to walk towards the door.

"Lindsay," Rico called out informally.

"Yes, Sir," she responded, turning around to face him.

"Thanks for your concern."

She smiled and then continued out the door to attend to her duties. He looked after her reflecting upon his opinion that she should've been born with red hair instead of her golden brown. Her green eyes and fiery disposition reflected her Irish heritage so well that she should've had the red hair to complete the ensemble. He lifted his arm gently sniffing at his armpit and winced, coughing in spurts. Rico stood to his feet, walked to the door, and cautiously peered out of his office looking both ways down each hallway. He waited just a moment for some crewman to go by so he could get to his quarters without offending anyone on the way. Once he saw that the way was clear. He went for it.

His solitude was to nurse his need to wallow in self-pity. It was a nasty habit unbefitting a man of his stature and accomplishments, and one that usually went unnoticed. This time, however, he didn't get away with it. In any case, he was satisfied that he'd spent enough time feeling sorry for himself and mourning the loss of his friend, Conrad. Now Rico could concentrate on exonerating his dearest friend's memory and restoring honor to his crew.

Upon arriving at his quarters he was greeted by his personal computer companion, Zeveney, which could do anything from hacking into other systems, create tactical schematics and simulations, to calling for pizza delivery when in port of course. In Rico's quarters Zeveney has a holographic interface that projected an image of a man in his late thirties with dark hair and mustache, presumably the image of the system's creator, but when Rico accesses Zeveney from a remote location, it's audio only with the voice resonating a rich baritone quality. Rico has had Zeveney reviewing all the records on Captain Conrad Banes, both past and present. With this information he hoped to extrapolate a profile, and pit it against the charges that brought him to his execution.

"Greetings, Captain Sanchez."

"Hello, Zev. Have you finished the profile on Captain Banes?"

"Yes, I have."

"Let's hear it."

"Excuse me captain, but my sensors are picking up a foul odor. It is rather putrid. Shall I call the maintenance department to track down and eliminate the odor?"

"That won't be necessary. The odor is coming from me. I'll just go take a shower."

"Yes, that would be a good idea," Zeveney said beginning to cough.

"Hey, knock it off. You're a computer."

"I am an artificial intelligence mainframe interface system, and strong odors interfere with my delicate senses, negatively affecting my concentration."

"It figures," Rico muttered under his breath, and then continued, "of all the Zeveney 7000 systems produced. I get the one with attitude."

"I am a Zeveney 7000-P, for personality." Its response was cocky and proud which only added aggravation in dealing with its otherwise informative and lively repartee.

"That's not what the salesperson said. You should have been called Zeveney 7000-A for attitude," Rico replied back while holding back a laugh.

"Do you wish to trade me in?"

"No, but before I get into the shower have you made any progress in getting a response from Admiral Griffin?"

"No response to any of your inquiries regarding Captain Banes."

"Okay, what about progress into the evidence files that convicted him?"

Zeveney acquired an indignant expression and refused to answer. Rico knew that if he were going to get any information from him at all it would be after he took his shower. Rico took off his clothes, gasped for a breath of clean air, and held them as far from his nose as he could until he could place them into the laundry receptacle. He then turned on the water in the shower stall to his favorite temperature and stepped into the stall with soap and shampoo in hand. After placing the soap and shampoo on a ledge, he bowed his head and immersed it into the stream of warm water pouring through the showerhead.

He could feel the grunge being washed away as it cascaded over his body and onto the shower floor where it was sucked into a drain and reclaimed. Normally he was in a hurry to shower and dress, but today he'd take his time. Once he lathered his hair and body, he then began to rinse off throwing his face and body parts in and out of the water like a hippo frolicking in a river. He turned off the water, grabbed a nearby towel, and began to dry himself in the steam-permeated bathroom. Rico opened the bathroom door to allow the mirror to clear so he could shave. After shaving, he splashed on some refreshing skin conditioner and admired himself in the full-length mirror with his naked well-toned body reflecting in it.

"It doesn't get any better than this," Rico suggested aloud to Zeveney looking for confirmation. Although most would think that such a statement would come from a self-proclaimed egomaniac, he was in actuality quite tongue and cheek about his looks. He made it a point not to take himself too seriously.

"I prefer a different set of circuitry," Zeveney admitted dryly.

"I'm the captain. You're supposed to agree with me."

"I am programmed to give honest responses."

"Okay, let's get back to business, what about the evidence files," Rico inquired, as he pulled out some clean clothes from a nearby dresser and began to get dressed.

"There are no evidence files."

"You mean that you haven't gained access to the files."

"No, I mean that there are no records stored inside the evidence files."

"How can that be?" Rico questioned aloud totally bemused by the mystery.

"There are two possibilities: one, the evidence is in a physical file and was never input into the system, and, two, there is no evidence."

"Okay, back to my first question from a different angle. Can you find any evidence in Conrad's records that would support the charges of high treason or the rumored collaboration which was not mentioned at his sentencing?"

"No sir, but I would like to point out that Captain Banes was constantly in the most extreme battles recorded during the war. It is possible that he experienced a trauma that could cause a sudden shift in his basic personality."

"I know those battles, and in each of them he was decorated for valiant conduct above and beyond the call of duty. Many of his crew, and mine, owe him their lives."

Rico's tone was quite defensive becoming rather melancholy. Zeveney picked up on the subtle changes in it and sought to rectify it.

"My comment was only meant to suggest a possible explanation. I did not mean to disrespect your friend's memory."

"You did what I asked you to do. To be honest, I'm not sure I'd believe any such evidence if I saw it anyway."

"Why?"

"Because a friend is chosen by your heart, and my gut isn't willing to turn loose so easily."

"You make a lot of decisions based on your gut."

"Yes, and though it's most often correct, it has been known to be devastatingly wrong."

"Do you believe your gut has misled you in regards to Captain Banes?"

"I'm saying that a zebra can't change his stripes."

"What does an extinct species have to do with anything?"

"It's an old earth saying that implies that if you know certain things about someone, even if there are facts to the contrary those facts are what is suspect not the person."

"So you choose to disregard the facts of the public Tribunal."

"Yes, I choose to disregard the facts because facts can be manipulated. I've never been more certain of anything in my life, and I'll not rest until I've proven Conrad's innocence," Rico answered.

"Do you have anything else you wish me to do?"

"Yes, begin compiling information on the Phoenix crew. Start with those closest in rank to Conrad. See if any of them had cause to set him up for a fall. Also, I would like to see where all the Phoenix crew was at during the Battle of the Breach relative to Captain Banes, and the enemy."

The Battle of the Breach was the last most devastating battle of the Rundi War. Since nothing was amiss prior to that engagement, it seemed logical to start their investigation with that battle. Perhaps something took place that no one or very few were aware of that compromised Conrad. Regardless, Rico wasn't taking anything at face value.

"You suspect foul play," Zeveney replied as a statement and not a question.

"Indeed I do. An honorable man doesn't betray his people, nor is a hero executed for treachery. Make certain you are not detected."

Zeveney didn't know how to respond, so he remained silent and began his covert task. Even though the Zeveney 7000-P system was quite fast, Rico's request was more than just plotting and adding numbers it was producing personality profiles that could signal a possible adversary. In addition, if this exercise turned up any leads it didn't mean that they did anything wrong. The only thing that this would do would give Rico a starting point for his unauthorized, off the books investigation.

Rico, who hadn't slept in a couple days, stopped to gaze at a photo on his dresser of him and Conrad at their Academy graduation party. He picked up the frame in his hand. He reflected upon the effervescent smile of his friend remembering the contagious nature of his laughter. He could almost hear the cackle that was so Conrad. He didn't realize it, but he'd started to tear up. He quickly set the photo back down, wiped the tear forming in his right eye, and saluted. Rico then crawled quietly into bed to get some well-deserved sleep. He was out almost as soon as his head hit his pillow.

Chapter 2

Rico slept for a full twelve hours. He couldn't remember the last time he had slept that soundly with no interruptions. Now he was ready for whatever awaited him on Epsilon 6. He shaved and washed his face, brushed his teeth, combed his hair, and then put on his formal uniform. Wearing that uniform would show he meant business with starched, pressed creases and a full display of medals and ribbons. He carefully adjusted each and every medal by hand to make certain that they were completely straight. After that he passed a lint brush over the formal jacket just to make certain that there was no dust on the garment. With one last glance in the mirror before leaving his cabin, he flashed a determined grin at himself.

"You are a handsome devil Rico Sanchez," he said aloud to himself. The Zeveney program made no comment about Rico's opinion of himself as he left his quarters.

***

On the large and spacious bridge of the Falcon, Lt. Commander Lindsay Macalister was in charge of final approach and docking to the Epsilon 6 station. This well seasoned crew trusted her just as much as they did Captain Sanchez. The bridge was especially busy today with many department heads making final reports to the appropriate bridge officer. When the door opened and Rico stepped onto the bridge Lindsay made certain that the proper respect was shown by the crew.

"Attention! Captain on the bridge!" Lindsay called out in full, concise military manner. All of the bridge crew that was not engaged in active maneuvers stood at attention to await the captain's greeting.

"At ease," Rico said, acknowledging their respect with a return salute. "What's our status?"

"We're on final approach to Epsilon 6. We've been given clearance to dock at bay twelve," Macalister answered.

"Very good," replied Rico as he took the opportunity to enjoy the full magnitude of creation displayed upon the view screen. The Epsilon 6 system was one of the most beautiful systems in the quadrant. The outer planets consisted of three gas giants, each a different color. The first was green like a primordial forest, the second, red, like a pomegranate, and the third, a lovely pastel pink with orange stripes. The inner planets were rocky, and two of the four had vegetation with a breathable atmosphere. The first of these two was called Cassiopeia and had an extensive network of beaches with white and black sands. The other was called Otadan that had two metropolitan cities and an agricultural community on the southern continent. Most of the soldiers would take their leave on one of these two planets.

Captain Sanchez wasn't planning on taking his full leave as there were too many unanswered questions about Conrad, and he was determined to find out what happened. Although captains rarely take leave the same time as their crews, this was a unique occasion, and he was admittedly in need of some rest. He would make certain to take at least one week for his own health's sake.

They were at peace with the Rundi, and for the first time in a long time there was a feeling of hope among the people. Yet for Rico, this feeling of hope felt artificial. He didn't quite understand it. All he knew was that his gut wasn't at ease with the trappings of this armistice. Perhaps his feelings regarding Conrad's demise was cluttering his judgment, but nothing he did could shake his uneasiness.

"Captain, where are you going to take your leave?" a young, wide-eyed ensign inquired pulling Rico out of his deep contemplation.

"I'll probably go to Cassiopeia and enjoy the sand and surf on some remote beach," Rico replied with a smile.

"Why doesn't that surprise me?" Lindsay chided, sarcastically.

"Some of us like our solitude," Rico defended. "In any case, my leave has been delayed for a couple of days."

"That's not fair. You've worked harder than anyone," the ensign spoke up.

"I appreciate that, but command has a different burden. I will, however, still enjoy most of my leave before we start are next mission."

"What about you commander?" the ensign asked of Lindsay.

"I was hoping to take in some of the beaches, but since my mother hasn't seen me in five years I'll probably split my time between both planets," Lindsay responded.

"Don't get too comfortable with that idea," Rico suggested.

"Why not?" Lindsay asked.

"I'll only delay you for a little bit, but it's very important that you accompany me to the Admiral's office when we arrive at the station after we have disembarked our honored dead."

"Why?" she asked curiously.

"After you park the ship, collect me from my office," Rico ordered with a half grin designed to pique her curiosity. He purposely didn't elaborate further, leaving her to wonder. He did this for two reasons; one, because he didn't feel like elaborating, and second, because he knew it would drive Lindsay absolutely nuts.

"Yes, sir," Lindsay acknowledged, begrudgingly. Rico was a man of few words, and would answer in his own way and in his own good time.

****

Within the hour the ship was docked safely, and the exchange of base personnel for Falcon crew began. The sound of laughter echoed here and there throughout the ship's corridors as crewmen ran to their bunks to get what few possessions they had and go planet side. The sound of a serendipitous crew telling each other their plans to meet with family and see sons and daughters they'd never met, born to them during the past two years made Rico smile. The only real sadness to the moment was the off loading of the dead, those who were killed in the final battle with the Rundi. Captain Sanchez had given strict orders that every respect would be given the dead as they disembarked the Falcon. All of his department heads were required to come and salute their fallen comrades as they exited the ship prior to leaving on their long overdue furloughs.

As the Falcon's officers lined up in silence along the gantry, the only sound that could initially be heard was the footsteps of the men and women carrying the bodies off the ship one body bag at a time. As each body passed, the Captain would click his heels and salute. His officers would follow his lead and salute in response. Taps was played during the entire ceremony until all the dead had been removed. Once the dead had left, the department heads were free to go on their leaves with the exception of Lindsay who stayed behind per Rico's request.

They walked wordlessly together to the Admiral's office. Past experience proved that unless Rico started the conversation, he wouldn't respond to any questions. He would give all the answers, but on his terms, and in his timing. Rico walked into the office of the Admiral whose secretary, Nancy, was busy at work filling out reports. She gazed up at Captain Sanchez, and immediately notified the Admiral of his arrival.

"Admiral Griffin, Captain Sanchez is here to see you," she announced without any prompting from Rico.

"Send him in," the Admiral responded without hesitation.

Rico seemed slightly surprised. After all the inquiries the Admiral had ignored he found it odd that he could just walk right into his office without a wait. He cut his eyes at Lindsay. That was Rico for, 'sit down and wait until I call you.' It was kind of scary that she understood him so well, but then they had been to hell and back together. They were closer than a husband and wife relationship, a soldier's bond that was not easily broken. Neither would think twice about surrendering their life for the other so she tried to make herself comfortable in the waiting room.

When Rico first entered the room, the very studious Admiral looked up from his paperwork and smiled. It was a smile of recognized familiarity rather than an expression of happiness. The Admiral looked older than he did the last time Rico saw him. There were more white hairs upon his head, and a few more lines upon his face. He waited for the doors to close before approaching his desk. The room seemed dimmer, but then again it had been two years since he had met with Griffin in his office.

"I'm glad to see you made it home in one piece," the Admiral began. Rico looked puzzled by Admiral Griffin's warm greeting. It lacked the usual formality of a face-to-face with the brass. "You seem on edge, Rico, sit down. I know you have a lot on your mind." The Admiral seemed almost jovial, a strange state of mind considering the circumstances.

"Let's say I'm curious. I fully expected you to dismiss me. You know why I'm here. My inquiry hasn't changed."

"You want to know the details surrounding the execution of Captain Banes," the Admiral surmised. He leaned back in his overstuffed leather executive chair with hands clasped together resting them upon his chest. Rico pulled his chair closer to the Admiral's desk before responding.

"Yes, I do."

"I'm sure your Zeveney program was quite successful in hacking the files. Why don't you tell me what you've found?"

"Nothing and you well know it," Rico answered with a growing undertow of agitation in his voice.

"Then you know what we know."

"You expect me to believe that you executed a man you've known for fifteen years for nothing. Hell, he even lived with you when his parents died for the first three!" Rico was angered, confused, and disgusted by the Admiral's lack of sentiment in this matter. Although Rico didn't expect to see a display of unrequited emotion, he did expect there to be a resonance of respect for Conrad's memory.

"Frankly, I don't care what you believe. What's done is done. Move on," the Admiral stated coldly, standing up as he turned his back to Rico. It took all the strength Griffin had to say those words without choking on them, and Rico picked up on that. The Admiral couldn't keep his forced resolve under Rico's inquisitor's gaze for long. In spite of the contradiction, Rico became enraged by Griffin's callousness.

"I can't move on!" Rico exclaimed, standing to his feet. "A man's life was taken in disgrace. A life that was honorable has been thrown to the vultures. I can't believe that he did, or even thought one of the things he was accused of by the Tribunal!"

"I'm sorry about Conrad, but there was nothing I could do," Admiral Griffin stated fighting back a cracking voice. The Admiral began to nervously thump his hands together. Rico could tell he was holding back, but what, he didn't know. For the first time Rico could sense an emotional undertow in the Admiral, but for some reason he was forcing it into deaf and dumb silence. Rico knew that Griffin wanted him to leave it alone, but he couldn't regardless of the consequences.

"At least let me see the evidence against him, and I don't mean the circus of lies spewed at the hearing. I want to see the actual evidence," Rico pleaded for this understandably simple thing that was not out of military order for him to request.

"I can't do that. The evidence was classified as above top secret and only eye witness testimony was allowed to be included into the public record. The evidence has been sealed by the president himself."

"Then tell me what you know."

"I can't."

"Damn it, Griffin!" Rico exclaimed slamming his fist on the table. "I've known Conrad for most of my life. He was like a brother to me and like a son to you. I don't believe that you think that he would ever betray either of us or the human race. At least let me read his last testament."

"I can't," Griffin informed, as he turned back around to face Captain Sanchez.

"You can't, or you won't?" Rico's tone was now accusatory and bordering on insubordination.

"I can't because he didn't make a final statement!" Griffin yelled back, defending himself on the only point he could truly divulge in complete honesty. Rico was allowed this emotional release because of how close they all had been. Captain Sanchez felt the Admiral deserved every angry dart that he threw, but knew that Griffin couldn't allow him much more.

Rico wanted to scream. The Admiral's emotional state was now a mixture of anger and fear. Rico had never seen that combination in the Admiral before. His anger was getting the better of him. That was not like him, and he struggled to bring it back under control.

"You know what happened and you know I won't let it go," Rico informed.

"I can't confirm or deny that statement," Griffin acknowledged, lowering his penetrating blue eyes praying that Rico would start reading between the lines and stop this foolish line of questions.

"After all we went through together, how could you let it end like this?" Rico asked leaning over the desk while trying to look into the Admiral's evasive stare.

Griffin's eyes would always tell the tale even when his mouth refused. Admiral Griffin was his and Conrad's mentor when they were at the academy. He put them through hell during basic, and even back then couldn't hide any falsehoods with his eyes even when it came to pulling a surprise party for Conrad's birthday.

"It's over. For your own sake, let it go, please," the Admiral implored, his eyes fighting hard to match his vocal tone. It was clear

22

that there were two dialogs going on here, but why? Rico couldn't begin to comprehend.

"I can't. You know I can't," Rico admitted. His tone was apologetic, but his determination never wavered. There would be no thwarting Rico's search for truth.

"Damn it Rico, you have to let it go!" Griffin urged, as if directing a drowning man to a life preserver who refused to be rescued. His eyes spoke volumes that his words could not, yet it was still not an understandable answer even to Rico's trained eye.

Pain had begun to etch deep lines onto the Admiral's face. Rico didn't notice it before until the lamplight on his desk exposed them. Perhaps the Admiral was indeed being coerced not to tell, being threatened by some terrible fate should he divulge anything. Although Rico couldn't prove that, it felt right to make that assumption. That at least, his gut confirmed without exception. Truth be told, no matter what the facts were, it wouldn't bring Conrad back from the dead. He, therefore, decided to calm down and focus on the living, the crew that was left in disgrace.

"What about the Phoenix? Have you found a captain for her?" Rico questioned, changing the subject slightly.

"No, no one wants the job because of the circumstances," the Admiral answered also beginning to calm.

"I'll take her."

"But what about the Falcon?"

"I have the answer to the Falcon sitting in your waiting room. Lt. Commander Lindsay Macalister, my first officer is ready for the Captain's chair."

"Nancy, send in the Lt. Commander," the Admiral called.

Lindsay stood to her feet hearing her summons. Nancy smiled at Lindsay. She cocked a half confident smile back, took a deep breath, and opened the door to join her Captain and Admiral Griffin. Upon passing through the threshold she immediately saluted her superior officers.

"Welcome, Macalister," Admiral Griffin greeted, his pleasant demeanor returning. Lindsay saluted the Admiral, and stood at attention. "At ease," he commanded seeing that Lindsay seemed to be waiting for her next order.

"Thank you, Sir," she responded, but was still very stiff.

"At ease Macalister," Rico said again reinforcing the Admiral's command. Lindsay relaxed slightly expelling a heavy sigh, but was prepared to go back to official mode at a moment's notice.

"Have a seat we've much to discuss," the Admiral began. Lindsay sat down. "Rico tells me that you're ready for command."

"Sir?" Lindsay questioned, gazing at Rico in surprise. His face was beaming like a proud papa.

"I'm assigning Rico command of the Phoenix. He has assured me that you will make the perfect Captain for the Falcon."

"Captain, Sir?" Lindsay questioned aloud. A smile soon began to cascade across her face as the information sank in that she was being promoted. The Admiral reached into his desk drawer and pulled out a box containing her new Captain's bars. He tossed them to her. She caught them, opened the box, and looked upon the shiny bars twinkling under the lights overhead.

"Congratulations Lindsay," Rico said, holding out his hand for her to shake it. She immediately began to laugh in spurts.

"Thank you!" was about all she could verbalize as she took Rico's hand.

"Don't thank me too quickly," the Admiral cautioned. "Although your crews will have their furloughs, you'll be going back to work very quickly. One of the provisions of the peace accord with the Rundi is that we remove all human colonists from the frontier area in the Alpha sector, specifically Hyperion. We have thirty days to remove the human presence or they will return with a vengeance and exterminate anything breathing."

"I knew this peace was too good to be true," Rico commented under his breath.

"It is a true peace, and will be a lasting one, provided we remove the human colonists."

"So the Rundi just moves in with no prior claim to the planet because they say so," Rico stated, his tone exuding his contempt for this directive.

"This was the agreement reached by our two governments. They claim that they need to establish a buffer zone between human and Rundi space so no further misunderstandings can happen between our two peoples. Once the space is established, no reason will be considered acceptable in violating it. Any human vessel that wanders into this space will be destroyed on sight."

"And if a Rundi vessel enters?" Lindsay asked.

"They promise to self destruct, and take out any human vessel that enters in to harm them."

"With so much at stake, I'd think you'd recall the furlough," Rico submitted.

"The colonists on Hyperion must prepare to evacuate. It'll take at least two weeks for them to be ready for evacuation, and for our ships to be converted to haul that many people. The Phoenix will be ready in seven days since she preceded all other ships into port. In addition, our people need the rest. We can't afford a mistake. One more thing, there'll be Rundi ships just at the edge of sensor range to monitor the evacuation. Once all human presence has been extracted they will move in to sterilize the planetoid. You are not to fire on any approaching Rundi ship."

"This plan is a recipe for disaster, Sir," Lindsay added.

"Indeed, that's why I'm entrusting the two of you with command of this operation. The Falcon and Phoenix will work in tandem with the Ares and Triton to evacuate these people. Understand the time constraints are absolute. The colonists and your ships will be ready in two weeks. That leaves sixteen days for the actual evacuation. There are no extensions to this time frame. Anything, or anyone left behind will be eradicated."

"Then I guess we better not screw up," Lindsay added.

"Indeed, anything else you wish to ask?" Admiral Griffin inquired.

"Yes, what are the Rundi giving up?" Rico questioned.

"Nothing to my knowledge."

"That seems a little biased," Rico commented.

"The Military doesn't make policy Captain Sanchez, we uphold it."

"Anything else that you need to share with us, Sir?" Lindsay asked.

"No, that about covers it. I'll have the particulars transmitted to your individual ships. Your contact on Hyperion will be Governor Paul Tarken who has been fully briefed on the situation."

"Good," Rico began with some pent up relief. "Lindsay, I'd like for you to personally transfer my Zeveney program from the Falcon to the Phoenix before you take your leave."

"Yes, Captain."

"It's Rico now, Captain Macalister," Rico corrected. Lindsay just smiled, and nodded in the affirmative.

"I'll make all the necessary updates in the system of your transfer to the Phoenix and Lindsay's promotion to command of the

Falcon. Congratulations, young lady, on a well deserved promotion. Dismissed," the Admiral ordered with a smile.

"Thank you, Sir. I won't let either of you down." She then saluted and left to see to her duties leaving Rico alone with the Admiral again. The Admiral could see that Rico wasn't turning lose of his gut concerning Captain Banes.

"Let it go, Rico. It's best for all concerned."

"I can't, but it'll not interfere with my duties. I just wanted to make that clear."

"For what it's worth, there have been none better than Conrad and I'll miss him too." The Admiral offered this statement like an olive branch, but it was a stiff gesture.

"I know. That's why I have to pursue this."

"Even if it costs you your life?" The Admiral asked, stopping abruptly. It was clear by Griffin's expression that he was afraid he may have said too much, but his eyes were trying to reach out like a warning for Rico to let it alone for his own sake. Rico caught the subtlety and lifted his eyebrows in curiosity. Now, he was certain there was more going on than what was released to the general public.

"Even if it costs me my life," Rico confirmed, and turned to leave.

"Your efforts would be better served restoring morale and honor to his crew."

"Correction Admiral, my crew. And yes, I will restore to them what was wrongfully taken," he stated looking back over his shoulder. Rico then left the Admiral's office without another word to go to the Java Bar and indulge in an espresso to help clear his mind. He hadn't had coffee in sixteen days, and today he would take several and savor each and every drop.

***

The Admiral knew it would be useless to try and stop him from trying to learn the truth, he just hoped he never would. After Rico left the office, a humanoid emerged from a side door. The individual was tall and wore a bulky hooded robe. The hood was drawn down completely covering his face. The sleeves were so long that the hem fell long past any hand that might exist. The bottom of the robe touched the floor. The robe itself was the color of magenta and had a rich gold brocaded belt studded with opals.

"You're Captain Sanchez is a stubborn man," commented the hooded figure in a raspy voice that was quite abrasive and deliberate in its delivery. His tone, however, still managed to command a powerful respect. "It would be a pity to have to kill such a man."

"Yes, Prefect, it would. Although if you told him the truth, he'd leave it alone," the Admiral explained.

"That would be a breach of the peace treaty between our two peoples."

"I know that," Admiral Griffin snapped. He was like a caged tiger ready to devour those that kept him under lock and key.

Glenda C. Finkelstein

"Are you prepared to kill him to preserve the peace?"

"No, I'm not," answered the Admiral, looking vainly upon the Prefect's hood-covered face. He was caught between right and wrong, and the greater and lesser evil. His eyes burned to pierce the facade of this member of the Rundi Parliament so he could see the true nature abiding underneath. Yet, he dare not lift a finger toward him.

"I believe, Admiral that was the most honest statement I've ever heard you make."

Chapter 3

At a pub called Quasar's on Epsilon 6's seedier side, the crewmen of the Triton, Ares, Falcon, and other ships waited for shuttles to either Cassiopeia, the tropical paradise planet, or, Otadan, where many had family. To make the wait pass by more quickly they sipped ale and boasted of their recent prowess in battle. Some even compared scars and recent injuries. With each passing gulp, the boasts became more grandiose. Most of them were content to simply get drunk, but occasionally friction would erupt between crews over who among them was considered the best.

A small group from the Phoenix crew was still there two days after their scheduled furlough release, having been delayed by the circumstances surrounding their late Captain's execution. To view the ensemble together they looked more like a group of misfits rather than loyal subordinates of what had once been called the finest crew in the fleet.

Lt. Edward Jarvis, a black male that stood at an imposing six-feet and four-inches tall with well-defined muscles had the look of a bouncer, but was not a brawler. He maintained that intellect was a far more powerful tool, than the business end of a weapon. He was Captain Bane's second in command, and scuttlebutt had basically tagged Jarvis with promotion after the death of Richard Benson, Captain Banes' first officer who was killed in action during the last Rundi offensive.

The lone female of the group was Lt. Janet Sadowski. At five-feet six-inches tall, Janet's feisty disposition matched well with her short-cropped brown hair and piercing brown eyes. She had no problem taking on anyone that looked at her cross-eyed. Her specialty was engines and she knew every part intimately from stem to stern. It was her ingenuity that had brought the Phoenix safely back home. It was an act that would normally have won her a commendation. Under the circumstances, however, she realized her actions would never be recognized. She had all the makings of a fine officer if she could just learn to control her mouth. Jarvis had made it his pet project to tame this woman. Unlike most whose

32

mouth overrides their backside, she could cash the checks she was writing.

The third member of the group was Wong Qwan, an Asian male of about five-feet and five-inches. He seldom spoke, but when he did you made sure you paid attention. Although he was no bigger than a minute with little visible brute strength, he could take out a barracks full of muscle bound soldiers with his keen fifth degree black belt skills. His specialty was ship's computer systems. In some ways he was considered, Captain Bane's favorite son. The Captain took a special interest in Wong's career after rescuing him from a life of boredom in the technology industry on Beta-Indie. Although no one really knew the whole story behind Wong's corporate past, Conrad trusted him explicitly.

As different as these three were, they shared a fierce loyalty to the memory of Captain Banes and would not sit idly by while someone defamed his name. The problem was that this incident was on the minds and lips of everyone these days. Whenever a uniformed member of the Phoenix crew was seen, people stared and whispered to each other. After a few beers, people stopped whispering. Several crewmen from the Triton had come in a few minutes earlier, and had already downed at least two beers each with a bourbon chaser.

When Jarvis, Sadowski, and Qwan arrived at the bar they noticed that the loudness of the room quieted when they stepped through the door. All eyes followed them to their table. Janet met each inquisitive gaze with a non-apologetic glare. Once they were seated, the room returned to its usual fervor.

"What can I get you?" questioned a scantily clad, overworked waitress with tussled hair and beer stains on her apron.

"Three beers," Jarvis answered. The waitress immediately left to fill their order.

"Did you see how they looked at us?" Janet asked the others, pointing specifically at the Triton crewmembers sitting across the room.

"It was hard to miss. Stop pointing," Jarvis ordered.

"I'd like to stuff those eyes down their gullets," Janet quipped, pulling her accusatory finger back.

"They can look all they want, it doesn't change anything," Jarvis responded trying to get Janet to calm down.

"I resent being looked at as maggot."

The waitress came back and sat three beers on the table. Jarvis paid for the round, and they began to drink them. Suddenly, from across the room, the same four crewmen from the Triton got up from their table and approached the trio.

"Trouble's coming," Qwan informed the others. The drunken group was coming from a table located in their blind spot save Qwan who had a lovely view of their table. Janet turned her head around to look at the approaching men.

"Just ignore them," Jarvis whispered. Janet just rolled her eyes at Jarvis. They were coming to the table. She knew there was no way they were going to get away with just ignoring them.

"Well, if it isn't the proud crew of the Phoenix," announced the ringleader of the foursome in a slurred sarcastic tone. Janet started to get up. Her legs pushed the chair away as she stood to her feet. It screeched across the hard floor causing those sitting at a nearby table to wince from the sound it made as the men came around to face them. Jarvis and company could smell the alcohol on their breath even from across the table. The foursome stood tall, or at least as tall as one can stand while swaggering.

"Damn straight, we're proud," Janet defended without apology, her eyes unwavering against the upshot young Lieutenant Travis' derogatory comment. His name patch was now clearly visible. Janet took a moment to glance at each one's name patch and committed them to memory.

"You shouldn't even be in that uniform after what your yellow bellied Captain done," Travis stated insultingly with sluggish speech and awkward grammar.

"Captain Banes was a great man," Qwan defended, standing to his feet.

"The bravest there ever was," Janet seconded.

"You gentlemen should move on," Jarvis advised, cautiously. They dismissed his suggestion with a sneer. Jarvis stood to his feet realizing that good sense was not going to win out. His full stature

35

unfolded before them like a ladder. The men gazed up at Jarvis, but they had too much beer in their bellies to exercise common sense.

"No, you're the ones who need to leave," Lt. Travis instructed with arrogance.

"We have just as much right to be here as you do," Qwan informed, in a calmness that few possess when relaxed, much less when challenged. His calm, however, was deceptive. Even though Wong knew his friends could handle themselves in a fight, he prepared to defend himself and his crewmates anyway.

"He was a traitor," announced crewman Capps. He spit some of the beer foam that had accumulated in the corner of his mouth on Jarvis' shirt with the deliberate pronunciation of each slightly slurred syllable.

"I think you should recant that," Jarvis informed, while wiping away some of the beer-laced spittle from his shirt.

"No." Travis answered on Capps' behalf, trying to get in Jarvis' face.

Suddenly, a fist was thrown nicking Qwan. Janet threw her beer into Lt. Travis' face. His buddy shoved the table knocking Janet onto her backside. Qwan kicked the man in the face and helped Janet back up to her feet in one fluid movement. Then crewman Capps punched Jarvis in the gut. Jarvis absorbed the impact, gave a look that implied, *you really shouldn't have done that*, and knocked him cold with a right uppercut. The scuffle bumped a couple of nearby tables, spilling beer in their laps, and a fight quickly broke out that embroiled the entire bar. Chairs, beer bottles, peanuts, fists, feet, and anything that wasn't tied down went flying.

Qwan began to take down each brawler one at a time with finely tuned karate precision. He managed to take out most of his opponents without injury to himself, but failed to duck as a chair went flying by cutting his arm. Before the military police arrived to break up the fight most of the Triton crew were lying on the floor, and the trio from the Phoenix were still standing. Janet had a busted lip and bruised knuckles. Although she was a girl and was military trained, it was her skills she acquired from her four older brothers that served her best in these situations. Jarvis sported a black eye and a busted lip.

When the Military Police arrived at the bar, everyone was carted off to security and placed in holding cells until their commanding officers could be notified. At this stage there was no more taunting, just groaning and moaning as the pain began to sober them up. Needless to say the Military Police were not thrilled that another incident involving the Phoenix crew had taken place. Although no official announcement had been made to the Phoenix crew, most base personnel had already heard the news that Captain Sanchez was now their new commander. Officer Brutus shook his head with dismay as he put Jarvis, Janet, and Wong in their holding cell.

"What's up with you?" Jarvis asked, nursing a swelling eye. He surmised from Brutus' tone that he possessed information they lacked.

"I don't envy you guys."

"So what's new?" Jarvis bantered.

"What's new is your new captain isn't going to be happy about this," Brutus explained.

"Our new captain?" Janet questioned, unaware that they had been assigned one.

"Yes, Captain Rico Sanchez."

"Oh, shit," Jarvis commented aloud.

The three looked at one another knowing their goose was cooked. Captain Sanchez had quite the reputation when it came to dealing with disciplinary issues. It had been said that one would rather do hard time than be under Captain Rico's boot. They all took a seat inside their cell to await the end of their careers.

Qwan's arm was bleeding and since the wound was not life threatening they wouldn't see medical until their captain bailed them out. With a practiced hand Janet withdrew a handkerchief from her pocket, folded it, and tied it taunt around his arm until he could be treated. This was something she had done many times before during the war. Wong didn't protest as it provided a moment of close contact with the one he's had a secret crush on for some time. Yet, outwardly he was nonchalant about it.

***

In the Java Bar on the opposite side of the station, Rico was waiting with great anticipation for his espresso. He could see the waitress from across the room heading in his direction. She was bringing to him the most wonderful of elixirs. At any other time he would have allowed himself the privilege of admiring the waitress' female form. This time, however, he'd gone a long time without his beloved espresso. The coffee had become more sensually stimulating than gazing upon the opposite sex. That thought greatly unsettled him. He'd definitely been too long without his coffee.

His eyes widened as the waitress set three small cups of espresso one at a time in front of him. He bit his bottom lip as he eyed the coffee. The steam wafted up from the froth just a few inches above the cup. He reached out bringing the first cup of coffee toward him. He leaned over it breathing in the scent of his favorite drink slowly and deeply into his lungs. Then he took the cup gingerly into his hands, closed his eyes, raised the cup to his lips, and tipped the cup so that the coffee trickled over his lips and teeth falling upon his tongue. He savored every tiny drop that fell into his mouth as it cascaded over his pallet and into his stomach.

Almost instantly he could feel the coffee revitalizing him. The waitress watched this patron. She had never before seen someone drink coffee and demonstrate such sensual ecstasy in its consumption. Although she found him handsome, it was his actions that intrigued her more than anything else. Once he had finished the first cup of coffee, he opened eyes to meet the waitress' curious stare. He suddenly became uncomfortable. It was similar to the feeling one gets when your mom discovers the girly magazines hiding under your mattress.

"I'm sorry, Sir. I never saw anyone drink coffee like that before," the waitress confided trying to discharge the awkwardness of the situation.

"I've been without coffee for sixteen days, eleven hours, and twenty minutes. Espresso is my favorite," Rico explained.

"Enjoy," the waitress conceded with a smile, his explanation was a fair and justified one. She recognized many of the medals and ribbons that adorned his coat and knew he, like all military personnel, were returning from battle. The waitress turned around to tend to other customers. Soon the Military Police entered the Java Bar intruding upon Rico's solitude to inform him of his new crew's antics. Before being able to drink the other two Espressos, the Military Police walked up to his table and advised him that he was required to accompany them back to security to claim his crew. He knew his duty demanded that he comply but thought it would be justified if he made the crew wait while he finished his Espressos. He ultimately decided it was best to deal with his crew's actions sooner rather than later.

Noticing the look on Rico's face, the waitress couldn't help but see his disappointed countenance as the police made their request. His sadness was displayed with such heart wrenching boyish charm that she had to intervene.

40

"Sir, why don't you go with these gentlemen, take care of your business, and when you return I'll have two fresh Espressos ready for you at no charge," the waitress informed with a kindly grin. It was the least she could do for a Captain of Epsilon 6 command who has served with such distinction.

"Thank you," Rico responded with a big grin beaming across his face. After expelling a sigh of both relief and aggravation, he went with the Military Police to the holding cells where some of his new crew was being held. Upon arriving at the brig he stopped at the front desk to check in, find out whom he was collecting, and what they did to receive a stay at the box motel. He carefully reviewed their names, glanced at their positions on the Phoenix, and their prior disciplinary records.

"What happened?" Rico asked the guard on duty.

"What usually happens in a bar, too much to drink and too much pride. No one really knows what started the fight because the military motto of guarding each other's back is keeping all parties quiet."

"Understood. May I see them?"

"Of course Captain, they're your crew now." The security guard rose to his feet and started to walk around the desk. "Excuse me for asking, but what did you do to earn the command of the most disgraced crew in the fleet?"

Rico looked into the guard's eyes with an upraised eyebrow. Although he expected comments like that from the enlisted ranks, he didn't expect it from security personnel. His assumption was that the bar fight was probably started by similar attitudes, but Rico came to get his crew out, not join them.

"I didn't do anything, soldier, I asked to be their new Captain."

The guard seemed stunned. He could see in Rico's steely-eyed expression that he should choose his next words carefully. The guard quickly veered away from Rico's gaze, and showed him where he could collect his crewmen.

"They're right back there in cell C-14. If you'll just sign here, you can be on your way. The lock will respond to your DNA."

"Thank you, umm," Rico paused to read his name patch, "Brutus," Rico said as he signed for his crewman. He was buzzed into the main holding area and preceded to cell C-14. Another security guard immediately accompanied him. He found his three crewmen sitting in various positions of disarray. He surmised that they were attempting to pass the time until their inevitable meeting with him. He could only imagine what was going through their minds about now.

Janet caught sight of him first and just knew that he'd have them doing garbage duty for the next three months. She elbowed Jarvis, who himself, reasoned that he could kiss any thought of being promoted to exec good-bye.

"Attention!" announced the security guard. Jarvis, Qwan, and Sadowski leapt to their feet. Their clothes were torn and full of stains from beer and blood from busted lips and noses.

"You may leave us," Rico ordered, addressing the guard. The guard saluted and returned to his station leaving Rico alone with his crew. Rico studied each one of them. It wasn't hard for him to figure out who was who. "Who wants to explain to me why members of my crew are sitting in a holding cell?"

No one answered. Each one looked over at the other and then back at Captain Sanchez without turning their heads. None of them wanted to explain, but Rico wouldn't accept their silence.

"I realize you don't know me, but I'm not going to accept your silence as an answer any more than Captain Banes would have. Some one had better start talking, or I will leave you here." Still no one responded. Rico decided to turn and walk away.

"Captain," Jarvis called sharply. Rico stopped, but didn't turn around until Jarvis started talking. "We were defending Captain Banes' honor. Some crewmen from the Triton disrespected his memory." He had Rico's attention. Rico slowly turned to face them so he could look them in the eye.

"Is this true?" Rico questioned of Qwan and Sadowski.

"Yes, sir," they responded together, but not in unison.

"I take it that you don't believe what Captain Banes was accused of."

"No sir, we don't, and will have words with anyone that says otherwise," Jarvis explained in further detail, cutting Janet off before she could insert her size six shoe into her mouth. He wasn't certain how Rico was going to respond, but it was the truth. Rico thought quietly for a moment.

"I admire your spirit, and share your view point. However, I'll not have my crew starting bar-fights. No one ever regained respect in such a manner."

"We didn't start the fight sir, we just didn't back down when challenged," Jarvis clarified.

"Yeah, but I'll wager that Lt. Travis will think twice before starting something again," Sadowski commented with a smile of satisfaction. All eyes focused on her. She didn't realize she had verbalized her thoughts. The smile left her face quickly as she cleared her throat.

"I know that the crew of the Phoenix is the best in the fleet. Furthermore, you don't need other's opinions to confirm or deny that fact. I don't care what people say about Captain Banes or you. You will ignore it, and that is an order."

"But sir they were wrong," Janet defended boldly. Rico admired her spunk, but if carried to extremes could be problematic.

"Yes, they were, but fighting isn't going to change their minds," Rico said. He opened the cell door with a wave of his hand. The lock responded to his DNA allowing the cell door to swing open. He entered the cell and began moving slowly from one to the

44

other making sure that his face was in their face. He studied their response to his words. "The only way to restore your own honor is to be the very best regardless of what people think, and doing it not for glory, but for the sheer fact that it's the right thing to do. Is that clear?"

"Yes, sir," they mumbled softly.

"I didn't hear you. I said, is that clear?"

"Yes, Sir," all three responded.

"Just so there is no misunderstanding, I don't care if they get in your face. You will walk away. If you don't, the next holding cell you find yourself in will be your permanent home. Are we clear?"

"Yes, sir," they answered, louder this time, but lacked confidence.

"I said, are we clear?" Rico yelled out as if he were drilling a team of fresh recruits.

"Yes Sir, Captain, Sir!" They responded back this time with loud, unwavering confidence accentuated with exacting military proficiency.

"Good, you're free to go, but not on furlough. You're to report back to the Phoenix and assist the base personnel in converting the cargo bays to receive refugees from Hyperion."

The three saluted and walked out of the cell single file. Jarvis was the last one out. He was amazed that they got off that easy considering their transgression and Rico's reputation.

"Jarvis, a moment," Rico called. Qwan and Sadowski looked back wondering if Jarvis was going to be punished further since he was the highest-ranking officer in the group. Jarvis gave a look of reassurance to them so they would go on ahead and report to the ship without him. He then turned around to face Captain Sanchez to receive any additional punishment he was going to dish out.

"Yes sir," Jarvis acknowledged, holding his breath while bracing himself for his demotion.

"I have only one question for you."

"What's that sir?" Jarvis inquired, having become uncomfortable under Rico's scrutiny. Rico had fallen silent for a moment as he studied Jarvis' reactions.

"Did you win?" Rico asked. Jarvis was taken aback by the question, and thought a moment before answering.

"Excuse me?" Jarvis asked just to be sure he heard the captain correctly.

"Did you win?"

"Yes, we won." There was no pride in his tone. It was simply an answer to Rico's question. A smile slowly grew upon Rico's face punctuated by a touch of pride. Even though the fight was not officially a good move, it was good to know that his people won the day.

"That will be all," Rico said dismissing Jarvis. Eddie didn't bother to inquire why Rico wanted to know, or why he smiled. It was enough that he was dismissed without further disciplinary action. Once Jarvis was out of earshot, Rico made a call to Zeveney.

"Zeveney," Rico began. He paused just a moment for Zeveney to acknowledge reception, but no acknowledgement was given. "Zeveney?" Rico called again, questioningly.

"Zeveney's currently offline sir," Lindsay responded.

"Lindsay?"

"Yes, Sir."

"Why is Zeveney offline?"

"You asked me to install him into the Phoenix. He has a very complex matrix. It was necessary to take him offline to insure that no data or formatting would be lost in the move."

"Very good, Macalister, call me when he's fully integrated into the Phoenix."

"Yes, sir. Oh, and by the way, I took the liberty to call the base movers to transfer your belongings to the Phoenix."

"Can't wait to move into your new quarters?" Rico asked, coyly.

"No, Sir, that's not it at all. I wanted to free up as much of your time as I could so you could enjoy some furlough too. You've had so much on your mind, I thought it'd..."

"Relax, Lindsay, I was just busting your chops. I appreciate it. When you've finished installing the Zeveney program call me. I'll be in the Java Bar with an Espresso or two."

"Yes Sir, Macalister out."

Glenda C. Finkelstein

Chapter 4

Lindsay wanted to complete the transfer of the Zeveney program into Captain Sanchez's new quarters with haste. When she took Zeveney offline back on the Falcon, she could see that it had been working on reviewing the evidence against Conrad. She should have known that Rico would be cross checking everything. She knew that he had an impressive security clearance, so she didn't think that he was doing anything improper. Equipment in hand she headed across the docking bay to the Phoenix.

Upon arriving in Rico's new quarters, she noticed that the movers were already packing up Conrad's things. Lindsay knew

49

that they were going to dispose of them, as there was no next of kin to send them to. This disquieted her. She knew that Rico and Conrad were very close since Academy days, and surmised that the careless disposal of Captain Banes' possessions would not sit well with him. With that in mind, she decided to intervene and allow Rico every opportunity to find the truth no matter how mundane. Even if it was just to bring his own spirit some comfort.

"Where are you taking Captain Bane's personal belongings?" Lindsay asked, feigning ignorance.

"We've been ordered to dispose of them, by Epsilon 6 Command."

"There was some confusion with those orders. I was sent here to put things straight. Leave the boxes in the corner."

"But Lt. Commander we've been ordered to..."

"It's Captain Macalister," she corrected pointing to her new Captain's bars, and then continued without hesitation, "and since I'm part of Epsilon 6 Command, I suggest you obey me before I put you on report."

"Yes, Ma'am," the mover said capitulating to her authority.

"Just box up his stuff, label them, and stack them in that corner. Captain Sanchez will want to inspect them, and will later dictate how they will be disposed. If you do a good job, I'll let Captain Sanchez know so he can send his regards to your boss."

"Captain Rico Sanchez?" he questioned, just to be sure he heard correctly.

50

"Yes, he's the new Captain of the Phoenix."

"Yes, Ma'am, right away," he responded and then turned to his men, "You heard the lady, I mean the Captain. Let's get busy."

Ah, the good ole Rico Sanchez reputation, Lindsay thought to herself. It was almost cruel to use it on these poor unsuspecting souls, but it was too enjoyable to feel guilty about.

While the men busied themselves with their new orders, Lindsay occupied herself with installing the Zeveney program. She was quite amazed at how different the two men actually were. You could barely discern a technological presence in the room. Although the Zeveney 7000-P was not a standard program, it was considered the Captain's choice of tech assistants. Conrad was known for being technologically challenged and preferred it that way. Lindsay soon discovered that there was only a small port left in the room for basic electronic devices. Most Captain's quarters are equipped with a wide array of ports and junctions which she was certain was standard, but was even more certain that Conrad went out of his way to have those basic electronic services removed. She needed a converter, and a tech to assist her.

"Bridge," Lindsay called from Rico's new quarters, "This is Captain Lindsay Macalister. I need a ship's systems specialist to bring a converter so I can install Captain Sanchez's Zeveney 7000-P computer companion in his new quarters."

"Acknowledged, Wong Qwan is our System's Specialist on the Phoenix and is currently on board. He'll be with you momentarily."

"Thank you."

While Lindsay waited for Wong, she watched the movers. They were quite proficient and careful with the Captain's things. She saw a photo on Conrad's bureau just as one of the workmen reached up to put it inside a box.

"Leave that," Lindsay commanded. He gently put the photo back down in its original position and continued his packing keeping one eye on Lindsay to see if she was going to say 'no' to anything else. If not for a different frame she would've thought that photo belonged to Rico. She knew they were close, but never realized just how much until recent days. Rico's behavior took a nosedive the moment the news was released that Conrad had been executed. It was such a shock. The man had just received only a few days before, a special citation that few survive to be awarded for conspicuous gallantry above and beyond the call of duty. She became lost in her thoughts while she pondered the irony of it.

Wong poked his head into the open doorway sporting his new bandage from medical, and looked about at the goings on. He surmised quickly that the woman seated on the chair near the console was the lady who summoned him.

"Captain Macalister, I presume?"

"You presume correctly."

"System Specialist Wong Qwan, at your service. I have your converter."

"Thank you Mr. Qwan," Lindsay acknowledged as she took the device from his hands. The workmen excused themselves having finished their task interrupting their greeting. Wong moved to the side to let them exit before extending his hand to Lindsay.

"Call me Wong."

"Okay, Wong it is," she agreed shaking his hand which was smaller than her own. He winced slightly. "I'm sorry I didn't see your injury. Did you acquire that at the Breach?"

"No, it's nothing really. It was my first bar fight."

"Oh," she was slightly embarrassed that she may have put him in an awkward position then tried to change the subject. "I'm surprised you're still on board."

"We still have a skeleton crew that remained behind due to the damages the Phoenix received," he informed. It was true in general, just not completely true. He had already shared more with her than he intended.

She smiled graciously at him not wanting to pry any further. Lindsay quickly dispensed with this small pleasantry and went straight to work. He watched her nervously as she began to try and install the converter. Although she was proficient, she was slightly clumsy with the equipment. Wong, on the other hand, was like an artist in the arena of technology. He had never seen a Zeveney 7000-P system up close and personal before. The amount of data

53

and processing speed it possessed was nearly incalculable. To put it in perspective it was like a student of art seeing a Picasso for the first time.

"You didn't happen to bring your tool box with you?" she asked. There was frustration in her tone, but it was directed at the equipment and not Wong.

"I have the tool you need right here," Wong offered, extracting the tool from the pocket of his work coat. She took the device from his outstretched hand. "Although I miss Captain Banes, I'm excited about having a Zeveney 7000-P system on board. Captain Banes was a bit of a dinosaur when it came to technology."

"Not Rico. I mean, Captain Sanchez," Lindsay corrected, quickly. She'd adjusted to the familiar too easily for her taste. "Crap," she commented as her hand slipped.

"Here, let me help you with that," Wong offered. She smiled, nodding in the affirmative.

They worked together as they talked, speaking in their techno babble speech that no one but a fellow techie would truly appreciate. Lindsay was quite charmed by this man. He was intelligent and agile around the equipment. Once the converter was installed, Lindsay proceeded to connect the interfaces, both physical and virtual. Wong watched so he would be more than ready to serve his new captain. He needed the brownie points especially after making such a terrible first impression.

"There, that should do it. Let's fire him up," Lindsay announced. Wong turned the power on. Zeveney came back on-line like a sunrise breaks the horizon. At first his presence was barely discernable, but soon reached full power. His brilliant, crisp image could be viewed so well that it was almost like a physical person took up residence in there. A wave of the hand, however, would disperse the suspended photons and you'd discover quickly that it was just a hologram.

"Lindsay?" Zeveney asked, slightly dazed. He was a little unsettled from the transfer.

"Yes, Zeveney, it's me. How are you doing?"

"I'm a little out of phase."

"Wong Qwan, the Phoenix Systems Specialist, and I just finished installing you into Captain Sanchez's new quarters."

"I see. It's a pleasure to meet you, Mr. Qwan."

"Just call me Wong," he insisted with a smile.

"You should adjust the calibration to two one-thousand's of a micron down," Zeveney suggested.

"Okay, but that's pretty minor," Wong conjectured aloud as he retrieved the necessary tool to make the requested adjustment.

"Minor for you, not for me. You would understand it better as indigestion."

Wong made the adjustment, and a sound very similar to a burp emanated from Zeveney. Lindsay stifled a giggle. It still amazed her how lifelike this program was, and yet, still just a bunch of algorithms.

"Better?" Wong questioned.

"Better," Zeveney said smiling. Lindsay just smirked at the exchange.

"Well, I need to get going. So long Zeveney, I believe I'm leaving you in good hands."

"Goodbye Lindsay," Zeveney addressed in farewell, and then turned his attention to Wong. "I'm sorry for your loss, Wong. Captain Banes was a good man."

Wong was taken aback by this machine's genuine, albeit awkward, attempt at manners.

"Yes, he was, he deserved better than what he got."

"Zeveney," Lindsay interjected, before leaving the room. "Captain Sanchez wants you to contact him now that you're back on-line. Also, let him know that I had Conrad's belongings boxed up and left in the corner of his new quarters for him to inspect."

"We'll do," Zeveney answered. Lindsay left the room with a parting smile. Wong just shook his head staring at the hologram. He'd heard wondrous things about the Zeveney program, but didn't believe it could live up to its reputation. It truly was the most lifelike system he'd ever seen.

"If you'd shut the door on your way out, I have work to do," Zeveney requested of Wong. He was surprised at Zeveney's awareness of privacy. Wong complied with the request. He left the room and headed straight for a library unit to beef up on the specs of this new system he just helped install. The electronic door closed and locked behind him. Zeveney was now alone to contact Rico at his discretion.

"Captain Sanchez," Zeveney called, opening a communication signal.

"Zev! You're back," Rico greeted with glee as if he were addressing a dear friend through his combadge he wore as one would cufflinks.

"Yes, thanks to Lindsay and Wong Qwan. How may I serve you?"

"I need you to prepare a report from the personnel folders of Wong Qwan, Lt. Edward Jarvis, and Lt. Janet Sadowski. Have their profiles ready when I arrive on the Phoenix to collect my things. I'll be going on holiday for a few days."

"I'll have them ready for you. Lindsay wanted you to know that she had the movers pack up Conrad's belongings and leave them in the corner of your new quarters," Zeveney responded.

"Thanks, Zev. Oh, one more thing. I want you to scan the quarters, Conrad's stuff, and mine when it arrives. See if there is anything amiss such as surveillance in the room before I get there. I have a hunch that things aren't as they would appear."

"You have found evidence to support your suspicions?" Zeveney questioned, cautiously.

"Let's just say that I'm more certain than ever that there is some sort of conspiracy going on, but I'm still gathering data and I'm not taking anything for granted."

"Your wish is my command," Zeveney acknowledged closing the signal between them. Rico was now alone with his last cup of Espresso. He drank it with as much enthusiasm as the first cup he consumed savoring every drop.

***

A couple hours later Rico boarded the Phoenix without much ado. Most of the crew was out on furlough and the base personnel were busy preparing the ship for the evacuation of Hyperion. Upon entering he surveyed his new quarters, had it not been for the Phoenix insignia on the wall he would have thought he was back on the Falcon. White boxes piled up on the starboard side were labeled Banes, blue ones on the port side were labeled Sanchez, and in the middle was his Zeveney 7000-P program hard at work compiling the information he requested.

"How are things coming along?" Rico questioned.

"Fine," Zeveney responded, and continued. The Zeveney program had one unique feature which delighted Rico, and that was when the program was really crunching numbers it'd hum like a human does when they're happy.

"Is the room clear of any spying devices?"

"Si."

"You're learning Spanish, that's great! Is anything complete yet?"

"Yes. No. I'm not sure…" Zev responded in broken one-word sentences.

"Zev, is everything okay? Do you need maintenance?"

"No, I'm puzzled."

"Why?" Rico questioned with delight. He didn't think there was anything that could stump this program. "Please state the cause of this puzzlement," he requested with boyish anticipation.

"That photo of you and Conrad Banes that belonged to Conrad is, on the surface, identical to the one you have with the exception of the frame."

"So why would a different frame bother you?"

"I discovered a message written directly onto the photo itself."

Rico walked over to the photo on the counter, picked it up in his hands, and carefully examined it. He couldn't see anything on the photo or the frame.

"I don't see anything," Rico admitted.

"Let me adjust the light to the ultra violet spectrum."

When Zeveney changed the light two words showed up clear as day on the face of the photo, 'morphing nymph.'

"What can you tell me about this cryptic term?" Rico asked.

"Not much other than certain species of insects called butterflies and dragonflies fall into that category. There are others, but those are the most common. The hand writing matches that of Captain Banes, but why he wrote it I can't begin to surmise. There is no mention on an interest in entomology. What is even more mysterious is the substance with which it was written is unknown."

"Unknown?"

"It's definitely organic, but of a structure I've never seen before. There's not a single match in the collective database library."

"Can you tell me what it resembles that you do recognize?"

"Blood."

Zeveney's response was short and to the point. The word lodged into Rico's brain like a hatchet lodges into the skull of some poor unsuspecting soul in some low budget horror film. He stood there unable to formulate a response. Until this moment Rico had hoped that all these incidents would turn out to be some horribly twisted unfortunate mistake, but now he knew that Conrad had left a clue in case something happened to him. That meant the actions taken by the military council were not only deliberate, but at the very least, added up to subterfuge. He was staring down the throat of a deadly conspiracy.

The worst thing about this epiphany was that he knew he couldn't go to command. Admiral Griffin was definitely a part of it. Rico just didn't know if it was willing or unwilling. His gut, however, dictated that it was probably unwilling. Yet, it still amounted to the same thing. Rico was alone in his search for the truth, and at the end of it, he too, may be killed to keep whatever secret the government was hiding. The Admiral's cryptic warnings began to take on greater significance with this new evidence.

"Zeveney, I want you to erase your findings, methods, and direction regarding this photo. In addition, should you receive a command from me or anyone else you will not scan that photo again. Unless I provide our secret password, is that clear?"

The Zeveney program started humming as it tagged various files. It knew that Rico didn't want anyone knowing what it knew, although neither of them could be certain who or how many that might be. Nor did they understand its significance at this early juncture.

"I've finished tagging...dumping files...encrypting algorithms...final wipe complete."

"Good. Please bring up the files you've prepared on Lt. Janet Sadowski, Lt. Edward Jarvis, and Wong Qwan."

"Pulled and ready."

"Give me a brief summary of each one beginning with Janet."

"Lt. Janet Sadowski, Engineer's First Mate. Captain Banes wrote a commendation for her, but she has yet to receive it."

"What was the commendation for?"

"She was commended for conspicuous ingenuity and performance above and beyond the call of duty. She repaired the Phoenix's engines enabling this ship to escape from a fighter barrage

61

during the Battle of the Breach in one piece. Had it not been for Lt. Janet Sadowski, this ship, and its crew would have been lost."

"Is the medal on its way?" Rico questioned. Zeveney didn't answer immediately. "Surely the Admiral wouldn't be that big of a jerk. Regardless of the circumstances surrounding Conrad, the entire ship's company owes their lives to that little lady," Rico stated aloud.

"I'll check," Zeveney acknowledged searching the base files as instructed for any soon to be released commendations. "No sir, the Epsilon 6 High Command…" Zev paused. He didn't want to relay any further information that would upset Rico.

"Continue," Rico insisted.

"They refused the commendation based upon the circumstances surrounding Captain Banes."

"Son of a…Hold that thought, and get me the Admiral," Rico demanded. Zeveney made the connection bypassing the secretarial communication line.

"Admiral Griffin, here," he responded to the intercom believing that he was talking with Nancy, his secretary.

"Admiral, this is Captain Sanchez."

"How'd you bypass?"

"Never mind how I got through. It has come to my attention that the High Command has refused to grant the commendation for Lt. Janet Sadowski submitted by Captain Banes."

"We thought it best under the circumstances."

"You thought wrong! I want a full commendation medal and accompanying paperwork on my desk for her by the time I return from my holiday. If it's not here, I will be paying you a personal visit!" Rico disconnected the communication lines abruptly.

"Yes, Sir," Admiral Griffin responded to a now dead line.

"Impudent isn't he?" stated the hooded figure lingering in the shadows of the room, his comment was more of an observation than a question.

"No, Prefect, the term is passionate."

"Are you going to grant his request?" Griffin started to chuckle. "What's so funny?" the Prefect asked.

"You really don't get it. Rico wasn't asking. He was demanding, and he had every right to demand what he did. Ms Sadowski did well and she should be recognized for it. I will have the medal and paperwork ready by the time he returns because it's the right thing to do. Besides you got your token sacrifice."

"Token sacrifice?" the Prefect questioned.

"Do you really think we are so easily broken that we would fold in humiliation because one man's reputation was defamed?"

"Don't let Captain Sanchez's passions sway you from your sworn duty."

"Just because I carry out my duty doesn't mean I have to like it, or you." Griffin replied leaving no room for misinterpretation of his opinion of his task or the Prefect.

"You humans are a strange lot."

"I'll take that as a compliment. If you'll excuse me, I have work to do," Griffin informed, his attitude having absorbed a little of Rico's passion. The Prefect just turned around in silence and walked away.

***

"Zeveney, would you please continue with the file picking up with Lt. Edward Jarvis?"

"Lt. Edward Jarvis has served on board the Phoenix since he graduated from the Academy. During the Battle of the Breach he was cited for rescuing the life of Captain Banes when he refused to leave the fallen body of his first officer, Lt. Commander Richard Benson."

"Is there a commendation for him too?"

"No."

"Why not?"

"It would seem that Lt. Jarvis used a right cross to convince Captain Banes to come along." Rico chuckled. He knew Conrad could be a horse's ass when he made up his mind. Although the end result was saving Conrad's life, striking a fellow officer isn't a commendation bell ringer.

"Any other disciplinary actions on Jarvis?"

"No, although he was cited numerous times for performing above and beyond the call of duty during the Rundi War."

"Very good. What about Qwan?"

"Qwan doesn't appear to exist prior to being transferred to the Phoenix three years ago from the Beta-Indie Technology Corporate Warehouse facility on Conrad's recommendation. He states that he was from the Uzzah Colony and any records on him would have been destroyed. That outpost took heavy losses during the Rundi War. He has a top-secret security clearance, and is technically still a civilian under contract to Epsilon 6 Command. Conrad took a liking to him, discovered his uncanny gift with computers, and put him to work."

"Strays," Rico muttered under his breath.

"Strays, Sir?" Zev questioned.

"Conrad always took in strays. I remember him keeping an abandon puppy hidden in his barrack's closet even though it was against the rules until his then girlfriend could visit and take it home with her."

"There's no record of that incident in Captain Banes' file."

"That's because the brass never found out. Albeit they had their suspicions, they just couldn't prove it," Rico explained, reflecting upon the time when the then Captain Griffin discovered his shoe missing. When another recruit found it the shoe had been virtually gnawed in two.

"There is one other odd thing in his file. It was a current entry under personal notes, and it makes no sense to me."

"What?"

"Conrad notes that he believed that something was going on between Wong Qwan and Janet Sadowski, noting Wong's propensity for losing at poker when Janet stood to win. Would you like me to put them under surveillance?"

"Hardly."

"Do you know what he meant?"

"Yes, Conrad was under the impression that Wong was sweet on Janet."

"Sweet?" Zeveney questioned.

"It falls under human interpersonal relationships."

"Oh, you mean human mating rituals," Zeveney corrected.

"I'd hardly call it a ritual. Rituals are consistent beautiful ceremonies with deep meaning. Human sexuality is clumsy, awkward, and more often than not, hurtful."

"I see. Do you require anything further?" Zeveney asked, trying to change the subject. He realized that this was one of those esoteric human concepts that simply made him feel inadequate. Realizing Zev had grown uncomfortable he gladly continued with additional business.

"Yes, make a notation in Lt. Edward Jarvis' file that he is this day promoted to Lt. Commander Jarvis, and is my new executive officer."

"Do you want me to inform him?"

"No, but summon him to my office. I'll tell him on my way out. Oh, and while I'm away, I want you to review the files for every member of this crew. Compile a list of anything that's odd or doesn't add up be it past or present. In addition, pull all the logs both professional and personal for all the officers, search for anything out of the ordinary. Do a compare and report anything that doesn't jive with other logs on the same incident."

"I've already tried to access Captain Banes' logs, but they've been hard erased. The data is irretrievable."

"I figured as much that's why we're coming in through the back door on this investigation. Leave nothing to chance or to assumption. While you're at it conduct diagnostics on the ship maintenance logs including the shuttles. Understand, Zev, you and I are the only ones that are in the loop on this, and it can't interfere with the evacuation of Hyperion."

"Understood."

"I know I've given you a lot to do. Please try and condense it for me when I return."

"You've yet to exhaust my computation capabilities," Zeveney stated proudly.

"Yes, but I'm not you. So I need it in nice bite sized chunks."

"Of course, Sir."

Rico grabbed a suitcase out of one of the boxes that he always kept packed for short holidays. As he headed out the door, he paused a moment leaning back inside the door. He started to walk over and pick up the photo, but decided not to. His head was buzzing with all the possibilities and he needed to clear his head before he started seeing a conspiracy behind every door. If he couldn't think clearly, he would be useless to his friend. Besides after basically announcing his intentions to the Admiral he needed to keep a low profile so that his response would seem to reflect the heat of the moment rather than his intense desire to get to the truth. Although he desired to stay and get on with the investigation, discretion and secrecy was more important at the moment.

"Keep the door locked. No one is to come in here while I'm gone," Rico ordered.

"Your wish is my command."

Rico withdrew from the threshold as the door shut and sealed behind him. He stopped by his new office where Lt. Jarvis was waiting. The Lieutenant was noticeably nervous when Captain Sanchez entered.

"Captain," Jarvis greeted, snapping to attention when the door opened.

"At ease Jarvis."

"Yes, Sir."

"It has come to my attention that you were single handedly responsible for saving the life of Captain Banes during the Battle of the Breach."

"Yes, sir, for all the good it did." Jarvis was angry that he had saved his Captain's life just so command could take it from him.

"Yes, well, unforeseen circumstances not withstanding I'm promoting you to the rank of Lt. Commander, and you'll be my new first officer."

"Sir?"

"Are you deaf?"

"No, Sir, but I didn't exactly make a very good first impression."

"No, but under the circumstances I'll let that slide. Your record is impeccable. But understand I'm not as easy as Conrad. If you ever strike me with a right cross, I'll bust you down to ensign so fast you won't know what hit you."

"Yes Sir. Thank you Sir," Jarvis responded, snapping to attention. A smile slowly crept across his face.

"Now get this vessel ship shape. She'll be the first one to arrive at Hyperion followed closely by the Falcon, Ares, and Triton. I'll be back in seven days for immediate launch."

"Yes, Sir."

Glenda C. Finkelstein

Chapter 5

Governor Paul Tarken had his hands full on Hyperion. While the local gentry were busy preparing for evacuation other more vocal groups were preparing for anarchy. The Miners Union would lose a very lucrative contract. Hyperion was the galaxy's lead producer of precious gems far more valuable than those that were once cherished on earth. Then there was the Farmers Coalition, which would also lose their livelihood. Hyperion had the most fertile soil of the 50 inhabited planets. It was so rich with nutrients that it was pitch black and grew vegetables at an extraordinary rate.

Glenda C. Finkelstein

Tarken had governed the planet's population of 80,000 plus since its' founding ten years ago. Hyperion saw little, if any action during the Rundi war and had no planetary defense systems. An agricultural planet was not considered a strategic target during the hostilities, and no defense was thankfully ever needed. He was still in shock, though, when Epsilon 6 Command gave him the evacuation order. There was no negotiation, no extensions, and no protection should something go wrong. If they violated this directive even accidentally, they stood alone against the resolve of the Rundi. Paul only had a small militia that was used to maintain civil order. It was never meant to be a military unit. Most of the time they were used for crowd control during festivals and holidays. The colony was peaceful, and saw very little "criminal" activity.

Paul had been hearing rumors of the Miners and Farmers intentions to defy the directive, but to date they were unsubstantiated as none of the information had come to him through official channels. He suspected they were still working things out amongst themselves, but really didn't know. Hypothetically, if they were divided it'd be easier to convince people to leave, but if they weren't he'd be hard pressed to convince them otherwise. In spite of the stirrings of trouble, Paul had no intention of notifying Epsilon 6 Command. He had enough to worry about without Military Command calling every five minutes for an update.

In an effort to calm himself, he decided to talk with Old Joe. He was a wise old man who had lived so long that he didn't bother to use his last name anymore, not that he could remember what it was now anyway. When Joe arrived, Paul's mind was whirling with all the known dilemmas along with all the 'what if' concerns stirred up by gossip. So much was looming in the near future that he could barely wrap his mind around it. He looked up when he heard the door open, but didn't look directly at Joe. His gaze was fixed on some distant troubled horizon.

Joe sat down across the desk from Paul calmly resting his old bones in an overstuffed armchair. His blue eyes were still clear and sparkled with spry like whimsy. Although his white hair was quite thin, it still held an old style he liked when he was younger. His body was tanned and wrinkled like soft leather. His skin color and texture blended in with the upholstery of the chair he sat in. His demeanor was gentle and wise, but allowed himself the liberty to be good humored. If he'd learned anything in his vast lifetime of one hundred and twenty-five years, it was patience and laughter. Joe didn't press Paul to speak. He knew the man would speak in his own good time and when the words had settled into a coherent form.

"I'm sure you're wondering why I called you here," Paul opened.

"Well, I assumed it had something to do with the directive to evacuate and the rumored grumbling of certain blowhards in our otherwise fine community."

"How'd you know?"

"I'm old, not deaf." Joe punctuated his statement with a wink. "People talk, but they don't always talk the facts, and that's what's really bothering you, the facts."

Paul looked hard at Joe. He was surprised that he was so intuitive, but then again it was this wisdom that he needed to consult. It was like the old man had invited himself into Paul's mind. The truth of the matter was that when you've been around as long as Joe, you learn to pick up on the subtleties of body language that most people ignore.

"Yes," Paul admitted, nodding his head in the affirmative. "I just can't seem to wrap my mind around why we have to leave Hyperion when there are other worlds closer to Rundi space that would make more logical candidates for a buffer zone. When I asked, 'Why us?' they simply told me to shut up and carry out the directive."

"Well, it sounds like we need to further analyze our situation. Perhaps things aren't as people would like to believe they are."

"What do you mean?" Paul asked, wondering where Joe was going with his line of reasoning.

"Let's go back to the end of the war two weeks ago. What was the announcement?"

"The war is over," Paul answered.

"Exactly, the war is over. They didn't say we won, and the war is over now did they?" All of a sudden understanding began to grow brighter and brighter as he continued to listen to Joe's words.

"In every conflict, there is always a winner and a loser even if it's not overtly discernable. Although the winning side might not have won everything they went after, they got more than what they started with. The loser even in a close match still has to give up something. If it's a draw, then both sides give up something to maintain the peace."

"So you're saying that we may have lost the war, and this is what we have to give up."

"Possibly, it would explain command's refusal to elaborate on the situation. People don't like to be told to do something without a reason. It's this lack of information which I fear has opened the door to rebellion." Joe's wise council was like water to a thirsty man.

"Rebellion or no, we've been told what will happen if we don't comply. Any human left here when the Rundi arrive will be obliterated."

"That's not a justification, that's an ultimatum. Never confuse the two."

"So what do I do, Joe?"

"The best you can with what you have to work with."

"That's not going to be easy. I've got four ships that will start arriving in just a few days including our disgraced flagship. I suspect two groups are going to try and defy the directive which will put the remainder of the population in jeopardy."

"When dealing with so many people there is always a danger that you'll lose some. I've heard old stories from earth that told of times when huge storms would come out of the oceans onto the land masses so strong they could level entire buildings. They too, were given evacuation orders, but some chose to stay in the path of danger."

"What happened to them?"

"The same thing that happens to all fools, their dead bodies was placed in body bags when the storm was over because they defied an evacuation order given to save their lives."

"Why?" Paul asked, shaking his head in confusion.

"No one knows why people get stupid. Humans aren't always the brightest creatures in the galaxy. You just need to understand that no matter how hard you try you're going to lose some in this evacuation, and it's not your fault."

"That thought doesn't make me feel any better."

"It's not supposed to. That's what makes you a good leader."

"Thanks Joe."

"Don't thank me. Knowing it doesn't make it any easier while you're going through it, but hopefully it'll help you sleep at night when it's all over."

"Understood."

"If you'll excuse me, I have to go and pack. I'm old and slow."

"Take care, Joe. I'll see you on the other side."

The old man just smiled. His toothy grin was filled with teeth still his own with only one missing bicuspid. They gleamed like pearls between his thin tanned brown lips. It was a crooked smile, but sincere and it warmed Paul's heart.

Paul waited until Joe was out of sight before closing the door. It had been a long day and he was ready to go home to his beautiful wife of twelve years, Samantha. They had no children, but were a happy couple devoting themselves to the good of others. She loved to cook, but then, so did he. Usually his position kept him too late to help with the cooking during the week, but he made up for it on the weekends. When he arrived at home, Samantha was putting the finishing touches on their meal. To them, presentation was just as important as the food they ate. Mealtime was very special to them. It allowed an intimate moment of sharing with one another about the day's exploits. Samantha also lit candles to keep the atmosphere of romance alive and well.

"Darling, you're home early," Samantha commented from the kitchen. When Paul came through the door she dropped what she was doing and greeted him like the lover of her heart and soul that he was.

"It's just five minutes," corrected Paul, waiting for his embrace and slow kiss. Each embrace from her reminded him that marriage was a deep and intimate relationship that was to be celebrated. He snuggled in nuzzling her neck. After caressing her silky ebony black hair that smelled of honey, he breathed her in.

Glenda C. Finkelstein

The scent of her made him feel whole. After their embrace, she took a moment to straighten his blonde hair with her fingertips. Although the couple had their disagreements and difficulties, they consciously worked to keep their union fresh and joyful. He looked into her sparkling brown eyes. They danced like fairies upon flowers in a forest.

"I made your favorite," she smiled, mischievously.

He sniffed the air catching the hearty aroma of Beef Bourguignon wafting in from the kitchen, "Mmm, lead the way," he requested, salivating over the coming meal.

He smiled as he followed her to the table, but Samantha could tell there was trouble in the waters of his blue eyes that usually reflected the world like quiet garden pools. She waited until he sat down before placing his food in front of him. He usually dug right into his meal, but he was listlessly pushing pearl onions about his plate without moving any of the food to his mouth. She gazed at him inquisitively over the flickering candles.

"What has you so troubled that you have to redecorate your plate?"

"Is it that obvious?" he asked. He didn't like bringing the day's troubles home with him. It wasn't that he didn't discuss his work or policy with her. It was just some days he enjoyed coming home to his personal sanctuary, but no matter how hard he tried the evacuation weighed heavily upon his mind. Realizing he wasn't

78

fooling her he took a mouthful hoping that the food would restore some calm to his person.

"Yes. Talk to me, Paul."

"What's your opinion about the end of the war?" Paul asked, wondering if she, too, had made assumptions.

"I'm happy it's over. Isn't everyone?"

"That's not what I mean. Do you believe we won or lost?"

"I assumed we won, but now that you mention it. No one has actually said either way. What do you believe?" Samantha inquired.

"I believe we lost. It's really the only explanation of why we have to give up Hyperion. Not to mention that we seem to be the only ones giving something up," Paul expounded.

"Now I understand why this troubles you. There are other worlds closer to Rundi space that would be more logical choices for a buffer zone. Hyperion is simply out of the way although rich in natural resources," Samantha surmised.

"Exactly. We've never been attacked, and we were here two years before the war started. What makes this place so special to the Rundi?" Paul asked, his mind reeling from the possibilities.

"Didn't Epsilon 6 also say that the Rundi would not take possession either?"

"Yes, that makes it even more mysterious of why we have to leave. They don't want it and they don't want us to have it either."

"I appreciate your need to understand, but it doesn't change the fact that we must leave," she reminded. She could see his frustration of wanting to represent and protect the rights of his people, and his hatred over his helplessness to do what the people elected him to do.

"I know that, but if I could just find a good enough reason maybe I could convince those who would choose to defy the order to comply and thereby save their lives too."

"Paul, most of the time your sensibilities give you a compassion that enables you to make good policy for the people, but at times like these, it can be your Achilles heel. The people need to see a resolute man determined to obey the directive. The fools will do what they will, but you can't allow yourself to make decisions in consideration of fools or problems that haven't surfaced yet."

Paul snickered at her words, but mostly at himself.

"What's so funny?" she asked coyly. After all, she thought her argument was well stated.

"That's basically what Old Joe said."

"He's a smart man," she acknowledged.

He smiled back at her. He knew they were both right. He hoped and prayed that he'd have the strength of character not to bow or flinch before the nonsense of fools in a public display. Paul needed to remain courageous even if he didn't feel it.

***

On the other side of the community, heavily muscled men meandered through the darkened dirt streets toward the mining caves that lay one mile just beyond the housing modules. Manny

Smithers, the leader of the Miners Union, had called this secret meeting of the Miners and Farmers to discuss their stand on the government-enforced evacuation. As the men gathered, they began to murmur amongst themselves. Although there were women who worked as Miners and Farmers throughout the Coalition of Planets there were none on Hyperion. Manny chose the caves because they were a good distance from the colony, and they could get as loud as they wanted and no one could hear them.

After a quick scan of the crowd gathered inside the largest and well lit cavern of the mines, he surmised that most everyone had assembled. He then took his thumb and index fingers, pursed his lips upon them, and whistled to get everyone's attention. The loud piercing whistle quickly silenced this raucous crew.

"I've called this meeting to discuss defying the evacuation order," Manny began in his gruff toned voice. He was in his early to mid-forties, and although sported one less finger on his right hand than he did when he arrived on Hyperion, was still just as headstrong as he ever was.

"How do you suppose we defy the order? I hear they're sending four military destroyer class ships to take us off," questioned an older, more sober individual, Jake Summers by name. He was a tall, red haired man whose long hair and beard was no longer discernable from one another. He sported two beady green eyes, and was Manny's senior by fifteen years. This was the man that Manny had to convince as most of the men looked up to Jake, and would follow his lead even though Manny was their elected leader.

"You'd be right, that they're sending four destroyer class ships to evacuate us, but their weapons are to protect us from the Rundi who'll be spying on the operation. Despite that, I don't believe they or anyone else in this galaxy has the right to demand that we leave our homes."

"Why?" A voice from the back of the cave questioned. The voice sounded familiar, but Manny couldn't quite place it. In either case he planned on answering it.

"Why indeed? We were here two full years before the war started. Never have we been attacked during the conflict, and now that it's over they want us to give up the choicest piece of real estate that exists in the Coalition of Planets. This planet was empty, save the native plants and some small rodents prior to us coming here. There's never been any Rundi presence, why now?"

"I don't deny what you say is true, but both Epsilon 6 Command and the Rundi Parliament made this planet off limits to humans at which time they intend to kill any of us that remain," added Shawn Burke for the Farmers Coalition.

"We've fought them before, Shawn. Hell, my son personally greased 23 of their pilots during the conflict. We can hold our own."

"What do we fight with, picks and shovels?" Jeremy Tate questioned. "The Rundi could kill us from orbit." He had a valid point, and Manny knew it but he had a plan to get around that.

"I'm glad you asked," Manny commented and then continued to explain the rest of his plan to the men. "First we must arm ourselves. There is an armory bristling with weapons that was placed here in case of a Rundi invasion for the militia to protect the people. If I'm not mistaken you, Mr. Tate, are a member of the militia."

"You're right I'm a member, but what good are guns. They can kill us from space," Jeremy reminded, as if Manny had lost his mind, or at least his hearing.

"The guns are to give us power over the crews that will be landing to assist with the evacuation so we can take control of at least one of the destroyers to defend our efforts here on the planet. I'm not suggesting we kill anyone. There are plenty of stun rounds in the munitions depot. We just want to get their attention, and subdue them if necessary."

"Okay, so you take control of a ship. What's to stop them from turning on us and leaving us here to die," Jake confronted. Murmurs among the men ebbed and receded in volume like a tide while they waited for Manny to respond.

"You forget that there will be hundreds of civilians already loaded aboard. They aren't going to fire on a ship full of civilians."

"Human ships no, but the Rundi will not hesitate to fire on us," Jake reminded.

"You have a valid point, but let Manny continue with his explanation, his plan intrigues me," Jeremy encouraged. Manny didn't expect support from the younger generation, but he'd take all he could get.

"In addition to our leverage on the craft in orbit, I suggest we kidnap the Governor's wife for leverage planet side."

The room fell so silent that you could have heard a pin drop into the loose dirt. The words fell upon the men's ears and hearts. They were stunned to hear such a statement from a man who had always maintained the letter of the law in any given situation.

"Kidnapping?" Jake questioned, in horror, finally breaking the silence. Although the miners were a rowdy bunch, none of them fancied themselves as criminals.

"I'm not suggesting we harm her. Just keep her with us until they bow to our demands. We have to show them that we're serious, and by taking the Governor's wife we'll have his full, undivided attention. He'll have to deal."

"This is treason," Jeremy stated with alarm, regretting his earlier comment to listen.

"No, Jeremy, just desperation. I'm trying to save our livelihoods. I've nowhere to go. Do you? This is my home. This is our home. We didn't set the terms of this agreement, but we can change it if we act together."

"You realize even if we win, we'll either be imprisoned, or dead," Jake added soberly. He wanted everyone to be fully aware of the brevity of the situation.

"Quite possibly, but I'd rather fight and die like a man for something I believe in than passively obey an arrogant directive made in chambers thousands of light years away. This is not their home. It's ours!" Manny's plea was both passionate and convincing.

"Say you do pull this off. Which ship do you intend to try and overtake?" Jake asked.

"The Phoenix of course, the most disgraced crew in the fleet should be easy pickings."

The room degraded into a jumbled mess of voices arguing, reasoning, and debating one another. Passions blazed both for and against the plan with reasons being brought forth to support both sides. This went on for about an hour before Manny brought the men's attention back with his piercing whistle.

"Enough talk, we vote. Black marble we leave here with our tails tucked between our legs. White marble, we fight for our homes and way of life. As with anything else that comes to a vote, when the verdict is read we obey to the death. Any who wish to leave may do so now. If you stay, you're bound by the decision."

All heads nodded in agreement, and none of them left even if they wanted too. Nobody wanted to appear cowardly. They clearly understood that those who stayed for the vote was bound by its outcome with his very life even before they were reminded. Yet whether they were for or against the rebellion, the vote was too important to walk away. They had to cast their lot for what they believed in.

A large clay pot was passed from man to man. Each one stuck his closed fist inside and released a marble. Once the object clinked inside the vase, the individual removed his hand, and passed it to the next. This was done with the greatest reverence, and there was no talking during the decision making process. After all the men had voted, the marbles were poured out into a wooden box and counted so that all could see the result.

"We fight," Manny announced aloud. It was close, and passed by a margin of two. The men were somber as they returned to their homes. At this point they were bound by their own code into silence. Anyone found breaking the vow with an outsider would be killed by one of their own.

Chapter 6

Rico arrived without incident on Cassiopeia. It was a true paradise and the most exotic among all the inhabited systems of known space. The sea was saltier than the oceans of earth that was said to teem with life, but here in these waters life was sparse and harmless consisting of tiny fish the size of your fingers that subsisted on tiny grasses that grew out about a hundred yards from the shore. The water itself was crystal clear and took on a lavender blue hue. It seemed to darken in spots due to the patches of black grass that the fish fed on in the deeper areas. The neighboring planet Otadan was barely visible, but the large hovering pink and orange-stripped gas giant accented the sky above the horizon. At night you could see the sparkling rings that encompassed the huge planet. During some months of the year Cassiopeia passed through them. These seasons made for some very romantic evenings on the beach.

Rico arrived the night before, and stayed at the hotel until morning. He woke early to be transported to a private straw hut for the rest of his stay. The hotels provided lifeguard services and staff to bring in food, clean the rooms, etc. The huts were spaced out quite a distance from one another to allow people a chance to relax outside of the usual beach crowds. Although things were spread out, people were free to walk, swim, and sun bathe anywhere they wished along the hundred-mile stretch of shoreline.

He passed a sigh of relief after settling into his new abode that resembled something out of The Swiss Family Robinson. The hut was surrounded by lush green and red foliage with lovely shade trees that seemed to be an odd mix between banana, palm, and willow trees. He left his uniform coat in his office on the Phoenix and carried only the required electronic devices for communication. He neatly packed away his pants inside his suitcase and donned his beach bum attire. He had no plans of interacting with anything or anyone save the hotel staff that would bring him his meals or extra towels.

Rico took a sniff of the salt-laced air that was evident even inside his hut, pulled on his navy blue snug fitting swimsuit, and stepped outside. The temperature was a lovely 80 degrees

Fahrenheit. He was so relaxed he didn't bother to shave. He took a moment to rub on some sunscreen before stepping out into the mid-morning sun onto the powdery soft pink and white sands of the beach.

"I could travel from one side of the galaxy to the other and never see anything more beautiful," Rico said to himself aloud. He was so awestruck by the sight that he let go his amazement audibly unaware that the sound would reach another human ear. Now that he was outside, he could taste the salt carried upon the breeze as the waves crashed gently upon the sands.

"Now that's the cheesiest pick-up line I've ever heard," came a female voice in response to his statement. A woman was sunbathing upon a reclining beach chair not far from his position. Rico looked over in her direction. A large rimmed straw hat covered her face.

"I'm sorry I didn't realize anyone was here. My comment was meant for no one but myself," Rico explained, respectfully.

The woman peered up from underneath her bonnet. Her eyes were a rich creamy jade green, with the pattern of flower petals within the iris. She proceeded to remove her headgear which allowed her waist length auburn hair to fall back down upon her back. Her skin was fair with few freckles that typically accompanied red tresses. Rico was mesmerized. She, too, seemed to be awed by his person. Her eyes began at his feet and moved up his body, pausing at the well packed manhood just underneath his swimsuit, and moving up to his well defined muscular torso, arms, shoulders, and then his lovely Roman chiseled jaw line ending at his medium, somewhat unkempt, pitch black locks of hair.

Suddenly, her face became flush as she realized that he was noticing her just as she was noticing him. In awkward embarrassment she removed her eyes immediately from him and stared down at the sand. She sat straight up in her chair and placed her feet firmly on the ground beneath her in case a hasty retreat was called for. Realizing that his statement was sincere and meant for the creation surrounding them, she sputtered an apology.

"I'm sorry. I thought you were the cabana boy. He's been pestering me all morning."

"It's okay, no harm done, but at the risk of sounding cheesy, I stand corrected. Now I've seen the most beautiful vision in the galaxy."

A blush of red filled her cheeks. "I better go, I've obviously disturbed your section of the beach," the woman admitted as she began to gather her things to move on.

"Don't go. Please, it's just me, and there's plenty of shoreline for two?" Rico questioned as an invitation. It had been a long time since he enjoyed the company of a woman. He could tell that she was not like other women. Even though she was obviously attracted to him, she respected his privacy to move on. That told him much about her. Most females would have been all over him to get a quickie. Although in his youth, he'd succumbed to such tactics, now in his late thirties, he'd grown to appreciate relationships and found them to be far more enriching and satisfying than a one-night stand. The war, however, left little time for either.

She, too, seemed to be taken back by his politeness. She stopped short of picking up the chair. She put the book she had been reading down on the seat and turned around to face him. He looked deeply into her eyes. They were more beautiful than any he had ever seen. His intense gaze was making her uncomfortable and he glanced over at the book.

"Very well, if we're going to share this stretch of ocean front, what shall I call you?" she questioned.

"The name is Rico," he informed, returning his less intense gaze back to her lovely face.

"Rico," she repeated aloud. The sound rolled off her tongue like a melodic song and he could tell that she drew pleasure just from hearing her own voice speak it. "Daphne," she returned, smiling up at him.

"Daphne, I like that name. So, what book are you reading?" he asked, truly interested in what she was doing. She seemed surprised by his question, usually it was, 'Are you married?' It was refreshing and she happily elaborated on the book thus far.

The two of them talked about everything under the sun including themselves, but neither of them made any comment about what they did for a living. They simply spoke about their families, likes, dislikes, embarrassing moments, and the like. They spent the day talking, walking, swimming, and before long the sun was beginning to set. Neither of them had realized the passing of time. Never before had either of them found a member of the opposite sex so appealing in so many ways. It was like their attraction went beyond the physical level and into their spirits and intellects.

Although both had experienced vacation flings before, there was something unique about this one. Their time together was so enriching and yet they had just barely scratched the surface of the other's life. They hadn't even learned the other's last name at this point, but knew all about their pets, their first grade teachers, etc. They were focused on learning about the person. Each one wanted to know what made the other happy, sad, or silly and not the titles that were given or salary level achieved to date.

Hours turned into days, and soon it was the last night before reality would call and disturb this happy and delightful moment of life. Vacation had come to an end and he would have to leave the following morning. Rico had a special dinner brought in with all the trimmings, wine and candlelight set up along the beach. The sun hung low in the sky, the table set up just at the edge of the water where the surf would gently cascade over their bare feet. A violinist played softly in the distance so as not to interfere with anything that might transpire between them.

They ate in silence, not a word spoken between them save their eyes, which spoke things that words could never formulate. The candlelight reflected in Rico's eyes seemed to become part of his passion, but it was something that came from his very soul and not just his libido. Daphne's eyes reflected wonder and appreciation for all that life could offer two people in love. After they ate and drank the last of the wine, they went for a walk melting into one another's arms. The rhythms of the waves slapping at the sand gave measure to the calls of chirping crickets and night warblers.

They returned to Rico's hut under the cover of moonlight. Rico initiated a passionate kiss. Daphne returned it with the same enthusiasm and joy. They began to undress one another slowly and carefully making the most of each moment. Each one savored every inch of skin holding on to the last vestiges of self control for fear that haste would dissipate their pleasure too quickly. Now they could feel one another's breath on their skin that heightened their senses. Heat exuded from their fingertips. With each highly charged caress becoming an epiphany of love their hearts were seared into one. They continued making love until the wee hours of the morning. When all their strength was spent they fell into a wistful sleep like a down feather floating softly to the ground.

The next morning the sun's golden rays poured into the hut filling it with warmth. Rico turned over. His arm fell upon the empty bed. He sat up and looked about the mattress and then the room. To his dismay Daphne was gone. He called out her name, but there was no response. She wasn't there. The only thing that testified to her presence was the hint of night blooming jasmine perfume still present on the sheets and her abandoned straw hat hanging on a nearby wooden chair.

Although Rico was at a loss as to why she'd leave without saying goodbye, he knew they had experienced something special these past few days. Last night more than just sex had transpired between them. Their hearts and souls had been knit together. Yet, she was gone without a goodbye just the same. It wasn't until this moment that he realized that they had never shared their sir names. He grabbed a pair of Bermuda shorts and went outside to see if he could find her. The only thing that greeted him was the salt breeze and a deserted beach.

"Daphne!" he called into the wind, once, twice, and again a third time. He realized that she had left, just like the receding tide. Although part of him wanted to be sad, the aftertaste was still so sweet he didn't want to spoil it. There was a part of him that knew she had her reasons, and something told him that they would meet again. He didn't have the time to look for her. His duty called to him and he couldn't allow himself to be distracted. He gathered himself and prepared to go back to work carrying with him the sweet aftertaste of love.

***

Rico's euphoria dissipated quickly upon arriving back on the Phoenix. It was near pandemonium as ship's personnel reported for duty and base personnel exited after turning the cargo bay into a mock refugee center so they could evacuate the people of Hyperion.

Rico hoped that the colonists were truly ready to leave and they wouldn't try to make some heroic stand for a lump of rock that really didn't belong to anyone. If it would keep the peace with the Rundi, it was worth giving up. Eight years of battle had left him weary, and he wanted it to be finished even though his gut felt the opposite was true. His first order of business was to restore to the crew of the Phoenix, the honor that had been stolen from them. His second order of business, if he got truly lucky, would be to find out what really happened to his friend, Conrad.

Rico headed straight for his office on the bridge, he wanted to be certain that Janet Sadowski's commendation was waiting there for him. When he entered he noticed a little girl, or so it seemed. She wore a uniform, but didn't look old enough to wear it for any other reason than to play dress up. The insignia on her sleeve indicated that she was a Yeoman and would be the only other person with authorized access to his office. She had light mousy brown hair, and brown eyes. Her mannerism was rather jumpy like a Chihuahua's.

"Yeoman, may I help you?" Rico asked. Startled she turned around and was so nervous that she could barely speak.

"Ca…Ca…Captain Sanchez."

"Yes, that's my name, and yours would be?"

"Oh! Sorry, Sir. This is my first posting. I'm uh…Yeoman Lisa Smith."

"What are you doing in my office Yeoman Smith?"

"I was just straightening it and cleaning out Captain Banes' old things, so you could put your own in," she explained apprehensively. Rico scowled. Her countenance fell quickly into panicked pandemonium.

"What have you done with Captain Banes' belongings?" Rico questioned, sternly. He was annoyed, but could tell that this barely dry behind the ears kid was trying to be helpful.

"Over there, sir," she answered pointing to some boxes in the corner, her voice beginning to waiver. He realized that she was innocently trying to do a good job and was probably not part of the conspiracy.

"I appreciate the fact that you wanted to make a good impression, but next time unless it is on your duty roster, don't do it until I order it done."

"Yes, Sir, I will put everything back."

"That won't be necessary," Rico began taking a calmer tone. He was afraid that she would go into cardiac arrest if she didn't calm down soon. "I'm looking for one thing in particular. Did a sealed envelope arrive for me from the office of the Admiral?"

"Yes sir. It's right over here," she informed, walking to the other side of his desk. She picked it up and handed it to him.

"Very good," he commended, taking the envelope from her. "Do you know if all personnel have reported for duty?"

"We're still waiting for one person, but she should be here any moment."

"She?"

"Dr. Lamb, our chief medical officer."

"As soon as she's on board, I want this ship underway."

"Yes, Sir," Yeoman Smith saluted. Rico returned the salute. She left to attend to her duties. Rico looked about the office. There'd be plenty of time to look through everything once the ship was underway he thought to himself. He shook his head realizing that he must be getting old when the new Yeoman looks like she should still be wearing pigtails. Then his mind reflected momentarily upon his first look at Daphne. He didn't feel old then. He felt invigorated and very much alive. Rico shook his head again as a dog would shake water from its body to try and bring his full focus back to the mission at hand.

Rico opened the packet and reviewed the contents. Everything was in order. He left his overnight bag sitting by his desk, slipped the envelope under his arm, and headed for the bridge. The hallways were full of people going this way and that getting the ship ready to set sail. Although Rico was very much aware of the fact that they were in space, the statement, 'blast off' seemed more like one mistake shy of an explosion and was much more comfortable with 'set sail'. He preferred the nautical terminology because it was the stars that guided the ancient sailors. Although man now sailed among them, instead of under them, they were still the guiding lights of the voyage.

Upon arriving on the bridge, the noise was nearly deafening as last minute checks were called out and performed. Suddenly, Jarvis noticed Rico's presence, and announced it clearly so that everyone would respond the first time. Jarvis' voice was quite guttural, and as soon as the name Captain Sanchez registered in the ears of the crew, they stopped, stood to their feet, and saluted. Rico looked about the bridge as if he were inspecting them. A look of satisfaction flashed briefly across his face. No one moved, uttered an audible sound, or even blinked an eye until Rico gave them permission to do so. Rico in return assumed his most militaristic and sincere stance and returned the salute.

"Is the crew all present and accounted for?" Rico questioned of Jarvis.

"The last member boarded just five minutes ago. We are fully staffed and ready to sail at your orders," Jarvis responded.

"Good, but before we get underway we have some unfinished business to take care of. Call Lt. Janet Sadowski to the bridge, and put me on ship wide intercom," Rico ordered as he flipped a nearby switch that would also allow the Admiral to hear everything that was about to transpire.

"Sir?" Jarvis questioned. It was highly unusual to call a member of the engineering staff to the bridge at this time.

"Now, Commander," Rico insisted.

Jarvis did as he requested, but his look of astonishment didn't recede. Janet's commander was equally inquisitive about what this meant. Janet on the other hand, was petrified. She thought that maybe Captain Sanchez was going to use her as an example of what not to do. Of all the times to get into a bar-fight, it had to be during a change of command. The whole way to the bridge she kept kicking herself for her lack of self-control. Upon arriving on the bridge she looked at Jarvis' stunned face. The expression was virtually the same as she engaged each member of the bridge crew. She took a deep breath before meeting the Captain's eyes.

"Lt. Janet Sadowski, reporting as ordered, Sir."

Janet stood at attention waiting for her captain's next orders. Captain Rico Sanchez held in his hand an envelope with the Admiral's seal. She just knew that this was a notice of court marshal. She swallowed what little bit of pride she had left and braced herself to face her darkest hour with some shred of dignity.

"Upon my accepting the Captaincy of the Phoenix, I discovered that there were some things that had been overlooked due to the circumstances of your former Captain. I took it upon myself to carry out his last wishes for this crew, and one of those was that crewman Lt. Janet Sadowski be awarded the Epsilon 6 Military Council Medal of Honor for performance above and beyond the call of duty during the Battle of the Breach which by her actions saved the lives of this crew. It is my most cherished duty to award this highest honor that a human can receive to a remarkable woman."

Janet's jaw dropped to the floor. She was amazed that Captain Banes had noticed with everything else that had gone on, and was even more astounded that the new Captain, the one who bailed her butt out of jail would see fit to follow through. Applause began to erupt throughout the ship. The clapping became more and more thunderous as Janet's smile became larger and larger. Then at the peak of pride and joy, a tear fell down her cheek. It was a mixture of heartfelt thanks for both captains and of sorrow for her former captain's passing.

"I...I...I don't know what to say other than thank you. I shall do my best to live up to the honor you've bestowed upon me."

Jarvis, would have sent his buttons popping across the room had there been any on his uniform. The pride he had in Janet was evident upon his face. Rico held his hand up to silence the crew so he could speak.

"I want this crew to know that Captain Banes was my dearest friend. He was like a brother to me. I don't believe for one second the things they accused him of, nor do I believe that this crew had anything to do with that action. In my mind and heart this crew is the best the fleet has to offer, and even if it costs me my last breath his and your honor shall be restored. Although as some of you may have already figured out, the rest of the fleet doesn't feel that way so we're going to have to earn it all over again. Even the smallest of things will have to be earned. No one will give us anything, and no one will take anything from us. We will do everything to the best of our ability and then do it better not because we have to, but because it's who we are; the best!"

A roaring cheer burst forth from his crew. They were in agreement with his words. This was needed fuel to fire a crew that had been to hell and seemingly left there to rot. Not so anymore as feelings of confidence began to infuse them again. He motioned again for silence, and inconspicuously turned off the transmission to the Admiral's office.

"Our current mission is to evacuate refugees from Hyperion to create a buffer zone between us and the Rundi. We have a specified amount of time in which to move thousands of people or leave them to be destroyed. It's imperative that you follow your orders to the letter without fail. Time is of the essence, and the Rundi will be watching our every move. This peace we have with them is only twenty-one days old. One wrong move and we could be back at war. As soon as we are underway, I'll be meeting with all department heads to explain the details that they'll be responsible for. That will be all, dismissed. Push off helmsman, and set a course for Hyperion."

"With pleasure, Sir," the helmsman answered with a huge smile. Hope had returned to the Phoenix, and just like her namesake from the ashes they would rise victorious.

***

This announcement was transmitted purposely to the Admiral's office. The mysterious Prefect listened carefully to Rico's speech. Although Admiral Griffin could not see the Prefect's face, he could tell by his silence and little spurts of air forcefully blown through his lips that he was not at all pleased with Rico's promises. This pleased Admiral Griffin and a sly grin began to creep into the corners of his mouth.

"Your Captain Sanchez is defiant from the beginning."

"You know very little about us," the Admiral stated. Griffin placed his hands firmly on the edge of his desk, stood to his feet, and turned to look into the face of the unwelcome Rundi Prefect.

"Perhaps you're right, your people are quite contradictory at times, but he's blatantly announced that he's defying your orders. He should be executed immediately."

"No," Admiral Griffin answered sternly. He drew close to the Prefect. He was so close that he could smell his breath even from behind his low hanging hood. "Don't you see the man is rallying his crew so they can perform their duty? They have been thrown into holding cells. Each one was questioned to the threshold of torture without so much as a kiss my foot and then released without explanation except to say that their Captain was to be executed for treason. I'll be dammed if I'm going to let you kill Rico for doing his job."

The Prefect was silent, but his posture remained resolute. Griffin could rip that hood right off his face, but he knew he'd said enough and it was forbidden to look upon their face. Without a word the Prefect turned and left through the back door to seclude himself away from the human contaminate.

Chapter 7

Inside the conference room, the department heads were gathered waiting for Captain Sanchez to arrive. When he came through the door, he scarcely noticed who was there or not there as he arranged his files in front of him. Before sitting down at the head of the table, he looked up gazing into the faces of his direct reports. Some he recognized having served with them on other ships, and some were new to him. Then near the end of the table his eyes fell upon a face staring back at him with a mixture of curiosity and dread. He suddenly felt warm all over, his knees began to buckle, and for a moment it seemed as if he had become transparent to everyone in the room. Everyone had to know what he was thinking that very moment when his eyes fell upon her. His thoughts couldn't even say the name, but his eyes betrayed him as they fell upon her nametag, Dr. Daphne Lamb.

Rico began to feel flushed. All eyes were looking at him. Part of him wanted to scream and part of him wanted to embrace her, but that would be impossible now. Regulations were very clear. A captain was not allowed to have an intimate relationship with any member of his crew. He opened his mouth to speak to his team and nothing came out. He felt as if his very legs would betray him and he would collapse onto the floor. He imagined them laughing at him as this woman made a fool of him on his own ship. He closed his mouth before anyone questioned him.

In an effort to recover from his shock he looked down at his files, and immediately sat down. He motioned to his new Yeoman to pass out a copy of his orders and specific mandates to each department head gathered at the table. He took a deep breath and then began his briefing. This time the words came, slightly vibrato at first, but then his full steady tone emerged victorious.

"As you all know, we're being sent in to evacuate the population of Hyperion. We are one of four vessels who will be engaged in this evacuation. The Phoenix and the Falcon have joint command of this mission. As far as we know things on Hyperion are moving along nicely. The populace has been preparing for this the entire time our ships were being refitted, and although we'd like to accommodate all their belongings, it's imperative that they only bring one suitcase. The deadlines are very tight with no allowance for an extension so there will be no time to debate with the people about the one suitcase rule. Tell them once. If they don't listen, they don't board the shuttles until they comply."

"Sir," Jarvis interjected. "This is an agricultural and mineral mining community. I realize these people have been here only ten years, but I'm sure they'll have crops and minerals that will need to be off loaded."

"You make a valid point, but time constraints do not allow for much of that. The nearest cargo ships were ordered in as soon as word came of the directive to evacuate. The ships were loaded to capacity with all that was ready. What wasn't loaded onto those vessels will have to be left in the fields to rot or for the Rundi to destroy."

"What about the sick and injured?" Dr. Lamb inquired, desperately trying to maintain a calm exterior. To the casual gaze of others in the room, she had outwardly succeeded for no one had picked up on her discomfort. She, too, felt equally transparent to those gathered in the room under his penetrating stare. Those deep brown eyes that she could so easily lose herself in still held and beckoned her reckless desires. Her blood began to warm and displayed itself as a slight blush upon her cheek. The other officers didn't notice as the room was a bit stuffy. At this juncture any

Glenda C. Finkelstein

unspoken emotion or unfinished business between them had to be left so.

"Command has already given two priorities in the evacuation order. The hospitals will be evacuated first along with mothers with nursing children. They've also requested that a triage team stand by planet side in case there is a panic near the end of the evacuation," Rico answered, trying not to look at her realizing that it was probably just as difficult for her as it was for him.

"Very good, Captain, I'll prepare my staff."

"In your departmental orders, you'll find the necessary contact people on Hyperion so you can coordinate your efforts more efficiently. Are there any other questions?" Rico asked, praying that someone, anyone, but her would ask one.

Several hands were raised. The Captain took each one in turn. The meeting continued for some time as they ironed out the finer details of the mission. Upon the conclusion of the meeting, he dismissed his staff save for Dr. Lamb whom he requested to stay behind. His request made her squirm in her chair, but she maintained her exterior professionalism. They waited for the room to empty before uttering a single syllable. Their eyes locked into the other's gaze unwavering, desperately trying to communicate all they knew they couldn't with their words.

"I didn't know you were stationed here," Rico began with his eyes darting toward his shoes. It was as if he was drawn and repelled at the same time.

106

"I didn't know you were either," she admitted, trying to reconnect to his lovely eyes.

"Yes, well," he paused just a moment looking back into her eyes dreading to ask the one question that was burning on the inside of him, the one he shouldn't ask, and the one he simultaneously didn't want a response to. "Why did you leave without saying goodbye?" he blurted. He could barely believe the words actually left his mouth.

His stare seemed to peer down into her soul which made her confidence fade. She looked down at her feet not wanting to engage his eyes anymore. He could tell that she was struggling to answer him. Her awkwardness was sincere with no intended malice evident. It was, after all, a relationship that was doomed from the start. She had a secret, one so terrible that she couldn't share it with anyone, especially him. These next few weeks would be torture for the both of them.

He took his finger and touched it to the bottom of her chin. He gently lifted her head. Rico's eyes pleaded with her. "Please, tell me," he begged.

"Because I couldn't say it," she answered numbly as she pulled away and started walking toward the door, her head hung low. She stopped just before exiting the room and looked back at him. "You can be assured that I'll perform my duties to the best of my abilities. No one will know what has transpired between us, and you needn't worry about your superiors finding out." She turned her back to him before uttering her last statement. "I never kiss and tell."

She tilted her head slightly and proceeded out the door never looking back. He started to follow, but realized it was better not to, nor say anything else. He wasn't allowed to touch her, and they had already said more than what they were allowed. He waited for a while just staring at the empty seats. His mind a blank until he realized he had a job to do and went to his cabin to brood just a little while longer before embarking upon his mission; both the official and unofficial one. Upon entering his quarters, the Zeveney 7000-P automatically came on.

"Greetings, Captain, welcome home."

Rico didn't respond, but went straight to a box that held some of Conrad's things. He rummaged around until he found an old bottle of scotch. He pulled it out of the box, removed the lid, and took a snort directly from the bottle. This was not normal behavior for Rico, and Zeveney immediately questioned it.

"Is something troubling you?" Zeveney inquired with all the concern one would hear in a friend's voice. It was so easy to forget that the Zeveney program wasn't a real human. It had been programmed with certain subtleties of human behavior that most computer programs couldn't process. Yet, in times like these when telling another human was out of the question that the program's true worth was appreciated the most.

"I finally find the perfect woman, and she's forbidden to me," Rico grinded out between clinched teeth. He took another snort, then capped the bottle, and threw it against the wall. It clanked, but didn't break against the cushioned walls tumbling to a stop near the sofa.

"I'm afraid that sort of problem is outside of my parameters of assistance, but I'm obliged to listen if you wish to expound further."

"I'll be fine in time. What did you find for me regarding the last known whereabouts of the crew in relation to Captain Banes and the Rundi during the Battle of the Breach?"

"There were two crew members that stayed by Captain Banes' side during the Battle of the Breach and his momentary disappearance from the battle prior to its conclusion."

"Disappearance?" Rico questioned. He'd never known Conrad to leave a battle for any reason, and was shocked by this revelation.

"Yes, disappearance."

"Names," Rico demanded. Zeveney responded to the order without offense.

"Lt. Edward Jarvis and Dr. Daphne Lamb were with Captain Banes during the battle and his excursion from and back to."

Rico cringed at the sound of Dr. Lamb's name. Of all the people he was willing to question, this was one he wished wasn't on the list. He resigned himself to talking with Jarvis, and only if he couldn't get enough information from him would he even consider talking with Daphne.

"The official records don't show that Captain Banes left the battle," Rico interjected. "I remember seeing him near the end. It was him who saved Lindsay from a land mine from which Conrad sustained minor injuries."

"According to the shuttle's bio logs, he, Lt. Jarvis, and Dr. Lamb flew from Pishon where the Battle of the Breach was raging, to Hyperion."

"Hyperion? Why Hyperion?" Rico's curiosity was growing. This little world seemed to be a growing enigma all its own. He wondered if it was connected to Conrad's death or just a coincidence, but returned his attention to Zeveney to listen to the full report.

"No data exists on why, just that they did. They remained for two hours and then returned to the battle. One other oddity is that the ship was heavier when it left Pishon than when it returned."

"How much lighter?"

"One hundred and thirty five pounds lighter."

"Cargo?" Rico questioned aloud. Although Rico couldn't begin to explain what cargo could be so important that you'd leave a battle, drop it off, and then return.

Zeveney paused a moment before answering as he reviewed the files. "No data," they said in unison. Zev was alarmed at Rico's knowing response. "I can only give you what is in the files,"

Zeveney explained. Rico could see that Zev thought he was somehow making fun of it.

"I know that. It's just that a pattern is surfacing causing my gut to twist, and that's never a good sign."

"Explain," Zeveney requested.

"It seems that you can access files and data up to the final battle, but anything during, or after that battle someone has tried to erase. Heck, maybe Conrad tried to erase it. I really don't know anymore."

"That I can confirm."

"Excuse me?"

"Conrad was the one who erased the regular shuttle log. The only reason why I picked up on the anomaly was that the ship automatically records the weight of the vessel as it leaves and when it returns as well as those present."

"Why would he erase the file?"

"I don't know sir. Perhaps Lt. Commander Jarvis or Dr. Lamb could answer that question."

"It's a proven fact that there is no such thing as a coincidence. I'm beginning to believe that all this is tied in with our current circumstances with Hyperion. I just don't know how. I'll tell you one thing I'm not going to take anything at face value. Contact Commander Jarvis and have him report to me here in my quarters. Upon his arrival, scan him for any covert listening devices."

"You believe that Jarvis may have a secret agenda?"

"Let's just say I'm not leaving anything to chance. Something's going on, and I need to know what that something is," Rico explained.

"I can sense your frustration. Do you need to take a break?"

"No. I don't need a break I need answers. Did Epsilon 6 Command know about the shuttle?"

"There is no evidence that their investigation went into that level of detail."

"Good."

Zeveney fulfilled his earlier request to have Jarvis report to Rico's quarters while they concluded their discussion of initial findings. Rico picked up the scotch bottle he had thrown and put it away. Jarvis couldn't come right away due to a personnel issue he had to resolve. He projected his time of arrival to within the hour. Rico decided to look through Conrad's personal effects while waiting for Jarvis to see if he turned up anything else that would be pertinent to this investigation.

Chapter 8

Governor Paul Tarken stood on top of his second floor rooftop balcony surveying the Hyperion colony surrounding him. The aroma of cinnamon rolls baking at a bakery down the street filled the air which coaxed many a pedestrian to wander in. The square and rectangular one-story modular buildings extended out from the city center like a labyrinth. The streets were gravel and dirt. They made it a point to keep the planet as natural and unscarred as humanly possible working in harmony with the planetary habitats. This was the lesson that humanity learned too late back on earth. The price was so costly that no human would dare pollute another world again. It had become such a vile offense that it was one of the few laws whose breakage warranted the death penalty.

Paul could hear the cold spring fed stream tripping over rocks and fallen trees just on the other side of the wall. Any other time he would have found comfort in the sound of flowing water, but tonight it tapped at his thoughts like fingers rapping upon a tabletop. Its relentless torrents laughed at him tormenting his mind as he wrestled with the anxiety of safely evacuating over eighty thousand people. If panic should sprout anywhere, he would be hard pressed to keep it in check. The thought of losing control was the reason he intended to call out the militia. His plan was to arm them with stun rounds and post them in key areas that would be problematic in a mass exodus.

What worried him most was the lack of opposition to the government mandate. Everything had become too quiet. The people were cooperative which should relieve his fears. Even the initial grumbling that was voiced in the gossip mills were now still. In many ways it felt similar to the deceitful calm that hushes nature just prior to a violent storm. His gut turned and twisted with the thought that he may not be as in control as he has been led to believe. In frustration, he gazed up into the moonless night sky in hopes that the stars would calm him. The stars above him were plentiful and shimmered with rhythms of pulsating light that displayed a whimsical fantasy. The bugs and snub-nosed lizards in the nearby bushes and trees sang so beautifully that it would rival the splendor of any songbird. Yet in spite of the stunning beauty, his spirit was still unsettled.

"So here's where you've snuck off to," Samantha interjected, coming up the steps with a cup of hot tea for Paul. He jumped. She leaped back spilling some of the hot tea upon her hand. "Ouch!" she yelped.

"I'm sorry, babe. You startled me," he explained, yanking a handkerchief from his pocket to dab the remaining droplets from his wife's hand.

"You act as if the mob had come for you," she commented unimpressed by his quick actions to wipe the hot liquid from her hand.

"Here let me take that," he offered taking the cup from her outstretched hand. Paul kissed her hand which disarmed any anger left in his wife's spirit. She pulled her hand gently away with a school girl's smile. He brought the cup up to his nose and sniffed at the wisp of steam erupting from its surface. A smile cascaded across his face when he recognized the scent of his favorite tea, chai.

"Why are you up here all alone?" she asked with concern.

"I needed to think," he explained.

"Think, or worry?"

"I just can't get anything past you can I?" He asked, gazing into her already knowing eyes and then confessed what she already suspected. "Okay, I'm worried."

"I thought so. I don't know why you continue to worry? The preparation for the evacuation is going more smoothly than you anticipated."

"You're right, it is. That's what has me worried," Paul admitted.

"Paul, you know I love you, but sometimes there's just no pleasing you."

"That's not it, Sam. It went from being almost riotous to a peaceful calm. It doesn't feel right to me."

"You think someone's trying to give us a false sense of security?"

"Yes, I do, but I can't prove anything. All I have is my gut, and it's doing somersaults right now."

"You're a good man, Paul. Whatever happens I know you'll do your best."

"I love you too," Paul announced as if it were the first time he'd ever said it. He set the tea down on a nearby table and pulled her close to him breathing in her scent. Her presence always managed to under gird him when he needed it most.

He knew the Phoenix would be the first ship to arrive and the evacuation would begin in earnest in the morning. Paul also knew that they would not have time for themselves as husband and wife for several weeks. He took the other cup of tea from Samantha, and placed it next to his. She looked at him curiously wondering what he was up to. Paul wrapped his arms around her encasing her like a

116

cocoon. He began to kiss her slow and gentle holding her in an embrace that quickly transformed into a passionate encounter. She responded to his touch like a candle ignites from the lighting of a match.

It didn't take them long to start undoing each other's buttons, belts, and zippers. He laid her down upon a pile of huge pillows under a covered canopy in the center of their rooftop balcony. They made love all night until their energy was spent, and slept peacefully inside the other's arms until the morning came.

***

Paul's gut served him well for the miners and farmers' terrible agreement would bear a higher price than any of them intended to pay. Their little rebellion totaled over two hundred members. They were very subtle about it patiently waiting for just the right moment to spring their trap. If they didn't, their uprising would stand little chance of succeeding. They had to gain control of a ship in orbit, and they were still more than a day away from that position. It was imperative that they acquired the weapons stored in the Munitions Depot prior to them being dispersed to the militia. To avoid any suspicion, those that had families prepared to evacuate just like the other inhabitants.

A little over a dozen men consisting of both farmers and miners led by young Jeremy made plans to raid the Munitions Depot before morning. This night was perfect with no moon to shine upon their endeavor. No one expected that the Depot was going to be hit and its weapons cleaned out. Since Jeremy was a member and had a key, it made the storage locker easy pickings. The only real challenge was removing the weapons without getting caught or tipping off the government any sooner than necessary. The Depot did have about three security guards that patrolled the building so timing and stealth would bring the largest payoff.

The guards usually patrolled for about an hour and a half past midnight, and then would enter into a friendly game of cards. This colony was not known for vandalism, theft, or dishonesty so it was more of a precaution against teenage pranks than a criminal element that concerned the guards the most. They were usually the only ones that stayed up all night. Most everyone else worked during the day and slept at night.

Dressed all in black, the perpetrators darkened their faces with the help of the soil. This would make spotting any of them while hidden along the tree line from a distance a near impossible task. The security lights along the corners of the building would provide them with all the light they would need to get into the arsenal. The men waited patiently for the guards to begin their card game before drawing near to the building. Manny kept watch for the guards while Jeremy unlocked the door, and with a hand held electric torch he reviewed the arsenal. He was careful to grab stun rounds instead of lethal ones. These were after all, their neighbors and families. They only wished to stay where they had made a home, they didn't wish to kill anyone.

118

Each carried at least six weapons using the rifle slings to hang them on their shoulders and a backpack to pack the ammo boxes in for each weapon. These would be delivered to the rest of the team before morning under the cover of darkness. Once all the weapons that were needed were removed, Jeremy closed and locked the door back. For this to work, no one could know prior to the arming of the militia that the weapons were missing. In addition to the fact that these weapons were not intended to be lethal they were easy to conceal by breaking them down into their component parts. This would enable them to smuggle them aboard the Phoenix without notice.

Jeremy tapped Manny on the shoulder and the two men disappeared into the night. These two men were in complete agreement with only one point of discord. Jeremy was opposed to kidnapping the Governor's wife. She was an innocent and he felt that would sway the people against them. After all, their greatest hope was that the other colonists would see their passion and join them. Holding a hostage could easily turn the people against what they were trying to do. They were after all patriots, not criminals.

Glenda C. Finkelstein

Chapter **9**

While waiting for Jarvis, Rico had been able to look through half of Conrad's boxes. Most of them contained clothes and personal mementoes which he wasn't sure what to do with as he had no family. None of them held any clues to his demise. Jarvis finally arrived at the Captain's quarters, and knocked on the door. Zeveney opened it and scanned him as he walked through. Jarvis was quite taken aback by the truly automatic response to his knock without the captain bidding him enter.

"You may proceed," Zeveney informed. Rico smiled. This was a good sign, as it indicated that Jarvis was indeed who he says he was.

"Please sit down," Rico entreated.

"Thank you, Captain."

"Coffee?" Rico offered.

"Yes, thank you," Jarvis responded. He looked a little confused. He had never before been invited to the Captain's quarters with such a personal touch, nor had he been told why he was summoned. After their initial meeting, he hadn't been around Captain Sanchez enough to feel comfortable in an informal setting.

"You seem tense, relax," Rico instructed.

"Sir, I'm confused. We should be preparing for the refugees, not having coffee."

"You have a well trained staff, don't you?"

"Yes, sir."

"Then they can deal with things while we talk. I told you I was going to get to the truth about Captain Banes' death, and I intend to do that. But, in order for me to do that, I need information that you may be aware of, and that is not found on any of the records I have reviewed."

Jarvis began to squirm shifting his weight from one side to the other. His mind immediately returned to the Battle of the Breach and the promise he made to Captain Banes. His struggle not to jeopardize the relationship he has with his new captain without betraying his old one was painfully evident upon his face. His eyes darted from Rico's inquisitive stare to the floor focusing upon a scuffmark on his right shoe.

"What kind of things do you want to know?" Jarvis asked his eyes still fixed upon his shoe. He bent down to wipe off the mark with his thumb.

"I want to know what happened at the Battle of the Breach."

Jarvis' fears had been realized. He bit his bottom lip, and hovered over his shoe a little longer than necessary so he could compose himself. He didn't want to dishonor the last wish of his former Captain.

"It was the largest land offensive of the war," Jarvis began more like a history professor.

"I'm more interested in why you, Captain Banes, and Dr. Lamb left in the middle of the battle, flew to Hyperion, and then returned before the battle was over."

Jarvis' eyes got as big as saucers. He was amazed that Rico knew about that. Even Epsilon 6 Command who had questioned them repeatedly about Captain Banes didn't know about that. "How'd you know?"

"That you left and returned," Rico stated completing his sentence.

"Yes. Even command didn't know about that excursion, and trust me they asked me everything including verifying my shoe size."

"Let's just say that there are things about ships that only Captains know. I also know that your shuttle was heavier when it left then when it returned by how much weight?" the latter question was directed at Zeveney.

"135 pounds," answered Zeveney.

Jarvis started to look pale as Zeveney's voice permeated the room. Jarvis started to stand up. He definitely looked cornered and a little scared. Fear was not something Rico would attribute to this powerhouse of a man.

"Sit down Commander you're not going anywhere until I get some answers from you."

"I can't."

"You can't?" Rico questioned, his tone was one that had just been challenged to combat.

"I promised Captain Banes I wouldn't."

"I can appreciate that, but I'm sure Conrad will understand."

"You don't understand. I can't," Jarvis explained almost as a plea for mercy rather than a statement of defiance.

"I'm not asking you to break a vow to your old Captain, but I need to know what your part in all of this was. I have to know I can trust you," Rico countered. The Captain was so close to him that Jarvis could feel Rico's breath upon his face laced with the smell of scotch mingled with coffee. He waited until Jarvis's eyes met his before he continued. "Surely you can tell me what your part was without violating your promise."

Jarvis swallowed hard before answering thinking and weighing everything very carefully. "Yes, Sir, I can tell you my part."

"Good," Rico acknowledged backing down and settling into his own comfortable chair. His eyes never left Jarvis face. Jarvis was quiet for a while. Rico gave him a moment to sort through his thoughts, but he was taking too long. "I'm waiting," Rico prompted.

"Is this on the official record, Sir?"

"No, this is my personal investigation. Anything that is said here is kept between the three of us."

"Three?" Jarvis questioned without thinking, and then remembered the computer companion. He looked over at the Zeveney system display that was smiling like a cheesy comic. "Oh, yeah, I forgot about the Zeveney 7000."

"That's Zeveney 7000-P," Zeveney corrected.

"My mistake," Jarvis apologized with a half smile.

"The battle," Rico prompted.

"Yes, the battle was the most violent assault of the war. The Phoenix was ordered into grid Alpha. We took a lot of heat off the Triton's landing zone. It was the first time that I, myself, engaged in hand-to-hand combat with the Rundi. They were outfitted in some deceptively lightweight material that our weapons had a hard time cutting through. The moment any of our lasers penetrated a suit, the body would vaporize. Dr. Lamb was sent in to see if she could recover anything at all about Rundi physiology. It was an impossible task, as the vaporized Rundi didn't leave so much as a bone fragment behind just a yellowish white powder."

Jarvis paused. Rico could tell he was thinking again. Part of him was back in the heat of the battle. Sweat began to break out on his forehead, and his eyes began to turn glassy as his thoughts retreated in time. Now he could smell the aromas of battle, blood, leather, and that chalky powder that would be picked up by the wind and fly up the nostrils reminding him of antacid. Rico could see he was losing him to the memory and called out to him in a calm voice.

"You're safe. I understand your objective now explain how you, Conrad, and Dr. Lamb managed to wind up together on the battlefield."

"Yes," Jarvis responded dreamily at first, but then returned to the present. "Captain Banes became very angry. His first officer, Richard Benson, was hit, and was pronounced dead almost immediately. Rich was my best friend. The shot took half my man's head off. He uttered a few words before he stopped with his mouth open and his left eye staring off into the distance. Captain Banes wanted a piece of Rundi ass bad, and he charged forward by himself. I was still holding my friend when Dr. Lamb got my attention and pointed to the captain's position. He was blazing a trail cutting through the Rundi lines greasing them as he went. I knew he wouldn't last long if some one didn't go after him, so I got up and ran to catch up to him. I nailed one of the bastards just before he tried shooting the Captain in the back. What I didn't
126

realize was that Dr. Lamb had followed me. It didn't take us long to realize that we'd been cut off from our unit."

Jarvis paused a moment to wipe the sweat from his forehead with his hand and then rubbed his hand against his trousers to dry them. Rico could see that this was very painful for him to recall, but he had to know what had happened.

"I know this is very difficult to have to recount this, but it is very important. Take a sip of coffee and a couple deep breaths," Rico entreated. Jarvis pulled his distant gaze back to look over at Rico and then down at the coffee on the table in front of him. He took a deep breath, held it briefly and then released it as he leaned forward to grab the cup. He lifted it to his lips and took a drink. He let the coffee ease over his tongue and down his throat. Its warmth calmed him, and the caffeine bolstered his confidence to continue.

"Good coffee sir."

"Why thank you," Zeveney spoke up.

"The computer made the coffee?" Jarvis questioned with doubt.

"Please, I'm a Zeveney 7000-P, do not insult me. It was quite the scientific achievement to devise a bold yet mellow coffee brew that would meet the captain's criteria."

"And a fine job you did too!" Rico saluted with his cup and took a drink.

"Where was I?" Jarvis questioned aloud, being unaccustomed to having a conversation with the furniture.

"You were cutoff behind Rundi lines," Rico prompted.

"Yes, I ran to help him when the Captain suddenly stopped short. I nearly knocked him over. He was hovering over a wounded Rundi, and was preparing to shoot it, but then he just stopped. Heck he had just left a trail of dead Rundi behind him." Even now relaying the sequence of events, Conrad's rational made no sense to him.

"Wounded?" Rico questioned, with piqued interest. He'd never heard of a wounded Rundi. He was very much aware of their typical self-destruction method leaving only powder behind. Never had he heard of anyone finding one wounded.

"Yes, wounded."

"Did you see what it looked like?"

"No, but I think Captain Banes did. He was kneeling over it like a nursemaid. He asked Dr. Lamb to treat it, but the Rundi refused. In a whisper that only the Captain could hear, he said that it told him that the only thing that could help it was the hot mineral springs on Hyperion. The captain scooped up the Rundi and found a break in the lines. We um, took it back to the Captain's shuttle."

"Why? What did Conrad hope to accomplish?"

"He said that if we could prove ourselves to be more than a warlike species by showing mercy to our enemy there might be hope for peace. You'd have thought it was Qwan or something the way he doted over it. He covered its helmet with a towel and wouldn't let either of us look at it for fear it would try to self-destruct. He hoped it would go back and tell the others about what we did, but it was a vain hope."

"It died," Rico surmised.

"Yes, it died. Right after we got to the springs and before the doctor could help it into the pool, but it didn't vaporize. It was bleeding pretty bad so we buried the body in a shallow grave in an old cave that the miners had abandon and then returned to the battle."

"Did you look at the body then?"

"No, the Captain thought it would be disrespectful." Jarvis paused reflectively then continued. "Did telling you my experiences help you?"

"Yes, it did. I'm curious when did you strike the Captain?"

"When we returned to the battle Captain Banes wanted to go back for Benson. I wouldn't let him. Our troops were dropping back. He went mad so I hit him and knocked him out for about five to ten minutes. By the time he came to, the cease fire had been communicated."

"Thank you for your honesty and trust. You're free to go."

"Thanks for the coffee, Sir."

Jarvis left the room. Rico looked after him for a moment before conversing with Zeveney.

"Do you want me to provide you with my analysis, or wait for you to expound upon your gut?" Zeveney questioned.

"Let me expound and then you can tell me what I left out."

"Very well, Captain, please enlighten me."

"Jarvis is not telling me everything he knows, even though what he told me wasn't a lie, he's holding something back."

"A plus for your gut Captain, there was a great deal of stress even allowing for battle stress when a soldier recalls specific battles. He was holding back. He did not, however, lie on any point."

"The real question is what's he not telling us and why. I mean beyond his vow to Conrad. There seems to be more than just a conflict of loyalty between Captains to his restraint."

"Agreed, I'd also like to submit to you that Captain Banes may have been guilty of the charges of collaboration and Jarvis is keeping any supporting evidence to that effect to himself."

"Never!" Rico yelled back at the program. His eyes bored a hole through the display with a fiery anger that was barely in check.

"I was not trying to upset you, but was only submitting to you one of the many possibilities for his silence."

"Then watch your wording. I'll not have you talk about him in that way. I'd have you dismantled and scrapped before I'll let you defame him any further."

"I'll be in sleep mode until you give me further instruction," Zeveney informed self-terminating his image. Although the Zeveney 7000-P program had no feelings to hurt, it did understand when Rico needed time to think.

***

Jarvis left the captain's quarters and headed straight to Dr. Lamb's office. She was busy preparing the medical bays to receive hospital patients. The activity kept her mind occupied so she wouldn't have time to reflect upon her earlier conversation with Rico. She didn't even notice that the door had opened and Jarvis was standing there watching her work. Suddenly she felt the weight of a stare upon her and she turned around. She half expected Rico, but was surprised to see the Commander. Jarvis looked pale.

"Commander, are you well?" Dr. Lamb questioned, walking over to him. She could spot that his forehead glistened with perspiration, but the temperature in the room was not hot. He looked at her for a moment before speaking, his expression solemn.

"The captain knows about our excursion to Hyperion during the Battle of the Breach."

Dr. Lamb put her notepad down and began to look as pale as Jarvis. She nervously took a cloth, wet it, and wiped the Commander's forehead.

"How?" she managed to ask, a tremor of fear wavered in her tone.

"There appears to be a shipboard recording device on shuttles that recorded our voyage. Captain Rico was serious about finding out the truth about Captain Banes. I just wanted you to know that I kept your secret."

"Thank you Edward," she said appreciatively addressing him in the familiar.

131

"Don't thank me. It's only my vow to Captain Banes that has stayed my tongue, a vow that I'll take to my own grave if necessary."

"Captain Banes was a good man," she added.

"I thought you should know in case Captain Sanchez decides to question you that I kept to the explanation Captain Banes gave us."

"I appreciate that."

"Don't think I'm getting sentimental, I just don't want to be questioned by him again if he finds a discrepancy. He's hell bent to uncover the truth."

"Knowing the truth could mean death for Captain Sanchez."

"I know that. What I don't know is if Captain Banes made the right choice to trust you," Jarvis admitted, then turned and left.

Dr. Lamb looked after him until he was out of sight saying under her breath, "Yes he did, and in time you'll learn that I made a good choice too."

The hallway was unusually empty for this time of day. She glanced briefly down at her timepiece and surmised that everyone was at their duty station. They'd arrive in orbit in just under two hours. Daphne returned to her own duties as the time was short, and she had no desire to entertain questions or doubts about what she did or didn't do on Hyperion.

Chapter 10

Governor Tarken was notified that the Phoenix was in orbit. In just a couple of hours the transports would be landing a few yards south of the city limits in the large open fields. Paul had his Chief of Security, Terry Biggs, call out the militia. They were ordered to report to the Munitions Depot to receive their weapons via the citywide alert system. While they were doing that, Paul and his wife, Samantha, were making preparations to receive Captain Sanchez and his assistant, Wong Qwan who would coordinate the evacuation efforts between the ships in orbit and Hyperion.

While Samantha fussed with the table display which housed a variety of pastries, fruits, teas, hard boiled chicken eggs, a delicacy on the frontier and of course, coffee; a messenger arrived at their home and knocked frantically on the door.

"I'm coming. What's the emergency?" Paul asked jokingly in response to the knocking rather than a premonition of what was about to be explained to him. The messenger paused a moment looking quizzically into the Governor's face before answering, wondering if he knew why he was there.

"Sir, Security Chief Biggs has sent me to inform you that the Munitions Depot has been robbed. We have nothing to arm the Militia with."

The statement fell upon him like a bucket of ice water. His shock was evident, as he did not move or speak for several seconds.

"Why didn't he call me?" Paul asked demandingly.

"He didn't want the information going over standard communications and insight a panic before we can gain control of the situation. He also didn't want to leave the scene so he can give this investigation his full attention."

The news even caught Samantha's ears as she stopped her fidgeting immediately and moved to stand next to her husband. Paul looked over at her to acknowledge her support, and then turned to look at the messenger head on. Paul's eyes glassed over with an unwavering determination. He was going to move forward with this evacuation, but couldn't afford a mass hysteria or panic from Epsilon 6 Command.

"Take me to the Depot," Paul commanded. His tone was absolute and filled with the authority that the people had given him to protect and serve them. He followed the messenger back toward the armory located about seven blocks north of the Governor's residence. He kept a brisk pace walking the mile long distance with little physical fatigue. People saw him and waved to him from their homes unaware of the danger looming close by. Governor Tarken responded sharply with a wave of dismissal rather than one of greeting. The people were familiar with him and knew that when he was focused on his duty he was not easily distracted. They dismissed his curtness due to the impending evacuation, but couldn't begin to fathom what was about to unfold any more than Paul could. They returned to their packing without further concern or offense unaware of the danger looming on the horizon.

"I'm sorry, Sir. I know this couldn't have happened at a worse time," Security Chief Terry Biggs apologized in greeting. He met him a block away from the Depot, and took over for the messenger who was quite relieved. Terry held out his big bear paw of a hand for Paul to shake. Paul took it. His displeasure was quite evident in his countenance, and was more interested in the coming explanation than a familial greeting. Seeing that Paul was not in good humor, Terry continued to explain on the way. "Whoever did it must have acquired a key because we can find no evidence of forced entry."

"Could it be one of our own?" Paul's question was asked in a hushed whisper and pricked Biggs to the heart. He took being Security Chief very seriously, and ran a tight ship. His face squinched up almost meeting in the middle of his chubby face. Although Terry was nearing retirement age, he was not a man to skate through his last watch.

"I suppose anything is possible, but I picked these men myself. They were interviewed and investigated by Epsilon 6 Command and yourself prior to their instatement. I know you're under a great deal of stress, but a witch hunt won't bring back the weapons."

"I'm not suggesting we conduct one, but people change. I'm forcing people from their homes. It's not outside the realm of possibility that one of them cracked under the pressure," Paul suggested as they arrived at the Depot. The door was ajar and the lights were on inside. Two guards stood watch outside the opened doors.

"It's possible, but we don't have the time to investigate it," Terry admitted.

"How much did they take?" Paul asked while they stood outside the Depot. Terry gestured for Paul to go in first so he could see for himself all that had been taken, but even he didn't know what the original inventory consisted of without the documentation in front of him. Terry tried to keep silent hoping that a picture would save at least a thousand words of ass chewing, but Paul's expression was unrelenting. He wanted a full report, and he wanted it from his Chief of Security.

"Virtually all the rifles are gone. They didn't touch the big weapons leaving us about a dozen of the smaller guns that are capable of firing stun rounds. However, they left us no stun rounds."

"Damn it!" Paul exclaimed, punctuating his displeasure with a punch to the inside wall. The metal wall gave way leaving a dent in the wall, but no sign of injury to Paul's fist. Even though Paul had a desk job, his physical prowess was not diminished and the Security Chief wanted no part of the receiving end of that punch.

"Your orders were quite specific banning the use of lethal rounds during this evacuation. At this point if things get out of hand we don't have anything to help bring the crowd back under control."

"I knew things were going too well," Paul said in disgust. "Have there been any reports of violence, the taking of hostages, threats, anything?"

"No sir. People are beginning to report to their scheduled evacuation zones as planned in an orderly fashion. The others that are not scheduled for a few days are doing what they're supposed to be doing. So far there have been no reports of rioting, looting, or anything out of the ordinary."

"And you have no idea who stole them or when?"

"We do now sir," a fellow guard interrupted, coming to report his findings. Biggs nodded for him to continue. "The surveillance playback doesn't give us a clear identity on who stole the weapons and ammunition, but we do know that they were taken last night. They were so well disguised we couldn't even tell you if they were men or women."

"And the guards you keep posted to prevent this from happening?"

"Saw and heard nothing. Whoever did this have been casing us for a while," the guard informed. Terry then took over the conversation. "If they knew the habits of my guards, then they were in and out before they made their second round."

"The time-stamp on the tape would confirm that sir," the guard added, to substantiate Terry's assumption.

"I don't like it Terry. Have your men keep their eyes open. Report anything unusual no matter how insignificant."

"Should we announce our situation to the people?"

"Hell no! In fact, I want you to pass out the lethal rifles, but no rounds. Maybe we can bluff our way through this."

"I'm not sure if my men can act that well."

"They'd better learn. People's lives depend on it."

"Yes Sir."

Paul came out of the Depot to face the militia who were still waiting for their orders and weapons. He looked at the men carefully wondering which one of them gave the thieves' access to

138

the Depot. He soon felt guilty for the thought as he engaged the eyes
of each loyal soldier. Paul was pretty much done with the invasive
stare by the time he reached Jeremy Tate's position. He was pressed
for time. Paul had to get back to his home to receive Captain Rico
Sanchez and company. Jeremy was quite relieved. He was
beginning to have doubts about his decision, but it was too late. He
was already committed. Paul walked to the front of the men to
address them.

"Gentlemen," Paul began. "It seems that someone has stolen
our non-lethal crowd control weapons and rounds. To what end, I
don't know. What we are going to do is give you lethal rifles, but
they'll be useless for I'm giving you no ammunition to fire. My
hope is that you'll be able to bluff your way through any situation to
regain control for the public safety. Perhaps the sight of these
formidable firearms will be a deterrent. Do not let the people know
you have empty chambers, for this to work they must believe that
they are loaded. Do you understand?"

"Yes, Sir," they responded, but it wasn't overtly convincing
when it rang in his ears.

"I said, do you understand?" this time Paul yelled it out in the
same manner as he heard drill instructors do at the Military
Academy. His brother went there, and the orders being coughed out
upon their troops had left an impression upon him as a teenage boy.

"Sir, Yes, Sir!" came the second and much more convincing response. Although this was militia and not regular army, all the militia had gone through basic skill and weapons training.

"That's better. As soon as you have your weapons, report to your assigned posts. I'm releasing you to Security Chief Biggs for final instructions."

Paul looked over at Terry and winked. That was Paul's way of saying that he didn't blame Terry for the mishap, and trusted him to pull his ass out of the fire. He just knew Epsilon 6 Command would certainly roast his balls as soon as word leaked out about what had happened. He then turned around to go back to his home. He was going to have to explain to Captain Rico Sanchez that he's been robbed, that the militia has no real firepower, and that he really doesn't know why or who did it. Although he had his suspicions, he had no real evidence to support it, nor time to investigate.

* * *

Before reporting to his assigned duty station with his useless weapon Jeremy Tate made a beeline for Manny Smithers' home. He knocked gently on the door. Manny opened it before the knocking could disturb his wife, Sarah, who was packing in the other room. Jeremy explained everything that happened in hushed whispers so that Sarah wouldn't hear. She was unaware of Manny's plan for the evacuation. Suddenly, Sarah walked into the room.

"What are you two men up to?" she questioned, believing that their whispering had more to do with poker than espionage.

140

"Woman! Are you trying to give me a heart attack? How dare you come in here without knocking!" Manny spit and sputtered his displeasure like a de-clawed house cat hisses at his shadow.

"Why Manny Edwin Smithers, I ought to take a broom to you for bidding me to knock before coming into a room inside me own house," Sarah chastised with a thick Irish brogue.

Jeremy looked at Manny and then at Sarah with a smile that pleaded for her to be merciful. He'd been in many bar fights and even a few skirmishes with the Rundi before he was wounded. Never had he been afraid of any of them, but he was afraid of Sarah. She was a woman who packed a punch.

"I was just telling Manny that the Phoenix has arrived in orbit."

"That announcement came over the loud speaker. Would you like to try again?"

"I owed him money on our card game last week."

"Now that I believe. You best be running along Mr. Tate. We've still got some work to do here."

"Yes Ma'am."

Jeremy shut the door and left to report to his post. Manny then turned around to face his wife of 25 years standing there with her hands propped up on her ample hips waiting for him to tell her the real truth. She was far from slender, yet her body was distributed showing in very womanly curves and an abundant bosom. Sarah was a woman of average height with golden brown hair that now contained within their shiny locks streaks of silver. Her face was spattered with a generous portion of freckles. The laugh lines around her eyes were still visible even when she wasn't laughing, as was her nature to do often. Those lines still adorned the most beautiful set of brown eyes Manny had ever seen. Those eyes of hers could melt his spine with a single look, and it wasn't a threatening one, it was a compassionate one.

"You don't buy Jeremy's excuse."

"After 25 years of marriage and two children you're finally getting a clue that I can see through any of your foolish pretenses."

Manny released a sigh knowing that he wasn't fooling her. He had to come up with something that held truth, but didn't give away their plan. He stared at the floor until he could see her feet standing toe to toe with his big steel-toed work boots. Her toes were painted and housed so daintily within the leather sandals that she liked to wear. Never had he known a woman to be so voluptuous, beautiful, and yet so strong. He took a deep breath before lifting his head to gaze into her eyes.

"Jeremy and a few others are going to go talk to the Governor to see if there's any way that we can keep our homes."

"Is that what's troubling you? You silly old fool, we've lived in so many places. We raised a family in several of them. When are you going to understand that home is where ever we are together?"

Manny just looked into his wife's eyes that were so pure and full of love with no pretense. He was, however, this time committed by his very life to follow through on his convictions. She was probably right that he was an old fool, for only an old fool would jeopardize such a wonderful marriage for a piece of land. Suddenly he reached out grabbing her with his rough hands and pulled her into his chest. He just hugged her like a small child would hug and nuzzle a stuffed animal.

"I love you Sarah Smithers. Whatever comes to this old fool of yours know that I have always loved you and will always love you."

"I love you too! Cheer up now, we've got to get busy. We're due to report to the transports at noon."

"I've a few errands to run, and some goodbyes to make."

"Go on, I'll have us ready to go when you get back. Be sure to keep track of the time."

"If I'm not back when it's time to leave, I'll meet you there or on board the ship," Manny insisted.

"Very well."

She kissed him on the lips. His eyes became shiny as tears welled up, but never overflowed their boundaries. She was definitely right, he thought, he was an old fool. He turned around and left before his entire spine melted in her gaze. He had a job to do and hoped that should he survive this rebellion of his, that she would forgive him.

Glenda C. Finkelstein

Chapter 11

As Rico and Wong set out for Hyperion in the Captain's shuttle, Captain Sanchez became lost in his thoughts preoccupied with the shallow grave holding the Rundi body. Rico knew that with the planet soon becoming off limits, his time was shrinking with this one and only opportunity to gather important biological data. Qwan, however, caught sight of a Rundi cruiser taking position on the edge of visual range and couldn't keep his eyes off it.

"That's a big ship," Qwan commented aloud. Wong's statement startled Rico bringing him out of his thoughts and leaned forward to see out the port side of the craft. He was amazed, impressed, and concerned all at the same time as he didn't recognize the type of craft.

"It's not the typical battle cruisers that we fought in the war. This looks much meaner, and yet it's not nimble enough to fight a battle," Rico added.

"You're right. It could be an invasion vessel with lots of room to store people, supplies, and shuttles. It's too big to land. Look at the starboard side. Those are some big guns."

"You have a point. Those weapons are huge and with that kind of firepower they could do a lot of damage even if they miss you," Rico commented.

"Unfortunately, the Rundi aren't known for missing what they aim at," Qwan commented. Rico just flashed a smirk at his statement.

"Sir," the pilot interrupted. "We're about to enter the planet's atmosphere."

"Thank you."

Rico and Qwan strapped themselves in and prepared for landing. A few minutes later the pilot landed the craft like a feather onto the terra firma. The Governor's Aids met them at the craft to accompany them to the Governor's home. Upon arriving at the house, they were formally announced to the Governor and First Lady.

"Welcome Captain Sanchez and Specialist Qwan," Samantha greeted, receiving them with gentile charm and sophistication. Paul stood beside her. Before responding, Rico and Qwan looked about inside the spacious apartment. The walls were painted in warm earth tones and furnished with deep mahogany wooden furniture and overstuffed leather chairs. The light bulbs shone through crystal chandeliers suspended from the ceiling and aromatic candles burned upon the tables.

"Thank you, Mrs. Tarken, Governor," Rico responded, bowing his head respectfully. Qwan also bowed. This form of greeting was now the accepted form of formal introduction and was used the majority of the time, however, the handshake was still popular especially among the men.

"Please come in and enjoy some breakfast which my wife has meticulously prepared for your enjoyment," Paul entreated.

"We'd be delighted," Rico answered. Although he was intent on finding where the Rundi was buried, he had a few days so he didn't have to be rude. The food did look awfully good. The two men helped themselves to the lovely delicacies that were spread out on the table which tasted as good as they looked. Paul waited for them to enjoy several bites of food and take a sip of coffee before he informed Captain Sanchez of the missing weapons.

"I'm very glad that you've arrived," Paul began, and then paused. Rico could tell by his tone that something was off. He flashed a look over at Qwan who immediately caught on to Rico's concern and put the pastry that he was about to eat back onto his plate.

"Is everything okay?" Rico asked suspiciously, sitting straight in his chair.

"Yes. No. I'm not sure," Paul responded. Rico put his plate down on a nearby table. He didn't like what he was hearing.

"Which is it?"

"I called out the militia this morning to arm them with stun rifles in case a panic should break out and we need to regain control quickly without harming anyone. When we opened the Munitions Depot early this morning, the weapons were gone."

"Any suspects?"

"Maybe, but all I have is rumor and nothing I can prove."

"Who?"

"All I have is some initial grumbling which all of us voiced, but that's all. I can't arrest people for complaining. Hell, I don't like having to evacuate either."

"Who?" Rico questioned again. This time he wasn't going to allow him to evade the question. Paul was still hesitant.

"You should answer the question," Qwan encouraged. He could tell that Rico was getting agitated.

"The individuals that actually raided the depot could not be identified. The Miners Union and the Farmers Coalition have been the most vocal about not wanting to leave. Yet none of them have any criminal background, and there have been no public threats or interruption of normal business."

"We're dealing with peoples' homes Governor. Even the weakest will still fight for his dwelling. In this case, their livelihood, as well as their residence, is being taken from them without warning and without a sufficient reason."

"Other than the missing weapons, nothing else has happened."

"Yet," Rico added to complete the governor's sentence. Paul squirmed in his chair. He was beginning to show dislike for Rico and the captain knew it. His reputation for stirring the pot undoubtedly preceded him and he wasn't about to disappoint. "What did Command have to say about it?" Rico asked with purposeful intent already knowing the answer.

"I haven't reported anything yet."

"Why didn't you report these incidents and the theft to Epsilon 6 Command?"

"The theft was only discovered an hour before you arrived at my door. As for the grumbling, I didn't want Epsilon 6 Command calling every hour on the hour for something I had under control. This evacuation is difficult enough without having someone looking over my shoulder every two seconds."

"Well, now you have me, and I won't be looking over your shoulder. I'm going to be in your face," Rico informed sternly. "Qwan, transmit a full report of this situation to HQ and to Commander Jarvis. Make sure that all of our people are on the lookout for those rifles. The last thing we need to do is provide a ship for a coup."

"My husband has done a lot in getting the people prepared. They are organized and ready to leave. There has been very little if any trouble. In addition, he's been able to provide a means whereby people can re-locate quickly and efficiently," Samantha defended.

"Mrs. Tarken, I'm here to evacuate over 80,000 people onto four spaceships before the Rundi, who are currently shadowing us destroy this place. They have enough firepower to cut this planet in two and exterminate what's left after the buzzer sounds. We can't afford a mistake."

Samantha swallowed hard, and took a seat only after her husband encouraged her to do so. She was a passionate defender of her husband's policies and practices. Qwan sent the particulars to each destination with his usual proficient manner. He then paused a moment to read an incoming message.

"Captain," Qwan began. "The Triton has just arrived in orbit along with another Rundi vessel."

"Is it the same type of ship as the one that's shadowing us?"

"No, Sir, they report that the new one is a standard cruiser, but scans indicate that it has been modified."

"Modified? How?"

"Over half the ship has been refitted to double the firepower of a standard Rundi cruiser."

"It would seem, Governor, that the Rundi are serious about this deadline. If you'll excuse me, I have some matters to attend to. Qwan you're in charge until I return."

"Sir?" Qwan questioned. He'd never been in a command situation before. Rico shot him a quick wink and a devious smile.

"I didn't stutter mister. You're the mathematical genius who'll make sure these people get off the planet and keep our shuttles from running into one another. Governor, please see to it that you set Qwan up with full radar and communications. As soon as Qwan is ready to go, the landings will begin. Please inform your people that the evacuations will start soon after."

"Yes, of course, but where are you going?" The governor questioned.

"That's need to know, and you don't. I will, however, be back in time for lunch. Mrs. Tarken I look forward to your lunch selection." Rico didn't want his abrupt departure to offend Mrs. Tarken. She was a charming hostess, and in spite of this rocky start didn't want to alienate the Governor. He was, after all, there to help him.

"You won't be disappointed Captain," Samantha responded with stunned sincere appreciation. His reputation of being a man of few words, and even fewer compliments was not unfounded.

Rico was concerned that if he put his investigation off, he may never get another chance to check out Jarvis' story. He wasn't expecting to walk into an incident in the first few minutes of his arrival. Things could go awry at any moment and a rare opportunity would be missed. Rico grabbed a pastry to go as he headed out the door.

As Rico walked the streets, his mind drifted back to his feelings for Daphne. These feelings were not going away, and were actually growing stronger with each passing moment. He also wondered if their encounter on Cassiopeia was accidental or orchestrated by fate. He knew that regardless of the answer his personal feelings had to be put on hold. His duty came first. They could sort out their relationship when this mission was over.

After walking several blocks, he contacted Zeveney to get directions to the location of the shallow grave. "Zev, are you there?" Rico questioned in a hushed whisper into his wrist link. The colonists watched him briefly with curiosity. They recognized the uniform and the rank, but were too busy with their own affairs to question why a Captain was walking down the streets of their fair colony.

"Zeveney at your service captain, I await your command."

"I need directions to the shallow grave," he whispered even softer, trying not to attract any unwanted attention. A small boy stopped and stared inquisitively at Rico for a few moments, but ran away when his mother beckoned him.

"Captain, I don't have those coordinates. I can only give you the landing site of Captain Banes' ship. You'll have to determine the most logical place to begin with from there."

"We'll start with that, but I also want you to integrate into the ship's sensors and scan the area in more detail. Perhaps you'll be able to find the grave before I get there."

"No problem."

"Also monitor all communications on Hyperion and let me know if you pick up anything that could indicate trouble."

"Are you expecting trouble?"

"Yes I am. The Munitions Depot was broken into and robbed. I don't want to be caught with my pants down."

"Pants down?" Zev questioned.

"It's just an expression…" Rico suddenly stopped talking. He had come to a crossroads and didn't know which way to go. Zeveney, who should be monitoring his progress, seemed to have forgotten that he was in route to the location and needed further instruction. Rico listened intently, but couldn't even discern the humming of Zeveney's drives running. There was nothing, but silence. "Zev! Did you understand my request?"

"Of course, captain. I was integrating."

"That's good, but I still need directions. I'm at a crossroads. Which way do I go?"

"Proceed due west about twenty blocks then follow the gravel road southwest towards the hills. From there you should be able to see a ridge of hills extending beyond the colony."

"Thank you. In the meantime, review the meeting I had with Jarvis' and see if you can discern any clues that would help narrow down my search once I arrive at the landing site. Call me when you've finished scanning and let me know what you've found."

"Yes Sir."

On his journey Rico looked about admiring the colony's achievements. They had a lovely community, and until today no reported thefts. He watched the shuttles landing just to the south of his position where crops had been just days before to evacuate the Hyperion refugees. He wondered how he'd feel if he was the one losing his home and occupation without so much as a, kiss my foot. Rico knew that somewhere among these people were those who thought they have a chance to save their homes. Unfortunately, he also knew that if they take that action, they'd most certainly lose.

The morning sun was climbing in the sky and it was getting hot. Rico needed to refresh himself. He wasn't used to perspiring except in the gym. The ship was kept at a comfortable temperature at all times. He needed to infuse his body with more than water and stopped at a fruit juice stand for a cold drink. The vendor was glad to sell him one since the evacuation had impeded his business. Rico, on the other hand, was quite thankful because it was so refreshing. The fruity taste of the wassa berry was reminiscent of pomegranates and was native to Hyperion. It was a favorite among the locals, and would only grow in Hyperion soil. All other attempts to cultivate the berry off planet were met with failure. Usually when a commodity was about to become that rare, the price would sky rocket, but in this case that would be useless as the law forbade such price gouging in times of emergency.

Rico finally reached the edge of town where a gravel road led out toward the hills. His boots made a crunching sound on the loose gravel that sank under his weight like beach sand. There was no one out there, but him. He could hear the singing of the snub-nosed lizards and the grunting made by the only mammal native to Hyperion that resembled a gopher called a Larnix. He'd never seen one, but believed he may have spied one just out of the corner of his eye before it darted into an underground burrow.

"Captain!" Zev called out loud and full of vigor. Rico nearly jumped out of his skin having gotten lost in the solitary beauty of this world.

"What the…?" Rico snapped.

"I have your coordinates." There was a lilt of accomplishment in Zeveney's voice that irritated Rico. This machine was at times, too human for his liking.

"Okay, where do I go?"

"Continue on your current heading for one hundred meters, and you should come to a cave opening. Inside is a hot spring."

"Good, and the body?"

"It should be in there."

"It should be?"

"Due to the composition of the cave, the ships sensors can't penetrate the rock from orbit. Jarvis mentioned a hot spring, and based upon the elevated temperature in the first cave that has to be it."

"Once I get inside will you be able to scan the body should I find it and confirm its identity by using my communication device?"

"Yes."

"Good, stand by."

Rico continued on until he reached the entrance to the cave. It was dark. He cracked a light stick that he retrieved from his belt so he could see where he was going. He could hear the bubbling of the hot springs. The odor of minerals began wafting under his nostrils. The odor was strong, but not overpowering. He could see evidence that people had been inside the cave. There was a military med kit with its contents strewn across the cave, probably from a curious animal, and of course refuse, fortunately dried.

"Zeveney, are you receiving any data from my wrist unit?"

"There's some slight interference, but it's starting to clear. Take seven steps to your left." Rico followed Zeveney's instruction. "Stop." Rico froze. "The body should be right under you."

Rico dropped to his hands and knees and began digging at first with his hands, and then spied a board that would assist him so he grabbed it and started moving the dirt and sand back. He dug for a few minutes until he hit something that wasn't dirt. He tossed the board away and returned to digging with his hands.

"I found it!" Rico announced, as he started to remove dirt from the face and upper torso. It was mostly bone so no visual

156

confirmation could be made, although the hair did appear to belong to a female. "Can you scan the body?"

"Yes, the transmission is coming through. Running DNA check."

"It looks human," Rico stated with some confusion. He was expecting a Rundi. Although he wouldn't know what a Rundi looked like anyway.

"You would be correct, Captain, the remains are human."

"Who?"

"Dr. Daphne Lamb."

"That can't be right. Run the scan again." This news baffled Rico. How could the good doctor be on board ship, and yet dead and buried, too?

"Complete, the results are conclusive. This body is Dr. Daphne Lamb."

"Then who's on the Phoenix?" Rico asked aloud. Zeveney started to answer, but Rico cut him off with additional orders. "Zeveney, integrate your circuits into the medical scanners in sick bay and scan our Dr. Lamb. Do not announce what you're doing."

"Yes, Captain."

"Wait, before you begin. Can you pinpoint the time of death on this body?"

"Yes, Dr. Lamb died on the last day of the Battle of the Breach."

"Thank you. Conduct your scan and get back to me."

All manner of scenarios were playing themselves out inside Rico's mind while he waited for Zeveney's report. Was she a spy? An imposter? Maybe she was planted by command to keep him from finding out the truth about Conrad. He really didn't know, and that caused his gut to twist and turn in contortions the human body was never meant to endure.

Whoever she really was he loved her. In desperation his mind leaped back to that night they made love. He could still smell her scent and feel the gentle sea breeze blowing across his body. His hand could sense her soft supple skin that was so smooth and warm under his caress. His heart was undone inside her embrace and the memory of their ecstasy was more precious than anything, and to think that it may have all been a lie was more than he could conceive. Yet he may have to…No, he'd not even think it unless his duty…

"I've completed the scan, but have experienced a strange flutter in my system," Zeveney informed, interrupting Rico's inner turmoil.

"Do you need repair?"

"No, the best way to describe it is to compare it to a human's sense of dejavu. I feel like I've done this scan before, yet no data exists to support that conclusion."

"I appreciate that feeling, but I need to know the results of the scan."

"Yes, of course. The Dr. Lamb, who's currently on the Phoenix, does not register on the medical instruments as human."

"That means she must be a Rundi."

"That would be a logical conclusion."

"Zev, I need you to scan the picture sitting on my bureau. There's a substance on it you scanned for me several days ago that I ordered you to delete from your data files. I also requested that you refuse this request. I'm giving you a priority override command code, 9 Alpha 5 Beta 3 Pi. Question: Does the substance on the photo match Dr. Lamb's blood?"

"Override code verified. Scanning… Your assumption is correct. In this data you asked me to delete, were you aware that there is a message on the photo written in Conrad's hand?"

"Yes, morphing nymph."

"Do you wish me to delete the information again?"

"No, but put it in a segregated encrypted file."

"Should I have Dr. Lamb placed under arrest?"

"No."

"But she's impersonating an Epsilon 6 Medical Officer."

"For all I know she's the reason Conrad is dead. If I act to hastily, I may risk losing the truth. I want her to join me planet side. I need answers, and she's the only one who has them."

"That's assuming a lot. Maybe this is what Commander Jarvis was holding back," Zeveney suggested.

"An argument for another day. Right now, I need to know how a Rundi took on the identity of my Chief Medical Officer and how this fits in with Conrad's death. This is probably the Rundi that he was trying to save and may have given his life to protect."

"What would you like me to do?"

"I'd like you to monitor ship's communications to see if there's any activity outside the norm with the Rundi vessels shadowing us."

"Will you be returning to the ship to collect her, or do you want Dr. Lamb brought to you?'

"I want her brought here, but I'll handle getting her here myself."

"Very well, call me when you need me."

Rico disconnected the communication. He knew he had to bring her here so he could confront her face to face. Only then would he be able to determine what's really going on. Officially, Zev was right. He should have her arrested, but something on the inside told him that would be hasty. He didn't want to use his shuttle. That would raise questions. None of which he was prepared to answer. This had to be done delicately and quietly. He thought for a moment, and then remembered seeing a pin on Yeoman Smith's lapel that indicated that she was a certified shuttle pilot. His new Yeoman was too new to question his orders. Rico opened a communication channel to the Phoenix.

"Phoenix," Jarvis greeted, responding to the hail.

"This is Captain Sanchez. Is Yeoman Smith available?"

"Yes sir. I believe she's in your office. Shall I connect you?"

"Yes, and secure the line."

"Yes Sir." Jarvis immediately complied with Rico's request and announced the incoming call to Yeoman Smith.

"Yeoman, are you there?" Jarvis questioned just to be sure he wasn't mistaken about her location.

"Yes Commander. How may I help you?"

"I have Captain Sanchez on a secured line for you."

"Very good," Lisa responded as she pressed a couple of buttons to receive the Captain's communication. "Hello, Captain Sanchez, what can I do for you?"

"Yeoman, I noticed the other day that you're a certified pilot, yes?"

"Yes sir. I'm certified on three different shuttle classes."

"Good, I need you to collect Dr. Daphne Lamb. I have a patient down here that is off the beaten trail that will need a doctor. I'll send you the coordinates."

"What's the condition of the patient?"

"Critical, but your priority is to get Dr. Lamb on the repair shuttle and only Dr. Lamb. Bring her here to these coordinates. Don't tell her where you're taking her, just bring her."

"She's going to have lots of questions."

"That may be, but you can't answer them."

"When do you want me to bring her?"

"Right now."

"Yes Sir. I'm on my way."

The Yeoman closed the channel and looked in the mirror with nervous eyes. The captain's request was highly unusual, but his tone dictated that she dared not disappoint him. She took a deep breath and headed for sickbay. Upon reaching her destination she entered from behind and watched Dr. Lamb for a moment. The good doctor was very busy preparing for the first wave of patients to be brought up. Lisa walked up quietly behind her in an effort to be as little of a distraction as possible. Daphne didn't see her and backed into Lisa. She was startled, as well as concerned that Lisa may have sustained an injury from being stepped on.

"Are you all right?" Dr. Lamb asked.

"Yes, I'm fine. I'm sorry to disturb you, but Captain Sanchez has ordered me to bring you down to Hyperion."

"Why?"

"He has a patient that needs your help."

"I can't leave at a time like this. I'll have one of my assistants accompany you."

"I'm afraid that's unacceptable. Captain Sanchez was quite clear that I was to bring you, and only you," Lisa explained. Her expression was intense and even her obvious youth didn't soften it.

Daphne looked into Lisa's eyes. She could see that although she was a fragile woman, she was resolute in following the Captain's orders. Part of her wondered if it was her time to be questioned like Jarvis had been, but doubted he would interrupt her valuable time for such a thing. Maybe there really was a patient, or, worse, maybe he'd discovered her secret. She made one last inquiry so she could be adequately prepared for this moment that she had been summoned to.

"What's the condition of the patient?"

"Critical," Lisa answered.

Daphne could see that this Yeoman, who was known for second-guessing herself, was quite certain of her actions in this instance. Although afraid, Daphne held onto a thread of hope that this man, Rico, whom she loved would not take a rash action against her without cause. For a brief moment she, too, returned to that grass hut on the beach and remembered what it was like to be surrounded by him and filled by him. His passion and warmth was like nothing she had experienced before. Suddenly she remembered that she had a duty to perform and was jolted back into the present staring into Lisa Smith's determined face.

"Let me get my med kit so I can stabilize the patient for transport to the ship." Daphne looked one last time into Lisa's eyes to see if anything had changed, but her gaze remained steadfast. She inhaled a quick deep breath hoping her concern was for naught. Maybe Captain Sanchez truly had a patient for medical transport that required extra attention, but her intuition said otherwise.

Glenda C. Finkelstein

The women boarded the repair shuttle, which was the only shuttle left that wasn't being used for refugee transport. Despite the fact that women are known for being chatty, neither female felt like talking save for the few statements protocol demanded that a pilot makes to prepare passengers for take off and landing. This silence allowed for each and every sound that the ship made to echo, even in this small space. It struck Daphne that there was little space on this little pod for a critically ill patient, but perhaps it was a child and doubted that Lisa would know who the patient was.

***

As they made their approach through the atmosphere of Hyperion, Daphne noticed that they were not on a trajectory that would land them inside the city limits. She could see that they were headed for the hot mineral springs. Her mind jumped back in time, and for a moment, she was there with Jarvis and Captain Banes making a rapid descent. It wasn't until she felt the dull thud of the pod touching ground that her mind came back to the present.

Yeoman Smith opened the doors bidding Daphne disembark first. The air of the planet quickly invaded the antiseptic odor of the pod, and the fragrant sweet smell of blooming tarts, a native plant, and the pungent peaty aroma of dirt flooded her senses. It was familiar to her and in spite of the butterflies in her belly, gave an odd euphoria of calm amid the rising waves of nausea. She stood to her feet and walked off the ship stepping gingerly onto the sand and gravel. Over near an outcropping of rocks that marked the beginning

164

of a maze of caves, caverns, and underground springs stood Captain Sanchez.

Rico stood alone looking at Daphne as she walked slowly, but steadily toward him. His eyes fixed upon hers. She was noticeably weary. Yeoman Smith took up position at the entryway to the pod, leaving Dr. Lamb and Captain Sanchez to their business. It was apparent by the looks exchanged between them that this was both important and probably personal.

Neither of them took their eyes off one another, each one searching for something, but neither wanting to give away what that something was. Daphne knew exactly where she was, but she would offer nothing voluntarily until he confronted her.

"Where's the patient?" she asked to break up the stifling silence.

"Inside the cave," Rico pointed, entreating her to accompany him.

"What's the patient's condition?"

"Dead."

"I came as ordered. I'm sorry I'm too late."

"You don't understand Dr. Lamb, the patient was you." He paused a moment to let the words sink in. Her eyes grew wide, and then settled back down. She held her tongue until questioned. "Would you like to explain to me how the dead body buried in the shallow grave that Jarvis told me about matches the DNA file for Dr. Daphne Lamb instead of the Rundi he told me was there?"

Daphne looked into Rico's eyes. They reflected his anger and hurt, but more than that, his compassion, that was actively battling to keep the other two emotions in check. She knew there'd be no talking her way out of it. The only thing that could save her now was the truth. Her time on the beach with him gave her a hope that he would give her an opportunity to explain herself. The only question now was would Rico have as open a mind as Conrad had?

"Since you already know that I'm not Dr. Lamb, and a Rundi I can only say that Dr. Lamb gave me a second chance to live. I can never repay her adequately, but Conrad…" Rico shot a look at her. She could tell that he was offended that she used his name in such a familiar way. She quickly realized her mistake and made the necessary adjustments. "I mean, Captain Banes. He believed that her sacrifice was not in vain, and was of her own free will."

"Did you enjoy playing human with me on the beach?" Rico questioned.

"You believe I'm a spy and set you up," Daphne stated, knowing the true intent of his question. "I'm not that clever. I'm a Rundi doctor who found herself in the wrong place at the wrong time. Captain Banes could have left me to die, but he didn't. When Dr. Lamb gave her life protecting me, the captain knew I would never be accepted by his people. That's when the decision was made for me to take on her physical appearance. Captain Banes gave me permission to do so in order to protect the life they had saved. Since I was already a doctor, it was easy to adapt to her role also.'

"As for the beach, I went to rest. My intention was to enjoy the time alone, return to the Phoenix, and before the ship left Hyperion to sneak back to the planet to be reunited with my family when they arrive. Everything else I shared with you, save my name and origin, was the truth."

"And what would that name be?"

"Zarta," she answered and then elaborated about her culture. "I have family and friends, just like you do. We have very similar family units with the same moral codes, and similar belief systems…" she paused a moment taking a deep breath before saying the next few words. "I didn't intend to fall in love with you. That's why I left without saying goodbye because I was torn. I miss my family, but I've never known love with anyone like I've known it with you. Besides, your attraction to me was based on a lie. You may not like my true appearance."

Tears began to flow unashamedly down her cheeks. She could sense that Rico wanted to come to her and hold her, but he maintained his distance. She ached to feel his arms about her, but knew he had his duty and it would come first.

"For what it's worth I sense no deceit in your current responses, but I need you to tell me what happened to bring you to this place during the Battle of the Breach," Rico's request was absolute. He couldn't allow his personal attachment to cloud his judgment nor be moved by her emotional display. He also hoped that comparing the two stories would confirm the truth.

"I was tending to my troops when one of our own explosive devices went off prematurely. I was hit with shrapnel in the lower abdomen. Our physiology is very similar in nature to two life forms from your home world called butterflies and dragonflies. We, however, have a layer of flesh surrounding our skeletal structure. Once the outer surface is breached infection begins almost immediately. The only thing we have to treat infection is the hot mineral springs like those found here on Hyperion.'

"I was not able to walk and in a lot of pain. Your troops were continuing to advance, and then suddenly out of nowhere your Captain Banes was standing over me. My first thought was that I was going to die. I was the perfect target. My people will usually self-destruct if they're wounded and believe an enemy might capture them, but medical personnel have no such device. I was at his mercy. He reminded me of a child investigating something new. Before I knew it he had called his own doctor to come and see to my wounds. I was scared, but realized that they were trying to help me although I couldn't understand why. I kept telling them that it was no use and that I had to be immersed into a hot mineral spring. I never thought they'd actually take me to one.'

"The next thing I knew Captain Banes had scooped me up into his arms and was running with Dr. Lamb and Lt. Jarvis following close behind. He brought me here, keeping my image from the prying eyes of Lt. Jarvis. Dr. Lamb was very kind to me. She got me into the water and kept me from drowning. Then something terrible happened. I'm not sure who it was, but someone from this colony happened upon us. They saw me and realized I wasn't human. They had to have been coming from inside the cave or Conrad would have seen them."

Rico shot another glare at her for using Conrad's name with such familiarity, but this time she didn't recant. She had every right to call him Conrad. She waited for Rico to capitulate that she had earned that privilege. After his silent objection was overruled, she continued to tell her version of the events.

"Dr. Lamb tried to get him to put the gun down, but he fired at me. Dr. Lamb threw her body in front of mine. She was mortally wounded."

"Hold that thought. Zeveney?"

"Yes, Captain."

"Can you confirm the cause of death on the body you've identified as Dr. Daphne Lamb?"

"Reviewing intensive scan... It's conclusive, Dr. Lamb died of a fatal gunshot wound to the chest."

"You may continue."

"I'm..." Zarta began to chastise him, but then remembered that he could just as easily have had her arrested. She took a deep breath and continued, "Conrad heard the shot. He immediately responded firing back killing my attacker, but it was too late to save

169

Dr. Lamb. I realized I was a walking target, if I didn't take human appearance I'd be dead and those that showed me mercy would die too. My people have the ability to force their flesh to take any appearance they wish within the limits of humanoid form. I asked Conrad if I could take Dr. Lamb's appearance. As I had never seen another human female, she was all I had to work with. He gave me permission to do so, and swore Lt. Jarvis to silence."

Zarta paused a moment to see if Rico had any other smart-ass comment to make before concluding her tale.

"You can confirm that there is a male human that was killed with a military issue weapon. He's buried on the opposite wall."

Rico took hold of Zarta's arm, walked across the cave, and over to the wall where Zarta indicated. He knelt down, held out his wrist, a scanning beam emerged scanning the area indicated, and then receded. She carefully pulled her arm free from his grasp and continued to walk around the cave. She was careful not to make any quick movements.

"She is correct Captain, including the way he died. The DNA marked round came from Captain Banes' weapon."

Rico stood back up to his feet. He gazed into her eyes across the cave. There were so many questions running around in her head wondering if he was going to arrest her. She could tell that he'd thought about it, but she's been able to prove that she was the victim.

"Your story checks out and is in loose agreement with Jarvis' account. I do, however, have one last question." He paused before asking it. She was ready to respond, and get this over with. "Were you the real reason that Conrad was executed for treason?"

"No, although I believe Jarvis believes I'm responsible, I'm not. I don't know why such a man would be killed. No one knows, save maybe the Prefect. When your people questioned me during that time they questioned me as if I were Dr. Daphne Lamb. If they knew who I really was, wouldn't they have arrested me or detained me?" She stopped with that question, leaving the impression there was one more question to ask or statement to make as she walked back across the cave to stand toe-to-toe in front of Rico.

"Probably," Rico answered. His voice was cold and distant. "What's a Prefect?" He asked.

"A Prefect is a Rundi official assigned to a conquered race to facilitate peaceful cessation of hostility."

"So what happens now, we become your pets or servants?" Rico's tone was full of disgust.

"No. That's not our way. We only wish to be left alone."

"We didn't know you even existed until your ships showed up one day and started shooting at us. Why did your people do that?" Rico asked with an undertow of mistrust for her species.

"I'm not privy to that. I'm a doctor that was drafted after the war began. Now that the war is over I'm ready to go home."

"We're all ready to put the war behind us, but it was never made clear that we had actually lost until this business with Hyperion," Rico stated aloud.

"I thought it was pretty obvious that you lost the conflict," Daphne was blunt, but not offensive.

"Not as obvious as you might think. Does this Prefect know you're here?"

"No my people believe I'm dead. Are you going to arrest me?"

"No, Zarta, I'm not. I'm going to honor my friend's decision. Return to the ship, I need my Medical Officer. I'll make sure you're left here so you can rejoin your people when the time comes."

"Why would you do that?"

"Because Conrad believed you were worth saving. If he trusted you, I who fell in love with you can trust you."

"Thank you Captain."

Relief passed over her face leaving a smile of appreciation in its wake. She engaged his eyes longingly wanting to recapture that last night on the beach. Those same desires were mirrored in his eyes, but she realized that this relationship was over. No matter how much they wanted things to be different, it couldn't. He was Captain of the Phoenix, and she was his Chief Medical Officer and a Rundi that needed to go home.

"Go on. There are people who need you," he insisted.

She looked disappointed at first, but knew she had received mercy. Zarta also knew that she had a job to do. In addition to Conrad and Daphne, she now owed a debt to Rico. She was determined to re-pay it as best she could for the gift of life and freedom that they so sacrificially bestowed upon her. Her heart, although filled with love for Rico, truly desired to return to her people. Deep down they both knew there was no place in the universe where they could be together without denying who they were, and the joy they had brought to one another would in time become loathing.

Turning to leave she headed for the shuttle pod secure in the knowledge that she put Rico's fears to rest and that the most precious secret of all was still intact. Rico accompanied her just far enough to clear it with Yeoman Smith to take her back to the ship. Rico remained behind to walk off his heartache so he could give full attention to the job at hand.

Glenda C. Finkelstein

Chapter 12

One week into the evacuation and everything was proceeding on schedule now that all ships are here and functioning at full capacity. The Phoenix was nearing its maximum volume and was making ready to depart for the Theta Sharon Transport Station where the refugees would be off loaded. The Phoenix would return for a second batch and to scan the planet for any remaining colonists removing them by force if necessary prior to the Rundi taking control. It was hoped that the latter would not be necessary.

On Hyperion, Wong had his hands full coordinating all those landings and take-offs. After a near miss between landing and launching shuttles from two different ships that fried everyone's nerves, Wong enlisted some help from Governor Tarken's team and the Falcon to avoid any such recurrence. Although Captain Sanchez was looking forward to touching base over a cup of coffee with his former first officer, Captain Macalister, the evacuation forced them to put that off to a later time.

Everyone aboard the Phoenix was very tired and at their wits end dealing with the refugees who were so numerous. Space was at a premium and no one could really wrap their mind around the fact that they still had room for two more transports full of people. Tempers flared here and there as the frustration level from the crew collided with that of the refugees. When the ship reached maximum capacity they were to leave orbit within the hour to offload their visitors and then return at full speed for yet another load.

In the cafeteria of the Phoenix, Jarvis and Sadowski was sharing some lunch in between shifts. Dr. Lamb entered the chow hall glancing over at Jarvis. She nodded a greeting with a shy smile. At first it appeared Dr. Lamb was going to join them, but changed direction to sit at a table near the door when Jarvis responded with a half-assed dismissal hand wave. Dr. Lamb took the hint. Jarvis was uncomfortable with her being summoned to the Captain on Hyperion last week. Jarvis was certain that the captain knew the truth about Dr. Lamb by now and yet had not confronted him about what he had withheld from him. It appeared to him that Captain Sanchez had shown her mercy and protected her just as Conrad had done. There were only a few days left and this charade would come to an end one way or another.

"I'll be so glad when Wong gets back. Poker just isn't the same game without him," Sadowski complained to Jarvis as she fixed her eyes on the distant horizon.

"Why is that?" Jarvis asked, but before Janet could answer him, she noticed Dr. Lamb passing by with a tray of food instead of joining them like she had done many times in the past.

"What's up with you and Dr. Lamb?" Janet asked, curiously as Jarvis gaze never left the good doctor until she sat down at another table. Jarvis noticed that Sadowski could see that her inquiry made him uncomfortable. This made her smile because it was rare to have an opportunity to aggravate him and realized he had given himself away.

"Nothing," he responded, attempting to recover from his obvious discomfort. His answer was short. He hoped that she would leave it alone, but knew she'd been waiting for an opportunity to turn the tables on him and she took full advantage of fanning the flames a little bit. He was always so calm and in control, and she, well, she was such a hot head. She took great joy in pushing the few buttons he had when they became available.

"You aren't sweet on her are you, because I believe she's sweet on the Captain?"

"Leave it alone," Jarvis insisted. He had stopped his spoon full of soup in midair to turn and face her eye to eye.

"I was just…" she began, trying to sink her teeth even deeper into the jugular of his attitude.

"I said drop it, don't' make me pull rank," Jarvis quipped sharply on the verge of raising his voice, cutting her off midsentence. Janet looked into his chestnut brown eyes. There was a storm raging just beneath his usually calm surface. She shrugged her shoulders and capitulated to the fact that this was the wrong time to push the issue.

"Someone got up on the wrong side of the bed this morning. I was just having some fun at your expense."

He glared back at her refusing to comment. She surrendered her mock battle with a placating expression. She appeared to be keenly aware of his internal conflict, but appeared to be clueless as to the nature of that struggle. Her surrender allowed him to cover-up his irritation by turning on the charm and switching the subject back to that of poker without resistance.

"You don't like poker anymore because you can't read Ensign David like you can Wong," he chided. A smile slowly cascaded across his dark face, but it was forced and the twinkle in his eye that usually accompanied it was missing. Janet didn't challenge the pretense and played along. Whatever she stoked in his usually stoic emotional arsenal needed to be left alone.

"You got that right. I've lost over 40 credits since Wong went planet side."

"Excuse me, I couldn't help but overhear that you play Poker," said an average looking man probably in his thirties. They could tell by his dress that he was one of the refugees. Although they had requested them to stay mainly in the cargo bay, the cafeteria was far from a critical or restricted area of the ship and they entreated him to sit down.

"Yeah, we play. Are you looking for a game?" Janet asked.

"You could say that." The man took a seat across the table from them, responding to their kind invitation. He made himself comfortable, and leaned back against the wall. "You're Commander Jarvis aren't you?"

"Yes and your name would be?"

"Sorry, the name's Tyler," he greeted with an outstretched hand toward Jarvis who didn't accept it. Jarvis looked at him with a wary eye. Something in his gut was churning about this man, but couldn't put his finger on it. Janet took hold of his calloused hand instead. "I was getting restless down in the cargo bay. I'm used to being in tight places, but not with so many people," Tyler continued without any discernable offense of Jarvis refusal to shake his hand.

"You must be one of the miners then. I'm Lt. Janet Sadowski."

"Yes, I am," he said confirming her assumption. "It's a pleasure to meet you both. To comment on your earlier conversation, I'd venture to say that Wong is sweet on you. That's why it's so easy to fleece him."

179

"You were eaves dropping," Janet charged, slightly offended.

"Let's face it there isn't much privacy anywhere on this ship. Is there?"

"He's got you there, Sadowski." She inflicted a quick glaring glance of aggravation at her commanding officer to which he seemed quite pleased. She was so easy to aggravate, and he derived way too much pleasure from doing so. *Oh, if he wasn't her commanding officer, she'd turn the tables,* she thought to herself.

"So, what kind of stakes do you play for?" Tyler asked.

Janet hesitated before answering his question. She was still surprised over his allegation that Wong let her win. She wasn't, however, opposed to the idea that Wong might be sweet on her. She cut a look over at Jarvis who she could tell was enjoying watching her squirm and then returned her attention back to Tyler.

"Just credits with a forty credit cap," she finally answered.

"Sounds pretty tame to me," Tyler commented.

"It's just for fun. What do you play for?" Janet asked inquisitively wondering if he was all talk. Jarvis just watched the newcomer's expression change from carefree to that of determination. His eyes glazed over wiping out any sense of compassion. The transformation was unsettling and quick.

"Me? I play for keeps," Tyler said as he pulled out a gun sitting straight up with the barrel aimed at Jarvis. It was time for the coup, and Tyler's job was to make sure that the bridge would not have their Commander. Janet had just taken a bite out of her chicken

180

sandwich when he pulled the weapon on them. Her eyes grew wide as she swallowed whole, the chunk in her mouth. He just laid a finger across his lips indicating that he wanted them to stay quiet.

"Everyone, stay where you are if you don't want anyone to get hurt," Tyler yelled out as he jumped to his feet keeping the weapon pointed at Commander Jarvis and Lt. Sadowski. He then instructed the doctor to lock the door so no one else could enter. The crew was in shock and didn't know what to do, but could see that Tyler meant business. When a crewman started to stand Tyler pulled out a small knife from his pocket and threw it, tacking the crewman's sleeve to the table. The crewman sat back down. Tyler motioned for everyone to sit and be still, promising that no harm would come to them if they just cooperated.

Jarvis eyed the weapon in Tyler's hand, and although the gun was not the typical projectile one of old, it did have the capability of killing. The only trouble was that there was no way to tell if he had loaded it with lethal rounds, or stun rounds. A week old report from the Captain mentioned stun rounds being stolen from the Munitions Depot, but that didn't mean they were in the gun. Sadowski started to stand up from her chair in response to Tyler's knife throwing demonstration. Jarvis grabbed her by the sleeve and made her sit back down. His eyes said everything his mouth couldn't order, and she understood every word sitting slowly back down in her chair. Tyler simply nodded with a wry smile commending Commander Jarvis for his wisdom.

***

After overpowering two security guards, Jeremy Tate, along with a dozen men used the guards DNA for the hand scan to gain access to the bridge. They moved swiftly inside and using the element of surprise took control quickly. Jeremy was calling the shots. He chose this mission over abducting the Governor's wife. An action that he still disagreed with, but he would prove his unfailing loyalty to his mentor, Manny Smithers, here on the Phoenix. With the bridge crew secured he had a couple of his men drag the two security guards inside with them and tie them up.

Yeoman Lisa Smith, who was manning the store until Commander Jarvis returned from lunch, was obviously shaken by the suddenness of the attack. She tried to resist Mr. Tate, but lacked the training to do so and was easier to manipulate than a seasoned war veteran would be.

"Seal off the bridge from the rest of the ship, and lock us in," Jeremy demanded.

Lisa shook her head having determined to put up some resistance, but it was apparent that she couldn't maintain it long. He fired off two shots near her feet. She could feel the power of the rounds as the hairs of her body stood on end, and the electricity crackling on the metal infused floor like loose kernels of popcorn. Their shoes protected them from any serious injury, but it still stung.

He leaned over glaring into her face. He was so close that it hurt to keep her vision in focus. Her resistance collapsed under his

182

unrelenting gaze. Trembling, she reached over to her console to lock down the bridge. A smile brushed across his face, satisfied that he had her attention and submission. He stood back up to give his next order. Jeremy was quite pleased if not relieved that he could manipulate this young Yeoman so easily.

"Take this ship out of orbit and align us into a position to acquire weapons range with the Rundi cruiser," Jeremy ordered. Lisa's eyes widened with horror. She withdrew her hand from the console, crossed her arms, and stayed put refusing to obey such an insane order.

"No," she finally managed to utter, her voice vibrated with the fear inside her.

"Do it, or I'll shoot your navigator," he demanded. Others of his group stood with guns pointed at various crew members.

"You better not shoot them. You need us," Lisa's voice quaked as she uttered sound advice to their attackers.

"Why do you think that we need you?"

"If you didn't then you would have shot us already."

"You're a smart girl. Isn't she boys?" the other men just smiled and nodded their heads. "You'd be right if I was steeling the ship and wanting to go somewhere, but all I really need is you."

He jerked her chair back around and drew her to within inches of his face. She could smell the earthy aroma of tobacco on his breath, and feel the moisture of saliva splashing upon her face as he spoke. Her eyes tried to evade his as she attempted to turn away, but he pulled her head back forcing her to look at him.

"Now, let's get back to your decision. Will you move the ship, or do I shoot your navigator?"

"No, I will not move the ship," she said, trying to sound strong, but praying that he was bluffing. She closed her eyes in an attempt to keep her resolve, but opened them when she heard his gun cock back. "It's suicide. The Rundi are..."

"Do you think I care what the Rundi are?" He questioned, cutting her off.

"They'll kill us," she pleaded for reason, but none was there.

"Move the ship's orbit," Jeremy demanded one more time. He could see that this little girl, who had given in so easily the first time, was becoming obstinate.

He lifted his weapon at Robert Johnson, the navigator, who sat up straight in his chair. He refused to show fear. Jeremy glanced into Robert's unwavering eyes, and to verify his aim. He then returned his full attention to Yeoman Smith before shooting Robert at point blank range in the temple. He fired. Lisa jumped. Although he was firing stun rounds, Robert would be unconscious for at least 12 hours and no one from a distance would be able to tell if he was alive or dead. Some of the crew members stood up to come to the aid of their comrade. They stopped in their tracks believing that he'd have had them shot too as the sound of several weapons cocking to fire upon them sounded in their ears. The crew stood down knowing that this intruder had the upper hand.

"I can't," she squeaked out amid waves of sorrow. Jeremy had another man prepare to shoot a woman crew member while he turned Lisa around in her chair to witness the next shooting.

"You can stop this," Jeremy whispered in her ear. Lisa sat silently, arms still folded in desperate defiance that was quickly beginning to melt. Her friend looked into her eyes pleading for mercy as she felt the cold barrel being placed upon her temple. A silent tear fell down her face. He just nodded his head and the man cocked the weapon. She closed her eyes.

"Stop!" Lisa Smith yelled as if an order to everyone. "I'll do it. Just back off!" she shouted. Jeremy nodded in agreement. His man backed away. The crew exhaled a collective sigh of relief. The crew still feared the worse in regards to Robert Johnson, but held on to a fragile hope that their navigator would be all right.

Since these guns were not projectile weapons, they didn't make an outward wound. They did carry a powerful electrical jolt encased inside a laser pellet that could short circuit a person's brain function. Depending upon the power of the jolt, it could render a person unconscious for several hours or kill them.

"Now make the adjustments."

Lisa nodded her fearful agreement to his demands and made the adjustments. The ship lurched as it moved into a higher orbit nearly stranding the last shuttle filled with refugees in space. They were unable to reach the ship forcing them to return to the planet for additional fuel. Although Lisa was a trained pilot for shuttles, the Phoenix was not a shuttle and the ride was definitely going to be bumpy. She had hoped that the bumpiness would allow the Phoenix crew an opportunity to regain control of the bridge, but her hopes were dashed quickly as the infiltrators regained their footing faster than the crew could get back to their feet.

Unsure of whether the other cruisers would pick up on their change in orbit, Lisa turned on their exterior lights that were only used when docking with a space station hoping that would catch their attention faster. She didn't know what these men wanted, and was scared beyond reason. After all, she was a Yeoman, an administrative assistant, not a military grunt.

***

The Falcon was the first of the main cruisers to notice the Phoenix changing position. Captain Macalister's navigator, Jim Bailey, was quick to inform her of the Phoenix's course change.

"Captain, the Phoenix is breaking stationary orbit. Their last shuttle was forced to return to Hyperion."

"I see it Mr. Bailey. Lt. Casey, open a channel to the Phoenix," Lindsay ordered, her eyes glued to the view screen.

"Yes, Ma'am," Lt. Casey responded. "Hailing frequencies are open."

"Phoenix, this is Captain Lindsay Macalister of the Falcon. Why are you breaking orbit?" Lindsay waited patiently for a response, but all she got was static. Her first thought was some type of technical malfunction, but then she noticed the parking lights. Not even a first year cadet would make the mistake of turning on the parking lights.

***

"Don't reply," Jeremy informed softly into Lisa's ear. He held his weapon at the back of Lisa's head. She remained silent as Captain Macalister repeated her hail several times. Jeremy bent over and scrambled the communications console so no one could use it but him. He also initiated a dampening field so no one on the Phoenix could receive or transmit unless he allowed it. Lisa held her breath as his strong arms leaned over her nearly smothering her. The light stench of body odor lingered until he backed away. She didn't release her breath to refill her lungs until he took a step back from her.

Her fellow crewmen shared her fear. They swallowed hard hoping that he wouldn't pull the trigger, and then released a collective sigh when he withdrew the gun from the back of her head.

"Phoenix, I say again, this is Captain Lindsay Macalister of the Falcon. Why are you breaking orbit?" The question resonated inside the nearly silent Phoenix Bridge followed quickly by hails from Hyperion demanding to know the same. Lisa sat motionless slowly shutting her eyes bracing herself for the inevitable shot in the head or the destruction of the Phoenix by the Rundi. Either way, their survival rate was about nil.

***

Again there was no response from the Phoenix to the Falcon's hails. Macalister looked over at Bailey who just shrugged his shoulders at her. He, too, was lost for an explanation.

"What are they doing?" she questioned aloud.

"I don't know, the maneuver was clumsy and unlike a well trained bridge officer. Regardless of the political mess and their unfavorable standing, the Phoenix crew couldn't possibly perform that poorly."

"Agreed. Get me Captain Sanchez on Hyperion."

"Got him Ma'am, he's standing by," Lt. Casey informed.

"Captain Sanchez, why's your ship leaving orbit?"

"I don't know. Wong caught the shift in orbit when one of our shuttles was forced to return to the planet. I've been trying to raise her without success," Rico commented.

"I can't raise her either. Can you make contact with Zeveney?"

"Already tried and failed. All communications seemed to be blocked, or they're just not responding. However, if I know my Zeveney 7000-P, I'm sure it's figuring a way to bypass this problem."

"Captain Macalister!" Bailey interrupted. "The Phoenix is arming her weapons."

"Captain Sanchez I've got to go."

"I heard. Do what you need to. I trust you."

The console went silent between them, but Rico and company were still able to hear what was going on aboard the Falcon.

"Target her weapons array," Lindsay ordered.

"Too late, she's fired at the Rundi ship!"

"Crap! What's going on over there? Don't just sit there, mister, follow that ship and take out her weapons. Get me ship wide communications."

"Yes, Ma'am."

"All hands, this is Captain Macalister. Report to battle stations, repeat all hands report to battle stations."

Alarms went off inside the Falcon. All hands reported immediately to their posts. Any shuttles that were in route to the Falcon were ordered to turn back around and land on Hyperion for safety. Mr. Bailey adjusted their trajectory so he'd have a clean shot at the Phoenix. He couldn't afford a mishap. Too many lives were at stake. The ride was a little bumpy for the Falcon crew, but it was necessary in order to stop the Phoenix. He took aim as the Falcon glided into position, and fired with absolute precision. The weapons array was taken out with their first shot, but the Phoenix held her position and refused to return to her prior orbit or respond to continued hails.

Glenda C. Finkelstein

Chapter **13**

Unable to sit idly by while his ship starts the next war, Rico ordered Wong to notify Admiral Griffin of the situation post haste. Paul tried to step up to help, but Rico was less than willing to accept Paul's help believing that Paul had dropped the ball on this one placing his people in jeopardy. He knew his crew both past and present, and knew something had to be terribly wrong as their worst fears were only beginning to be realized.

On Epsilon 6, an alarm sounded rousting Admiral Griffin from a sound sleep. He reached over thinking it was his alarm clock, but the alarm kept sounding even after he turned the darned thing off. It was then that he realized that it was the emergency military channel. He sat up in bed to turn it off, when suddenly the Rundi Prefect walked uninvited into his room. The glare from the lights just outside his door caused him to shield his eyes from the pain of harsh brightness accosting his sleepy vision.

"Don't you people ever knock?" Admiral Griffin grumbled as he looked at the Prefect.

"Your ship fired at my people."

"What?" The Admiral was stunned. Part of him hoped and wished that this was some cruel dream that he'd be laughing at later, but it wasn't. The throbbing headache just behind his eye sockets was proof of that. Not to mention the sight of the garish hooded figure in front of him. Whatever lurked under the Prefect's hood couldn't be worse than his horrible choice of colors.

"Captain Sanchez's ship to be exact."

Griffin's attention was brought around quickly to the crisis at hand, his senses being jolted back into consciousness by the threat of a crumbling peace accord. His office was the only one that had knowledge of this incident since everything flowed through him and the Prefect. The rest of Epsilon 6 Station was peacefully unaware of the precarious situation unfolding on Hyperion.

"There has to be a reasonable explanation. I'm sure no hostility was intended."

"They fired at a Rundi cruiser. This is an act of war."

"Hold on a moment," the Admiral insisted, jumping onto the floor. His plaid pajamas seemed to detract from his military rank. "Let me find out what's going on before you go jumping to conclusions."

"It doesn't matter. My people will eliminate the threat."

"You can't do that. You have to stop them and give me time to figure out what's going on."

"It's our way. I couldn't stop them if I wanted to."

"You son of a…" he didn't bother finishing the statement as he stomped toward his office to answer the call from his people, and to see if there was anyway they could make it out of this with their peace intact. A peace that Conrad gave his life to acquire. The Prefect followed, but at a safe distance. He wouldn't put it past the Admiral if he should respond with his formidable right hook that he had heard so much about.

Griffin slapped the communication channel open while simultaneously activating the view screen.

"Talk to me, Rico."

"Admiral, we have a situation."

"Yes, I know we have a situation. Your ship fired at a Rundi Cruiser. What the hell is going on out there?"

"I wish I knew sir. I'm down on the planet and my ship has stopped answering hails, has changed orbit, and fired its weapons. Captain Macalister has rendered the Phoenix's weapons useless and is taking up a defensive position between the Rundi and the Phoenix. Both ships are full of refugees."

"A fine mess you've gotten us into."

"Me? Look I'm here following your orders. We need your help!"

"I have none to offer. It's up to you. If you can't come up with a miracle in the next ten minutes, then the peace we've known for all of a month will be gone. They will return fire."

"You have to stop them, sir. They have to understand that the Phoenix is no longer a danger."

"I wish I could."

"What about the Prefect, certainly his word carries some weight?" Rico asked. Griffin was so stunned by Rico's certain knowledge of an individual that no one outside of his office was supposed to know about that he froze up.

"How did you know about the Prefect?" Griffin finally stammered.

"We're out of time Admiral."

"Hold," the Admiral ordered, as he silenced the audio and darkened the view screen. Rico just threw his arms up in the air in total frustration. *How could he put him on hold at a time like this?* The Admiral turned around to the Prefect. "Order your people to stand down."

"I can't," the Prefect responded. His tone was almost apologetic.

194

"You can't or you won't?"

"Your Captain Sanchez is full of surprises. No one outside yourself and the President should know of my existence."

"Is that all you care about, your precious rules, secrets, and code of honor? There are innocent people on that ship, and you're going to let them die. You heard the Captain they can't raise them, and they're no longer a threat. It's possible the ship is experiencing mechanical failures due to the refit. Is that a reason to go to war?"

"I'm sorry. I can't help you."

The Prefect turned around and started to walk away. The Admiral had his fill of the Rundi's high-minded notions of superiority. He followed him grabbing him by the arm, jerked him around, and let fly that famous right hook of his. The Prefect was knocked upon his self-appointed superior ass and the Admiral dared him to get up.

"I'm sure that just violated a few rules in your government's handbook. You want to fight then let's fight, but you leave those people in peace. My troops will regain control of the situation. There's no need for another war."

The Prefect looked up through his veiled face at the ferocious tenacity of Admiral Griffin. He didn't move, nor did he attempt to stand. The Prefect was unprepared for such an outburst at that moment, but he wouldn't underestimate him again.

"You can beat me and even kill me if it'll make you feel any better, but regardless of why the Phoenix fired at my ship. They will fire back. You can provide them no reason to stay their hand. Even if I gave the order, they'd ignore me as I have no power over our military leaders."

"Then find me someone who does!"

"It'll be too late."

"I suggest you try anyway."

The Admiral grabbed the Prefect's arm, pulled him back to his feet, and sat him down at a communications terminal. All Griffin did was point at the terminal and stare with an unrelenting, I don't give a crap about the rules, expression. It was enough for him to at least get the Prefect to go through the motions, but Griffin knew it was useless and quite probably too late to stop the killing.

Chapter **14**

The maneuver jolted the Phoenix causing anything that wasn't tied down to slide off the tables and onto the floors. Janet looked up at Commander Jarvis whose eyes had not left Tyler's. It was as if they were having a staring contest and she knew without a doubt that the Commander would win. Janet tried to move her arm into position so she could dislodge the weapon from his hand, but he was too alert for that.

"I wouldn't," Tyler cautioned. He gently adjusted his aim to make Janet think twice before trying anything again without disengaging his eye lock with Commander Jarvis. She removed her arm resting it back at her side.

The miners and farmers had most of the key crew members pinned down, so any thought of rescue from somewhere else was out of the question. This didn't mean that the crew wouldn't try to regain control of the ship. They just needed to play their cards more carefully. Manny had hoped that the Phoenix crew would feel beaten down and worthless, but he guessed wrong. The crew had been through tougher scrapes than this, and they weren't about to let them get away with kidnapping a ship full of refugees.

A good number of the crew and passengers sustained minor injuries when the Falcon took out the Phoenix's main weapons, but life support was maintained. The jolt to the ship was enough to knock anything that wasn't secure to the floor including people as no one was prepared for the attack from their own fleet.

What the vast majority of the crew on board the Phoenix didn't know was that their efforts to regain control were about to be snuffed out by the Rundi's response of being fired upon. Although in this case, ignorance was indeed bliss and the crews' hopes of retaking the Phoenix remained strong. Most of the refugees were oblivious to their impending doom except in the cafeteria where a view screen had shown what was happening outside. Dr. Lamb could see the Rundi ship and the growing glow of their weapons that were preparing to return fire. She knew it was a matter of moments and they'd be in range and at full power. Her people would fire at them destroying the Falcon and the Phoenix along with all hands on board both ships. Since there was only one man with a gun in the cafeteria, Dr. Lamb decided to take action.

Seizing an opportunity in the chaos which ensued after the Falcon took out their weapons systems, Dr. Lamb jutted toward the automatic door. Although Tyler had her lock the door to prevent anyone else from entering, the door's safety mechanism always allowed for egress. Tyler was startled by Dr. Lamb's actions, but was too busy trying to regain his own balance to shoot her. He took his eyes off his prisoners for only a moment. That's when Lt. Sadowski grabbed hold of the gun jerking it from him. Commander Jarvis clocked Tyler's jaw sending him reeling back against the wall with a thud. He slid back into his seat slouched down. Lt. Sadowski handed the weapon to Commander Jarvis as he stood to his feet. The rest of the crew applauded their actions breathing a collective sigh of relief.

"Quiet, we're not out of this yet. That Rundi cruiser is powering her weapons. If she fires at us, we're all dead," Commander Jarvis cautioned.

"I didn't hear any shots fired from the hallway when Dr. Lamb made her escape, that means the way is clear," Lt. Sadowski informed.

"A sound assumption," Commander Jarvis agreed. "Stay in pairs, report to your duty stations and report to me the status of your areas using your personal communicators. Change the frequency to sub-channel fifteen. I'm hoping that they're not familiar with covert communication protocol. For them to have gotten this far they have to have control of the bridge and other key areas of the ship. I mean to take it away from them, but I don't want to lose you or our refugees in the process. No one acts without my direct orders, is that clear?"

"Aye, sir," the group said in unison, adjusting the frequency of their personal communicators. They all started to leave, but paused when Sadowski asked a question.

"What about you?" She was curious for there were no other bridge personnel in the cafeteria for Commander Jarvis to buddy up with.

"I'm hoping that security will already be waiting outside the bridge. There must be more gunmen up there then what were holding us here. Sadowski, see if you can disconnect the power from the weapons in case the Falcon didn't take them all out. If we're helpless, maybe the Rundi won't fire. Move out!"

They left together spreading throughout the ship as ordered. Commander Jarvis knew his hope was in vain. He knew that the only thing that could protect them from the wrath of the Rundi was the presence of another Rundi because they always fired back. He also hoped that he understood what Dr. Lamb was doing, or this would be a very short rescue mission.

Just as Commander Jarvis had surmised, Dr. Lamb had made a beeline to Rico's quarters. It was the only place on the ship that she believed she might get a signal through. For her idea to work she had to have Zeveney transmit on a Rundi frequency. If any equipment on board this ship could do that, it was the Zeveney system. She tried to go in, but the door was locked. She frantically knocked on the door hoping Zeveney would respond and open it.

"Zeveney, it's me Daphne. Please let me in. I need you!"

The door opened. She stepped inside. Zeveney's image was at full strength watching her every move. She looked about making sure that there was no one else in the room or following her in case the hijackers knew about this program. Zeveney didn't greet her waiting for her to initiate an instruction.

"I need an open communication channel that the bridge can't override," she requested.

Zeveney did a quick check on ship's status to determine why she would be making such a request. "There's a dampening field around the ship preventing communications. Why?" Zeveney questioned. He wasn't aware that the ship had been compromised as he was in sleep mode.

"The ship's been commandeered by hostile forces. They fired at a Rundi cruiser. If I don't tell the Rundi that I'm on board, they will fire and destroy this vessel in addition to the Falcon."

Zeveney immediately checked out her story as she relayed it, integrating into the various ships systems. He seemed to be taking longer than necessary.

"We don't have the time. You have to trust me. I'm the only chance this crew has of surviving."

Daphne looked into his photon formed face. Her eyes pleaded with him. It took a moment, but he decided to comply with her request.

"There is a tiny fluctuation in the dampening field that we could get a communication through."

"I need it in a Rundi frequency."

"But such a configuration would render me useless in a few short minutes."

"I only need a few seconds. If it's not a Rundi frequency, they won't believe me. Besides it'll only damage your sensory capability. You'll still have full computation mode."

"But my remote abilities will be useless. I won't be able to assist my Captain."

"Rico is a big boy and can take care of himself. Hurry, Zeveney, the clock is ticking."

"Very well, I'm reconfigured. You may begin," Zeveney capitulated. The Rundi frequency was too strong for Zeveney to transmit for long. In addition, the ship's sensors couldn't detect the wavelength modulation while the dampening field was on so no one but Daphne and Zev would know it was sent.

"Thank you," she said, and then began to speak in her native tongue hoping and praying that it wasn't too late to stay their hand.

***

"Captain Macalister!" Bailey called out frantically excited.

"What now?" Lindsay questioned, wondering what else had gone wrong.

"It's the Rundi ship. She's standing down."

"What?" the captain questioned with skepticism.

"The Rundi are standing down," Bailey confirmed.

"That's not possible. They never stand down."

"Possible or not, they're returning to their position and are powering down their weapons."

"In eight years of war I've never seen or heard of them doing that," Lindsay uttered both as a proclamation of disbelief as well as the first proof that miracles might truly exist in this universe. The Falcon bridge crew released a heavy sigh of relief, as did everyone on the Phoenix that knew what was going on.

***

Rico and Wong had been listening to the chatter aboard the Falcon. Rico seemed to be so surprised that the Rundi stood down that he pinched himself to be certain he wasn't dreaming. He winced realizing he was awake. Then his mind rested upon that of Daphne being on the ship. *Could it be her presence?* He wondered to himself.

"Wong, can you confirm what the Falcon just relayed to us?"

"Yes, Captain, the Rundi are standing down and returning to their previous position."

"What's going on up there on my ship?" Rico questioned aloud.

Suddenly an image was displayed upon the view screen. It was Jeremy Tate, holding a weapon to the head of Rico's Yeoman. Their relief turned quickly back to the cause of their dire straights. Even Admiral Griffin had a front row seat to the transmission, but didn't interfere. He trusted Rico to regain control of the situation.

Jeremy was wild eyed and determined, but was equally scared for all his outward portrayal of control. Rico was a seasoned warrior and recognized his fear. He knew that this man was far more dangerous than any hired gun because scared men were prone to unpredictability.

"Who are you, and what do you want with my ship and crew?" Rico asked boldly and calmly showing no outward sign of his own concern for the lives under his command that precariously hung in the balance. His steady timber gave his bridge crew hope that he could and would rescue them. His practiced demeanor demonstrated to both friend and foe alike that he would not be shaken, threatened, or forced to act against his conscience.

"My name is unimportant, but my cause isn't. We don't believe that the Rundi or Epsilon 6 Command has the authority to remove us from our homes."

Rico looked over at Paul Tarken demanding his assistance. It no longer mattered who was at fault. The only thing that mattered now was the lives aboard the Phoenix. Paul knew who this gunman was and stepped forward to whisper his name into Rico's ear. Rico held his anger well during his discourse with Jeremy for he knew it would not be well received. On the contrary if Rico lost his temper, he'd just be adding fuel to Jeremy's misdirected fire.

"Whatever your disagreement with the councils of both races, this is no way to state your opinion Jeremy. May I call you Jeremy?"

"I don't care what you call me. We will not leave Hyperion, and are prepared to fight and die for our cause."

"You hold innocent lives at gun point, and threaten to destroy the peace we have acquired with the Rundi and..."

"Your crew isn't innocent," Jeremy blurted out, cutting Rico off.

"I was referring to the refugees that are already on board the Phoenix. You know them they're your neighbors, and probably your friends and family too. You nearly killed them and the Falcon's crew when you fired on the Rundi a little while ago."

"It was not our intention to fire on the Rundi, but at the Rundi to warn them to stay away. We only want to stay on Hyperion and be left alone to work and live."

"I'm afraid that won't be possible Jeremy. The Rundi are still coming only seven days from now and only half the population has been evacuated. They'll kill whoever is left," Rico informed.

"I don't think so, because we not only hold 'innocent lives' as you call them up here, we hold them down there too. You'll stay

205

to protect them. It's your duty." Suddenly the screen went dark, and panic filled Rico's mind.

"Son of a bitch, get him back!" Rico commanded, yelling at Wong, his cool level head dissipating as fast as Jeremy's image did.

"I can't sir they've turned it off from there. Unless they choose to answer my hails, we have nothing."

"What about contacting individual crewman?"

"The ship is too far away for us to make contact with any one crewman. That's probably why they moved the ship, unless, you can get through to Zeveney."

"I've tried, I can't get through. It's just dead air," Rico informed.

"I wonder if he was bluffing when he said they held innocent lives down here too?" Wong questioned.

"Captain Sanchez," Lindsay interrupted the conversation on the open frequency.

"Yes, Lindsay, what have you got?" Rico asked, hoping her interjection was a precursor to an idea.

"We can attempt to land an insurgent crew on the Phoenix. I'm sure they could break in through the maintenance hatches. I have a team standing by."

"That's a good idea, but it's risky. I don't want to force their hand until we know how many aces they have. Keep your team ready. I'll contact you."

"Will do Captain Sanchez, Macalister out."

"Keep this channel open," Rico ordered Wong.

Suddenly a messenger came rushing in going over to Paul's side. He gave him a piece of paper. Fear swept across Paul's face as he read the letter. Rico believed they were about to find out the answers to their questions.

"They've got Sam!" Paul exclaimed. Rico didn't follow who Sam was to the governor. "My wife!" Paul clarified in horror.

Rico could see that Paul was near tears. Samantha truly was the love of his life, and the words he uttered were laced with fear, but tempered with anger, the kind of anger that wells up in a man when those most precious to him are violated. Even the most meek, will become like a lion in order to rescue those they love.

"What are their terms?" Rico asked as if he didn't already know the answer.

"To keep Hyperion. It's all or nothing."

***

On the outskirts of town, a frightened Samantha Tarken finds herself inside a cave with her eyes blindfolded. She realized that she was inside a cave because the men's voices that filled the cavern echoed off into the distance. No other structure on Hyperion gave off that acoustical signature. There were too many people talking at once for her to discern a familiar one among them. She remembered little from the time they grabbed her inside her own home until she awoke here in her darkened consciousness. Her head throbbed, a side effect of the sleeper drug they forced into her system.

The offbeat rhythm of gravel and dry dirt giving way under the weight of a heavy, industrial boot broke through the fog of indistinguishable noises, stopping beside her chair. She tilted her head slightly to listen carefully hoping for any clue as to who had her, and why. Suddenly a heavily calloused hand lighted upon her head. She jumped only as far as her bindings would allow causing the chair to which she was fastened to jerk.

"I'll not harm you," announced a powerful male voice. Its deep base tones made his speech clear even in his hushed whisper. He placed his hand upon her head again and began to untie her blindfold. The untying of it pulled some of the hair on her head stinging the scalp as it was pulled away. She squinted and blinked her eyes several times trying to get her pupils to adjust to the subdued lighting of the cave. Even though its brightness paled in comparison to the Hyperion sun, it was still quite bright when compared to total darkness.

She contorted her face trying to keep the throbbing pain of a headache at bay while simultaneously adjusting to the light. Slowly her vision cleared and she could make out individuals. She could tell by their attire and the comfort they had in such constricted spaces that they were miners. Samantha turned her head to look into the face of the one who had removed her blindfold. It was Manny

Smithers, the legal representative of the Miners Guild on Hyperion. She had met his wife at least twice before.

"Why did you kidnap me?" she asked calmly. Many women would be panicked in a situation such as this, but Samantha was no ordinary woman. She was a military brat, and a politician's wife. If she had learned anything in her life, she learned that in any given situation a calm head would always be more successful.

"Leverage."

"Leverage for what?"

"We're not leaving Hyperion, and neither are you. We will not be forced from our homes."

"We don't have a choice. My husband made that quite clear."

"You misunderstand my meaning. We fully appreciate that your husband has no authority to violate the peace accord, but we will not roll over and allow them to take from us our homes and our way of life."

"If we don't leave, we'll die."

"We're prepared for that."

"I'm not, nor do I believe Sarah is prepared to die."

"You remember me." Manny was surprised that a bureaucrat's wife would have taken the time to commit their meeting to memory.

"Yes I do. You and your lovely wife are known for being reasonable. Don't do this. Let me go, and I'll not press charges."

"My wife has no idea where I am or what I'm up to. She is free and as for me, my life is forfeit and begrudgingly so is yours. Without you, we'd have no hope of getting their full undivided attention."

"They'll send out search parties."

"They've got no time. They have to get all those people off the planet... Well, at least those who are willing to give up their homes to the enemy. Besides, Epsilon 6 Command must protect civilians against attack."

"We didn't win the war, that's why were losing Hyperion, and now you think by starting another fight we can win?"

"As for me and my comrades, the war never ended."

"You can't possibly think you can win this? Our military vessels have been converted to people transports, and those that aren't, are too far away to help."

"Throughout human history there have been many a hopeless battle fought and won."

"True, but more were lost than won. You're a reasonable man. Stop being selfish. Think of your wife."

All of a sudden rage filled Manny's face, and brought himself low so he'd be at eye level with Samantha before he responded to her verbal challenge to his character.

"I'm giving up everything I know and love for a cause I believe it's just, that's not selfish."

Chapter 15

After receiving the last batch of transmissions from
Hyperion, the Admiral sat staring at the hooded figure of the Prefect
who had not spoken for two hours. The silence was quite unusual
and annoyed Griffin more than his quips had. Finally, he had all the
silence he could stand.

"Well, aren't you going to say something?" Griffin
questioned.

"My people withdrew," the Prefect announced aloud,
addressing himself more than Griffin. His voice saturated in

disbelief. "I have to make contact with my people," he continued. He seemed oblivious to Griffin's presence.

"Yes, they did withdraw," Griffin confirmed, taking this as a good omen. Perhaps Conrad's sacrifice was not in vain after all. This thought comforted him, but only slightly.

"But there's only one reason why they would have done so," the Prefect uttered pausing for a long while before completing his thought. "But that's not possible."

The Prefect seemed dazed. Griffin thought his right hook did more damage than he had intended. Although he was concerned that the Prefect may be losing it, he wasn't concerned enough to apologize for his actions. He had it coming. Griffin's anger had abated for now, but he'd be more than happy to oblige another round should it be necessary.

"Snap out of it, man! We've got a crisis on our hands." Griffin insisted, trying to get the Rundi Prefect to engage in constructive problem solving.

"What?"

"You heard the report. The Miners have taken hostages. We've got to figure out a way to get those people out of there."

"These people need to be eliminated. I'll have my cruiser deploy a landing crew, have them search out these Miners, and destroy them."

"You'll do no such thing."

"We're losing valuable time, Admiral. Those people need to be sanctioned."

"Although I'd appreciate any constructive help you could provide, I don't want your people anywhere near Hyperion until our allotment of days is up."

"You asked for my help."

"Yes, I did, but help that actually saves lives and doesn't take them. These aren't criminals. They're scared civilians."

"You humans draw some unusual conclusions."

"How so?"

"You seem to separate criminal actions from criminal humans. Isn't a crime a crime regardless of whom perpetrates it?"

"To us a criminal is someone who does wrong without consideration for the welfare of others and seeks only their own gain. The act alone is not enough to make one a criminal depending upon the circumstances and motives involved."

"It sounds like justification to me."

The Admiral got up to leave the room. He was so tired of the Rundi's position that they were the only sentient life form entitled to the privilege of true choice.

"Admiral," the Prefect began, but waited for his undivided attention before continuing.

Griffin turned slowly around his hand balling up into a fist ready to cold-cock the jerk again if he uttered one more word out of line.

"Have a talk with Captain Sanchez. I want to know how he knows about me."

"That really bothers you, doesn't it?"

"It should bother you, too. If he knows about me, he may know about Captain Banes."

"You and your secrecy make me sick. He should know about Conrad. What he did for us, his honor, and his sacrifice."

"That's enough, Admiral. I'll tolerate your lack of anger control, but I'll not have you dictate the Rundi conscience."

"From what you've demonstrated, I'm beginning to wonder if the Rundi have any conscience at all," Griffin blurted feeling tired, angry, and cornered. The Rundi claimed such high ideals, but seemed to know little about mercy. Nor did they seem to comprehend abstract ideas and problems. Everything in the universe doesn't always fit into nice neat packages. He could scarcely believe that the Rundi backed off, and the Prefect seemed equally baffled. It was almost enjoyable to see him off his game, but he would have preferred it to be under different circumstances.

The Prefect started to announce a rebuttal to Griffin's sharp edged comments, but decided that discretion was truly the better part of valor and let the Admiral go. In like manner, the Admiral stopped talking. The Prefect was as confused by human behavior as Griffin was by Rundi behavior, and noticed that even when pursuing the most honorable path humans will trip and fall inside their weaknesses so easily. They both wondered if the other truly understood the whole of honor and duty.

***

On the Phoenix Jarvis was working alone outside the locked bridge. He knew what he wanted to do, but didn't have the expertise to do it. He was also worried about Janet. She should have been here by now. This would be a piece of cake for her. Suddenly a hand lit upon his shoulder, and he jumped bumping his head on the bulkhead.

"Sorry, I didn't mean to startle you," Daphne apologized. She reached up to see if he'd sustained any real injury, but he swatted her away.

"Since we are still in one piece, I can assume that your message got through."

"Excuse me?" She was taken aback by his knowledge of her actions.

"I fought the Rundi for eight years. I know that they always return fire unless there's a Rundi in the firing line."

"It's against our code to knowingly kill a fellow Rundi. Sentient life is sacred to us," Daphne confirmed.

Jarvis was disturbed that she could still say such a thing. After all that Conrad did, it should be enough to prove that humans were sentient also. Considering their close call, it was clear that the Rundi didn't accept his former Captain's sacrifice as proof that they, too, were sentient. Unfortunately, he had no time for debate. He had to regain control of the ship. They might not be so lucky a second time.

"As selfish as this may sound, I'm glad you're on board," Jarvis finally admitted.

"As your people say, don't sweat it."

Jarvis seemed more appreciative of her honesty than offended. Again Jarvis went to work fumbling clumsily around the wires and mechanisms inside the exposed wall. Dr. Lamb watched for a moment. She could tell that he was uncertain of himself yet he continued anyway.

"What are you doing?" she finally asked.

"I'm trying to reconfigure the ventilation system. If you could acquire a tank of sleeping gas from sickbay, and bring Sadowski up here I might be able to put everyone on the bridge to sleep without any loss of life. Then we can break through the door, restrain the assailants, and get this evacuation back on schedule.

"I can understand you not wanting to harm your crew, but why the care for those who've put you in danger?"

"You heard their demands over the ship-wide intercom. All they want is there homes. These people aren't criminals, they're scared civilians who believe they've been deserted by their government and given no good or noble reason as to why they must leave when there was clearly no Rundi presence before they came here."

"You mean your people would cooperate if given a good enough reason to sacrifice their livelihoods?" Dr. Lamb questioned. This thought amazed her, and even entertaining it made her feel like a rebel. Although she could attribute noble behavior to a few humans, she never thought about them collectively demonstrating nobility. The idea intrigued her, but their circumstances would not allow her an opportunity to study such a phenomenon first hand.

"Yes, and as much as I appreciate this conversation, I really need Sadowski and the sleeping gas." Jarvis flashed an urgent smile pausing to rest his arms.

"I'll be right back."

"Dr. Lamb."

"Yes?"

"Be careful. There may be more of them throughout the ship. Several people were supposed to have joined me already, but haven't yet."

"I'll be careful," she said smiling. For the first time Jarvis seemed to truly be at ease around her. She had grown comfortable with these humans, but they never ceased to surprise her. Her people had no idea just how wonderful they really were, and she was convinced that Hyperion would undermine anything they had hoped to achieve with them. There was so much they could teach the humans, and after having lived among them, so much the humans could teach the Rundi. This time, however, the Rundi's need to have this planet under their sole jurisdiction was too great to gamble on the human's theoretical nature of nobility.

Daphne tried to keep her mind on task as she navigated the hallways that led to sickbay. She entered sickbay to discover that everything was under control. Her people were caring for the indigent from the planet without any hostile force looking over their shoulders. She stopped only briefly to glance at a status monitor. All were currently stable. Daphne grabbed a tank of sleeping gas, and a small hand held heart activator. It just might come in handy should she run into any undesirables along the way. It was compact and carried a powerful electric jolt. Her staff didn't make much fuss about her presence. No one knew what was going on, or who had the upper hand at this moment. They, therefore, kept their attentions focused upon caring for the sick and injured.

When Daphne arrived on the engineering deck she could hear Lt. Sadowski talking to someone. She assumed it was one of the hijackers due to the heavy tension in Sadowski's voice. Daphne sat the sleeping gas tank down quietly and moved to where she could get a better look at the situation. Sadowski had a lug wrench, and the perpetrator had a large screwdriver. They were walking around each other in a circular pattern. Both were breathing heavily having already struggled with one another.

The weapon he had been carrying was lying on the ground not far from Daphne's feet. It appeared to Daphne that Sadowski had been quite difficult for the man to handle. He already had a

218

couple of bruises forming on his face and Sadowski's uniform was torn exposing her shoulder. They continued walking around each other like two opponents in a boxing ring with eyes fixed. Their breathing was beginning to slow. Neither of them was ready to give up. Both ready to jump into action in the blink of an eye. Since neither was going to give way, something had to tip the scales, and that something was going to be Daphne.

Dr. Lamb knelt down and picked up the weapon. The man heard the noise and instinctively turned to see the cause of said noise. Sadowski ignored her instinct to be distracted long enough to knock him to the ground with a roundhouse kick to the jaw, a little maneuver she learned from Wong. The man hit the ground hard enough that his face bounced off the floor a few inches spewing spittle and blood from his mouth. The hit finished dislodging a tooth that her kick had started. Sadowski followed through her maneuver to meet this new threat only to discover that it was Dr. Lamb.

"Thanks! I needed that," Janet announced, as a wave of relief passed over her face.

"You're welcome. Commander Jarvis needs your help getting into the bridge. I'll escort our visitor to the brig," Daphne informed. Janet glanced back at the man wallowing on the floor. He spit out the dislodged tooth along with some drool and blood. She was satisfied that he was sufficiently subdued for the doctor to handle by herself.

Daphne smiled at the man. Her expression was one of pity for him and pride in the Lieutenant. He turned his head ever so slowly to look up at her from the floor moaning as he moved. He rolled to his side grabbing at his jaw with his hand making sure it still functioned.

"Thanks again," Janet said, turning to go to the bridge.

"Wait," Daphne called after her.

"What?"

"Take that tank of sleeping gas with you. Commander Jarvis needs it." Daphne indicated the placement of the tank with a nod of her head. Janet turned around, grabbed it, and headed to the bridge while her would be perpetrator was trying to get to his feet. She stopped briefly at a junction where two hallways intersected to retrieve a hand pistol from a locked case. Janet was slightly winded by her altercation, and didn't want to exert any further energy. Daphne waited until she was completely out of sight before giving any instruction to the hijacker.

"Easy does it, mister. There'll be no fast moves or I'll shoot you."

"I won't be moving fast lady, but I'll take you shooting me over that girl's kick any day of the week. What is she some sort of lethal weapon?" he questioned wiping a trickle of blood from the corner of his mouth. He rubbed his face trying to feel the imprint of her shoe upon his skin, but a reflective surface nearby confirmed that no shoe print was visible and only blood was flowing from his cracked lip.

"No, just the youngest of four brothers. Stand up slow, and I'll not call her back," Daphne threatened. He surrendered placing his hands behind his head.

"Yes, Ma'am."

***

"It's about time you got here," Jarvis complained. "What kept you?" He questioned, seeing Janet strutting down the hallway with the tank of sleeping gas in her left hand.

"I ran into some trouble, but Dr. Lamb has him now."

Jarvis smiled. He recognized the afterglow in Sadowski's face from a fight won. How a woman like her ever learned to love fighting as much as a testosterone charged male, he'd never know? She seemed so unlikely to the task. Her petite frame harbored a volatile, yet, powerful turret of controlled fury the likes of which he'd never want to be on the receiving end of.

He explained to her what he wanted done. She took a look at what he had already accomplished and chastised him for getting several conduits and wires messed up. Although he had made things more difficult, it didn't take her long to correct his errors and make quick progress. Watching her work was like watching a surgeon perform a delicate operation, her every move was masterful and artistic.

Glenda C. Finkelstein

Chapter 16

It was now dark on Hyperion. The Phoenix incident put them behind schedule. With so many people still needing to be evacuated no one was released to search for Samantha. Paul knew that despite his personal tragedy, his duty to the people of Hyperion came first. The shuttles from the Ares and Triton continued to land and take off during the night. Since Paul wasn't needed during the night shift, he tried sleeping. It was, however, a useless gesture as he tossed and turned upon his empty bed. Just outside his room and also not able to sleep, Rico sat cradling a cup of lukewarm coffee moving the cup back and forth between his fingers. His mind tried to formulate a plan to get control of his ship, get the evacuation back to full schedule, and rescue the Governor's wife. Yet nothing was materializing in his gray matter.

He ordered the Triton and Ares to scan what they could of the colony, but came up empty. They were at a loss as to where to begin the search for Samantha Tarken and time was too precious to waste. Rico, himself, was in turmoil since they lost contact with the Phoenix, and was having trouble staying focused on the task at hand. The near destruction of his ship by the Rundi weighed heavily upon him as well as his inability to make contact with Zeveney. He thought harder and harder as if stretching his mind would make the answer come, but all he gained for his efforts was a headache.

"Captain Sanchez!" Wong exclaimed, barging into the room. Rico was so startled that his hands jerked sloshing the nearly full cup of coffee he'd been kneading between them. The liquid flowed unabated upon his sleeve and the nearby table falling in rivulets onto the floor.

Rico stood up with a silent curse on his lips stopping short of releasing it when he saw that Wong's eyes were filled with dread. Wong tried to help Rico sop up the expanding mess by grabbing a nearby stack of napkins. The napkins however, seemed inadequate to the task of cleaning the mess.

"What do you want?" Rico finally managed to ask through clinched teeth.

"Admiral Griffin is waiting to speak to you on a secured line..."

Rico looked at Wong as he paused for a moment. The captain realized that there was something more to his announcement other than the waiting Admiral. An upraised eyebrow was all the permission Wong needed to share the remainder of his purpose for bursting into the room.

"And we have a storm system moving in fast. It'll soon be too dangerous to transport refugees to the Ares and Triton. I just gave the ground order."

"How long will the shuttles be grounded?"

"The storm system is huge, violent, and slow moving. At best I'd say we're looking at two to three days."

"Damn it!" Rico cut loose his earlier reservation, then realized cursing wouldn't make the storm subside any more than it would buy them more time to evacuate. He needed to get his ship back so they could unload this first batch at Theta Sharon Transport Station. The trip was only about ten hours via the dark matter corridors. He took a deep breath and expelled it within the confines of a heavy sigh.

"Finish cleaning up the mess," Rico ordered gruffly. He proceeded to stomp off like a child going to his room under protest.

"Yes Sir. I'm sorry for startling you."

"Forget it," Rico responded, less rigid then he was a moment ago. Considering the day they had and the night they were heading into. A spilled cup of cold coffee was pretty insignificant.

"Sir?" Wong questioned, hesitantly.

"What is it?" Rico asked, seeing the look of worry on his face.

"Do you think everyone's okay on the Phoenix?" His question undeniably driven by his feelings for Janet was not without concern for his remaining crewmates.

"I'm sure Janet is just fine," Rico answered as if he'd just read Wong's mind.

Wong breathed a sigh of relief then realized that he hadn't asked specifically about Janet. "How did you know?" he inquired, amazement prevalent in his tone.

"You're a mathematical genius and you always let her win at poker," Rico answered. The stated observation invoked a fleeting smile from Wong. Captain Sanchez flashed a quick smile back at him before leaving the room. Wong thought for a moment. This time he smiled at himself wondering if she knew how he felt about her.

"Do you think anybody else has figured out that I like her?" Wong called after Rico.

Rico turned rolling his eyes to the back of his head. Wong took that as a yes and went back to cleaning up the mess he had caused. Rico continued on down the hall and entered the small room

226

that had been converted into a communications hub. Griffin's face filled the small view screen hanging on the wall. Rico took a seat, verified that the connection was secure, and greeted the Admiral.

"Hello, Sir. To what do I owe the honor of this late night call?"

"You look like hell, Rico."

"Tell me something I don't know," Rico insisted through his bloodshot sleepless eyes. The bags that had accumulated under them were growing heavier by the moment.

"I take it you still have no contact with the Phoenix."

"No Sir, but the Falcon has taken up position to keep the Phoenix and Rundi from firing at one another again. Although the distance is considerably farther than we'd like, we were able to divert the last of the Phoenix refugee shuttles to the Falcon."

"Aren't you afraid they'll steal the Phoenix?"

"No, they're interested in making a stand. People who take that action seldom run away, but that's not why your calling me is it?" Rico asked. He knew the Admiral almost as well as he knew Conrad. There was a burning question trapped inside his bureaucratic mind, and he could tell he didn't want to ask it.

"I can't get anything past you can I?"

"Nope." Rico's callousness of speech denoted his exhaustion more than it denoted disrespect for the Admiral's rank.

"I'm curious about some knowledge you seem to possess. When you reported the fact that the Phoenix had been commandeered by hostile forces and were about to be fired upon by the Rundi, you made reference to a Prefect and for me to get him to intercede."

"Yes, what of it?"

"Prefect is a term you shouldn't know. It's top secret with no files in our databases."

Rico tilted his head down to look at the desk. He didn't wish for Admiral Griffin to see his troubled brow, but perhaps the wrinkles caused by his lack of sleep would keep any such subtleties at bay. He had trusted Daphne, but didn't realize until just now that she had trusted him. He was certain now that the only reason the Rundi didn't fire was that they must have figured out that a Rundi was on board the Phoenix. *Maybe she used Zeveney to send a signal to them*, he thought. That would explain why he couldn't be raised even through a dampening field. A Rundi frequency would fry a good portion of his systems and would not be able to communicate beyond the ship again after doing so.

This discussion resurrected a memory from early in the Rundi war. He withdrew into this recollection as he remembered an early battle of the war. One of his crewmen had gotten trapped behind enemy lines. In order to protect himself, he'd grabbed a Rundi holding him between himself and the enemy. The Rundi lowered their weapons and didn't fire until their comrade had been released. That being the case Daphne had to have sent word to the other ship that she was there. This Prefect must be quite intrigued how the Phoenix managed to acquire a Rundi, but he wasn't about to make their job any easier by volunteering information. He may trust Daphne, but that didn't mean he trusted the Rundi at large.

"Admiral, I need to inform you that there are some severe storms moving in. We will have to halt the evacuations until it's safe to resume." Rico made this statement for two reasons: one, it was important, and two, he was trying to change the subject so he could formulate a response that would be both plausible and keep Griffin in the dark.

"How long?"

"Wong estimates two to three days. We'll need more time for the evacuation."

"We don't have more time. I told you before you left that there would be no extensions. Stop stalling and answer my question," Griffin insisted.

"I've fought the Rundi for eight years. Zeveney has done a remarkable job of collecting data on the Rundi for me. Let's face it Epsilon 6 Command files are not the only place in the galaxy to get information. You've even admitted how talented my computer companion is. Why is it so amazing that he found something secretive?"

"You're certain this is where you got your data from."

"Yes. Will you get us additional time?" Rico asked again. *Surely the Rundi scanners could verify the approaching storms,* he thought. The humans didn't manufacture them, and even with no

229

problems the projections of successfully evacuating all colonists from Hyperion in the established time frame was daunting at best.

The Admiral looked away from his terminal as if he were searching for permission to answer. Rico watched his eyes carefully. They were etched with pain and even a little disgust, but were bent on keeping their secrets. He could almost make out a reflection in them, but nothing discernable just a ghastly magenta color.

"No, I can't get you additional time."

"I'm not buying it, Admiral. You can tell that Prefect of yours that I'm not leaving until the humans have been safely evacuated." Rico surmised that the individual Griffin was seeking permission from was the Prefect, and even if he refused to answer directly his reaction would give the answer for him.

"You'd jeopardize everything Conrad did to secure peace?" Griffin asked angrily. He couldn't believe the words left his mouth. The Prefect stood to his feet, ready to disconnect the Admiral should he need to.

"Conrad," Rico let the name hang in midair. "Very interesting." A smile slowly crept across Rico's face. "So Conrad contributed to this peace we have. Tell me Admiral, what does Hyperion have to do with Conrad or the Rundi?"

At first the Admiral was silent. He nearly gave away the farm. It took him a moment to collect his thoughts. He'd forgotten just how good Rico was at word games. The man could get under your skin so easily. Yet, Griffin had to regain control of the conversation fast to keep Rico alive.

"All I meant was, Hyperion was a concession for the peace treaty, and Conrad just like many other soldiers gave their lives toward that pursuit. That's all."

"Why Hyperion? There was no evidence that the Rundi had ever set foot on this planet, built anything, or even harvested crops. Why is this planet so important to them?"

"Careful Rico, you're bordering on treason."

"Answer the question."

"You have your orders."

"Yes, I do, but I don't have to follow them." Rico's tone suddenly became very confrontational.

"If I have to, I'll relieve you of duty and put you in the brig."

"Then come and get me," Rico challenged. Griffin was incensed.

"Don't push me. I'll only give so much allowance for your Latin temper."

"I'll do what I can to keep things inside the parameters of this mission, but I warn you. If the Rundi ships approach the planet before all the humans have been evacuated, I'll blast their self-appointed, superior ass into the next galaxy."

Admiral Griffin attempted to sound a rebuttal, but wound up looking at a blank screen. The Prefect just glared at the Admiral through his ornate hood. This Rico was far more dangerous than the

Prefect first thought. Although he was angered, he would not have his people violate the humans allotted time for evacuation. When they did, the Prefect wanted the law on their side. He would, however, be more than happy to call this human's bluff. The Rundi's need to have Hyperion was too great to risk showing their vulnerability to the humans, and the timing was non-negotiable.

The Prefect didn't buy Rico's answer about how he knew of his existence either. He was, however, convinced that Captain Sanchez knew that he had a Rundi aboard. What the Prefect didn't know was if the Rundi was there of their own accord, or if Rico had taken one prisoner. In either case, it was a moot point at this juncture for he had no way of contacting the one Rundi aboard the Phoenix. He'd bide his time for now, but would make certain that the Rundi was released before the Phoenix left Hyperion. He excused himself to make contact with the Rundi ships in orbit of Hyperion since his usual channels were unresponsive to him.

***

Rico immediately contacted the Captains of the remaining ships and placed them on full battle alert. He was tired, hungry, and pissed off with little patience for bureaucratic crap. He gazed out the window watching the tempestuous winds gusting to 95 mph. The fury of the lightning strikes, and the deafening thunder that followed descended upon them from the heavens without mercy. The storm raging outside only seemed to reflect his emotional state. All he could do now was wait and hope that his crew would regain the upper hand. Time was growing short, and he knew the Rundi would never back down from his challenge. Then again, he wasn't planning to either.

***

Jarvis and Sadowski were successful in putting those on the bridge to sleep. The security personnel finally reported to him on the bridge after having secured critical areas of the ship from the hostile refugees. Sadowski collected the weapons while Jarvis sorted through the bodies making certain that the refugees were transported to the brig before the sleeping gas wore off. Dr. Lamb rejoined them to verify the health of the bridge crew. The navigator, Robert Johnson, had to be taken to sickbay right away as his vitals were dropping fast. The remainder of the crew was fine and were coerced awake by the odor of strong smelling salts.

Lisa Smith sat up looking about the bridge in a daze. She could see familiar faces, but it took a moment for it to register that the attackers had been subdued. She went to stand, but a dizzy spell forced her back down to the floor where she had fallen.

"Easy, Yeoman, take it nice and slow," Jarvis ordered. His rich voice seemed to envelope her in comfort and the assurance that the crew was back in charge of the Phoenix.

"Commander, thank heavens. I thought we were goners."

"Commander," Sadowski interrupted. "The communication's panel is locked out," she informed after unsuccessfully attempting to fix it.

"Yes," Smith responded. "They encrypted the access, but I don't think you can convince them to undo it."

"Sadowski, I want you to go to the Captain's quarters and see if we can get through using Zeveney," Jarvis ordered. She nodded her understanding and sprinted off to Rico's quarters.

"Commander," Dr. Lamb interjected. "The bridge crew needs to report to sickbay before resuming their duties. I need to make sure that no one has sustained any ill effects from the sleeping gas."

"Very well, you heard the doctor. Get checked out, if you're cleared report back to the bridge," the Commander ordered.

***

Upon arriving at the Captain's quarters, the doors opened. Janet thought that was rather odd, but she went in. What met her eyes made her stomach sink to her feet. There was glass, crystals, and wires all over the place. Using her wrist communicator she reported what she found.

"Commander, I've got some bad news," she began, but hesitated.

"Out with it already," Jarvis insisted, waiting impatiently for Janet to get on with it.

"It's Zeveney, Sir. He's been destroyed."

"How bad?"

"So bad, that the only one that might stand a chance of bringing him back on-line is Wong. It's not just the software, but parts are strewn everywhere mixed with broken glass."

234

"Great, just great. We've got control of the ship, but we can't tell anybody!" Jarvis fussed. He began to pace up and around the bridge helping each crewman back into their chairs as they regained consciousness.

"Sir, what about the shuttle craft?" Lisa offered questioningly.

"I owe you a drink," Jarvis said with a smile of determination. "You get to work on getting this bridge back in operation but after you get checked out by medical, and I'll go tell everybody were okay."

"Sir, where's Robert?" she questioned looking about the room for him.

"Dr. Lamb's got him. You do your job, and she'll do hers."

"Yes Sir."

***

Jarvis headed to the shuttle bay, climbed in, and launched. Once away from the ship's dampening field he opened a channel to Hyperion and the Falcon. He didn't want to be mistaken for an escaping refugee. After several hails, Wong's familiar voice was heard as well as an acknowledgement from the Falcon. It wasn't long before Captain Sanchez was on-line and Jarvis began the task of bringing him up to speed on their status. The captain ordered them to head for the Theta Sharon Transport Station to drop off the refugees and transfer the prisoners to the Epsilon 6 Security Force stationed there. Since the storm had set in, Jarvis would have to conduct the questioning on behalf of Captain Sanchez.

Rico was very disturbed that Zeveney had been trashed. Even if Daphne used Zeveney to produce a Rundi frequency, he'd still be intact. It would explain much, but it also raised new questions. *Did the hijackers destroy him?* He prayed that Jarvis would be successful with the questioning of the prisoners, and answers would be forthcoming soon. They had to know where their Hyperion counterparts were holding Samantha Tarken. Time was not a luxury and Rico was counting on Commander Jarvis to get those answers. Otherwise the usually in control Governor Tarken may turn mercenary and set out on his own.

He also had a burning desire to speak with Daphne, but that would have to wait until the Phoenix returned. She may not know about military issues, but she may know why this planet was so important to her people. Something was amiss and it tormented his gut. In addition, he wasn't pleased with the news about his navigator, Robert Johnson. He was a good man. He hoped that Daphne could bring him around.

After so many hours of fruitless waiting, Paul had become impatient and was increasingly difficult to manage. Rico, on the other hand, was trying not to belt the man for he had fried every last nerve ending Rico had. Wong tried to add levity to the situation, but only managed to make things worse. He soon realized he should just sit and watch the radar while waiting for the weather to clear. At least there Wong wouldn't be in the firing line.

Wong wished he were playing cards with Janet instead of being stuck on this world. Just the memory of her poker tells, the bluff that was never a bluff, and the twirling of her hair with her index finger whenever she had an ace made his heart ache. Wong promised himself that he would make sure he shared his feelings with her when this mission was over. He came close to losing her today along with the opportunity to share his heart with her.

Glenda C. Finkelstein

Chapter 17

The Phoenix was underway to the Theta Sharon Transport Station to offload their current population of refuges accompanied by the Triton. It had been several hours since they had regained control of the ship, but they still didn't have full communications. Jarvis was confident that if Sadowski couldn't repair it, she'd install a bypass and it would be operational by the time they reached the station. He was dreading the thought of having to question the prisoners for deep down he agrees with them, but not their actions. The right thing done in the wrong way, still equates to a wrong.

Perhaps if Robert Johnson weren't in critical condition it'd be easier for him to stay focused.

He walked the halls surveying the damage while security personnel processed and prepared the prisoners for questioning. Jeremy Tate was to be the first one up for interrogation since he was the one calling the shots aboard the Phoenix. Jarvis hoped he'd be able to break him and extract the vital information needed to rescue Mrs. Tarken. Unfortunately, he had a limited amount of time before Epsilon 6 would take charge of them. He had to get a confession before then. He also didn't relish the idea of coming back empty handed to Captain Sanchez.

While Jarvis had his duties, so did Dr. Lamb who was working steadfastly on Robert Johnson. His vitals were very weak, but she was determined not to lose this patient. His heart and respiration rates seemed to be stabilizing. She hoped they would continue to strengthen in the next couple of hours, but the honest truth was they could go either way. She refused to leave his survival in the hands of a simple monitor and stationed a nurse to watch him constantly for the slightest change.

Daphne was washing her hands after working on him when Commander Jarvis came quietly into the room. He was relieved that there was no damage in sickbay. He looked over at his crewman carefully watching the expression of the nurse standing vigil at his side. Daphne looked up into the mirror and saw Jarvis in its reflection and knew his concerns even before he voiced them.

"I'm hoping he'll live, but it's going to be, how do you say? Touch and go for the next six hours."

"If he lives, it'll be one less charge that the Miners will have to face."

"Your expression tells on you Commander. You want them to pay for what they did to Richard."

"They will see justice."

"Justice is what thinking beings hide behind when their hearts cry out for vengeance. The violence of it, although satisfying in the moment, challenges your nobility as a sentient species. The primal rage being forced into submission by intellect and moral sensibilities, and yet, unsatisfied with its outcome even when justice is served."

"You seem to understand us very well for an outsider."

"Perhaps we share more than either of us care to admit," Daphne offered. "Who will you be questioning first?"

"Mr. Tate. He seems to be their leader, up here anyway," Jarvis informed just as two women entered sickbay.

"Would that be Jeremy Tate you're speaking about?" questioned one of the women her voice covered in a rich Irish brogue. Jarvis and Daphne turned around in unison.

"May I help you?" Jarvis asked. Suddenly the pregnant woman who was with the one who had asked the question, screamed out in pain just as her water broke. Dr. Lamb immediately came to her aid.

"Come this way," Dr. Lamb entreated to the woman in labor.

"I'm sorry, Commander, I didn't mean to eaves drop, but Jeremy Tate is my husband's apprentice and I'm curious as to why you'd be referring to him as a leader."

"And you are?"

"Sarah, Sarah Smithers," she answered, and then continued. "I've been very concerned about my husband. He hasn't boarded this vessel and I fear he may still be on the planet."

"Are you aware Mrs. Smithers that Jeremy Tate is the one who led the rebellion on this ship and nearly got us shot out of the sky by the Rundi?"

"I heard rumors in the cargo bay, and hoped that it wasn't true. I pray you Sir, let me speak with him."

"I'm afraid I can't allow that. He's a prisoner."

"Mark my words Commander, he's a stubborn man, and you'll not get a word out of him. When you've come to that end, you'll call me."

"Why would I do that?"

"Because he fears me, Commander, I'm a woman to be reckoned with, and I'll know where my husband is."

"I believe you, but for now you may want to stay with your friend."

"That I will," Sarah said smiling as she waltzed away just as bold as she could be. Jarvis was impressed, and bet she could cash the checks on her threats. He kept her demand in his back pocket as he left to question the prisoner. If Mr. Tate was as difficult as she said, he'd need all the aces he could get.

Dr. Lamb tried to calm the scared young woman down. Even though she was a Rundi, she was a doctor first and compassion was not a human only trait.

"What's your name?" Dr. Lamb asked. Her voice was calm and soothing.

"Tina."

"Is this your first child, Tina?"

"Yes. I'm scared. My husband was supposed to be here, but he had to stay behind with the Militia. Where's Sarah?"

"I'm here, Tina. Just relax and let the good doctor do her job."

"You'll be fine. I'm going to give you a little something to help you relax. It's harmless and it'll make the birth easier."

Tina shook her head wearily refusing, but Sarah confirmed the good doctor's words and she allowed the injection without further protest. Soon the injection began to take affect and Tina began to relax. Of all the similarities the Rundi and Humans shared, reproduction was not one of them. Humans gave live birth. The Rundi, however, laid eggs. The parents didn't come back for their children until they had emerged from the pupae at which point they were at the same developmental stage as a human child of three. The parents and offspring would identify one another through scent alone. Then and only then were they given names. A ceremony of joy and tears would be conducted to rejoice with those who found their children and to weep for those whose children did not survive.

She wondered if humanity felt the loss of young ones as poignantly as the Rundi. Daphne began to reflect inwardly upon her own situation, but was immediately drawn back by a call for help a few beds over. It was the nurse standing vigil over Robert Johnson. He was going into cardiac arrest. Dr. Lamb nearly flew across the beds to get to her patient. Her nurse was already preparing him for a heart re-start.

"What happened?" Dr. Lamb questioned.

"I don't know. He stopped breathing. I began forcing oxygen into the lungs through the air bladder. Then his heart started defibrilating."

Daphne felt for a pulse, but there was none. "It's stopped completely," she added. She was thankful that the vital internal organs of both humans and Rundi were virtually identical as she began administering CPR. After a couple minutes it was clear that wasn't going to work. She lifted her arm up and pounded upon his chest in hopes of jarring it back to beating. It didn't work. She tried it once more, still no response. She grabbed the electric paddles.

"Clear!"

Everyone jumped back. Daphne touched the paddles to his chest and ignited their energy. His body lurched up off the table and fell back limp.

"Still no pulse," the nurse informed.

"I can see that. Clear!"

Again Daphne did the same thing with the same results. She put the paddles down and grabbed a nearby syringe and administered a dose of adrenalin also with no success. "Come on! Beat damn it!" In desperation she grabbed the paddles again. "Clear!" Again nothing happened. She didn't want to give up. "Clear!" No response.

"Dr. Lamb. He's gone," the nurse informed, as she took hold of her shoulder. Reluctantly Daphne put her hands down signaling defeat. Her expression was a mixture of both anger and helplessness.

"Call time of death, and bring the scanner so I can conduct a brain scan," Dr. Lamb ordered as she put the paddles away.

The portable scanning machine was brought to her and she discovered the reason for their inability to resuscitate him. His brain had been fried in the area that regulates his autonomic functions. She put the device down, and with great reverence covered his head with the sheet. The average Rundi may not have mourned his passing, but to a doctor, to lose a life is a tragedy regardless of the life lost.

Dr. Lamb returned to Tina to check on her progress. Sarah Smithers seemed highly concerned by the events that had just taken place only three beds from them. Only the squeezing of Sarah's hand by Tina brought her back to them. Daphne stopped to wash her hands and glove up before conducting a pelvic exam on Tina. She tried to appear unaffected by the tragedy that had just taken place in the shadow of this joyous occasion.

"You're halfway to full dilation. It shouldn't be too much longer," Daphne informed trying hard to be encouraging. Tina just shook her head. Life and death were two sides of the same coin. It seemed at times ironic when they passed together in a single moment of time. In some ways it was comforting, and in others disturbing. The cycle of life was a circle, but some parts of it can't be seen past the horizon guarding its exit well.

"Who was that?" Sarah asked in a hushed whisper, pulling Daphne out of her contemplative state.

"That was Robert Johnson, our Navigator. He was a good man. He didn't deserve to die, though I doubt the hijackers care either way," Daphne informed, her voice full of disgust for the act that destroyed such an honorable man. She'd had coffee with him many times and listened to him brag about his children and wife living on Otadan. It was odd how moved she was over the death of a human. In her heart there was no difference between the loss of this human and the loss of Rundi family and friends over the years.

Sarah's face suddenly turned green. It was difficult for her to imagine that Jeremy would do such a thing. *What had her husband gotten himself into this time?* She wondered, hoping that he wasn't involved with this little coup. Yet, she knew in her heart that he probably was. Tina's contractions brought Sarah and Daphne out of their inward concern. Daphne busied herself with caring for this patient so she'd have some joy to offset this terrible loss.

***

On the engineering deck, Janet had finished her shift and clocked out having completed a full by-pass of the communications system and shut down of the dampening field. She grabbed a tray full of coffee cups from the cafeteria and filled them with hot coffee. The aromatic steam wafted up from the surface inviting anyone who caught the scent to come and partake of the rich elixir. She was heading for her friends in the weapons bay.

"Sadowski, what do you think you're doing?" the Chief Engineer bellowed. His presence startled her. She sat the tray down and saluted her commanding officer.

"Sir, my shift was finished so I thought I'd take some java to my friends who are pulling double shifts repairing the ship's weapons. I thought the break and the java would help keep them alert, and if they need it, lend a hand," Janet answered.

"Good thinking, Sadowski, as you were."

"Yes Sir," Janet responded with a smile. She grabbed the tray and headed for the weapons bay.

Upon arriving in the weapons bay, Janet was amazed at what she saw. Most of the mechanisms looked melted. There was broken glass, shattered support beams, and wires in a pile of what looked like pasta near the center of the room. The coffee's aroma had made it to the nostrils of the crew a few steps ahead of Janet. Mike peaked

247

out from his place inside a crawlspace to see Janet standing with a tray of their favorite drink.

"Yeah, now this is what I call a rescue. Hey guys! Janet's here with the coffee."

Whooping and hollering could be heard from inside the walls and in no time at all like ants marching from their mound they headed for Janet. With smiles of appreciation they each grabbed a cup and plopped down where ever a clean spot on the floor allowed them to enjoy this rejuvenating beverage. All that is, but Sophie, Janet's one and only female friend. Janet was used to hanging with guys and most women felt intimidated by her. Not Sophie. She could go toe to toe, and still be the best of friends. Janet finally saw her friend still hip deep in wiring and lying on her back. She was trying to work on the mangled control panel. Janet walked over and waved the drink under her nose so that the vapors would find Sophie's olfactory nerves.

"Umm…" came Sophie's response.

"Come on, my friend, you deserve a break," Janet entreated dangling the coffee like a carrot in front of a horse. A grin cascaded across Sophie's face, as she pulled herself out of the nest of wiring.

"It's about time you got here," Sophie quipped.

"Sorry, I got here as fast as I could. I thought engineering needed repair. How can you fix this mess?"

"We can't. We're trying to get the bad components out so we can install new ones when we reach the station. I just hope Theta has everything. If they don't, we're screwed."

Janet heard what her friend was saying, but wasn't listening. Her mind was on Wong who was still on Hyperion. She missed him, and was worried about those storms that were moving in.

"Are you listening to me, or are you thinking about your lover boy on the planet?"

"Excuse me?" Janet questioned. She wasn't sure she liked Sophie's tone.

"Don't act coy with me. I'm your best friend. You're worried about Wong."

"Of course I'm worried. I'm worried about everybody." Janet tried her best to misdirect her friend's assumption. She was still getting used to the idea of liking Wong, and wasn't prepared to deal with others questions about it.

"There are no bridges out here so stop trying to sell me one."

"What bridge?" Janet asked.

"Do you really think no one has noticed how close you and Wong are?"

"Actually I'm beginning to think everyone noticed, but me."

"Dang, Janet, you can be such a ditz."

"I don't mean to be. I just get queasy when I think about settling down, and having kids. I come from a big family, and I don't want any of my own. I want to be like Jarvis. He's free and can go on whatever adventure he chooses because he is free."

"You really don't know do you?" Sophie questioned.

"Know what?"

"About Jarvis."

"What about him?" Janet asked, wondering what Sophie was getting at.

"He was a family man."

"You're kidding." Sadowski could barely believe her ears. At no time had he ever mentioned a family, and she'd served with him for at least six years.

"No, I'm not. This so called adventurous life he leads is not by choice."

"He would have said something to me."

"Maybe it hurts too much for him to talk about it. Remember the passenger ship Daylan?"

"Who doesn't, that was the first human vessel attacked by the Rundi. That's what really started the war not that fiction they're trying to sell us on now."

"Jarvis' wife and newborn son were on that vessel."

"There were no survivors," Janet announced aloud as if it were breaking news all over again.

"No there weren't, and Jarvis has never gotten over it."

"I never knew that," Janet responded in a daze. It was almost too much to absorb, but it explained a lot. "You better get back to work. Do you need a hand?"

"No, but thanks anyway. And thanks for the java. It really hit the spot."

Although she was sad for Commander Jarvis, it made her reflect upon the thing she and Wong had never shared. Janet wanted so bad to call Wong and talk with him, but they'd be in the dark matter corridor in just a few minutes and no communications would be possible while inside the corridor.

***

In the interrogation room Commander Jarvis was still questioning Jeremy Tate. He was no further along than he was two hours ago. The room was nothing but a solid white box and was even starting to get on the Commander's nerves. Jeremy was resolute in refusing to answer any question. He was everything that Sarah Smithers said he'd be, and then some. Oh how he wanted to belt this upstart kid. Although Jeremy was far from a child, his innate ability to aggravate his interrogator was not unlike the grating of a child asking, 'Are we there yet?'

Security called Commander Jarvis out of the room. At first he was upset, but the interruption gave him a needed break. His expression turned to stone when they told him about Robert Johnson's death. Jarvis pounded his fist against the sparsely covered desk of the security office uttering a menagerie of curses. His outburst left an impression upon the desk. He looked down at the damage and then at the eyes of his Security staff. No one said a word. He took a deep breath before going back into the interrogation room.

Jeremy could see that there was a change in the Commander's countenance. The look in his eyes told Jeremy that this man was over playing games. He would have what he wanted to know. At first Jarvis just paced the floor back and forth. He was trying to formulate a statement that would allow him to show the full extent of his rage, yet demonstrate that he was in full command of the situation. He had refrained from any torture techniques, but was about to employ them like he did against the desk.

"Congratulations, you've just added murder to the charges against you and your men. Our navigator was just pronounced dead. He was a family man with a wife and two beautiful daughters."

Jeremy looked stricken at first, and then began to soften slightly.

"No one was supposed to get hurt," Jeremy finally uttered in disbelief. It was the first words he'd spoken in the interrogation room.

"But they have," Jarvis said jerking Jeremy's chair around to face him. "How many more lives will be added to this list of people who weren't supposed to get hurt?" There was fire in Jarvis' eyes now, the kind that would sear an image into the optic nerve of Jeremy branding him with the guilt of taking an innocent life.

252

"We just wanted to stay, and be left alone," he defended.

"Your words are empty," Jarvis clarified.

"What do you want me to say? I never wanted to kill anyone!"

"The moment you chose to join their action anything that follows is on your shoulders."

"We just wanted to be taken seriously," Jeremy added.

"Where are they holding the Governor's wife?" Jarvis asked, probably for the hundredth time.

Jeremy could feel Jarvis' breath upon his face and could taste the milk and sugar that he had put in his coffee a few hours ago. The saliva bubbles that had landed on Jeremy's face began to pop breaching the perimeter of his own mouth releasing the now sour odor.

"This wasn't what was supposed to happen," Jeremy muttered in garbled and slurred syllables, the guilt of his actions sinking into his consciousness and creating extreme emotional upheaval.

"Where are they holding the Governor's wife?" This time Jarvis was shouting at him, his patience at an end. He grabbed Jeremy's shirt balling it securely inside his clenched right fist. He lifted him off his chair. The strain of the cloth was evident. The Security personnel watched in fear as Jarvis seemingly began to lose control. "I'm only going to ask once more then I'm going to use you to mop up the floor. Where is the Governor's wife?"

"I don't know," Jeremy confessed. His quickness to respond did not lend credence to his words. Jarvis slapped him with his other hand. His face swung to the side under the force of it. He slowly turned his head back to engage Jarvis' unrelenting glare.

"You're the leader of this rebellion! You really expect me to believe you don't know," Jarvis stated with disgust. He thrust Jeremy back into the chair. He hit the chair so hard that it screeched several feet across the floor. It was the kind of sound that regurgitates one's nerve endings like nails on an endless chalkboard. The sudden pressure caused the chair leg to bend and then snap. Jeremy hit the floor with a loud thud. He was stunned at first, but Jarvis didn't care and moved in close to his face.

"I don't know!" He screamed up at Jarvis hoping that he'd back off. The suddenness of his outburst only caused him to back away briefly. He quickly regained his position.

"I don't believe you."

The realization of his actions was beginning to take hold. Tears of grief and guilt welled up in Jeremy's eyes. Despite this display of emotion, Jarvis was unmoved. He kicked him in the gut. Jarvis then lifted him off the floor and punched his face sending his head twisting under the brunt of the impact. Blood and spit flew from his mouth as teeth were forced against flesh and skin collided with his rock hard fist. Jeremy fell limp and Jarvis released him. His hands were still bound so it took him a minute to push himself back up to a sitting position. While the blood trickled down his chin dripping upon the floor, Jarvis studied him.

Jeremy was finally talking, but he still wasn't saying anything. Jarvis had Sarah brought immediately to the interrogation room. She gazed through the one-way glass at Jeremy. His face was bruised and bloodied. He was sitting in a replacement chair. The broken one was sitting just outside the door. This hardly looked like the same young man who was at her home just a few days ago. Commander Jarvis was standing over him just glaring at him as if trying to peer into his very soul. Sarah swallowed hard. Whatever Jeremy's original intent, they were far beyond that as events continued to spiral out of control.

When she initially offered to question the boy, she didn't realize he'd look so bad. Because of the nature of his crimes, she couldn't cry that his rights had been violated. He had given up any such rights when he hijacked the ship. Sarah indicated to the men that she was ready to go in, but before stepping through the open doorway she inhaled a deep breath and barely expelled it for fear of losing her own nerve.

"Mrs. Smithers welcome. You know Sarah Smithers don't you Jeremy?"

Jeremy just nodded yes. His jaw was soar and his lips swollen and didn't wish to engage in conversation unless it was absolutely necessary. He stared at the floor refusing to look at her.

She took the other chair that Jarvis had used and pulled it up beside him.

"Look at me, Jeremy Tate," Sarah commanded. Her voice bid him like a siren bid the sailors of old to their doom. He reluctantly turned his head to look at her, but kept his eyes lowered. "I said, look at me," Sarah insisted. Her voice was authoritative, but still maintained a compassion that she hoped was not misplaced. After struggling for just a moment, he obeyed and looked her in the eyes.

"I'm so sorry, Sarah," Jeremy blurted.

"I know the kind of man you are Jeremy Tate. What possessed you to lead the men in revolt against these people and endanger everyone's lives?"

"I believed our cause was just. No one was supposed to get hurt," he confessed to her through a torrent of silent tears that were a mixture of sorrow, anger, and shame.

"Where are they keeping Samantha Tarken?"

"I don't know."

"You're lying," Jarvis jumped in.

"Commander a moment if you please," Sarah insisted. Jarvis backed away to the wall, but didn't lean against it. He was ready to pounce upon any misspoken word that Jeremy might utter.

"Why don't you know?"

"Because our leader wouldn't tell me. He said it was better that way so if anything went wrong they still had a chance to make a stand."

"Jeremy, things have gone more than just wrong and I need to know whose lead you are following?"

"I can't say," Jeremy stated as if pleading with her not to pursue this.

"I know you're an honorable man. It's your duty now to tell the truth or that man's soul who died will forever be a blot against you." Sarah pulled her chair next to his and took hold of his hand.

"Manny is our leader. He's the one who divided up the assignments and coordinated the kidnapping of Samantha Tarken. I'm sorry Sarah. I'm so sorry," he confessed weeping upon her shoulder like a small, frightened boy. Tears, snot, blood, and drool seeped upon her shoulder as Jeremy buried his head there. In shock, Sarah stood to her feet not wanting to believe what Jeremy said, but knowing full well that he spoke the truth. She withdrew leaving him to sob in mid-air. His crying was inconsolable. In retrospect of her and Manny's last conversation, she knew what he said was true. *Stupid old fool*, she thought to herself.

"Who's Manny?" Jarvis asked.

"Manny is my missing husband, Commander."

Glenda C. Finkelstein

Chapter 18

On the outskirts of the colony deep inside the caves, Manny and his subordinates were discussing their inability to communicate with their people on the Phoenix. The lack of communication caused a great deal of unrest among the men. Manny sent Thaddeus to the surface to determine why they had lost communications and if anyone had become nosy near the cave entrances. Thaddeus made haste for the situation was deteriorating fast. While he was gone, the men offered up all sorts of scenarios. Each one becoming more hostile as fear began to paint a very bleak picture of their situation.

"There's something wrong," Jake suggested.

"What would you have me do?" Manny questioned.

"I don't know exactly, but kidnapping the Governor's wife wasn't a good idea. We should have never done that," Jake argued.

"If we hadn't, they'd have left us here to die. She's the only thing that will keep them here and fighting for us," Manny defended.

"What about our boys on the Phoenix?" Kent questioned.

"They've been captured, or they would have called again," Jake answered, cutting Manny off before he could answer.

"What proof, do either of you have? I thought I was dealing with men not boys. You knew this wouldn't be easy, and now you want to throw in the towel because of broken communications. Regardless of what has or hasn't happened there's no going back. If they failed, then it falls to us to finish it."

"The fact that we can't contact them should be evidence enough that we have failed," Jake insisted.

"Except that's being premature," Thaddeus announced coming through the entryway. He was slightly out of breath due to his haste to bring the answers back to Manny quickly.

"Report," Manny demanded anxiously.

"There's a strong electrical storm that's set in. I doubt even Hyperion command has good communications right now."

"You see, you worry for nothing," Manny announced, chastising his men in a disgusted tone. The near shouts that started to erupt prior to Thaddeus' return were now droning down to a dull murmur.

260

Samantha could hear the arguing where she was still tied up in an adjoining cavern. She was concerned that this situation could deteriorate quickly. She could easily find herself in the midst of a civil war. She was tied too well to slip out of her bonds, but perhaps she could get one of them to remove them. After all, it seemed that Manny's abduction of her was still a contention among them and she might be able to play up that angle and find an ally.

"Excuse me," Samantha called out to the men guarding her.

"Yeah," the young man responded. Samantha glared at him for being so unmannerly. "I mean yes Ma'am," he corrected.

"That's better. I need to go."

"I can't let you go."

"I'm not asking you to let me go, I'm telling you I need to go."

At first it didn't appear that they comprehended what she was getting at. She looked at them for a minute, and realized she needed to be more specific. Yet her breeding kept her from becoming vulgar.

"You know, full bladder."

"Oh!" said the other, "She's got to piss."

"We don't have facilities down here."

"I'll take going behind a rock, but I need to go."

"Sure Lady, but I'll have to keep an eye on you," the young man said as he loosed her bonds. She glared up at him.

"I'm the Governor's wife. I'll not have you watching me go. Besides, where am I going to run down here? I have no clue where I am."

"She's right Pete. We're down in the entrails of the mountain. She'd never be able to find her way out."

"Very well, but don't go too far. There are other dangers besides us down here."

"I won't," she assured as she stood to her feet. Her legs could barely support her weight having been tied up for so many hours. Her feet tingled. The tingling sensation ran up her calves and into her thighs with each step. She walked about a moment to get rid of the sensation. Once she was certain that she could navigate, she squatted behind a huge outcropping of rock to urinate. She hoped her legs wouldn't betray her and collapse out from under her. Samantha knew the young men were right about her not being able to find her way out, but she could hide herself. At least they'd lose their edge of being in control. Perhaps that would bring the situation to a quick resolution once the rescuers figured out where they were.

Her mind lingered upon the thought of rescuers coming to save her. She knew that Paul would come looking for her, but didn't know when. Then again they might not come at all. The need to get the population to safety may out weigh her need to be rescued. She shuddered to think what the Rundi would do to them if they found them still here when they arrived. Her belly began to get queasy at the thought, but she quickly grabbed hold of that dangerous thought

262

and put it away. She had to stay focused on the fact that she would be rescued or escape on her own. Right now, she was a bargaining chip. They needed to end this situation quickly and if she could remove herself from the equation, they might surrender faster.

Samantha walked into the darkness taking care to keep all worrisome thoughts locked away. It didn't take her long to find herself removed from the men and immersed in total blackness. Much of the noise she heard previously was now barely audible. She hoped she could hide herself without allowing herself to be too far distant from the men, but she quickly discovered that she was lost and had no way of determining a direction. Her nerves quickened within her, but she refused to call out for help and give away her position.

"Come on Lady, you're taking too long," Pete called. "Mrs. Tarken?" he questioned. Both young men bolted around to the other side of the boulder only to discover a wet patch of dirt that smelled of urine, and no Mrs. Tarken. They followed her footsteps for as far as the loose dirt held out, but quickly lost her trail. There were several tunnels that went deep into the mountain and none of them were lighted or well mapped. They called into the tunnels, and heard only their own voices echo back. They left their post to report to Manny what had happened. Even if she took advantage of them being gone there were other guards posted throughout the maze toward the surface.

"You lost her?" Manny questioned with anger. Needless to say Manny was not happy with the news. These tunnels were dangerous for them much less a greenhorn. She would surely get herself killed. He truly didn't want any harm to come to her for both their sakes.

"Yeah, we lost her. We untied her so she could piss, and she must have gone down one of the uncharted tunnels since she didn't come back by us."

"Why would she do that?" Manny asked aloud to himself. He threw his arms up in the air punctuating the question.

"Perhaps because we kidnapped her," Pete suggested believing that Manny was looking for them to answer his question.

"Fool!" Manny shouted in disgust. This coup was so not going as planned. Instead, it was falling apart around him. All he wanted was to save their homes and livelihoods. He never wanted to cause harm to anyone. "Damn it! Take the men, some lanterns, and search as far as you can. We have to find her!"

"Yes Sir."

They immediately followed his orders. Her odds of survival were not good. Manny didn't fancy the idea of going head-to-head with Paul Tarken should his wife not be alive when he finds them. Any defense or reason would be null and void.

***

By the time the Phoenix embarked upon her return voyage to Hyperion, repairs were complete, new weapons installed, and communications were fully restored. Jarvis gave a full report to Captain Sanchez on the results of his interrogation of Jeremy Tate. He also mentioned that what little success they had would not have been possible without the assistance of Sarah Smithers. She made a formal request to be present when they locate her husband, Manny, pledging her cooperation to Commander Jarvis and Captain Sanchez. Needless to say, Rico was not convinced that she would be useful in such a task and was unhappy with Jarvis' initial results. The only bright spot in knowing who took Samantha Tarken was that they might narrow down the search parameters, but it might not be enough to rescue her before their time ran out.

The news of Richard's death weighed heavily upon Rico's mind, but grief would have to wait. He was only the first fatality and wondered how many more would perish before the evacuation ended. He wasn't at all pleased with himself for losing his temper. Putting everyone on alert and challenging the Prefect may actually work against him in the end. The deadline would most certainly be made a hard deadline with no recourse for postponement, not that it was anything else but that to begin with.

Captain Sanchez didn't relish the thought of turning tale and allowing the Rundi to kill those left behind, even if they were misguided fools. Nor did he savor the idea of re-igniting the war just for a handful of people. Most of all, he didn't want to leave anyone behind who were being kept against their will. Part of him wondered if there were any more surprises, and prayed that all the cards were now on the table.

The storm was still rather fierce, but was showing signs of clearing. When the Phoenix and Triton arrive back in orbit the evacuation should return to full swing. Rico had Wong run several sets of scenarios, and under any of them they'd just barely be able to make it off the planet with the population intact. Their success would depend upon nothing else going wrong. He hoped they could find Samantha quickly and convince her captors to surrender her without the loss of any more lives. Richard's death was one too many. Regardless, the timing of the final evacuation would be extremely close leaving no margin for error.

At Hyperion command Paul was listening intently to the report that the Phoenix filed with Captain Sanchez. Now that he knew whom it was that they were dealing with he had a good idea of where they would be holding Samantha. He also knew that the ship's scanners in orbit of Hyperion would be useless in helping them locate her due to the mineral composition of the mountains. He pulled out several maps to show Rico the large number of tunnels and caves. Only then did Rico begin to understand Paul's agitation. The caves were numerous, the tunnels long, dangerous, and maze like.

The task before them to accomplish within the incredibly shrinking time constraints was nearly impossible. Paul was jumpy and on edge. When he walked, he paced turning back and forth.
266

When he stood still he bobbed about like a boat rocking back and forth upon the waves. When he sat, he would reposition himself a dozen times. When he spoke, it was as if each syllable was jabbed at the recipient. Rico was close to punching his lights out, but stopped short realizing that Paul didn't have the military training to contend with the pressure he was currently undergoing.

"Why don't you try some of this?" Wong suggested holding out a small cup filled with what appeared to be water. He was tired of watching the two volcanoes bubble toward eruption.

"I'm not thirsty," Paul snapped back, continuing to pace.

"It's not water," Wong informed calmly, holding the cup out again. Paul slowed his nervous twitching for just a moment and took the cup from him. He sniffed at it, and realized it was rice wine. He looked into Wong's eyes as he touched the cup to his lips and tilted his head back to imbibe the liquid in one swallow. The warmth immediately cascaded through his body with the speed of a tidal wave and began to numb nerve endings as it proceeded throughout. A sense of calm began to flood his body, and it craved more.

Paul held the cup out for a refill. Wong obliged and filled it. Paul took another gulp then sat down on the sofa, the elixir making him a little light headed. He sat the cup down on the end table, leaned over into his hands, and placed his forehead into them. A mournful cry erupted slowly from his grieving form like lava being spit gingerly upon a volcanic slope. Rico and Wong watched helpless to alleviate his pain. Although crying was not something men do often, there are times that it was useful to relieve stresses that interfere with clear thinking. Such was the cleansing sob, of Paul's cry.

"I suppose I'm not very tough in the eyes of the military," Paul admitted, feeling weak under Rico's militaristic stare.

"No one expects you to be a tough emotionless being. You have demonstrated a tremendous amount of courage in the face of extreme circumstances that have placed your personal and professional lives at odds with one another," Rico consoled, patting him on the shoulder as he took up a seat next to him.

Paul lifted his head to look at Rico. His hardened demeanor seem to soften in this moment and Paul knew that he wasn't speaking just to sound comforting, but was speaking from his own personal pain. Wong took this opportunity to excuse himself, and take his turn manning the radar and communications consol in the office a couple of doors down.

"I can't leave her here."

"I never planned on it," Rico informed.

"What?"

"I can be a mean and unemotional son of a bitch, but I'll be damned if I'll leave anyone behind that didn't choose to do so. You pulled out those maps to establish a game plan to rescue Samantha from the Miners who hold her. You say you know this Manny Smithers. How well do you know him?" Rico asked. Paul looked confused at first, but then realized why he was asking the question.
268

He wiped away the silvery tears that still clung to his unshaven face, and in so doing uncovered yet another layer of courage.

"I've negotiated contracts with him several times, and have dealt with him on some disputes."

"Okay, that's good. So you probably have a good idea of how the man thinks. Knowing that, where do you think he'd hold up?"

Paul stood up with renewed vigor and walked over to the table where the maps were spread out. He stared aimlessly at first, and then with confidence pointed to an area on the map narrowing the twenty plus possibilities to six, but just as suddenly as his confidence came, fear crawled up and slapped him around bashing at his certainty.

"What if I'm wrong? I can't afford to make a mistake. Too much is at stake. There's no time," Paul muttered in rapid succession.

"Forget the situation. Samantha is safe. You must believe that. Now just by the facts and your knowledge of this man. Where would he go?" Rico's voice rose up with authority as if he were giving an order. The sternness was enough to help Paul regain his focus. This time Paul grabbed a pen and circled the area on the map where he believed Manny would be narrowing down the search to three possibilities. Although it still wasn't accurate enough to successfully do a search and rescue in the time allotted, it was a start.

There was a slight noise coming from just outside the door in the hallway. The men stopped talking and listened for a moment. Realizing that it was probably nothing but the wind, Paul continued with his deliberation.

"Considering the time of her disappearance and when they announced their demands I estimate they wouldn't be more than six miles out. They'd want to be in a place where communications wouldn't be too hampered, but far enough out of reach where a quick search and rescue wouldn't turn up anything. They probably weren't counting on the storm. With the kind of communication devices they possess the storm has most likely prevented them from making direct contact with their people on the Phoenix. That makes them just as in the dark as we are right now."

"Good, that narrows it down and equalizes the playing field."

"No it doesn't. Not enough anyway, these tunnels are deep. They'll only be found if they want to be."

"Tell me about your wife. What's she like?" Rico asked trying to broach the crisis from another vantage point.

"You met her."

"Briefly. What I'm asking, is do you think that she's ballsy enough to take advantage of opportunities should they arise?"

"My Sam is a woman to be reckoned with, but even if she manages to escape her captors. She'd never find her way out of the tunnels alone. Manny's even lost well trained miners in those tunnels."

"Well, she is a politicians' wife. Perhaps she'll win an ally."

Paul looked up at him and smiled at the thought. If anyone could convince someone to do something, it'd be his Samantha. It warmed Rico's heart to see a smile return to Paul's face as his own heart was pricked. He would soon leave his own love here to her fate, and with her his heart would stay.

The sound of coughing soon caught their attention. It seemed to be coming from the front door near the floor. Rico motioned for Paul to move behind a wall in case this was a rouse to acquire the Governor too. Rico drew his weapon, and opened the door in one quick motion. An old man lay curled up on the floor, soaked by the rain. His clothes clung to him like plastic wrap. Paul recognized him.

"Joe!" Paul exclaimed, running to the old man's aid.

"Medics to the Governor's quarters," Rico called into a call box. There was some medical staff stationed in the building and he wanted them there pronto.

"Joe what happened?" Paul questioned. He could tell the old man was fading. The forces of nature were stealing the last vestiges of this man's ancient strength.

"I...know..." Joe coughed again, violently riveting his body.

"Bring water," Paul ordered of Rico.

"No," Joe commanded, weakly lifting his hand to take hold of Paul's arm and draw him close. "Sam taken."

"Yes, we know."

"She's…at…Wi-…dow's Rock…" Joe spoke in broken syllables as his last breath expired.

"Joe!" Paul exclaimed, shaking him as if to wake him, but he wasn't asleep. The medics ran toward their position and jumped into action. Paul was nearly thrown to the side by the head doctor. Rico had the good sense to stand against the wall the moment he heard their thundering footsteps. Wong heard the commotion and stuck his head out the door. He was concerned and walked over to Rico's position to check it out.

"What happened?" Wong asked.

"The old man, he just collapsed. I think he's dead," Rico informed briefly, keeping his eyes focused upon the medics and Paul.

"He's gone," The head medic announced to the others. "What happened?" the medic asked of Paul as he stood to his feet.

"We heard a noise at the door. We ignored it thinking it was the wind until we heard coughing. When we opened the door Joe was on the ground coughing in violent spasms. He could barely talk. I think he succumbed to exposure to the elements."

"Joe's a tough old bird, he's been rained on before," the medic commented.

"Yeah, but he's been out in it for hours so he could bring me information about where the kidnappers are keeping my wife."

"Why didn't he just call?" the medic questioned.

"I can answer that," Wong interrupted, and then continued. "The lightning took out several communications hubs on the southern section of the city. We know about it, but it was too dangerous to send out repair crews. Even your transportation system was not functioning there. The only way to get word out was to walk it here."

"One hundred and twenty-eight years old, and he's taken out by rain," the Medic commented, shaking his head in disbelief.

"And a lightning strike, look at the burns on his left shoulder," Wong pointed out. "If he was close enough to get burned like that, he should have been fried then and there."

"One hundred and twenty-eight years old?" Rico questioned aloud.

"Yes, he was the oldest colonist on Hyperion. As for you doctor, I expect a full autopsy on the exact cause of death. Just because he was old doesn't make it any less important that we determine the true cause of death," Paul insisted.

"Yes sir, although it'll have to be performed aboard one of the evacuation ships."

"That's fine, but I want the report sent to me."

"Yes sir."

They carefully lifted Joe's body onto a gurney, covered him with a sheet, and carried him off. Paul looked after him until he was out of sight. The loss of Joe stung, but Paul couldn't allow any additional emotion into his pot of soup. He had to stay focused. Joe gave his life to bring him the information to save Sam, and he wasn't going to let his sacrifice be in vain.

"Captain," Wong began. "You should know that the storm is beginning to clear in the northern end of the city. It should be safe enough to resume evacuation in that section in two hours."

"Good, get hold of the Ares, give them the coordinates so they can be prepared. Notify the other ships to stand by as the weather clears I want them ready to launch."

"Yes Sir."

"Oh, and get your stuff ready you'll be accompanying me back to the Phoenix. Contact Captain Macalister and have one of her crewman take over traffic control. I'm going to need you to fix Zeveney, and find out who destroyed him."

Paul looked confused at Rico's orders to Wong. Even Wong looked a little dazed, but followed them to the letter without another word. Rico returned his attention to Paul to greet his confused stare.

"I thought you were going to help me," Paul commented with great disappointment.

"I am, but you'll have to lay the groundwork."

"I don't understand."

Rico motioned for Paul to follow him as he returned to the table where all the maps were. Paul followed, but still didn't know what Rico was up to.

"Joe mentioned Widow's Rock."

"Yeah."

"Show me."

Paul pointed to a place on the map. Rico smiled.

"It's in the same area that you narrowed down," Rico offered with a sly grin forming on his face. Paul started to smile, but quickly caught it midway and returned to a more serious expression.

"That may be, but this group of tunnels is by the far the most treacherous of them all. If Joe's right and Manny's hold up inside them, we won't get them out unless they choose to come out."

"That's why I'm going back to my ship. I have one ace up my sleeve and I'm hoping it will give me the bargaining power to get them to surrender. In the meantime, I want you to take whatever militia you think you'll need and set up a perimeter as soon as the weather permits. Then I'll need you to do the hardest thing you'll ever do." Rico paused a moment. Paul was impatient pushing Rico for information.

"What?"

"Wait for me before you make your move."

Paul looked down at the map evading Rico's eyes and twisted at his wrists with his hands. He didn't want to wait, time was growing short and he wanted a piece of Manny's ass for taking his wife from him. Paul was not a strategist, and he knew it. Rico seemed to be a man of his word so reluctantly Paul nodded his agreement. Rico's expression indicated that he wasn't satisfied with merely a nod.

"I'll wait," Paul forced between clinched teeth.

"I'll not be long," Rico promised as he turned to leave. He walked down to the communications room where he joined Wong and waited until the relief watch arrived.

"Captain," Wong greeted as Rico entered the cramped room. Rico watched Wong coordinate ships like a conductor orchestrates a symphony. It was art in Wong's hands, for anyone else technology was just a tool.

"Remind me to promote you when this is all over."

"Promotion, Sir? What for?"

"For bringing out your cherished rice wine."

"I thought the governor could use it. I thought you were going to punch his lights out if he didn't calm down some."

"Exactly, Mr. Wong," Rico concurred with a smile and Wong smiled back.

Chapter 19

Commander Jarvis waited in the docking bay for Captain Sanchez and Wong Qwan to disembark their shuttle pod onto the Phoenix. Rico smiled up at Jarvis, and sniffed the air of the ship. He was planet side too long for his taste. The smell of a spaceship was comforting to him, and there wasn't a single aroma out of place. He was home. Commander Jarvis walked with the Captain up to his office filling him in on the progress of ship's status while Wong was released to attend to the repair of the Zeveney 7000-P computer assistant.

Wong entered the Captain's personal quarters and was taken aback by what he saw. There was debris everywhere he looked. He stepped inside allowing the doors to close behind him. Wong just stood staring at the jumbled mess that used to be the Zeveney 7000-P. After a moment he felt the weight of someone's gaze, and heard the sound of a gentle exhale. He looked about the room and saw Janet standing in the corner smiling at him. He flashed a big grin back at her. With no hesitation, he dropped his tool kit, grabbed Janet in his arms, and planted a kiss on her. She retuned the kiss.

"Welcome back," Janet greeted.

"It's good to be back," he responded, and then kissed her again.

"You better get to work or the Captain will get pretty terse. I tried to organize the debris as best I could."

"This is organized?"

"Yeah, you should have seen it before I organized it."

"Damn," was all Wong could utter. He began his work straight away. Since Janet was off duty, she stayed around to see if she could help him. He was grateful for the help, and doubtful that he'd be able to resurrect the Captain's precious computer assistant. He would, however, pull out every trick he knew to fix him and attempt to find out the identity of the one who destroyed it.

***

After Jarvis finished briefing the Captain, he left to find Mrs. Smithers. Rico wanted to talk with her himself to see if she really was ready to do what he needed her to do. In the meantime, Rico waited in his office for Dr. Lamb to join him. He missed her. He wanted to see her alone for two reasons, the first was that he truly wanted to be in her presence and hold her one last time. The second was to find out if she knew why Hyperion was so important to her people and hopefully share that information with him. Only the truth, Rico believed, would be able to sway the men who were holding Samantha Tarken to release her.

The door opened suddenly, startling him from his contemplation. He looked up and met Daphne's warm inviting eyes. They always displayed compassion. Even when she was upset they never became angry. His body became flush with warmth. He had to say something soon or go into meltdown. She, too, was also flushed with warmth, filled with the love that was forbidden them.

"Daphne," he entreated. "Please, sit down."

"Welcome back, Captain."

"Thank you."

An awkward silence followed their pleasantries. Rico didn't know how to begin to ask her. If she knew, she might not be at liberty to share it without retribution from her people. She picked up immediately on his anxiety.

"Just say what you have to say," she invited. Her voice was so gentle. He wanted to hang on to every sound, scent, or movement she might share in these dwindling moments. He was overwhelmed by the value held in each passing second, and could feel the time ticking away as if the sands of time were pouring through his fingers, helpless to slow them down.

"Do you know why Hyperion is so important to your people?" he finally asked. He engaged her eyes so she could see the sincerity and the need he had to know the truth. She quickly looked down at her lap. His desperation was clear, and although she trusted him as an individual the secret she held was all that stood between the Rundi's survival and extinction. "Please, I must know or an innocent woman may needlessly die." After another small silence, Daphne swallowed hard. Rico could tell that she was about to place all her trust into him which even at that moment appeared to be a heart wrenching decision.

"Yes, I know why, and I'll share that with you with the understanding that what I share is so important that our very survival as a people depend upon it and you must promise to fulfill your word to give us the planet just as you have promised to find the real reason for Conrad's death."

"I promise," he uttered, softly and reverently.

"Although the Rundi and the humans share many things in common, we differ greatly on the point of reproduction. Where humans give live birth we Rundi lay eggs. When they hatch, our children are in a larval stage and are nothing more than mindless creatures that do nothing but eat. After a time the larvae develop into a pupae. It's only after they emerge from their pupae, that they resemble the humanoid form similar to my own. At that point they are the equivalent of a human child of about three."

"I can appreciate the differences, but that still doesn't explain the need for Hyperion," Rico interjected.

"I'm getting to that. Our people go through reproductive stages at the same time every seven years. Our spawning ground is Hyperion. When we came to lay our eggs we found the humans there. Our cradle of life had been blatantly violated so we attacked the first human vessel we came into contact. During the conflict we were cut off from Hyperion. We tried other places, our eggs failed with a 100 percent mortality rate. The nutrients found on Hyperion are unique, and can't be duplicated synthetically. After we lay our eggs Hyperion's eco system is decimated by the larvae. It restores itself in two years and by the next cycle is ready for another batch. That's why the human colonists never saw any evidence of our presence. We don't build on Hyperion. We incubate our young on Hyperion."

"I'm beginning to understand."

"Are you truly? Remember when I told you that our larvae period is a time of mindlessness."

"Yes."

"Understand that the larvae will eat anything and everything. Even we do not stay once the eggs are laid. We leave a sentry in orbit to protect the young from anyone who might happen upon them unawares. We only return when they start emerging from their pupae, and parent and child find one another by scent. This is why all your people must leave. If they don't we the adults are not coming to kill them, our young will do that based upon instinct alone."

"I don't know what to say."

"Your expression says it best. You're repulsed by this knowledge. I should have never shared it with you."

"No I'm not repulsed. I'm a little shocked, but I'll get over it."

"I thought you were truly ready to be equal with us," she quipped.

"Where did that come from?"

"You have a hard time accepting what's different from you," Daphne stood up to leave. Rico reached across his desk to grab her arm to prevent her from doing so.

"So do you."

"I beg your pardon." Daphne was highly offended.

"You get a little too lofty sometimes. In order for two different species to fully understand one another, they need to first establish trust. I can't speak for the rest of your people, or for mine. I can only speak for myself. We have established a trust or we would not have shared what we did."

"That's when you thought I was human," she stated with latent sorrow in her voice. Rico walked around his desk, to come face to face with her.

"Human or Rundi, we were strangers to one another. I fell in love with you, and I'm still in love with you. I give you my word that this world will be returned to you and your people." His last few words were uttered in hushed deliberate whispers.

He nuzzled her with his nose then pressed his lips upon hers gently at first, taking her into his arms pulling her close. She melted into his embrace and reciprocated the love, tongues entwined and hearts raced as if they could mold themselves together into one being. He realized that what he initiated was outside the rules, but his heart dictated to damn the rules.

"We can't do this," she finally whispered, pulling away from his embrace.

"It's our last moment together as two people with no governments, agendas, or orders. Now tell me again how unequal we are," he insisted. Love was a greater force than even biology or duty.

"I'm sorry, I didn't mean to... I do love you..." her voice trailed off as they exchanged one last kiss.

"I know," he said. "Right now the only thing we have left is our duty. We have less than two days, and I'll need your help to resolve the situation on the planet so both our peoples can live."

"My duty will be honored," she vowed.

"As will mine. Now, go get ready to accompany me to the planet in just a few hours."

"I understand."

During this last embrace they each cemented into their consciousness the taste, the smell, and the warmth of the other. Suddenly a tremendous sorrow fell upon Daphne and she pulled herself away leaving Rico alone to himself. Daphne left his office abruptly and passed Jarvis and Mrs. Smithers in the hallway. She was on her way to her quarters to prepare herself to go home. Jarvis saw that she was upset, but she gave him no room to inquire as to why. He held his concern for now because his duty was pressed for time. Since they were expected, Jarvis didn't stop to knock.

"What!" Rico responded sharply to the intrusion.

"You ordered me to bring you Mrs. Smithers," Jarvis responded, uncertain why he was getting such an attitude from the Captain. In retrospect, it probably had more to do with Daphne than himself. Realizing that he had been abrupt, Rico adjusted his tone. He could see that Mrs. Smithers was a woman of fire and was prepared to give as good as she got.

"Please sit down, Mrs. Smithers. That will be all Commander."

"Sir," Jarvis responded back in quick militaristic proficiency saluting as he left stifling his initial need to respond in like manner. Rico returned the salute, but waited until they were alone before he spoke with Mrs. Smithers.

"Mrs. Smithers, I'm going to be blunt with you. I wasn't enthusiastic about you wanting to join us in confronting your husband."

284

"With all due respect Captain, I don't much care whether you like it or not. My husband is a very stubborn man, and if he's going to respond to anyone, it'll be me. Heck, if it weren't for me you wouldn't know what to do now."

Sarah was quite sure of herself and demonstrated a formidable demeanor. Rico could plainly see that his rank meant little to her, and that if she was going to respect him he'd have to be tough with her.

"Mrs. Smithers, I'm not," Rico began.

"Sarah," she interrupted, eroding his firm demeanor.

"Excuse me?"

"My name is Sarah."

"Very well, Sarah, I'm not a man who will be bullied or ordered by a civilian. The only reason I agreed to take you is that you may have the means to get your husband to surrender peacefully, but should he refuse I have neither the time nor the patience to be toyed with. I will shoot him if he gives me cause."

"Shoot him!" she was stunned and prepared to defend her man.

"With a stun round of course, but even those can have unexpected complications."

"Like with your navigator," she admitted, her defensive tone dropping from her voice.

"Yes." Rico paused a moment reflecting upon Richard's memory.

"I understand," Sarah offered, respectfully.

"I want to make sure you do. He kidnapped and is holding Samantha Tarken, the Governor's wife hostage. I'll have her released and those that are holding her will come back to the ship and face the charges that have been levied against them, with or without their consent."

"My husband may be many things, Captain Sanchez, but he'll face the consequences of his actions like a man. You can be sure of it."

"If you can get him to cooperate, I promise that I'll testify on his behalf at his hearing. If he doesn't, there's nothing I can do for him."

Sarah contemplated Rico's words carefully before responding to his offer that she knew was very generous under the circumstances.

"I very much appreciate your kindness when I know you probably think very little of my husband. He may be a fool, but at heart he's a good man."

"I realize that he's trying to save his home and his way of life, but there are things he doesn't understand that I hope to explain to him when we meet. Things that will make him understand why his action is so futile. There are other needs involved greater than his own and you must help me convince him of that."

"I have your word as an officer that you'll stand in his defense at the hearing if he cooperates."

"Yes."

"Then I'll ask, but one favor of you."

"What is that?"

"I've been married to Manny many years. I'll know if he's going to cooperate. If I sense that he's dug in his heels, then I'll signal you by kissing his cheek. Until then I ask that you hold your fire for he will test you at first."

"You're everything Commander Jarvis said you were. They don't make women like you very often, and if you don't mind me saying, Manny is a fool to put himself in a position to lose you."

Sarah smiled a sorrowful smile. "Yes, well, if he's a fool what does that make me?" she asked. Rico knew when to hold his tongue. "When do we leave?"

"Within the hour," Rico informed with a heightened respect for this civilian woman.

"I'll be ready."

***

The Prefect was sitting at his computer terminal going over the latest report from Captain Sanchez. His body language didn't hide his frustration with the information contained therein. He stood up to go find the Admiral and put pressure on him to expedite the situation on Hyperion. What the Prefect didn't realize was that the Admiral was already standing behind him and he nearly knocked him down when he stood up out of his chair.

"What nonsense are these reports?" the Prefect questioned without apology for stepping on the Admiral's toes.

"They are their best effort projections of being able to meet your deadline," the Admiral responded, stifling a curse word.

"This is unacceptable. This leaves no room for error."

"The storm had a great deal to do with that don't you think?"

"It's not the storm it's this futile attempt at rescuing Governor Tarken's wife that is fouling up the progress."

"I would think that by now you would understand Captain Sanchez better than you do."

"What do you mean?" The Prefect questioned demandingly.

"Captain Sanchez will get every person off that planet even Mrs. Tarken on time."

"The only thing that awaits him is execution."

"I beg your pardon. What for?"

"For holding a Rundi hostage aboard the Phoenix."

"That's enough I'll not let you stand there and accuse my best Captain of kidnapping."

Admiral Griffin got as near to his hooded face as he dared, shoving his pointed index finger into the Prefect's chest with every syllable uttered. He refused to let another fine officer without cause go to the slaughter just to appease some calloused unfeeling alien administrator in order to keep the peace. Griffin was going to make sure that the human race would not be dictated to by anyone else other than their own conscience.

288

"The only reason my ships withdrew and didn't fire on the Phoenix was because we received a distress call from a Rundi that was on board the Phoenix. Had there been no Rundi presence, the Phoenix would now be dust. I want him arrested forth with, and my people allowed to land now."

"That's not the only explanation of why a Rundi is on the Phoenix, maybe you planted a spy to watch him."

"We don't spy. We are not the criminals. Your Captain Sanchez violated the peace accord. Now carry out your orders Admiral."

The Prefect turned and left Griffin alone. Although he didn't want to believe the Prefect, the Admiral couldn't dispute his statement. The Rundi always returned fire when fired upon. The presence of a Rundi was the only explanation, but who or how seemed to revel about his mind like a drunken sailor on weekend leave. He so much wanted to contact Rico and ask, but it was too late. He'd already gone planet side, and Griffin had his orders.

***

Wong and Janet had been working ever since Wong's return from Hyperion without success on the Zeveney 7000-P. It was in many respects like working an archeological dig site with tweezers and a toothbrush. The components of the Zeveney series computers were unlike any other and were formed mostly from crystals. They had to be aligned in a specific order with no flaws. Of the many crystals they had collected so far, half of them contained cracks incurred when someone trashed the system. If the flawless crystal alignment weren't enough, the case they were housed in maintained a precise atmosphere devoid of microscopic contaminates. It was a safe assumption that all the crystals were now growing forests of microbes.

"I need a clean room," Wong commented.

"You need more than that. We may never find some of these crystals," Janet commented from her Sherlock Holmes position on the floor. She peered up through her hand held magnifying glass to meet her beau's frustrated expression.

"There's no way I'm going to be able to repair this system. I might be able to salvage its memory and transfer it into another unit, but this one is D.O.A."

"The Captain's not going to be happy."

"His happiness doesn't change the facts."

"I think the Captain needed to know who destroyed him more than he needed him repaired. To be honest I think he suspects an inside job," Janet suggested.

"I can't believe you think that the Captain believes it was one of our own."

"I guess I really don't, it's just he's so tense and angry. His reputation is one of power and control, not emotion."

"He's been stuck in a room with a politician for days while his ship was taken over by hijackers. He's entitled to some emotion.

Besides, we might be able to find out who did it once I get Zev's memory transferred."

"What's that up there?" Janet questioned, pointing up to an odd device sitting inconspicuously atop a bureau.

"Wong, you're an idiot!" Wong commented aloud to himself.

"No you're not," Janet consoled.

"That thing up there is a remote viewer transmitter. If we can find the memory crystal, I should be able to hot wire it and play back the last few minutes of what happened prior to Zeveney's destruction. At least we'll know who did it."

Glenda C. Finkelstein

Chapter 20

Captain Sanchez returned to Hyperion accompanied only by Sarah, Daphne, and Yeoman Smith as his shuttle pilot. His stay aboard the Phoenix was so brief that he didn't even sleep in his own quarters. He thought it best to leave Wong to the business of repairing Zeveney. Besides, the best he could muster for sleep was a power nap, and even that was fraught with nightmares. Smith set the ship down just a few yards away from Widow's Rock where Governor Tarken and a small handful of militia were waiting for their arrival. If all went well they'd rescue Samantha, take the miners into custody, and Daphne would be left there to await her people's arrival.

Paul walked over to where the shuttle had landed to greet Rico and company. He had never met Dr. Lamb and introduced himself accordingly. Captain Sanchez responded to his initiated pleasantry with his own on behalf of Dr. Lamb. She was courteous, but Paul could tell there was a lot on her mind. To Sarah Smithers, Paul bowed respectfully, but uttered not a word. It was evident to all that Sarah had hoped for more, but under the circumstances was not offended by his silence.

"I was beginning to wonder if you were coming," Paul began.

"I gave you my word," Rico responded with slight surprise.

"When you said you had an ace up your sleeve. I didn't think it would be your ship's Doctor and Mrs. Smithers."

"Dr. Lamb is here in case your wife needs a physician."

"That's thoughtful Captain, but I have one of my own standing by."

"Of course, but what you don't know is that Sarah has agreed to get her husband to cooperate with us," Rico informed. Paul glanced at Sarah. She seemed determined, but he wasn't as convinced as Rico that she'd be anything more than a nuisance. "Have they spotted you yet?" Rico asked, trying to assess the current situation.

"I'm not sure, but considering the noise that shuttlecraft made, they have now."

"Governor," Terry Biggs called, waving his hand to get them to come over to him where there was some cover. He made it clear that he wanted to be by Paul's side when they rescued Samantha from the Miners. It was the least he could do since he felt so responsible for the situation they were now in.

"What is it Terry?"

"Someone just stuck their head out for a peek. They saw the shuttle land."

"Good, it's time we made contact," Paul said, as he started to advance toward the cave.

"Easy does it Fido," Rico commanded, grabbing Paul's arm. Paul just glared at him. "I can't have you becoming a target. If you'll please take your position behind your Security Chief we'll advance together. It would also be better if you let me do the talking."

"Why?" Paul asked, demandingly.

"Because you're the Governor and I'm not emotionally involved with the hostage."

Paul knew Rico was right. Sometimes he really hated being a head-of-state. In this moment he was more husband than Governor. Terry, however, seemed relieved by Rico's command. They moved cautiously across the open area leading up to the cave's entrance. Rico made sure that those inside the cave could plainly see that they were not making any threatening moves.

"That's far enough," announced a voice from inside the cave. The group halted. "What do you want?" The voice questioned. Paul thought the voice sounded familiar, but couldn't put a name to it.

"We want to talk to Manny," Paul announced, cutting Captain Sanchez off. Rico glared at Paul. The Miner made radio contact with Manny, and he authorized a limited number to be brought to him. They could hear Manny's response allowing them to proceed and they began walking again.

"Not all of you," the Miner cautioned, causing them to stop again.

"How about just the four of us?" Rico suggested questioningly, cutting Paul off before he could speak again. The man verified it with Manny before agreeing to the proposed number.

"Okay, four."

Terry attempted to be the fourth man, but Paul refused to be left behind and even Rico didn't argue the point. Rico, Paul, Daphne, and Sarah kept walking forward leaving Terry and the other militia guards standing in the middle of the clearing. They continued inching slowly toward the cave. Upon entering the cave, Paul waved at Terry, indicating the number of guards inconspicuously with his fingers. It gave Terry knowledge that he could use should they need to overpower them and take control of the cave entrance. For now, however, Terry would bide his time. The Miners immediately made sure that none of them were carrying any weapons by padding them down.

Rico and company were led down a winding maze of tunnels. It seemed that they would never come to another chamber much less find Manny and Samantha. They knew they were going deeper because the temperature began to drop. Paul could tell that Sarah was uncomfortable in these tight spaces as she was increasingly jumpy. Sarah nearly came unglued when Paul accidentally brushed her elbow. She turned to find Paul's apologetic expression. After accepting his silent regret, she pulled her outer garment tightly around herself in an attempt to keep out the cold. Finally, they reached a chamber where several men were cloistered together. Although Manny figured that two of the four would be Rico and Paul, he didn't count on a woman or his beloved wife to be with them. Paul surveyed the chamber looking for any sign of Samantha.

"Sarah? What in the blazes are you doing here?" Manny questioned with grave concern.

"Coming to get you," she bantered back. Her voice was thick with disapproval. Manny turned a deaf ear to her. He'd finally got the government's attention with an opportunity to negotiate. He wasn't going to give it up easily.

"Where's my wife?" Paul interrupted.

"Your wife's around."

"Give her back!" Paul exclaimed, lunging toward Manny. Rico was quick to restrain Paul. He resisted at first, but then regained control. Rico released him only after he was sure that he'd stay put. Manny just stepped back allowing Rico to run interference. His men lifted their weapons in response to Paul's action, but Manny ordered them to lower them with an arm gesture. After all, if the circumstances were reversed, he'd be no less passionate about Sarah's return.

"If I do that, what's to stop you from shooting us or leaving us here to die?"

"If everyone would just calm down," Rico interjected, cutting a quick glance at Paul.

"That's cute. A captain whose lost his ship is giving an order," Manny taunted, believing he still had the upper hand.

"I'm not sure who you're talking about. The Phoenix is under my command. Your little raiding party has been arrested, and is on their way to Epsilon 6 Command for trial and incarceration."

"I told you they failed," Jake Summers jabbed.

"Be quiet," Manny insisted, curtly. He had lost his greatest advantage, and didn't want to do anything that could further undermine this last hope.

"The group led by Jeremy Tate is facing murder charges for the killing of Robert Johnson, our navigator," Rico informed.

"You lie," Manny countered. "I only sanctioned stun rounds to be used."

"He's telling the truth," Sarah confirmed. In spite of the fact that Sarah was with them, he knew she'd never lie for them. Manny wasn't about to surrender, even if Sarah did confirm that the information was accurate.

"Even a stun round can be lethal at point blank range," Daphne informed.

"And who might you be?" Manny asked sternly. He understood his wife's presence, but failed to understand this additional female.

"I'm Dr. Daphne Lamb, Chief Medical Officer of the Phoenix. I'm the doctor that tried to save him after your men pulverized his brain."

"That wasn't supposed to happen!" Manny exclaimed. His anger was laced with remorse, but not repentance.

"That's just what your Jeremy Tate said," Rico informed.

"Manny," Sarah began. "Listen to them. Stop this foolishness before anyone else dies."

"We had a good life here Sarah. Why can't they just leave us alone?"

"Because the Rundi need it more," Rico interjected. Daphne looked over at Rico with concern. The Rundi need was far too great to share it with brigands bent on defying a government decree.

"Why?" Manny questioned

"You claim to be protecting your way of life correct?" Rico questioned.

"Yes, I am. We've worked this land, and have built a community. The government has no right to put us out of our homes with no explanation."

"You have a strong belief in family," Daphne surmised aloud.

"Yes, Sarah and I have raised a family of our own, and have built a life here out of nothing. Family is the most important thing in the universe."

"What if I were to tell you that babies have died because they can't get what they need from here?" Rico submitted.

"Babies? What babies? No one said anything about babies dying. If what they need is here, we'll send it." Manny's demeanor switched quickly from revolutionary to missionary.

"The babies need Hyperion."

"Again what babies?" Manny questioned seemingly in vain.

"Rundi babies," Rico stated.

"How is protecting my home harming Rundi babies?" Manny asked. His confusion was evident in his tone and bemused expression. Daphne began to twitch.

"Hyperion is the Rundi nursery. Without it, the infant mortality rate is 100 percent," Rico explained.

"How can that be? The government said nothing about that." Manny looked over at Paul who seemed to be just as confused as Manny.

"I don't believe our own government knows the truth."

"Then how do you?" Manny asked, his shock turning to suspicion.

"The Rundi's reproductive cycle is different from humans," Daphne interjected, remembering Jarvis' comment about human nobility. Besides, secrecy didn't really matter in these closing hours. Her people were coming. "Humans give live birth, but the Rundi lay eggs. Our young need the nutrients found here to survive. They can't be synthesized despite our best efforts. Without Hyperion our children die," Daphne added.

"Our children? How would you know about such things? Is it because you're a doctor that you think you know so much?" Manny was intrigued, but still suspicious.

"No, it's because I'm a Rundi."

Everyone looked at Dr. Lamb in shock. Rico was unnerved by her confession, and feared an immediate reprisal. The men in the room as well as Paul and Sarah were no less shocked by her admission. Yet, none of them reached for a weapon. They seemed more confused than alarmed.

"You look human to me lass," Manny observed.

"Looks can be deceiving."

"You're just saying that to get me to surrender. I don't buy it. Everything seems too noble as if designed to appeal to my sensibilities."

Sarah was unaware of the reasoning behind the surrender of Hyperion to the Rundi so she could neither confirm nor deny to her husband the validity of it.

"Manny Edwin Smithers," Sarah called. This got Manny's full attention. She could see that reasoning wasn't working so she decided to appeal to his survival instincts. "Captain Sanchez has pledged to testify on your behalf if you give yourselves up and hand over the Governor's wife unharmed."

Manny tried to evade his wife's eyes. They were the one thing in the universe that could make him melt and was the reason he'd sent her away in the first place. Yet, there she was pleading with him. His upper lip began to quake.

"You're lying all of you!" he exclaimed lashing out even at Sarah. Although the moment it left his mouth he knew he shouldn't have said it. He stood there with his lip quaking, his gaze locked with Sarah's. She stepped forward and slapped him. He took it without reprisal.

"She speaks the truth," Rico said, taking Sarah by the shoulders and pulling her back. "End this now, while there's still time," he gently encouraged.

"Enough with the whys, where's my wife?" Paul questioned, interrupting this dance of confessed reasons. His tone was neither diplomatic nor calm.

"I can't give you what I don't have myself."

"What?" Paul questioned. He was incensed and didn't bother to hide it.

"It's the truth," Jake added. "The little minx escaped. She's lost somewhere in the tunnels. We've tried for days to find her."

"Be quiet Jake," Manny insisted.

"Will you give yourselves up?" Rico asked, trying to get back to the matter at hand. Manny looked at Sarah.

"It really makes no difference at this point. We can't give you Mrs. Tarken because we don't know where she is. A greenhorn can't last alone for long down here. So I suppose we're looking at two murder charges. All I was fighting for was to keep our way of life, and all I've managed to do is destroy it." Manny's eyes began to water with tears of regret, but kept them from overflowing their levies. He then looked at his men. "Lay down your arms. We're surrendering."

"I can't accept she's dead," Paul insisted, addressing Rico. "We've got almost a day. No one leaves here until we find her," Paul ordered. He wasn't asking for permission, he was invoking his authority as Governor to command the rescue of his wife.

"I hadn't planned on it," Rico said correcting Paul's misguided assumption, and then turned his attentions to Manny. "We're going to need your help to navigate these tunnels," Rico informed.

"We'll help you find her under one condition."

"Although you're in no position to make a request I'll hear it anyway," Rico granted. He needed their expertise to find Mrs. Tarken.

"If we find her, I'll be the only one to face charges."

"I can't promise anything, but I'll do what I can."

"I guess you are an honest man after all. Men, you heard the agreement lay down your arms and grab your flashlights and tools. No one leaves until we find her. Jake radio our surrender to the men upstairs, collect the weapons, give them to Terry Biggs, and get the rest of them down here to help with the search."

"Yes sir."

"I can help you find her," Daphne offered.

"You?" Manny questioned. Although Paul didn't utter a word, he agreed with Manny in this case. "You know nothing of these tunnels."

"I told you I'm a Rundi, and our senses are better tuned than a human's. Besides your well-trained men haven't found her, perhaps she didn't want to be found. I can find her regardless."

The group just looked at Daphne in disbelief of her grandiose claims. She stopped trying to convince them and proceeded to get undressed. This action took everyone, especially Rico by surprise. At first it was just her outer jacket, but then she started unbuttoning her shirt and removing her pants and undergarments.

"What do you think you're doing?" Rico questioned in horror, quickly removing his outer jacket to cover her nakedness.

"It's time for me to shed this outer skin. Remember this image isn't mine, it belonged to your Dr. Lamb," she whispered softly into Rico's ear. His nobility amused her, but it was unnecessary.

The Miners just stood there with mouths agape. Her naked form stood in the midst of them unashamed. Rico still tried to provide some modest screen with his jacket. Then suddenly the beauty that was there began to fade. The skin began to bubble like blisters and chunks of skin started to fall from her body and peel away as someone would peel away a winter coat. There was a brief foul odor that accompanied the process as her body excreted a type of acid and the biomaterial that made up her human looking flesh fell to the floor in smoldering clumps disintegrating into a white powder.

Underneath the human covering was a creature of even greater beauty, revealing a chocolaty brown skin that glistened with an oily sheen. Markings not unlike the most beautiful of butterflies adorn her body. Gone were the mammary glands, but her overall shape was still decidedly feminine. Her face became a graceful countenance of elongated symmetry with oval eyes whose pupils filled the entire socket and lovely markings of blue and yellow that gleamed and shimmered. Her movements were fluid and graceful. Although her vocal cords were well equipped to form the clicks and squeals of her species, they were adaptable enough to form frequencies and sounds that humans could interpret as language. Yet, another reason she was able to pass as a human so well.

Her beauty awed Rico. He had secretly wondered if he had fallen in love with her physical beauty as a human or her soul. Now, seeing her like this, he realized that he had fallen in love with her soul for she was just as beautiful to him now as she was in her human disguise. They set out immediately into the deeper tunnels knowing that they had very few precious hours left. Manny commanded that his wife wait there. The deeper tunnels were no place for her.

***

On the Falcon orbiting Hyperion, Captain Macalister was closely watching the progress of the evacuation. They had fallen behind schedule. The Ares was finally full and Lindsay ordered them back to Epsilon 6 for processing. Theta Sharon Station was still too overloaded to take any more. Although the Falcon, herself, was filled to capacity, Lindsay was not going anywhere until Rico was back aboard the Phoenix and they, too, were ready to leave orbit. Lindsay was also keeping a close eye on the Rundi ships.

"Mr. Bailey, is it my imagination, or are the Rundi ships coming closer?"

Mr. Bailey immediately checked the readings on his console. "Confirmed, Captain, they're coming closer."

"How fast?"

"Three quarter impulse speed."

"They're a little anxious. I don't like it."

"With all do respect, Ma'am, I don't think the Rundi care."

Lindsay let out a snicker, "I think you're right, but do keep an eye on them. At that speed they'll be within our orbit in fifteen hours."

Jim just nodded in the affirmative while Lindsay returned to her chair and looked over the evacuation progress report one more time. They were doing better than this before the storm. The only difference was that Wong Qwan had been the traffic controller. Although there was no time to take him back to the planet, they could switch the hub to the Phoenix. After all, the majority of the people were off, it was just the stragglers left. She knew that Rico had his hands full with the Miner situation and the recovery of Mrs. Tarken. It was up to her to get the evacuation back to full swing so they could retrieve their ground crews too.

"Casey, get me the Phoenix. I want to talk with Wong Qwan."

Casey nodded and soon had Wong on the view screen. Lindsay explained what she wanted, and within a matter of minutes the ground hub was abandoned save for the radar systems that were redirected and fed to the Phoenix. In a matter of minutes, they began to improve the speed at which the shuttles were landing and taking off. Lindsay just smiled, "The man's an artist."

"Captain Macalister."

"Yes, Casey."

"I have a priority communication coming in from Admiral Griffin. He's requesting a secure line."

"This can't be good," Lindsay uttered under her breath. "I'll take it in my office."

Lindsay retired to her office, and opened up the communication console. The Admiral's image was large filling every available space of the view screen. His furrowed brow seemed to speak all by itself.

"Admiral Griffin, to what do I owe the pleasure of this communication?"

"I'm ordering you to cease evacuation in six hours and arrest Captain Sanchez immediately."

"Excuse me?" Lindsay could scarcely believe what she heard. She could tell by his expression that he had never been more serious. "Are you aware that Captain Sanchez is currently with the team that is rescuing the Governor's wife?"

"Yes, I know where he is. The evacuation is taking too long. You need to be done now!"

"We have twenty-two hours left. I'll not allow you to take away the original allotment of time. We're too close to finishing."

"You're falling behind."

"We were, but if you'll check the numbers again you'll see that we have made adjustments and are back on schedule. I'm not going to interrupt the flow to arrest Captain Sanchez."

"This is a direct order."

"What has he done?"

"Kidnapped a Rundi."

"You're joking," Lindsay's disbelief was evident to the Admiral.

"I've never been more serious."

"Rico would never do such a thing," Lindsay defended.

"We have received confirmation that a Rundi is on board the Phoenix. A distress signal was sent from there to the Rundi ships in Rundi and on their frequency. No human can fake that."

"I have served with Captain Sanchez my entire career, and in circumstances that were less than desirable. He'd never kidnap anyone. I cannot and will not believe he's done any such thing."

"Are you calling me a liar?"

"No sir, I'm suggesting that you're mistaken about the facts surrounding this anomaly."

"He's violated the peace accord by holding a Rundi. You will cease the evacuation and take Captain Sanchez into custody."

"What about Mrs. Tarken and the rest of the people?"

"Too many resources have been sent to acquire Mrs. Tarken already. She'll have to be left behind as well as the remainder of the population."

"Over my dead body," Lindsay announced.

"I beg your pardon."

"It's you who should be begging mine. Our people, including those who are rescuing Mrs. Tarken, will be given every second we were originally allotted. I'll not allow the Rundi to land one moment early."

"I'll have you court marshaled."

"Be my guest."

"It doesn't matter whether or not you care about your position. The Rundi are coming now whether you want them to or not," the Admiral informed, hoping she would see reason.

"Then they'll die trying." Lindsay slapped off the communication link and stomped back onto the bridge. At this point she didn't care if her career lay in ruins and the peace treaty not far behind it. She was not abandoning the people of Hyperion or Rico to the Rundi invasion fleet.

"Captain Macalister," Casey frantically addressed. "The Rundi are on the move. They're increasing speed."

"Sound battle stations. Have the Triton and Phoenix continue the evacuation double time. Take us out of orbit and position us to meet them halfway."

"Yes Ma'am" Casey acknowledged. Jim heard the orders and immediately obeyed. Lindsay strutted around the bridge with an all business attitude stopping briefly at each station. She was ready to kick butt and take names.

"Captain, it's the Admiral again."

"I'm not home. Close the signal down and keep me in touch with the Triton and Phoenix."

Casey hesitantly complied, hanging up on the Admiral. She then blocked the Epsilon 6 official channel and opened lines to both remaining ships. Commander Jarvis examined the situation. There

310

was no way the Falcon could withstand four Rundi cruisers alone. Commander Jarvis tried futilely to contact Rico on the surface, but Rico and company was too deep inside the mountain. Jarvis also had his orders to stay put and complete the evacuation. In Rico's absence, Lindsay was the officer in command and he was compelled to follow her orders.

"What's going on? Why is the Rundi fleet moving in ahead of schedule?" Jarvis asked. The Triton Captain listened intently for he, too, needed to know the answer.

"Rico's been accused of kidnapping a Rundi. They say that gives them the right to move in ahead of schedule."

Jarvis just leaned back knowing that it was a lie, but understood why they got that idea. What saved them last time won't save them again. Besides Daphne was on Hyperion and there was nothing to stop them from shooting this time.

"That's not true," Jarvis defended.

"I know that, but we have to find a way to stop the Rundi from coming in too soon. You'll probably be ordered to take over for me and fulfill the Admiral's orders."

"You're my commanding officer in Rico's absence," Jarvis acknowledged.

"Mine too," Captain Spencer added.

"Remind me to give you both commendations in whatever service we may find ourselves serving in. I don't want to start another war, but I will if I have too. I'll not abandon those people or Captain Sanchez."

"What about using the Loki mines? You can position them a good distance out to buy us some time before being forced to engage," Captain Spencer suggested.

"Yeah, that just might work. All we need is to keep them at bay long enough to get our people out of there. Phoenix, did you copy that?"

"Yes, Captain Macalister. We'll deploy to your left flank, if the Triton will cover your right flank, you can cover the front. That should slow them down especially if you set them up far enough out to buy us some time before they reach firing range."

"Agreed, thanks for the input gentlemen. Jarvis, do you have any word on Captain Sanchez's progress with the Miners and Mrs. Tarken?"

"Negative, they're too deep inside the mountain to make contact. I did, however, alert his shuttle pilot Yeoman Smith to our situation."

"Good. Do what you can to hurry them along, and say a little prayer. We'll need all the help we can get. Also, there's no time to take people and luggage too. Whoever is left must leave everything behind that way we'll be able to double up on the capacity for each shuttle. I don't know how long we can successfully hold them off."

"Consider it done," Commander Jarvis confirmed.

"Casey open hailing frequencies."

"Open Captain."

"Attention approaching Rundi vessels. The human evacuation is continuing. We have twenty-one hours and fifteen minutes left on our designated allotment of time. Do not come any closer. If you do, you will be fired upon. I do not wish to engage your ships, but I will defend our right to remove the colonists prior to your acquisition of Hyperion. I say again. Halt your advance until the human colonists have been evacuated."

Nothing but silence greeted Captain Macalister's ears. She watched the view screen and waited to see if they were going to respond to her. She motioned for Casey to mute the Rundi hailing frequency.

"Jim, are the Rundi ships stopping?"

"No, but they have reduced speed considerably."

"How is the mine deployment coming?"

"They're almost in place."

"At the speed the Rundi ships are traveling. How long before they encounter the mines?"

"If their current speed remains constant, you bought us an additional six hours."

"Six is better than none."

Glenda C. Finkelstein

Chapter 21

The Admiral was incensed by Lindsay's refusal to obey his orders. His authority amounted to nothing. He had no power to refuse the Rundi demands, and he had little sway with his troops who openly ignored him. Truth be told, this was one time he was glad to be ignored. Yet, at the same time it grated against him. He didn't want the Rundi to take Hyperion any second sooner than Lindsay did. The Rundi Prefect was outraged by how little command Griffin held over his own people, but his temper tantrum held little consequences in the Admiral's office. The Prefect retired to his own quarters to brood. This peace accord was becoming more intolerable with each passing moment and Griffin wanted to regurgitate every directed order he followed up to this point.

The Rundi would reach the mines Lindsay had deployed to slow them down in just three hours. These little beauties would return fire instantly the moment an enemy vessel acquired target lock using the exact same levels it would receive along the same trajectory. This would cause a feedback within the weapons systems of the firing ship rendering it inoperative. The Loki mines were developed near the end of the Rundi war so they hadn't been used too often. In any case their strangeness was enough to make the Rundi think twice about engaging the human ships immediately.

The Rundi couldn't afford to be too hasty. Their cargo was too precious to risk an engagement, but the fear that the humans wouldn't leave nipped at their heels. Despite the fact that Lindsay and the others didn't know the real reason why the Rundi had slowed their progress, it was enough that the mines bought them much needed time to complete their mission.

The Triton signaled that they were now full so Captain Macalister ordered them back to Epsilon 6 with their cargo of refugees. The Phoenix, although half full to capacity with refugees, was simultaneously loading the remainder of their ground crew. Each shuttle full brought them that much closer to being ready, but there was still no sign of Captain Sanchez or news of the Governor's wife. This weighed heavily upon all of them. They tried scanning the surface from orbit, but the tunnels were too deep to be seen by even the most intense scans. They had to wait. Unfortunately, Rico believed he had far more time than he actually did.

***

Deep inside the mountain Daphne was using her finely tuned abilities to search for Mrs. Tarken in ways humans couldn't. All Rundi were equipped with sonar ability. This capability enhanced their vision in darkness due to the fact that the sonar receptors converted the sound into sight. She had searched for several hours with the aid of Manny and his men, but it was becoming futile. They were running out of tunnels to explore and then, just by chance an odd sound returned to Daphne. Further investigation indicated that there was an underground river flowing not far from their position. The rushing water was interfering with her ability to locate Samantha. Yet it wasn't just the water that had unnerved her. They had experienced several minor tremors, and the Miners were carrying on in hushed whispers about the possible outcomes of this search.

"Please be quiet," she ordered.

They immediately stopped their conversations. Another tremor hit and they could feel the vibrations under their feet. It was stronger than the others. Small rocks and sand fell from upper chambers through holes and fissures that older quakes had opened. Rico was unnerved. He was used to being in outer space not under the ground. Waves of fear of being crushed under the rocks began to sweep over him. Only his military training allowed him to maintain his outward level of calm. The Miners began talking again about the need to be quick. They didn't want to wind up buried so far inside the mountain.

"I said be quite!" She repeated, harshly. The men ceased their talking like school boys obeying a strict teacher. Even the tremor seemed to obey. She concentrated for a moment. The rushing water was interrupting her senses similar to a television screen having static. It seemed like she took a long time, but she had to isolate the interference in order to focus her vision. Perhaps then she could see clearly enough to hone in on Mrs. Tarken. Daphne surveyed the chamber again this time with clearer vision. A few yards away was a pile of rocks that had fallen through from the chamber above no more than a day or two ago. Near the bottom of the pile was Samantha Tarken. She'd almost missed her.

"There she is!" Daphne informed. The men immediately responded to her announcement by shinning lights on the subject. Her voice was timbered to squelch any excitement. She could tell that Samantha was not fully conscious and was pinned under several pounds of rocks. She was badly injured.

"Sam!" Paul yelled out darting forward. Manny grabbed him.

"Hold on, Governor. You better let us get her out. There are more rocks that could come a tumbling down any moment. Too many of our colonists need you."

Manny turned his flashlight toward the ceiling of the chamber. The rocks were still dribbling from above. A few more inches and the ground would give way to a large boulder precariously perched on the edge. They worked against time and the forces of nature methodically digging her out. Another seismic quake began to rain sand and larger pebbles as they dug. The boulder wobbled slightly, but it still maintained its position high above them. Manny urged his men to accelerate their progress. They were running out of time.

They finally freed Samantha and pulled her from the rubble. She was badly hurt. Manny scooped her up in his arms just as another more powerful seismic tremor hit. They barely got out of the way as the remainder of the back ceiling came tumbling down. Jake, however, wasn't fast enough having stepped into a crevice. He couldn't free himself. One of Manny's subordinates saw it, but things happened too fast to go back for him.

"Manny, it's Jake!"

Manny turned around with Samantha still in his arms. In the time that it took him to turn around it was already too late. He was helpless to save him as the boulder fell upon him squelching Jake's cries for help. The men ran toward the safety of the tunnel opening. Once inside the tunnel, Manny handed Samantha to Paul. They all coughed bitterly trying to clear the dust from their lungs. Paul pulled Samantha close to himself and kissed her forehead. She opened her eyes. They were weary, but they began to brighten slightly when she realized that it was Paul who held her.

"What took you so long?" she asked in a dull whisper. In spite of her pain, she managed a weak smile. He smiled back. The exertion of that small thing caused her to slip back into a deep sleep.

"Come on, we have to quicken our pace. It isn't safe," Manny insisted.

They began the long treacherous journey back to the surface. A couple of Manny's men were injured and bleeding. Daphne could tell that if they didn't stop Peter's bleeding soon, he wouldn't make it to the surface.

"We must stop," Daphne announced.

"Why?" Manny questioned.

"Your man is about to bleed out."

"Peter?" Manny questioned. All of a sudden Peter passed out.

"I need someone's shirt," Daphne informed kneeling down to tend to his wound. Manny immediately took his off and handed it to her. It was full of dust and sweat, but it would hold the wound closed until they could get him to the surface. Manny and Rico hovered over her.

"It won't hold for long, but it may get him to the surface. He'll need to be carried."

"I'll do it," Rico announced.

"No," Manny interrupted. "I'll carry him." Manny wasn't taking no for an answer. This was his man. He was responsible. The word *responsible* clanked around his brain for a while. It had a bitter aftertaste.

"As you wish," Rico said, stepping back.

Manny bent down and prepared to lift Peter over his shoulder. Although Manny was in his late forties to early fifties, his muscle tone was as good as any twenty-year old, a benefit of his occupation. His well-defined muscles rippled with each movement. Even though Manny was well up to the task, Peter was a big man and was cumbersome to carry. They continued to make their way to the surface.

The journey was becoming more arduous with each passing step. Rico could tell that Paul was getting tired. He offered to carry Samantha for a while. Paul was grateful, but refused the gesture. He thought to offer his aid again to Manny, but Rico wasn't up to the task of carrying such a huge man as Peter through these tight corridors.

On the surface, Yeoman Smith was facing a barrage of hails from both the Phoenix and the Falcon. At this point Rico and the others were still too deep for radio contact, and she was panicked to think that the Rundi were on their way. Lisa didn't know that they had found Samantha and were working their way back up. All she could do was relay that their status remained unchanged.

Glenda C. Finkelstein

At this point, they were the only people left on Hyperion. Her orders were clear. Stay until the rescue team returned. Standing alone just outside the ship she couldn't even see the Militia guards posted at the cave entrance. It was an odd sensation to think that on the entire planet she was the only one on the surface.

Another underground tremor hit. This time it was shallow enough that Lisa could feel it. Even though the tremors were nothing dangerous above ground, she was quite unnerved that her people were still underground. Little did she know how right she was as the last shockwave caused a cave-in which blocked their escape to the surface. A call for help went up from the behind the pile of rocks. The Miners had men stationed at various places throughout the maze to mark the way out. Since these tunnels were uncharted the biggest danger prior to the tremors was getting lost.

The men stationed at the next turn heard their cries and notified the next few in the tunnel to come help. They came quickly and began to dig them out. While they were digging, Lisa became frightened by the solitude and the impending early arrival of the Rundi. She ran to the cave entrance leaving her post to find out for herself the status of the rescue team. The hails from the Phoenix who recorded the tremor now languished in ignorance of their safety.

"Yeoman Smith, are you there?" Jarvis called to an empty shuttlecraft. "I'm going down there," he announced aloud to his own bridge crew. The ship-to-ship open communication channel caught his statement.

322

"No, you're not," Captain Macalister ordered.

"I can't reach anyone now," Jarvis explained.

"I know," Lindsay added.

"There's only an hour left when there should be six," Jarvis reminded.

"I don't need to be reminded of how long we have left before we're forced to engage the Rundi. No one is to go down to the planet."

"Why?"

"They are all that's left. If they don't make it off, then the losses are minimal," Lindsay explained. Part of her couldn't believe those words left her mouth, but it was a sound decision.

"I can't believe you just said that."

"Believe it mister. You want to give them the best chance at survival? Then stay at your post. I can't hold the Rundi off by myself. Captain Sanchez can handle himself."

"You're right," Jarvis said, plopping back down into the captain's chair. He hated that she was right. At this point it would only aggravate the situation and put more lives in harm's way.

***

Yeoman Smith reached the cave. She was on the verge of an emotional breakdown. Never did she think she'd be in a situation like this. She was an administrative assistant for goodness sake, not a seasoned combat officer. Terry Biggs greeted her at the entrance.

"Woman, what are you doing here?" he asked, grabbing her by the upper arms. She pulled away. Her nervousness and fear was apparent.

"The Rundi are coming," she uttered. Her voice quaking.

"Yes, we know the Rundi are coming."

"No, you don't understand. They're coming now!"

"What?" Terry questioned.

"You heard me," Lisa jabbed.

"They're not due yet."

"Yeah, well things have changed. Where are the captain and the governor? Where are the Miners?"

Her distressing news and her demanding questions were more than he could deal with. He entreated Sarah to step in to deal with her.

"Yeoman," Sarah began.

"My name is Lisa."

"Lisa, your Captain, the Governor and Mrs. Tarken are on their way back to the surface as we speak. There was a cave in that happened just a of couple levels down. The miners are digging them out now. Try to calm down."

"Calm down?" she questioned as tears began to flow from her eyes. "No one was reporting in. Everyone was hailing me, and then the tremors started. I had to find out what was going on."

"It's okay child. I'll walk with you back to the shuttle to make a report. That should help put everyone's fears to rest," Sarah offered.

"You don't understand the Rundi are coming in less than one hour."

"The men are digging as fast as they can," Terry informed. "As soon as they are out, we'll get them to the shuttlecraft."

"Okay," Lisa nodded. She was still breathing pretty heavy and fast. She wiped the tears away that had erupted so suddenly. She didn't begin to calm, however, until they reached the shuttlecraft. Sarah waited to see if Lisa would open hails, but she didn't. Sarah then took control of the situation.

"Commander Jarvis, are you there?" Sarah asked, opening the hailing frequency. Jarvis was confused at first when he didn't hear Lisa's voice.

"Mrs. Smithers?"

"Yes, Commander."

"What happened to Yeoman Smith?"

"She's right here with me. She had a bit of a fright, but everything is okay."

"What's your progress?"

"You're not much on pleasantries are you?"

"We're out of time."

"Yes, so we've been informed. They have found Samantha Tarken, the Miners have surrendered, and they're on their way back to the surface."

"They need to hurry up."

"Yes, we know, but there was a cave in blocking their egress. The Miners are digging them out now."

"Casualties?"

"None that I'm aware of save Ms Smith's nerves." Sarah smiled, patting Lisa's arm as she said it. She wanted to reassure her that everything would be okay. This wasn't the first time that Manny had been trapped behind a collapsed wall. Although under the circumstances, she knew it'd probably be the last.

"Do you need assistance?"

"No. The tunnels are very small, and we already have the experts here."

"Do they know they're out of time?"

"Yes, Commander, they're aware. However, you can only dig so fast."

"Thank you for the report. Have Captain Sanchez notify us as soon as they're aboard the shuttlecraft."

"Of course Commander shuttlecraft out."

Lindsay, who had been listening in, was relieved. Her faith in Rico was always well placed. She relayed the circumstances of their last group on the surface to both the approaching Rundi vessels and Epsilon 6 Command, but neither responded. She maintained her position refusing to give way.

Glenda C. Finkelstein

Chapter 22

Not long after their communication with the shuttlecraft on the surface, the Rundi vessels arrived at the Loki mines deployed by the Falcon, Triton, and Phoenix. They halted their progress. Their time had run out and no additional reports of success from the shuttlecraft were forthcoming. The Rundi ships just sat there ominously hovering in place. No probes were launched. No hailing calls. Nothing was happening. A strange silence fell upon the Epsilon ships. No one spoke as if that sound would signal an attack from the Rundi.

Unbeknown to Lindsay and the others was that the Rundi vessels were in the same predicament. Their cargo of pregnant females was not the horrific invasion force imagined by the humans. In like manner, the Rundi couldn't fathom the fear the humans felt at the thought of losing those still on the planet should they land. So they, too, waited in paralyzed silence.

On the planet Rico and company made their way out of the tunnels. They limped back to the shuttlecraft carrying their wounded. Upon reaching the craft, Yeoman Smith's relief to see Captain Sanchez and the last of the Hyperion refugees was evident upon her face. She was delighted that they had all made it out safely and stepped out of the vessel to greet them. They were filthy. The whites of their eyes seem to glow, set inside dust encrusted faces. As she scanned the people boarding the craft her eyes fell upon the Rundi that she didn't know was amongst them. Lisa was caught off guard by the sudden appearance of this alien. After the trauma that she'd experienced on the ship and the unnerving situation on Hyperion, she just couldn't take any more and passed out believing that the Rundi fleet had already started landing. Rico tried to catch her, but he wasn't fast enough and she hit the dirt with a dull thud.

"Poor thing," Sarah commented. She knelt down beside her to examine her head for any injury sustained in the fall.

"Take her with you and get her strapped in," Rico ordered.

"Of course Captain, but you better contact the Falcon. The Rundi fleet is closer than they should be." Sarah said as she obeyed

330

his order. With the help of Terry Biggs, Sarah got Lisa to a chair and strapped her in. Rico turned his attention to Daphne. He gazed upon her beauty attempting to etch it upon his retinas. In this moment, he had no regrets for taking the time on the ship to say farewell properly. Goodness knows they didn't do it on the beach. In comparison between the two farewells knowing why made the pain of separation more manageable. He knew this would be the last time he would see her. He didn't want to leave her there, but he knew he had to.

"Thank you for keeping your word," Daphne began, seeing that Rico was momentarily lost for words. She could tell that his duty was now urgent and she had to fade quickly out of his mind and life.

"Thank you Daph— Zarta," Rico finished with her true name. She smiled. He then climbed into the cockpit and opened the hailing frequencies to make contact with the Falcon. "Falcon do you read? This is Captain Sanchez."

"Rico!" Lindsay yelled through the communications channel accompanied by a visual image. She immediately began to chastise him. "Where have you been? Why did the Admiral want you arrested for kidnapping a Rundi? Why did you take so long? Why didn't you keep in touch?" She asked. She fired off her questions in rapid secession like an automatic pistol without taking a breath, nor allowing for a response. Zarta was still hovering in the doorway.

She lingered because she really didn't want to say goodbye either, but knew it was their destiny to go their separate ways.

"Lindsay!" Rico greeted with a smile, his white teeth glowing amid the dust. "I think that's the first time you've used my first name."

"What?" she questioned in bemused frustration. He obviously didn't understand the levity of the situation.

"Hold for just a moment," Rico said. After muting the microphone, he turned his attention toward Zarta. "I'm going to need your help with the authorities," He requested, knowing Zarta overheard the conversation.

"When my people land I'll make something up as to why I was on your vessel that will not compromise you or Conrad. By the time you reach Epsilon 6 Command the kidnapping charges will be dropped."

"Thank you, from both of us."

"Captain," Jarvis interrupted, trying to re-establish communication with Rico. His rich voice muted the noise inside the shuttlecraft. "We have a real touchy situation up here."

"Report," Rico commanded.

"The Falcon and the Rundi are nose to nose. Captain Macalister had to deploy Loki mines to slow them down."

"Have there been any casualties?" Rico asked.

"No," Jarvis replied. Rico expelled a sigh of relief. He glanced over at Zarta who was understandably nervous.

"Where do we stand with the evacuation?"

Lindsay piped in, "You're all that's left sir."

"Then recall the mines, allow the Rundi to pass, and withdraw to a safe distance immediately."

"But Sir, I'm not leaving without you."

"No buts, by the time you recall all the mines. We'll be in orbit and docking with the Phoenix."

"Aye aye, Captain."

Rico closed the channel and turned to take one last look at Zarta. Their eyes said everything their words could not. She stepped off the ramp as Rico closed the doors. He looked at the console and rubbed his hands together.

"Well, it's been awhile, but I still have my pilot's license," he said, grinning with glee.

The passengers were less than enthusiastic, as his bumpy take-off confirmed their fears. Zarta backed far away from the shuttle and watched it until it was no longer visible and waited anxiously for her people to land. The Rundi ships passed slowly between the Falcon and the Phoenix without a single shot being fired. It was an ominous sight to watch the crossing from the vantage point of the shuttlecraft as the heavily armed Rundi cruisers passed just meters over them. Everyone simultaneously expelled a sigh of relief after they had gone by.

Before docking with the Phoenix, Captain Sanchez made it very clear that no one was to discuss the transformation of Dr. Lamb to that of Zarta. If they were questioned about what happened to Dr. Lamb, they were simply to respond that she was lost in the mines on Hyperion in the rescue of those injured. The statement was indeed true with the exception that the real Dr. Lamb perished a little over two months ago. Rico wasn't sure how Zarta would explain herself and get him off the hook, but he would be careful to honor her trust so she would not experience any repercussions. After all, he had no idea how the Rundi would react to her helping humans.

Even though their peoples were at peace, Rico still wasn't convinced that it was a lasting peace. It was thoughtful for Zarta to remember Conrad's memory as well. His reputation had seen enough damage. In all the commotion he'd nearly forgotten his pursuit of the truth concerning Conrad. His heart flinched that it could have ever taken a backseat in his consciousness. Although he now knew the full truth about Hyperion, Rico wondered just how many other truths still waited to be uncovered. It was much clearer now why the war started and was probably the same reason it ended. Although it still shed very little light on how Conrad fit into this picture. His best friend's involvement in this situation still ate at his gut like a parasite. There was still a huge piece missing to this puzzle.

As they began docking maneuvers with the Phoenix, Rico wasn't convinced one way or the other that these people would keep silent about Zarta. He had no authority over them, but he hoped that they would cooperate. Most of them would be secluded in the brig with no exposure to the general population. In addition, they were probably too worried about their own hides to talk about a forbidden subject. If keeping quiet about their Rundi encounter were in their best interest, they'd probably do it. In any case he would make certain that this gag order was an essential element of leniency.

After seeing the Shuttlecraft had docked safely, Jarvis signaled the bridge to withdraw from orbit and set a course for Epsilon 6 Command. He then left the bridge to greet Rico and company personally. Jarvis met the Captain in the docking bay with a full security detachment to escort the Miners to the brig. He also brought medical personnel to deal with the injured.

"Welcome back Captain," Jarvis greeted, giving a formal salute to his returning captain. Rico saluted back, but it lacked the energy that normally accompanied his demeanor.

"Thanks, Commander. I'm just glad to be here on my ship, and back in space."

Jarvis was quick to note that everyone was covered in brown dust so thick that it was hard to recognize anyone. He tried to figure out who was who, but it was nearly impossible. Their introductions waited until medical personnel secured Samantha Tarken and the two injured miners. Rico motioned for Terry Biggs to come up to the front.

"This is Hyperion's Security Chief Terry Biggs. Terry, this is my first officer Commander Edward Jarvis."

"Pleased to meet you, Sir," Terry greeted, sticking out his hand for Jarvis to shake.

"Likewise," Jarvis responded, looking down at the grime and filth on Terry's hand and flashed a smile. Terry looked down at his hand and realized why Jarvis was so hesitant to take hold of his outstretched hand. He chuckled, and smiled back then bowed in place of the handshake.

"Perhaps I should get cleaned up first," Terry suggested, his teeth gleaming in contrast to his earthen face.

"My men will escort the prisoners to the brig. We have facilities to get them cleaned up and processed. We also have some extra quarters for yourself and your officers," Jarvis informed, bowing in response.

"Very good Commander. Men, help the Phoenix crew identify the prisoners and then report back to me for a shower."

"Yes, sir," they responded in unison.

The Hyperion security detachment went to work straight away. The Miners were at this point tired, and were no trouble to get them where they were supposed to be. Jarvis' men affixed restraint cuffs on them and escorted them in an orderly fashion to the brig.

"Joe," Jarvis called to his security man.

"Yes Sir."

"Please make sure that Terry and his men are made comfortable."

"Aye, Sir."

Now that Jarvis was satisfied that the formal duties of securing the prisoners and visitors were dealt with he turned back to Rico. "Would you like me to brief you now, or would you prefer to get cleaned up first?" Jarvis asked.

Rico looked down at his own hands that were nearly the same color as Jarvis' hands. He then caught a glimpse of himself in a reflective surface. He was a wreck. Now that the adrenalin had worn off he could feel the sand next to his skin. It began to itch and scratch in places that ought not to have any chafing.

"I think I'll get cleaned up then you can tell me what the hell happened up here."

"Yes Sir." Jarvis saluted his Captain as he retired to his quarters, but paused. "Sir, what is the official word on Dr. Lamb?"

"She died in the line of duty. I'd like for you to start the paperwork for a commendation," Rico requested. His tone was reverential for the life that the true Dr. Lamb saved and those her benefactor rescued from certain death.

"Will do."

Jarvis lingered behind long enough to make certain that everyone had disembarked the Shuttlecraft. He noticed Sarah Smithers sluggishly looking after her husband from a distance. Although Jarvis had never seen Manny, the melancholy expression upon her face gave his identity away. She waited patiently until the restraints were fixed upon Manny's wrists before standing to her feet. Manny, avoided looking at her. He was openly ashamed and mournful. Jake, a family friend, had died right in front of his eyes because he couldn't follow the Epsilon 6 direction to evacuate.

Sarah trailed behind the security guard escorting her husband with her head hung low. Jarvis reached out and gently took her by the arm. She wasn't quite as dirty as the rest of them, but you could see where silent tears had cleared a path down her dusty face. She was reluctant to meet his gaze. He'd have every right to be condescending with her, but he wasn't. There was compassion in his eyes so merciful that she broke down and sobbed upon his chest. Manny heard her sobs and turned to look upon his wife. He knew he was the cause of her sorrow. He was not in a position to comfort her, and he was grateful that Commander Jarvis did. Yet, his heart was pricked because he was the one who was supposed to comfort her, and couldn't. Of all the things in the universe he'd lost, the one thing he couldn't bear to lose was her love.

The guard allowed a brief moment for Manny to look at his wife, but then urged him forward. They had a schedule to keep. Sarah didn't turn around, and Manny didn't call after her. Manny continued without further prodding with a tear welled up in his eye, but commanded it to stay put. Sarah pushed herself away from Jarvis' massive chest, but didn't turn to follow her husband this time. She couldn't bear to watch the love of her life being led away.

"Why don't you get cleaned up?" Jarvis suggested. Lisa, having just come to moments earlier hovered close to tend to Sarah, like Sarah had tended to her.

338

"I should go to the brig."

"You don't belong there. You're tired. I've prepared guest quarters for you. I even got some lavender bath salts set aside for you, compliments of one of my staff."

Feeling a presence close by, Sarah turned around and saw Lisa. She smiled at Sarah with a kind, healing sort of smile. Sarah was taken aback by their hospitality to the wife of the man who instigated the whole revolt. The crew of the Phoenix had no cause to show her kindness, but she was grateful for it nonetheless. For the first time in her life she felt very alone.

"You don't strike me as a family man. How do you know what a woman likes?"

"A long time ago I, too, had a wife. She loved lavender, especially when she was tired or upset with me."

A weak smile broke the sullenness of her face. "Past tense Commander?"

"My wife died several years ago. Manny didn't die. He's going to need you."

"Part of me is so ashamed and embarrassed. The man that you've arrested seems like a stranger to me. His actions caused a lot of good people a lot of pain."

"True and he will have to live with that for the rest of his life. He does, however, have one thing in his corner."

"What's that?" she asked, sniffing back some snot before it ran out her nose.

"He has a good wife. A wife that has the power to bring back that man she loved."

Yeoman Smith, who had been hanging back, came up alongside her and took hold of her arm to help her to her quarters. They walked a little ways before Sarah stopped and turned around.

"Thank you, Commander."

Jarvis smiled kindly at her. She then turned back around and went with Yeoman Smith. He gazed after her until she was out of sight before tending to his own duties.

***

Upon entering his cabin, Rico was appalled at the pile of shattered crystals strewn across the floor. He nearly jumped out of his skin when Wong stood to attention. Rico hadn't noticed him in the corner of the room still hovering over a pile of crystals. Wong looked at Rico and barely recognized his captain underneath all that dirt. He had been waiting for him in silent dread.

"Captain, it's good to see you back aboard."

"At ease Wong. When you said that Zeveney had been destroyed, I had no idea it was this bad."

"I can't repair him sir. Even if I hadn't been taken away from this project to put us back on schedule with the evacuation, I still would have been unable to repair him. I have been able to salvage his memory, and I can transfer it into another unit, but it'll never be the same computer companion that you knew."

"Any luck with finding out who did it?"

"Yes sir. I was able to pull the information off the security feed."

"Has security reviewed it?" Rico asked. Although he was curious, he was also tired, hungry, and very dirty.

"No, Sir. I thought it best that you view it first. You may not wish to turn it over to security after you see it."

"I don't understand."

"You will when you view it, Sir."

"Why so cryptic?"

"It'd be better if you take a look for yourself. I'll not be far should you need me."

Wong turned and left without another word. After seeing what was on the tape, Wong wished he hadn't. Knowing the humanity of one's Captain is not a person's first choice. They're supposed to be larger than life, and a notch above the others. To actually know firsthand that the Captain is just as human as any man is sobering for his troops. Then of course, there was the knowledge that could turn everything upside down including the peace treaty. He returned to his post as if in mourning leaving the Captain to his own discovery.

Rico was concerned by Wong's actions. Although his body cried out for that warm shower, his mind demanded he view the recording. He looked at the recording crystal and loaded it on a desktop view screen. He soberly watched the events that took place in his room while he was marooned down on the planet unfold before him. At first it was just images of his room then Dr. Daphne Lamb entered.

"Dr. Lamb," Zeveney greeted.

"I need an open communication channel that the bridge can't override."

"Why?" Zeveney questioned.

"The ship's been commandeered by hostile forces. They fired at a Rundi cruiser. If I don't tell the Rundi that I'm on board they will fire, and destroy this vessel."

Rico watched as Zeveney began checking out her story as she relayed it, he recognized that irritating hum when integrating into the various ships systems. He was going to miss even that. It was now quite noticeable that it was agitating Dr. Lamb too.

"We don't have the time for you to double check my every word. You have to trust me. I'm the only chance this crew has of surviving."

Daphne looked into his photon formed face. Her eyes pleaded with him. It took a moment, but it decided to comply with her request.

"I've cleared a communication channel that can penetrate the field."

"I need it in a Rundi frequency."

"But such a configuration would render me useless in a few short minutes."

342

"I only need a few seconds. If it's not a Rundi frequency, they won't believe me. Besides it'll only damage your sensory capability. You'll still have full computation mode."

"But my remote abilities will be useless. I won't be able to assist my Captain."

"Rico's a big boy and can take care of himself. Hurry, Zeveney, the clocks ticking." Rico smiled at her comment and continued to watch.

"Very well, it's reconfigured. You may begin," Zeveney capitulated.

"Thank you," she said, and then began to speak in her native tongue.

"You're welcome," Zeveney responded waiting for her to complete her signal. After her transmission Zeveney commented about the drain on his systems. "I feel a little strange."

"I'm sorry Zev, but it was the only way to keep them from destroying us."

"It's okay, but you're not you."

"I beg your pardon?"

"When I scanned you, I noticed another DNA pattern in your system."

"I don't know what you're talking about," Daphne protested. Rico could tell that she was not being truthful with that statement, and so could Zeveney.

"I believe you do. You're carrying within yourself, the DNA patterns of Captain Sanchez."

"You can't tell him."

"I must tell him everything. I'm a Zeveney 7000-P the latest of computer systems designed for military Captains."

"You can't tell him that I'm pregnant and he's the father."

"For humans this is happy news."

"Not this time Zeveney. We aren't supposed to be compatible. Humans aren't supposed to be sentient."

"I see."

"No you don't. If Rico finds out, it would further complicate an already complicated situation. We can never be a family. I don't even know if our offspring will survive. No. It's best that he doesn't know. Anymore than he should know that Conrad was tricked into surrendering his life for a peace that was a pretense to acquire Hyperion. Once my people have what they came for, they intend to attack again. If Rico finds out the truth about Conrad's death, the Prefect will kill him. I can't let that happen. I love him. I can't stop my government, but I can protect the man I love."

With these final words, Daphne grabbed a heavy lamp and began to destroy the Zeveney system. Tears of remorse gushed from her eyes in torrents of despair. She struck the system until she had no strength left and collapsed onto the floor sobbing. In silence Rico turned off the recording. He stared at the view screen with his own shadowy image reflecting back. He was already physically tired, but nothing prepared him for the numbness he felt at this moment.

His mind toyed with the idea that he could turn his ship around and annihilate the eggs and quite probably the mothers from orbit, but they weren't guilty of anything. Genocide was not honorable. He wondered, though, just how long the Rundi would take before launching another unprovoked attack that would destroy the peace that Conrad gave his life to establish. The humans had been used from the beginning, and now that he knew the truth he was most assuredly a dead man. The thought of fathering an alien infant seemed of no consequence at this moment. After all, he'd never be able to see the child. And like she said, it probably won't survive either by design or governmental decree.

"Wong," he called through a communication channel.

"Yes, Captain," came his dead panned response. He could tell by the tone of his voice that he had seen the full recording.

"Come to my cabin."

"On my way."

It didn't take Wong long to return to the Captain's quarters. He entered without knocking, knowing that he was expected. The Captain's demeanor was somber as if he were at a funeral.

"How much did you see?" Rico asked.

"All of it," Wong answered. He was almost ashamed. The contents were intimately personal and equally militarily top secret.

"Have you told anyone about its contents?"

"No, Sir. I thought it best that you make the decision of whom to tell."

"I'm about to place you in a very difficult circumstance that may put you in conflict with the rules of our society and your own conscience."

"My life is yours, Captain. I owe it to you and Captain Banes' memory."

Rico smiled at his level of complete loyalty just as a father would take pride in a son. At least he knew that Wong was willing, and was not feeling coerced. Although he may regret it later, he had to do what he had to do. Rico had to stop another war any way he could. The stench of death from the last one was still strong in his nostrils, and the cost of stopping it was dearer still. All of a sudden the actions of the Miners weren't as terrible as he first thought. They didn't fully trust the peace anymore than he, but at least they had the balls to challenge it. Why didn't he? The self imposed question rattled around his brain like a chain falling down a storm drain.

"Under no circumstances are you to reveal to anyone for any reason the contents of this file, or make a copy. As far as you are concerned you do not know about its existence or its contents. This is binding for as long as you live, and no request, torture or legal obligation can be allowed to force it from you. You will protect this secret even if it means you must die. Do you understand what I'm asking of you?"

"Yes Sir."

"I want you to make a copy of this recording," Rico ordered, testing his response.

"I'm sorry Sir. I don't know what you're talking about. I can't make a copy of something that doesn't exist."

"Good man. You're dismissed."

"Aye, Sir."

Wong left. Rico locked the door after him and headed for the shower. His room seemed emptier with Zeveney gone. In many ways he was more alone than he had ever been in his entire life. Anger, sorrow, contempt, and uncertainty swam around in his head like fish circling a bowl. His clothes were permeated with dirt. He even discovered a pebble lodged in a place that smarted when he removed it. How it got there, he didn't even want to guess. He half expected to be two different colors, but the dust had forced its way through the fabric of his clothes and covered his skin.

He turned on the water. When it finally reached optimum temperature he stepped into its rejuvenating flow. It cascaded over him washing away some of the grime, but he had to lather and scrub his skin hard to get it all off. His mind reviewed every piece of evidence over the past thirty days. Nothing prepared him for what he had just learned, but now he couldn't just hate them for being the enemy. He had feelings for one of them, and fathered another. Yet, for all these emotions, his duty was his driving force. His friend had to be vindicated, and this peace that he gave his life for had to last.

Glenda C. Finkelstein

Though the cost of its survival would be dear, its failure would be dearer still.

For the first time in his life his gut was at odds with his intellect. His gut screamed out for vengeance, but this was not the time. Justice would be a truer comrade in these next few days than vengeance. The military system, however, was not as chased as justice was, and he'd have to find a way through the maze. He could be angry with Zarta for keeping all this to herself, but in hindsight he found her to be very brave. After all, she had no way of knowing how he would respond to this knowledge. He doubted that his knowing earlier would have changed anything.

Even though the shower had revived his body, it was his soul that needed the invigoration. His next decision and his alone would bring long lasting peace or devastating war. He stepped out of the shower grabbed a nearby towel and wrapped it around his waist. Without drying himself he stepped out of the bathroom and onto the living room carpet. The carpet sopped up the water dripping off his body. He glanced over into a nearby mirror and gazed upon his wet body. His chest hair was laying flat against his skin and the hair on his head hung in clumps with water dripping freely from the ends.

"Coffee," he commanded. The silent response was yet another reminder that he hadn't fallen asleep and dreamed these circumstances. Zeveney was gone. He took the towel from around his waist and began drying himself. After getting dressed and combing his hair, he made his way to the chow hall to acquire a cup of coffee. It wouldn't be nearly as good as what Zeveney would make, but the most important ingredient, caffeine, would be there.

His crew greeted him, and he nodded in return with restrained courtesy. Word traveled fast that the Captain was up and about. Jarvis made haste to meet up with him so he could brief him on the particulars of their situation. Rico took his coffee to go and stopped briefly in the hallway to stare out the window. They had entered the dark matter corridor where no light was visible. He often pondered how such a place existed where time and distance have absolutely no meaning. Even though he'd traveled them numerous times, it always seemed to awe him with its expanse of nothingness existing in the midst of normal space.

"Captain," Jarvis greeted. "Good to see you about."

Rico heard him, but didn't acknowledge him right away. He finished his pondering, and then turned to gaze into the worried eyes of his first officer.

"Ship's status?"

"All is well sir."

"Then why do I sense some anxiety in your voice?"

"I'm concerned about your arrest order that Captain Macalister disobeyed. This could end her career before it has had a chance to start."

"Let me worry about that. Besides, it will all be taken care of by the time we reach Epsilon 6 Command."

"I don't mean to dispute you captain, but your voice doesn't express your usual confidence that everything will be okay."

"Then trust my words. I'm very tired."

"If you're tired sir, then take a moment and take a nap. You've earned that."

"I couldn't sleep if I wanted to. I'll be in my office catching up on reports. I don't want to be disturbed until we reach the Epsilon system."

"Yes Sir."

Jarvis turned to leave. "Oh, Jarvis," Rico called.

"Yes Sir."

"Nice job with getting control of the ship back."

"Thank you, Sir." Jarvis saluted this time with a touch of pride that Rico noticed his hard work in this recent crisis before taking his leave.

Rico watched after him. He then began walking slowly toward the bridge where his office was located, sipping his coffee. Jarvis was soon out of sight. Rico himself took advantage of this moment to take in all the sights, sounds, and smells of his ship. Being a Captain was a privilege, and one that would quite probably end when they docked with Epsilon 6 Station. He would miss this, but his commission would be a small price to pay to keep the peace. In his solitude he would rehearse every innuendo and possible direction. He'd weigh every outcome and hoped when he was finished that he'd have a plan that would preserve the peace and restore his friend's honor. Any other concerns at this time were secondary.

Glenda C. Finkelstein

Chapter 23

Zarta stood watching the skies long after the shuttlecraft was out of sight. For a brief time she was the only sentient life form on the planet. She kept gazing into the sky while she walked to make sure that there was nothing that could bear witness of her next action. Before her own ships landed she made haste to find a place to lay her own egg. Fearing reprisal from her people she hid her egg inside one of the manmade structures just inside the town limit. She doubted her people would even care that these buildings stood at this point. She also knew that they would never want to contaminate their young with anything human so she was pretty certain that her

353

egg would remain undiscovered until it was too late for them to do anything about it. Content with the fact that she had done everything possible to insure the safety of her unborn child, she returned to the nearby woods waiting in silence for her people to come.

When the ships first started landing she was anxious to make contact with the Prefect stationed on Epsilon 6. Her attempts to enter one of the shuttles nearly caused her to be trampled to death by her fellow females, some with eggs already halfway out. They needed to nest quickly, and there wasn't time for the usual drama in claiming tiny territories. It was first come first serve or whoever dropped an egg first. In all the pandemonium, no one really noticed her. She had been missing since the Battle of the Breach and was presumed dead by her family.

Once all the females had evacuated the landing pods she looked around for someone to report in with as well as to secure a communication console. No one was interested in her presence. There were thousands of females laying eggs, and all eyes were on their safety. She was amongst her own people and was not considered a threat to security. Since she was not in the midst of any trauma, she was ignored by the male physicians busy with the others and the pilots who were taking a moment to relax.

She walked into the nearest shuttle and took a seat in front of the abandoned communication console and opened hailing frequencies. This was not uncommon for a Rundi female to do after depositing her egg. The Prefect's familiar voice acknowledged the signal expecting it to be a physician reporting in. He was startled to hear Zarta's voice. She identified herself twice before it truly sank in that the one whom he believed was dead was actually alive. After establishing her identity, she confirmed that she had not been kidnapped demanding that the charges against Captain Sanchez be dropped.

"How did you wind up with the humans?" the Prefect asked.

"At the Battle of the Breach I found myself behind enemy lines. The humans were coming toward me. I saw a human female not too many yards back and I transformed into her image. They thought I was their lost crewman. During the past few weeks I've avoided prolonged contact with them so as not to blow my cover. I hopped a ride on one of the last shuttles and hid in the woods until our ships landed," Zarta answered.

"You are certain that your cover wasn't compromised."

"Father, you have known me long enough to know that I would never compromise our people. As a physician I didn't have the ability to terminate myself, all I could do was blend in until I could escape."

"Captain Rico Sanchez never suspected that you were one of us?"

"No, he didn't. Although he is a pain in the thorax, he's not guilty of the charges. We can't charge an innocent person, even a human, with a guilt that is not his. We are better than that."

"I can see how our military got the wrong idea about Captain Sanchez. I will make certain the charges are dropped. I will see you soon when you and I return to Rundi Prime."

"I look forward to it."

"As do I, working with the humans…well I'm not telling you anything you don't already understand. I'm in much need of a respite. Prefect out…"

She breathed a sigh of relief when the screen went dark. The Prefect never asked her if she had laid an egg due to the fact that she was not in the company of her own kind when she would have been fertile. Her egg, in that case would be sterile and rot. Zarta knew that it was still a while before the egg hatched. With the mixing of the species, it may not survive beyond the larvae stage. She'd have to wait just like all the other females. Her mind filled with dread should the child survive, and the questions that would follow. *How apparent would his mixed heritage be?* She wondered. The volume of worries nearly consumed her. The only way she would ever survive this was to force herself to deal with one worry at a time.

Zarta so wanted to be that good little Rundi that never questioned the status quo. Her experiences, however, had led her down another path, one that challenged her core beliefs and prejudices. Even though she knew that her people planned to rekindle their war with the humans, she had time before she was forced to make a choice. Right now all she wanted to do was go home to her family.

***

The Prefect sat at his communications console still in shock that she had survived alone for so long among the humans. He set aside his previous suspicions of Captain Sanchez. He believed that it must have been very difficult for her to live among the humans. He, himself, had issues and he only dealt with one. Any mistakes she may have made that allowed her to wind up with the humans, was penance paid. After terminating the communication, he sat in his chair uttering a prayer of gratitude. Tears streamed from his eyes as the reality that his daughter was alive resonated in his heart and mind.

He wasn't totally convinced that she was telling him everything, but she was his daughter. She had no reason to lie to him. She had to be tired both physically and mentally, and knew that she would fill in the blanks later. He couldn't imagine the difficulties she had to have endured while with them. In any case, he would drop the charges of kidnapping and repeal the arrest order for Captain Sanchez.

When the repeal landed on Admiral Griffin's desk, he was relieved. It didn't, however, alleviate the unpleasant duty that lay ahead of him concerning Lindsay Macalister. She blatantly refused to obey orders. He couldn't let that slide even though he agreed with her. In many ways he hoped the Falcon never returned to port. The disciplinary actions that would fall upon her were severe. She'd be lucky to stay out of the brig, and her term as Captain was permanently over.

Admiral Griffin transmitted the repeal of the arrest orders. Both the officers of the Falcon and the Phoenix breathed a sigh of relief. Lindsay, regretfully, couldn't be totally relieved. She knew her career was all but over. Being Captain was a difficult position. Rico made it look so easy. She knew it wasn't and knew that Rico had his moments. Still her gut insisted she did the right thing. *Her gut!* She nearly fell out of her own chair with that thought.

She'd stand by her decision and accept the consequences that came with it. She had no plans, however, of entertaining any impending doom in her imagination prior to reality presenting its own. She decided to contact Rico and congratulate him on the repeal of the arrest order.

"Hello, Captain Macalister," Jarvis greeted.

"Commander, I'm trying to reach Captain Sanchez, but I'm getting no response," Lindsay informed.

"He's been hold up inside his office for nearly a day. He won't respond to anything, not even a coffee break."

"Sounds like he's brooding again."

"Brooding?" Jarvis questioned curiously.

"Yeah, it's this strange habit of his. He usually does it just before doing something incredibly brave or stupid. Does he know about the pardon?"

"I sent him an electronic notice which he acknowledged. I thought he'd be happy, but nothing. I was just getting ready to call and ask you about his hermit behavior. You've served under him longer than I. What should I do?"

"There's usually a reason for his brood, but for the life of me, I have no idea what that reason could be this time. I typically just let him brood."

"I just feel awkward."

"Don't, he is who he is. If you're coming to him with something that pertains to his duty, he'll let you in."

"And if it's just concern."

"Then you get what you get."

"Sounds a bit like Russian Roulette."

"Feels like it sometimes too," Lindsay added with a smile.

Jarvis just smirked as he closed hailing frequencies. He didn't know what there was about Rico that made him feel so intimidated. The commander could face a fortified hill of Rundi under heavy fire and he didn't quiver as badly as he did barging into Rico's office. After a determined exhale, he pulled himself up by the bootstraps and entered Rico's office.

Rico was not moved by Jarvis' entrance. He didn't even look up from the reports he was reading until Jarvis cleared his throat. Rico gazed up from the reports to meet Jarvis' awkward stare. Commander Jarvis just stood there in frozen silence.

"May I help you?" Rico asked.

"I've come to brief you on what's happened while you were on Hyperion."

"Then do so," Rico invited. He doubted, however, that what he had to say could add to his secret knowledge or alter the course he had to take.

Jarvis fidgeted with his document reader. "Yes, well, Umm."

"Commander, why are you acting like a first year cadet?"

"I'm sorry, Sir. It's just that I was nervous about interrupting your brooding."

"My brooding?" Rico questioned with surprise. "You must have been talking with Lindsay."

"Yes, Sir, I was. It's just you isolated yourself after returning from Hyperion, and I was supposed to brief you but I didn't get the chance to complete the briefing."

"Then brief me."

"Epsilon 6 Command has repealed the arrest order for your person. The remaining prisoners have been cleaned up and are being questioned. Mrs. Tarken has stabilized." Jarvis rattled off in sequence until his breath expired and then stopped talking. He just stared at Rico who listened, but didn't seem to pay attention.

"Is that it?" Rico asked.

"Well, yes. No. Yes."

"Is it yes, or no?"

"Sir, I'm concerned about Captain Macalister. She violated Admiral Griffin's direct orders by refusing to arrest you."

"I'm well aware of that. You let me handle Admiral Griffin."

"I also wanted to find out if Dr. Lamb was really okay. I heard it was pretty bad in the tunnels."

"It's just as I stated in my report. Dr. Lamb died on Hyperion in the line of duty," Rico said with a wink confirming to him visually that his concern was unnecessary. "As for any other concerns, the repeal of my arrest order is proof of a happy ending."

Jarvis understood Rico's cryptic response. Since he knew that Dr. Lamb was a Rundi, he realized that they couldn't take the chance that the Captain's office was clean of spying devices. They had to keep up the ruse that Dr. Lamb was human, if only to protect Zarta.

"I'm sad that we lost her. We owe our lives to her."

"Yes, and she'll have a heroes memorial service when we return to base."

Jarvis stood up. He still looked a bit unnerved. "Sir, are you going to do something brave or stupid?"

Rico laughed. He was both taken aback by the question and entertained by it as well. It felt good to laugh. He couldn't remember the last time he laughed. Jarvis finally laughed too. His relationship with Captain Sanchez had never really been established and the awkward tension was finally broken between them. Although Jarvis wasn't Lindsay, he was a good man who had done a great job.

"Probably a little bit of both. When we return to base I'm going to entrust you with something very special. My orders will sound odd, but I need you trust me even if it sounds stupid. Lindsay will confirm that my stupid can still get us to where we need to go."

"Yes Sir."

"Why don't we go down to sickbay and check in on the Governor and his wife?" Rico asked.

"I'd like that."

They left Rico's office together. It was odd the way they joked with each other on the way. It was like they were drinking buddies. Rico used this opportunity as a release valve allowing all the pressure that had been building up inside him to be released. He couldn't afford to let it continue building. His actions upon reaching Epsilon 6 Command would have to be cold and calculating. He couldn't afford an emotional imbalance that would impede his progress. With any luck he might make it out with his life intact.

Regardless, however, of what happens to him. He couldn't allow the Rundi to get the upper hand by another surprise attack. He owed it to Conrad to try and save the peace. He willingly gave up his life to prove that humans were worth the sacrifice. His love for his fellowman was beyond reproach in that he, who was innocent, allowed himself to be ridiculed and executed so that the rest of humanity could live.

Jarvis' deep belly laugh brought Rico out of his inward journey. His laugh was so infectious that it was difficult not to join

362

in. Jarvis knew that Rico was planning something. He could see it in his eyes. Captain Sanchez's passions ran deep and there was a lot that he wasn't saying. At least now Jarvis felt that Rico could come to him no matter what. He had no basis in words for such a feeling. It was a gut thing. Although Jarvis' gut was not as famous as that of Rico's, it still judged a fellow man truer than any other measuring rod.

Upon arriving at sickbay they were greeted by Dr. Davis who'd been tending to Mrs. Tarken. There was a feeling that something was off in the room. No one else had died. Perhaps it was the absence of Dr. Lamb. Rico could see it in the faces of the nurses. There was a need to express sorrow, but permission had not yet been granted. They were still charged with completion of the mission. Until their patients were transferred to base medical, they couldn't afford a dunk into the pool of emotional loss. He could see their professional detachment in the dullness of their eyes. They were just going through the motions with no real meaning behind them.

Jarvis and Rico could see Paul Tarken hovering over his beloved wife against the far wall. Dr. Davis tried to give them some privacy in the limited sickbay facility. He was trying to be sensitive to their feelings concerning being treated next to those who had abducted her. Rico stepped forward with Jarvis on his heels. His gate and manners became gentler as they approached the couple.

"How is the first lady doing today?" Rico asked, softly and full of encouragement. She gazed up in the direction of Rico's voice. Paul's body had blocked her line of sight and couldn't see them approaching.

"I'm not the first lady any more, Captain Sanchez."

"I disagree. You will always be Paul's First Lady."

"Indeed she is Captain," Paul concurred.

"How are you feeling?"

"I'm sore, but comfortable. Dr. Davis says I'll need surgery for the leg and several months of rehab before I can walk again."

"Mrs. Tarken, were any of your injuries sustained at the hand of any of the Miners?" She looked bewildered by the question. They had kidnapped her. Sensing her confusion, Rico reiterated his question. "Did they abuse you?"

"Captain," Paul cautioned. He was not about to have his wife questioned. Not until she was better. "Can't you question her later?"

"I'm afraid I must know certain things now."

"It's alright Paul," she said reaching for his arm. She had a sense of duty, and she would do her best to fulfill that responsibility. "No, Captain. Other than being kept there against my will, my injuries were only sustained by my own stupidity in trying to escape."

"I disagree. If they had kept their grubby paws off my wife, she'd not be laying here in this hospital bed now."

364

"Manny Smithers sustained losses when he committed his men to the action of saving your wife from a rock slide."

"Manny needs to pay for what he did. His actions hurt a lot of people," Paul countered. His disgust was evident. He harbored a great deal of resentment against the Miners for taking his wife when they had served them so well for so many years.

"True, but he also desires to take sole responsibility for his actions allowing the rest of his men to go free or have reduced sentences."

"What about Jeremy Tate? He ordered your navigator shot producing injuries that caused his death. Are you eager to allow him to go free to grant Manny's request?"

Rico was pricked. Paul was walking a fine line between justice and vengeance. Captain Sanchez was trying to keep them in balance. He thought long and hard before opening his mouth carefully choosing each and every word. "As I told Mr. Smithers in the cave, I would do what I could depending upon the situation. Some of his men should bear a stiffer burden than others. Yet, not all of them are guilty of all charges."

"Guilt is guilt."

"Justice without mercy is just vengeance, and will devour the victim as easily as it devours the perpetrator."

Mrs. Tarken dozed back off to sleep. Paul dared for Rico to wake her. Rico realized that more than just physical healing would need to take place. Perhaps in time, Paul could sift through his emotions and find it within himself to forgive the Miners. Otherwise, he would grow bitter and be ineffective in any public office. He turned around and left with Jarvis.

Their next major stop was the brig. Rico stopped to look over and evaluate the prisoners. Terry was in the interrogation room with Manny. Captain Sanchez stepped inside the observation room where Sarah sat in the darkened room listening to the exchange. Her husband dressed in prison garb and handcuffed to the table. She was now clean with every hair in its place. Her clothes starched and pressed. Her face stained with silent tears mourning the fall of her good husband.

The technicians in the room ignored Rico's presence, but Sarah gazed up at him. No words were exchanged between them, but gratitude and mercy talked freely without the limitations of human speech. Knowing Paul's anger toward Manny and after dealing with his own, he knew that this ordeal would be hardest on Sarah. She would have to face public ridicule for loving a man who made a desperate mistake. Judging by his responses to Terry's questions, he was taking full responsibility for the uprising. That would make things easier, but it would still be a long road. Rico gave a sad smile that emoted compassion as he patted her gently on the back. She nodded her understanding of his gesture as he and Jarvis left.

Even though Manny's little coup failed, his actions brought about knowledge that might have never been known. He may have actually saved more lives than he cost. His intentions were noble, not criminal. Yet, he would spend the rest of his life in prison never knowing the truth primarily for doing the right thing, the wrong way.

Rico, too, was faced with a terrible dilemma. He wondered if he could trust Admiral Griffin, or if he was truly compromised. His plan would have to take both possibilities into account. He couldn't afford a mistake or the humans would be at the mercy of another surprise unprovoked attack. He also didn't want to start a war with the humans as the aggressor. He wanted to keep the peace by getting the Rundi to understand that they were more alike than different, and that Conrad's death was sufficient to prove it for both sides.

Rico continued to tour the ship stopping in at each department to chat with the crew. Jarvis simply walked along side him watching him and engaging in the conversation when it was warranted. When they arrived at engineering, Janet was hard at work. Rico watched her for a moment before announcing his presence. It was like watching a dance rather than work. The moment the crew noticed him they stopped and stood at attention.

"At ease," Rico ordered with a smile.

"Captain!" Janet exclaimed with glee. She immediately left her tools and walked over to him clutching a report scanner in her hands. "I'm so glad to see you. I submitted a leave request for Wong and I. He didn't think you'd approve it, but after this mission the two of us need a break."

"Crewman, mind your place," Jarvis scolded.

"It's okay. She's got a point. I've read the reports. They did well on this voyage and are deserving of a vacation. If you got a copy of the request handy, I'll sign them now."

"Oh, thank you, Captain!" Janet said shoving the report scanner into his hands.

"You just make sure that you and Wong have a good time."

"We will, Sir!"

While no one was looking Rico grabbed a small laser driver, slipped it into his pocket, and excused himself to continue his tour. Jarvis began to notice a pattern developing. His exchanges with the crew were personal, not professional. He thanked each crewman for their diligent efforts in this recent crisis commending them for a job well done. Although Jarvis hadn't known Rico as long as Lindsay had, he was quite certain that this one-on-one personal touch was not his style. Then it hit him. Rico was saying goodbye. Lindsay was right. Whatever Rico was up to was going to be both brave and stupid.

Suddenly an announcement came over the ship-wide intercom. The Phoenix had re-entered normal space and were beginning their approach into the Epsilon 6 System.

"That's our queue," Jarvis reminded.

"You head on back to the bridge. I have one more duty to attend to then I'll join you."

"Very, well. See you on the bridge." Jarvis' smile was genuine, but it was full of questions. Ones he doubted he would get the answers to.

Rico gave Jarvis a farewell salute which was returned with much respect. He waited for him to be out of sight before returning to his own quarters. Upon entering he was reminded yet again of just how alone he was. The room was still a mess. He walked through the shattered shards of glass that crunched under his boot embedding themselves deeper into the carpet fibers. He looked at the boxes that contained Conrad's things and found the box he was looking for. He reached his hand inside and pulled out the bottle of scotch.

He lifted it up to the light gazing through the glass bottle at its amber color. With the bottle tightly grasped in his left hand, he headed over to the cabinet. He rummaged around looking for a glass, but all he could find was a ceramic coffee cup. Rico inspected it. Even though it wasn't a glass, it was clean. He set both the bottle and the cup on the counter. He then opened the bottle of scotch and poured some into the cup. He held it by the cup itself and not the handle. After all, this was scotch, not coffee and some measure of protocol must be maintained.

He walked out of the kitchen alcove and around to the credenza where the photo of he and Conrad stood as a memorial. He picked up the photo in his other hand. He studied it in an effort to recapture that moment in his mind, the smells, the sounds, and emotion of the moment. Although pictures are grand for capturing moments in time, they miss so much. For a brief moment, the laughter of that time from other classmates filled his empty room, but quickly faded as another intercom announcement echoed through the halls of the ship. He had to hurry. Time was growing short.

He set the photo back on the credenza. He took in a deep breath and exhaled it before lifting his cup to his fallen comrade. "To you Conrad, my dearest friend and brother, who gave your life as a ransom for many. Now it's my turn to keep the sanctity of your sacrifice and abandon myself to your cause."

He waited for just a moment for his words to fall into the expanse of eternity. Then he took a swig of the scotch. It was a sturdy mouthful, worthy of the toast to which it was dedicated. He then set the cup down, and reported to the bridge.

Chapter 24

The Falcon was on final approach to the Epsilon 6 Station with the Phoenix an hour behind it. Rico arrived on the bridge in full command of his faculties. Gone was the familial sentiment. The only thing present in his demeanor now was his duty. Jarvis announced his presence.

"Captain on the bridge."

The crew snapped to attention, unless their present task prevented it. Captain Sanchez gave them a cursory gaze stopping at Commander Edward Jarvis. He was impressed with this man. His performance during this crisis showed effective command ability as well as strategic thinking. He demonstrated that he could keep his head without lashing out emotionally. All the qualities a good Captain should possess.

"How close are we to docking?"

"Just under an hour now Sir," Jarvis answered.

"Good, Yeoman Smith, I want you to transmit this message to Admiral Griffin's office in text read out only," Rico ordered, handing her a small piece of paper.

"This message, Sir?" she questioned. The Message simply read, 'I'm coming,' and she wanted to be certain that the statement was his complete message.

"I didn't stutter Yeoman."

"No, Sir, you didn't. I'll send it right now."

"Very good, Yeoman. Commander, a moment in my office."

"Of course."

Jarvis followed Rico to his office. As soon as they exited the bridge, Rico got down to business in a tone barely above a whisper.

"I've come to the conclusion that you are a man that I can trust. You've been faithful to me, and to Conrad. I'm going to entrust you with a very sensitive and delicate mission." Rico paused as he reached inside his pocket and pulled out the recording that Wong had given him. He held it out for Jarvis to take. Jarvis extended his hand and took it. He examined the recording crystal cradled in the palm of his hand.

"What do you want me to do?"

"That depends on what happens to me." Jarvis looked at Rico blankly. "That crystal is the only one in existence. You are not to look at it, or tell anyone that you have it. If all goes well, I'll return to collect it at which time you'll forget that I ever gave you anything."

"If you don't return to collect it?"

"Then you'll take that chip and broadcast its contents in full on every transmission channel we have including those that have been compromised by the Rundi without edit or preview by you. You will see it at the same time everyone else does. You must make sure that the transmission is sent in full, or all that we have achieved to date may be lost."

"I don't understand."

"I have reason to believe that our government may have been compromised by the enemy. If I'm wrong, then I'll be back to collect the chip. If I'm right, then the contents of that chip will be the only thing that saves us from future destruction."

"You found out why Conrad was killed," Jarvis surmised.

"Yes, I did, or at least as close to it as I will ever get."

"There's a lot more going on than anyone realized, isn't there?"

"I can't stop you from expounding upon the possibilities, nor can I elaborate to confirm or deny those at this time." Rico paused a moment. *Damned if he didn't sound like Admiral Griffin,* he thought to himself. He could scarcely believe he spoke those words. Could

373

it be that the Admiral was innocent after all, or was he a pawn in some political game? Rico returned to his conversation suppressing further questions. "I need you here as my failsafe. Do not release the crew except for Wong and Janet until the outcome of my fate is determined."

"The Refugees?"

"You can release them. They've been cooped up long enough. Base security will be by to collect our prisoners, and medical will transfer Mrs. Tarken and the others to the hospital."

"What else can I do?"

"Nothing. Just serve me as you did Captain Banes. That will be more than enough."

"You have my word," Jarvis said, snapping to attention.

***

Admiral Griffin was sitting in his office reviewing reports and pondering how he should handle Captain Macalister's breach of conduct. As much as he didn't want the order obeyed, he couldn't have a Captain in his ranks that wouldn't comply. He really liked her, and felt she was a good officer. Yet if he allowed this breach to go undisciplined he'd be setting a very dangerous precedent.

He was glad the Hyperion mission was finally over, the peace was still intact, and Rico had been cleared of any wrongdoing. Perhaps now the Rundi Parliament would be satisfied, and he could send his Rundi Prefect overseer packing. He'd like nothing better than to get back to the business of exploration leaving the relocation of the Hyperion Colonists to Social Affairs.

His reprieve, however, would be brief. His office would be supplying the evidence for the prosecution in the upcoming Hyperion Rebellion trials, but that was just legal maneuvering, and no war would loom over their heads because of it. Although relieved, he could feel the ulcer that had developed in his stomach over these many weeks beginning to churn over Macalister. He reached into a small cabinet and pulled out a bottle of antacid. After uncapping it, he took a swig right from the container. Griffin made a face that would rival a toddler's first experience with spinach. He capped the lid after taking a second swig, and put the medicine back in the cabinet.

Nancy knocked on his door.

"Come," he called.

"Admiral, this just came over the communication's line." She handed the palm reader to Griffin. He read the message displayed and whom it was from. "Sir, I realize that Captain Sanchez is usually full of himself, but isn't, 'I'm coming,' a redundant statement?"

"This is Rico's way of telling me to keep my calendar clear. My office will be his first stop when they dock."

"Who does he think he is?" She scoffed.

"Captain Rico Sanchez," was Griffin's only reply. He cut a quick smirk to qualify the statement. He was accustomed to Rico's arrogance, and was one of the few men he knew that could cash that sizeable check.

Nancy released a frustrated sigh of contempt for this arrogant Captain. "If he were anymore arrogant, he'd be even more insufferable," she muttered under her breath. "Did you make a decision regarding Captain Macalister?" she asked, knowing that the Falcon was in the process of docking as they spoke.

"Yes, I want a security escort to bring her here to my office the moment docking is complete."

"And if Captain Sanchez arrives while Captain Macalister is with you?"

"Then she'll wait in the waiting room with you until we're done."

"Very good, Sir."

Nancy turned around and left. Griffin knew Sanchez got under her skin. He always seemed to obtain two reactions from women, contempt or avarice. No matter how they perceived his personality, Rico remained true to himself. People either loved him or hated him with no middle ground, but regardless they always knew where they stood with him.

With everything that had gone wrong, Rico still managed to come out of it smelling like a rose. He and his team got the colonists off the planet just in time to avoid another war. Griffin couldn't help but wonder if Rico had found the truth he was looking for and hoped he hadn't. Of course, he could never be sure unless Rico told him.

Perhaps that would be the safest course of action. Don't ask, and he won't have to tell.

Per Griffin's orders a security contingent gathered in the docking bay waiting for the Falcon to open her doors after she completed all safety checks. Nancy alerted Captain Macalister that she would be escorted to the Admiral's office. Lindsay was so nervous that at times she forgot to breathe. She watched her people as the crew made their final checks to verify that the Falcon was secure into the Epsilon 6 dock. Lindsay had never really gotten used to the idea of them being her people until now. It would be a brief realization. She knew that she'd never sit in the command chair again. The only thing she didn't know was how severely command would discipline her.

Now that safety checks were complete, Lindsay's first officer ordered the crew to attention. Regardless of the penalty for doing what she did, this was the crew's way of telling her that they supported her as Captain. There was a pride in their shinning faces as she walked by. She wanted to etch this moment into her memory. This show of respect and honor moved her. She felt a tear well up in her eye, but she dare not let it fall. A tight smile and returned salute was the appropriate response. She walked with head held high off the bridge and to the upper level exit ramp where security was waiting at the bottom.

Several stories below them Lindsay could see and hear the mammoth cargo bay doors of the Falcon opening. The metal moaned and squeaked under the power and weight of its own size. Its thunder rolled through the docking bays spacious facilities. The area itself was fifty stories high and four football fields in length and width, and was one of ten such bays. Echoes from the ships massive doors filled the room to capacity, but was summarily deafened by the exuberant cheers of the refugees disembarking their cramped quarters.

The Refugees poured out of the Falcon like water breaking through a levy. She hadn't realized there were so many. Occasionally a small child would look up into the heights of the bay and see Captain Macalister standing at the top of the crew ramp. They smiled and waved at her. She looked down at them and realized that they were safe because of her. Regardless of what happens to her now, she could honestly say it was worth it. Lindsay then looked upon the waiting security personnel at the bottom of the ramp. She paused momentarily to take one last look at her ship, took a deep breath, and then disembarked.

"We're here to escort you to Admiral Griffin's office," the head guard announced. The guards took up position on all four sides without laying a hand upon her.

"I'm ready," she responded. Her words were in such contradiction to the way she felt, but she was a Captain with all the duty and responsibility that entailed. Lindsay believed for the first time that she truly understood the meaning of the word 'duty'. It seemed so simple when the orders were easy, but it was when they

378

weren't so easy that the true worth of duty was measured. Yet, if she were to be faced with that situation again, she'd make the same choice. She had no regrets. The Service could survive either way, but she alone had to live with herself.

They were nearing the Admiral's office. Her heart beat in rhythm with the steps of her stride. The pounding of her heart got louder and louder in her ears drowning out the thud of her boots clacking upon the marble floor. She thought her eardrums would burst by the time they reached the Admiral's office door, but suddenly the pulsation stopped. Her racing heart calmed. She breathed in deeply then exhaled. She watched and listened to the guard announce their presence.

The calm was deceitful for as soon as the door opened, she could feel her heart thumping in her throat again. She must have looked odd to the guards with her throat bulging each time her heart beat. Admiral Griffin was seated at his desk. The two front guards stepped forward first. She then stepped into the Admiral's office with the rear guard closing her only route of escape. The guards stood at attention waiting for Admiral Griffin's instruction.

"Leave us alone. Wait in the reception area. I'll call you when we're finished."

The men saluted, pivoted, and retreated from the room leaving Lindsay alone with the Admiral. The door finally closed behind them. The sound of the locking mechanism falling into place seemed more like a rifle bolt being pulled back. It might as well be a gun. This meeting would surely end her career. His expression was one of pain like a father shows disappointment in a child. She expected anger. A lump filled her throat. She couldn't even swallow her own saliva. There were times she hated being a woman. A woman's natural tendency to express emotion was not the kind of thing that would benefit her at this moment. *Oh, to have that testosterone fortitude,* she thought to herself.

"Please sit down," the Admiral entreated. She slowly took a seat, half expecting it to administer an electric jolt. After all, this was the proverbial 'hot seat'. She wanted to respond verbally to his kindness, but nothing sounded right upon reaching the edge of her lips. "You do know why you're here?" he asked, his words carefully chosen. His voice was calm, cold, and emotionless.

"Yes Sir."

"Why?" He asked. His question was simple and his tone demanded an answer. She knew he would not tolerate a one or two word response. Lindsay opened her mouth to give him her reasons, but they sounded more like excuses so she closed it. She tried to evade his stare, but he wouldn't allow her. He stood up and walked to her side of the desk. He knelt down peering up with his inquisitive blue eyes straight into her green eyes. His gaze bored down into her soul to retrieve that elusive truth that he had to obtain at any cost. His manner was half pleading and half unfeeling.

"I…" she stammered, succumbing to the weight of his unspoken plea.

"Go on," he insisted after she stopped. It was as if he latched on to the one singular word and would pull on it until the rest of it came out.

"I couldn't obey your order. I knew Captain Sanchez wasn't guilty, and we still had people on the planet."

"I gave you an order. Who are you to judge guilt or innocence?"

"I was his shadow during the Rundi war. I've been with him in far dire circumstances than the Hyperion mission. He'd never kidnap anyone. Besides the order was rescinded so technically I obeyed the correct directive."

"Technically my ass!" he exclaimed standing to his feet. "You not only disobeyed a direct command. You then severed our communication lines."

"I admit I may have overdone it."

"That my dear Ms Macalister is the understatement of the year." He bent over her chair thrusting his face into hers resting his hands upon the arms of her chair. She leaned back as far as the chair would let her go, but she did not evade his gaze again. "I can have you thrown in prison, court-martialed, or anything in between."

"Yes, sir, you can. What are you going to with me?"

"I'm not sure yet. I'm still waiting to hear why you did it." He removed his hands from the arms of her chair and stood erect.

"I told you why."

"No you didn't. You told me things I already knew. I want to know why you did it!" His words were delivered in loud military staccato, and any gentleness that may have remained from the prior demands evaporated.

She glared into his now angry blue eyes, and saw the unwavering determination in them. Lindsay knew that no matter what the penalty, they could only punish her once. She drew in a deep breath chasing away any fear that remained to allow her reasons to rip full force without apology.

"I had the Rundi headed for the planet before they were supposed to, a hostage that was in the process of being rescued, and orders that were being given that defied the parameters of our original mission. The lives of the refugees aboard the remaining ships and on the planet were my responsibility. I couldn't abandon the remainder of those people, or the man who had saved my life and countless others time and time again to be slaughtered because our government lost their freaking minds! I was the one in the thick of it. My making the right decisions was the only thing that would keep our people alive and keep the peace! I didn't give a damn about what you bureaucrats thought!" She finished with passion, and then added, "Sir!"

Admiral Griffin stepped back a moment, he wasn't prepared for that kind of response from this usually meek woman. She obviously had more balls than he had given her credit for when Rico suggested he make her a Captain. He stood up straight assuming the

382

posture of command and returned to the other side of his desk. Lindsay watched him take his seat and start typing into his note pad. After making his entries, he simply stared at his note pad for a long while continuing to tap on its side. Finally, the tapping became too unnerving.

"Sir, please," she begged, placing her hand upon his to stay it from making contact with the note pad again. Her tone had lost its passion. She had spent her fury and had again returned to the mild young woman he was comfortable with. He knew what she wanted, and truly had no idea what he should do with her. Her logic was sound albeit poorly handled on dealing with the bureaucrats. She had proven herself capable of handling a difficult situation on the front lines, but order had to be maintained within the ranks.

He looked into Lindsay's eyes one last time then opened a communication line to his secretary. "Nancy, please send in the guards."

Lindsay squirmed in her seat. "What are you going to do with me?"

"I honestly don't know."

The doors opened suddenly. Lindsay jumped even though she was expecting the guards to enter. She remained seated. She wasn't sure where the Admiral was having her taken, and she wasn't all that eager to learn. The guards marched inside the open door in precise cadence, and once inside stood at attention awaiting their orders.

"Your orders, sir?" questioned the head guard.

"I have assigned quarters to Ms Macalister in the Ambassador wing. I want you to take her there under house arrest, see that she's comfortable, and don't let her leave. When I'm ready I'll summon you to bring her to me."

Lindsay was slightly relieved to know that they weren't taking her to the brig. She was, however, puzzled that the quarters where she would be kept under house arrest was so lavish. Lindsay stood up slowly. She started to turn, but then maneuvered back around to face him.

"Admiral Griffin," she began. Her voice was soft, but resolute. "You must know before you make your decision, that if I was faced with these exact same circumstances again, I'd change nothing."

Griffin lifted his head and nodded. "Thank you for your honesty Ms Macalister."

Lindsay then turned back around and took her position amid the four guards. They walked out of his office without another word uttered between them. Griffin looked after her until the doors closed behind her. He was impressed that she didn't fall into the typical female tactic of tears. She had learned much from Rico over the years. Griffin hated disciplining female officers. He was tempted to go too soft, but then there was the danger of coming down too hard for fear of the former.

He glanced over at the status board to see that the Phoenix had finished docking. At any moment his door would spring open and Rico would be in full Rico mode. He looked back over his shoulder at the door the Prefect used to enter his office. It was closed for now, but he knew that it would soon be opening. How he dreaded this moment these past thirty days. He hated being a puppet to both governments, and he hated having to discipline Captain Macalister for doing the right thing. Griffin was trapped by secrets. Just like a big cat that finally realizes that he's been cut off from the wide-open plains, he stood to his feet and began to pace back and forth while wringing his hands.

Glenda C. Finkelstein

Chapter **25**

Rico waited by the external hatch until the ramps were secured. The cargo bay doors of the Phoenix opened several levels below his position. Rico watched through the view port as the refugees scurried out of the cargo bay onto Epsilon 6 like ants marching out of their mounds in search of food. He knew there were several thousand on board, but they looked more numerous from his current vantage point. Soon the flow of people leaving his ship mingled with the remainder of those still leaving the Falcon. His mind drifted to Lindsay wondering how she was holding up under the disciplinary scrutiny of Admiral Griffin. The man could be a hard ass, but he was fair.

Rico made it clear that his crew was to stay on board ship with the exception of Janet and Wong who were preparing to leave for their belated vacation. After watching the refugees, he turned around to engage the owner of the weighted stare he felt so firmly upon his back. It was Wong. Although Rico thought he'd be with Janet, his presence wasn't a surprise. He uttered no word to his Captain, maintaining his pledge to him. He was the only one who truly understood the brevity of Captain Sanchez's position. Even Jarvis didn't suspect the depth of the conspiracy they were swimming in. Rico cut a quick wink and half smile at Wong who received it with somber appreciation. He gave only a nod in return to assure the Captain that he understood his silent message.

Finally the green light turned on and Rico could open the crew doors and exit the ship. There was no security to greet him. This was one more confirmation that the arrest orders had indeed been rescinded. He uttered a small thank you to Zarta in his mind, but dared not ponder her too long. He had some very difficult things to hash out with the Admiral and he couldn't afford a distraction.

His gate was deliberate and steady. The sound of his footsteps on the iron ramps that would normally echo in the large room was muffled by the noise of the refugees below. He couldn't remember a time he had seen so many people in one place. Rico looked about for the security force that would take charge of the

388

prisoners and the medical personnel that would off load the injured, but saw none. They were probably waiting for the crowds to die down first. He didn't envy the task that Social Affairs faced with getting all those people relocated. He doubted that Epsilon 6 had the facilities to house all of them. There'd be a lot of people loitering about the station over the next few days.

Once he reached the steps the familiar vibrating clank filled his ears for he was far enough away from the multitudes for the acoustics to resume its familiar sounds. Luckily for him, the crowds were moving in the opposite direction than he. Rico had no wish to be distracted by anything. He was focused and bent on uncovering the last vestiges of truth that the Admiral must be keeping to himself. Rico wouldn't stop until he knew for certain whether the Admiral was the real traitor, or if he was an unwilling pawn in this highly complex political game.

He turned down the last hallway where Admiral Griffin's office was located. There were no guards in front of his office door to bar his way. That was a good sign, but then again it may simply serve to lull him into a false sense of security. He would make a mental note to take nothing at face value. Besides, he still had his ace in the hole should he not emerge from the Admiral's office. Rico knew one thing without a doubt. They'd either leave together, or Rico would be dead.

***

Back on the Phoenix Jarvis secluded himself inside Rico's office. He had ordered everyone to prepare for inspection. After the mess left by the departing refugees, it wasn't an illogical order and it kept everyone busy leaving him alone to keep vigil over the fate of humanity entrusted to him by Captain Sanchez. He had been toying with the crystal inside his pocket rolling it from his index finger to his pinky and back again. He finally tired of that and pulled it out. He studied it carefully. It was rather unremarkable, just a standard computer memory crystal. Yet encoded within its microscopic framework were powerful secrets.

He pondered what those secrets might be that even the Rundi must be made aware of in order to avert some future disaster. His mind raced through all the possibilities, yet, for all the things he came up with, he dismissed them as too wild or not wild enough. He considered viewing it himself, holding the chip between his thumb and index fingers just above the player. It hovered for what seemed like an eternity, but then withdrew his hand.

"No, I'm going to serve Captain Sanchez like I did Captain Banes," he said aloud to himself as he placed the chip back inside his pocket. Jarvis stood to his feet and exited the Captain's office. He decided to busy himself with his duties. At least if he was busy, the temptation was not so great.

**

Rico entered the Admiral's outer office cautiously. He looked about the room and saw Nancy at her desk working on some

390

report. He glanced about the area to discover that it was only the two of them in the room. Nancy looked up from her work to see that the pompous one had arrived. She stopped her task and buzzed him in.

"He's ready for you," was all she said. Her demeanor was filled with her usual disdain for his person. He knew he got under her skin and rather enjoyed it. Most women just melted in his presence. Not her. She was a challenge, although, not a romantic one. Yet, it was refreshing to know that not all women could be so easily charmed by his beguiling ways.

"Thank you," Rico responded politely somewhat relieved that things were as they should be. Although his manners were refreshing, this one instance was not enough to undo all of those other times when he was gruff or condescending. Nancy simply rolled her eyes as she watched him go into the Admiral's office.

Rico entered Griffin's office with care. The Admiral immediately looked up from his desk when he heard the doors open. His eyes locked with Rico's. Both men gave no indication that there was anything else but duty to be dispensed with. Rico cut off access to the Admiral's office as he turned the internal locks securely behind him. He wanted no interruptions.

"Nancy has a key," Griffin informed with some annoyance.

"True, she does," Rico responded, whipping a laser driver out of his pocket that he picked up from engineering during his tour of the Phoenix. He then melted the locking mechanism in place.

"Don't be alarmed Admiral. This is just to make sure that we clear the air without interruption."

"You do like your theatrics don't you?" Griffin asked, but already knew the answer.

"At least I'm entertaining," Rico quipped.

The Admiral simply shook his head. '*At least he knew what he was*,' Griffin acknowledged to himself.

Rico turned back around to face the Admiral. He wanted to look Griffin in the eye man to man. He studied every line in the Admiral's aged face. He looked older than he did thirty days ago. Griffin reached toward his cabinet. Rico jumped, and positioned himself for hand-to-hand combat. He had intentionally left his weapon on the ship. He didn't want a misunderstanding to become a regrettable mistake.

"Relax, Rico, I'm not the enemy. I'm just getting my antacid," Griffin informed, pulling the bottle out from its hiding place. He uncapped it, took a swig, and made his usual sour expression before returning the bottle to the cabinet.

Rico continued to study him for a moment longer. Most people would be feeling uncomfortable by now, but he was convinced that Griffin was not about to make the first move. This was Rico's game, and he wasn't about to foil his plans.

"You're not going to ask me are you?" Rico questioned.

"No, I'm not."

"Very well then, we shall start with your involvement."

"My involvement? My involvement in what?" Griffin questioned. He didn't like Rico's accusatory tone.

"The Peace Accord of course."

"You've lost me. We have peace, and no thanks to you and Captain Macalister, we still have peace."

"That's where you're wrong Admiral. The Peace Treaty is a lie." Rico let the word 'lie' hang out there for a moment until it sank into the Admiral's brain. He wanted to study the Admiral's reaction. He could see that Griffin was clearly taken back by this news. Of all the things he expected to hear from Rico, this wasn't on the list. His mental checklist was an open book as he ticked off each item. Griffin clearly expected to hear Rico ramble on about how they covered up Conrad's sacrifice to appease the Rundi Parliament, or even the truth that the humans had actually surrendered. It was clear by the expression on his face that he never doubted, even for a moment, that the peace wasn't real.

"What are you talking about?" Griffin asked with the shock clearly evident upon his face.

"I'm talking about truth. I know that Conrad gave his life to redeem the rest of us from destruction at the hand of the Rundi. That was the test of sentience. They didn't expect us to step up and when we did, or should I say, when Conrad stepped up that wasn't good enough anymore. They still had to be superior to us so the only way they would accept our surrender was if Conrad went to his death as a traitor. A most disgraceful death, but one the Rundi could live with."

"You seem to know much about what happened. I'm still waiting for the lie."

"Bear with me a moment longer Admiral, and I'll get to that. Now that you know that I know what happened, perhaps you'll be more forthcoming with my next question." Rico paused. His eyes locked with Griffin's looking for any hint of dissembling. He had to know whose side Griffin was really on.

"Ask your question," Griffin demanded. He was becoming increasingly irritated with Rico's scrutinizing gaze.

"Why did the Rundi require that we give them Hyperion?"

"It was just a concession of real estate spelled out in the peace treaty along with several others."

"The others had strategic value, but Hyperion was the odd one out. It served no strategic value. Although rich in minerals and agriculture, it had no evidence of a prior civilization. In addition, the Rundi had no need of such a planet. Probe data gathered along the border clearly shows that the Rundi Empire have many such treasures."

"I honestly didn't think anything about it. The colonists had only been there about ten years, but still they were a small contribution to our economy."

"Let me enlighten you. Hyperion is the only planet in the galaxy that the Rundi can successfully breed. Their entire species
394

produces offspring every seven years. During the war Hyperion was cut off, and they lost an entire generation. I have obtained information that as soon as they have successfully birthed this generation they will attack us again."

"Why would they do that?"

"Because our existence challenges their belief that they are the most sophisticated and sentient species in the galaxy. Until we came along, they thought of themselves as the center of the universe and the only ones with a true soul."

"Actually we prefer the term gods," the Prefect commented, having slipped silently into the room from the back door.

Rico looked over at the hooded figure hovering in the shadows. Griffin's mouth fell open in stunned disbelief. The Admiral withdrew into a silent argument wondering where he failed Conrad and when he became a puppet.

"You must be the Prefect."

"You of course, Captain Sanchez, require no introduction. I've been watching you closely. You realize of course, I can't let you leave this room alive."

Rico smiled at his arrogant dictate. *'This Prefect should have paid more attention if he thinks I'm leaving here in a body bag,'* Rico thought to himself.

"Why don't you step forward and face me, and take off that garish hood," Rico suggested.

"It'd be my pleasure to accommodate your last wish."

"We'll see about that. Although unlike Conrad, you'll have to earn it this time," Rico encouraged, gesturing to him to bring it on.

"You may want to reconsider your course of action," the Prefect cautioned, taking off his hood.

"My dear Prefect, before we embark upon our next actions. Consider this. I could have turned our ships around and killed your children from orbit along with their mothers. In addition, I could have made the planet unable to support them for hundreds of generations, but I didn't. I don't kill families."

"You may live long enough to regret your mercy," the Prefect commented as a sly grin began to grow ever wider upon his dark face.

"Of all the things we humans regret, mercy isn't among them."

Griffin sat in his chair as if tied to it unable to move. He watched helplessly as Rico and the Prefect drew closer to one another. Conrad had given his life to provide a lasting peace, but it was all a lie. Conrad's blood was on his hands. Griffin signed the execution order. Even though Conrad told him to do so, it offered little solace to Griffin's grieving spirit as everything he gave his life for was disintegrating in front of him.

The Prefect closed the distance between them. After seeing Zarta, Rico knew a little bit about what to expect, but Griffin had no such preparation. The Rundi male possessed a pronounced mandible like some terrible ant, and was not nearly as beautiful in color and

396

form as the females. His body was well muscled, and lean. He began to pop every joint in his body in preparation for the coming scuffle. When he finished the Prefect demonstrated his power by pounding on a nearby credenza with a clenched fist. It shattered into splinters under the force. Rico realized that he couldn't match the Prefect's power, but perhaps speed would be his greatest ally. Just like human body builders, the Prefect possessed great strength but little agility or so he thought.

Nancy heard the horrible racket. She called through the doors. "Admiral, is everything alright?"

The Prefect looked over at Griffin. The Prefect's pupils were nearly as large as his eye sockets. Rico noticed that the pattern on this Rundi was much bolder and the colors of red and orange flashed brighter just prior to his obliteration of the credenza. Perhaps he could use that flash of brightness to evade his punches.

"Admiral Griffin?" she called a second time.

"I'm fine," Griffin finally called back. His voice was saturated in horror.

"What happened?" she asked.

"I knocked over the planter," he finally managed to explain.

"Do you want me to call maintenance?"

"No!" came his excited response. Nancy wearily returned to her desk. She was uncertain what had really happened, and knew it probably has something to do with Rico. Still his voice didn't have that rigid assurance that would lay her concerns to rest.

"Was that supposed to scare me?" Rico questioned, baiting him to attack first.

Suddenly the Prefect lunged at Rico with extended forearms. Rico jumped back avoiding the initial thrust. The Prefect's maneuver was not intended to make actual contact with Rico. He was using it as a measurement of how finely tuned Rico's reflexes were. Now that the Prefect had Rico avoiding one move, the Rundi fired off a punch with his left fist that connected with Rico's jaw. The hit knocked Rico back a step. Once he regained his balance, he responded with a right upper cut glancing the Prefect's mandibles. The connection scraped Rico's knuckles.

The Prefect recoiled with a modified roundhouse kick to Rico's head. The foot connected, and Rico went sailing into the aforementioned planter. Before Rico stood back to his feet he grabbed a handful of dirt from the planter and threw it at the Rundi's face. When the Rundi went to cover his face, Rico let go with a kick to his chest bending his opponent over. He then followed it quickly with a second kick to the head. The Prefect was knocked into a porcelain vase that went sailing against the wall. The shattered shards ricocheted and sliced the Rundi's side.

"It's not as easy as you thought it was going to be, is it?" Rico asked. The Rundi gave a visual response that would equate to a human's expression of, 'You've got to be kidding me?' but was probably more accurately translated as 'bite me.'

Despite the fact that Rico got in some lucky shots, the Prefect recoiled and came back with some surprisingly quick and powerful moves. He then grabbed Rico by the breast of his shirt and coat, and in one move lifted him off the floor and threw him hard against the ground on top of the glass shards. Rico arched his back in response to the razor sharp splinters penetrating his back. Luckily the shards were small, and other than some minor lacerations it didn't inflict serious injury. Griffin was speechless as he watched the two men fight. Again Nancy was rousted from her chair to investigate the noises coming from behind the office doors.

"What is going on in there?" she asked, panic prevalent in her voice.

Griffin couldn't even form the words to give a response, and Rico was too busy re-evaluating his opponent to answer. Nancy tried opening the door herself by jiggling the handle. It was locked. She returned to her desk to activate the electronic lock. Again the door was still bolted. This time she retrieved the key. She inserted it into the keyhole, but it wouldn't budge. It was fused shut. Now she was worried.

"Admiral Griffin, Please respond!" she pleaded yelling through the door. The noise continued. She believed that Rico and Griffin were the ones going to blows. She immediately called Security to come to her aid.

Rico stood to his feet quickly to avoid a chair about to be thrown at him. He had blood dripping and oozing here and there and a bruise beginning to form on the side of his face. He was breathing heavier than the Prefect. They started circling each other again. The Prefect still held the chair in his hands.

"You're just going to sit and watch?" Rico asked between inhales and exhales of air. His annoyance displayed without apology.

"Yeah, you're doing fine," Griffin answered.

"How about you Rundi? Are you ready to call it quits and go home?" Captain Sanchez questioned.

"I'm ready to go home, but when I do it'll be when you and Admiral Griffin are dead. Then we will be back for the rest of you to finish what we started."

"Why? What did we do to you?" Rico inquired. His tone relayed his ignorance of the real motive behind the Rundi attack.

"You exist."

"That's it? That's our only crime. Living?"

"Yes, and since you're not sentient no harm no foul."

"Isn't killing sentient beings a violation of one of your highest laws?"

"Yes. No Rundi would dare slay a sentient being. We must take our own life if it should harm another."

"The act of sacrifice is a mark of sentience. Correct?"

"It suggests that the possibility is there, but it's not conclusive evidence."

"So basically, unless one is a Rundi or is biologically compatible with a Rundi we can kiss our ass goodbye."

"Essentially, yes." The Prefect answered, but was concerned with Rico's choice of words. Rico acquired a sly grin. He had hoped to protect Zarta, but not at the expense of the human race.

"I suggest you call Zarta."

"Who?" The Prefect questioned, feigning ignorance.

"Don't play coy. It doesn't suit you very well. Zarta contacted you to tell you that I didn't hold her against her will so you would drop the arrest orders."

"What does that have to do with anything?"

"Did she go into any detail about how she came to be on the Phoenix?"

"No, but she assured me that the crew didn't know."

"That's true, the crew didn't know, but Conrad did. He was the one that risked his life to save her."

"She would have told me."

"I don't think so. After listening to you talk, I doubt that you share her feelings about us humans." Rico had the Prefect's full, undivided attention.

"Zarta is a skilled and loyal Rundi. Whatever ploy she used to keep you from harming her, I assure you was just that."

"No surprise there but let me fill you in on the details anyway. At the Battle of the Breach, your weaponry exploded by accident, wounding Zarta. Conrad found her on the battlefield and brought his own doctor to see to her injuries."

"Your doctor could do nothing," the Prefect interrupted.

"I was getting to that. He took her to the mineral springs on Hyperion to heal her body. A human attacked her and Dr. Lamb laid her life down to protect her. Zarta took the form of Dr. Lamb so she could blend in. By the time they returned to the battle, there was no way to return her safely to her people."

"So your Captain Banes was kind and your Dr. Lamb foolishly laid down her life for someone that would never return the favor."

"How little you understand us. Zarta cared for sick and injured during her stay aboard the Phoenix."

"Of course she did to keep her identity a secret."

"She also went on vacation to the same planet I did. She and I fell in love."

"You're lying. She could never fall in love with a non-sentient species."

"But she did, and I'm the father of her child."

"Don't you dare utter another word," the Prefect cautioned with finger pointed at Rico.

"Our two species are compatible."

"No! My daughter would have said something," the Prefect stammered. He was stunned by Rico's admission. The ramifications of this could be devastating for the Rundi people. If they were

402

responsible for the killing of sentient beings, their entire race would bear the weight of that sin.

Rico was shocked to hear that Zarta was the Prefect's daughter. Griffin was even more stunned to know what all had gone on without his knowledge. The fact that Zarta was his daughter could help them, but it might hurt them also. The next few minutes would be critical. In frustration the Prefect threw the chair to the side and lunged for Rico grabbing him by the torso. They fell to the ground releasing primal yells as they rolled around knocking into the desk, chairs, and walls. Neither could get a good punch in. It was blind rage.

***

Outside the office Nancy continued to listen. She had stopped calling out believing that the Admiral was too busy to respond. At least the noise confirmed that he was still alive. Security came to Nancy's call for help immediately, but they couldn't get the doors opened either. Nor could they get the Admiral to respond. The doors to his office swung outward so they couldn't kick them in. Realizing that they would need a laser torch to cut through, they demanded that maintenance make this a top priority. Unfortunately all maintenance staff was on the other side of the station hip deep in refugee issues.

They were ordered to leave their current post and come at once. This, too, was difficult, as they had to wade through the throngs of refugees wandering aimlessly through the station to make their way to the Military wing.

***

The Admiral had tired of watching them flail about the floor. This was getting them nowhere. Griffin pulled out a laser pistol from a secret compartment under his desk and fired it just above the Prefect and Rico. The shot was more dramatic than lethal bringing about its desired intent.

"What the..?" Rico called, as he pushed the Prefect away. The Prefect released his hold and drew back to a more defensive position.

"What's the meaning of this?" the Prefect demanded.

"It's time we stop fighting. Call your daughter, and have her confirm or deny what Rico said."

"No," was the Prefect's answer.

"That's unacceptable."

"I can't."

"Sure you can," Griffin countered.

"He just doesn't want to have to face the possibility that they've been killing sentient beings. It'll make them human," Rico interjected. His quip aggravated the Prefect and that delighted Rico.

"Either you make the call, or I send you home in a body bag." Griffin's tone and attitude was filled with concrete resolve. If Rico was right, then the truth had to be told or everything that Conrad gave his life for would be meaningless.

404

"Very well, you leave me no choice."

The Prefect walked slowly over to the communication's console. In just a little while Zarta's beautiful face filled the view screen from aboard the Rundi ship still in orbit of Hyperion. She looked blankly at her father, Rico, and Admiral Griffin. The Prefect so wanted to speak in their native tongue, but the Admiral would surely view that as subterfuge.

Zarta drew a deep breath. *They knew about her egg*, she surmised. It was the only explanation. She had hoped to face this later, but that was not going to be possible. At least now, no one could destroy the eggs for everyone was back in orbit. Zarta's father could see by the look upon her face that what Rico said was true, but he was forced to ask it.

"Zarta, Captain Sanchez claims that he mated with you, and that you laid a viable egg."

"Yes," was all she said, her tone was full of shame.

"Did he force you to do this?" He asked.

"No, father, he didn't force me."

"Then why? Why would you do such a thing?"

"I love him."

"Love? These humans know nothing of love."

"That's where you're wrong," Rico interjected.

"Do you have any idea what you have done?" The Prefect asked of Rico.

"I believe I may have inadvertently saved my species from extinction at the hand of the Rundi," Rico answered.

"Was that your objective?"

"No, my intent was to love your daughter. At the time I didn't know she was a Rundi."

"And now?" The Prefect asked.

"My love for her has only gotten stronger."

"Yet, you left her behind. If you loved her, you would have kept her with you."

"She would be alone here. I loved her too much for her to be alone. So I returned her to her people."

"And the offspring, what of this child?"

"I didn't know about the child until after I left her there."

"If you had known?"

"I would still have had to leave her on Hyperion or risk the death of the child."

"You do realize that laying a viable egg is not enough. It must be able to survive on its own until it emerges from the pupae."

"Which brings us back to Rundi and Human relations…Are we destined to go back to war?" Griffin asked.

"Only if the child dies."

"And Zarta?" Rico asked. He could see the fear in her eyes. The communication lines still open. She watched carefully the interaction between her father and Rico.

"I will deal with my daughter in my own way."

406

All of a sudden the noise of a cutter slicing through the door interrupted this conversation of truth. The Rundi was startled. No one, but Admiral Griffin and President Charles Patton was to know of his existence. If that secret were broken, even by accident, the peace that they stood to gain by this new knowledge would be threatened. The Admiral quickly turned off the communications console and escorted the Rundi to the back door.

"When will we know if there will be a lasting peace between us?" Griffin asked tossing his cloak to him.

"When Zarta returns to Hyperion to find the child. If he or she is alive, then the peace will last forever. If it's dead, then reprisal will be swift, violent, and unrelenting for you have contaminated my daughter. No Rundi in his right mind would ever choose to mate with her again, and I will avenge her suffering."

The Prefect closed the door and proceeded to his vessel that was docked nearby. Normally this exit had a standard escape pod docked in case of an emergency, but was replaced when the Prefect arrived allowing him private access to the Admiral's office. As soon as they secured the door behind him and turned around, security burst through the main door with weapons drawn.

"Admiral, are you all right?"

"I'm fine Jackson."

"Captain Sanchez?" Jackson asked in stunned amazement. "You look terrible. What happened in here?"

"Well, I…" the two men began to explain at the same time then stopped.

The other guards with Jackson looked about the room. It was a mess. Broken tables, vases, and planters along with dirt and shards of porcelain and glass littered the floor. Virtually every square inch of the Admiral's office was trashed with the exception of Griffin's desk. Rico had cuts, bruises, and tears in his uniform. He was also dirty. His hair was disheveled. Yet, the Admiral still maintained his spit and polish image. Rico showed signs of exhaustion, but the Admiral seemed rested. Griffin and Rico looked at one another. They both couldn't answer because they might get their stories mixed up so Griffin let Rico go first.

Rico paused a moment before responding. Griffin motioned him to go on so he took it and ran with it. "I'm sure you're wondering why everything in here and myself is such a mess," Rico offered.

"Yes, sir, we are," Jackson confirmed.

"I was demonstrating some new defense tactics to the Admiral. I guess I got a little carried away," Rico explained with a smile.

"A little carried away?" Nancy questioned. "I should've known better with you in here. You scared me out of ten years of my life which I can't spare. Don't you ever do that again," Nancy chastised, shaking her index finger in Rico's face.

"It won't happen again," Rico capitulated.

"It better not, or I'll put you on report," she spouted, pivoted, and then strutted out of Griffin's office at full speed with nose held high in the air.

"Jackson, you and your men can stand down," Griffin ordered.

"What about the door?"

"Maintenance can come back later and fix the door."

"Very well, you heard the man. As you were," Jackson ordered. The Maintenance men gladly returned to their previous projects on the other side of the station, and his fellow security men returned to theirs as well.

Griffin and Rico were alone. Rico stood there looking at the Admiral. "What?" Griffin questioned.

"What do we do now?" Rico asked with grave concern.

"We do nothing. I will make my report to President Patton, and await his instruction."

"Fair enough. Have you decided what you're going to do with Lindsay?" He asked. Since it would be some time before they would know the Rundi response, he figured he should concentrate on things he could do something about now.

"No, I haven't. I've been a little busy," Griffin answered sarcastically. Rico raised his eyebrow.

"Can I make a suggestion?"

"Like I have a choice?" Griffin bantered back.

"You always have a choice, but you always listen because I know what I'm talking about," Rico said puffing up his chest with pride. Griffin just smirked while Rico continued. "She not only did a good job she made some tough, correct decisions, and you know it."

"That may be, but because she disobeyed me she'll never sit in the command chair again. I don't even know that anyone would take her as their exec."

"I'd take her."

"You already have a first officer."

"I've been meaning to talk to you about that."

"I thought you liked Commander Jarvis," Griffin said. He was concerned that something else had gone wrong that he hadn't found out about yet.

"Relax, it's nothing bad. Jarvis' performance during this crisis is proof that he's ready for a command of his own. He'll make a fine captain."

"What are you suggesting?"

"That you promote Jarvis to Captain of the Phoenix. Let me return to the Falcon, and I'll take Lindsay as my exec. That way everyone gets to save face, and Lindsay gets to stay with the corp. Besides she disobeyed for me and I won't turn my back on her now."

"Sounds like you've been thinking about this a lot."

"Yes, I have. I did what I set out to do for the crew of the Phoenix. They distinguished themselves with honor during the Hyperion crisis. It's time for me to go home."

"And Conrad can rest in peace?"

"I'll not say anything to anyone about what I found out. I'm content knowing that he did the right thing, and hopefully I was good enough to honor his sacrifice."

"Very well, I'll have Nancy call ahead to the guards and release her into your custody. After you pick her up, you can meet me in the bar and I'll buy you a beer."

"Make it an espresso, and you're on."

"An espresso it is," Griffin confirmed. He just shook his head as Rico left the room. *That man and his coffee,* Griffin thought to himself. Before leaving the room Griffin gazed up into the ceiling of his office looking straight into a concealed camera. He knew that President Patton had watched everything, and there would be no report.

Glenda C. Finkelstein

Chapter 26

President Patton turned away from the display monitor where he had seen everything transpire to face a man sitting across from him on the other side of his desk.

The President was reflective of what had just taken place. The man sitting across from him waited for the President to start the conversation.

"I have to hand it to you Conrad. You were right about your buddy Rico, and about the Rundi not being totally forthcoming."

"Like Rico, I trust my gut. Although I'm concerned that if the child does live, that my existence might void the treaty."

413

"Not a concern. You died. I had you resuscitated, your appearance altered, and your vocal cords realigned. I couldn't allow one of my most valued officers to be sacrificed on a maybe. I need you."

"So, Conrad Banes is truly dead."

"Yes, I'm afraid so, and Rico can never know that you're alive."

"What am I supposed to do? I may look and sound different, but my DNA can't be altered. The moment I leave this station it'll be recorded."

"In addition to giving you a new identity, I had a microchip installed that will send out a false DNA reading to the scanners."

"Okay, I can leave the station. Thanks, but I've spent my entire life training to command."

"Your talents will not go to waste. I'm placing you in command of the covert Viper Squadron. I need you to monitor things on Hyperion. I want confirmation of the child's death or survival accompanied by irrefutable evidence. I don't want our dear Prefect to do something stupid to protect his daughter and damn the rest of humanity to hell."

"That's not going to be easy."

"That's why I'm giving you the assignment."

"So what's my new name?"

"Jack Blackstone."

"It's different."

"It'll go better with your rogue cover."

"When do I leave, and where do I rendezvous with my team?"

"You will leave in just a few minutes after I test something out first."

The President just smiled at Conrad. He then opened a communication line to his secretary Irene, out in the lobby. "Irene, is my three o'clock here?"

"Yes, Sir."

"Send him in."

The door opened just a few seconds later and in walked the biggest shock of Conrad's life. It was Wong Qwan. He smiled at President Patton like they were chums. Conrad tried to stand, but his butt was clenching the chair. Surely Wong would recognize him. Wong glanced over at the man in the chair and nodded cordially to him, but there was no recognition on his face.

"Wong. I'd like you to meet my newest undercover agent, Jack Blackstone."

"Pleasure to meet you sir," Wong greeted. Conrad lifted up his hand to take Wong's and shake it. He finally managed to stand to his feet.

"Likewise," Conrad answered.

"Do you have the recording?" Patton asked.

"Yes, sir. I have everything that was recorded by the Zeveney 7000-P when Zarta was destroying the computer, as well as his memory chip. Although she damaged the system, the memory files are intact."

"Good. You may go now Mr. Qwan. I don't want to keep you from you overdue vacation."

"It was good meeting you, Mr. Blackstone."

"See you round," Conrad responded casually.

Patton waited for Wong to leave before expounding upon the myriad of questions rolling around in Conrad's head. "Yes, he's one of my best operatives. People trust him. He also didn't recognize you." Patton smiled. He then handed Jack the recordings that Wong had delivered. "Hopefully there's enough here to help you with your mission."

"My team," Conrad inquired.

"You'll find them on Beta-Indie."

Conrad Banes stood up, took one last look in the mirror hanging on the wall, and left his old identity there. He was now Jack Blackstone, and the future of mankind rested on his shoulders again.